FROM
DISTANT
STARS

Also by Sam Peters from Gollancz:

From Darkest Skies

FROM DISTANT STARS

SAM PETERS

GOLLANCZ

LONDON

First published in Great Britain in 2018 by Gollancz
an imprint of The Orion Publishing Group Ltd
Carmelite House, 50 Victoria Embankment
London EC4Y 0DZ

An Hachette UK Company

1 3 5 7 9 10 8 6 4 2

A CIP catalogue record for this book
is available from the British Library.

ISBN 978 1 473 21478 1

Typeset by Deltatype Ltd, Birkenhead, Merseyside

Printed in Great Britain by Clays Ltd, St Ives plc

www.gollancz.co.uk

For Pete, Nigel, Sam, Ali, Alex, Tony and John. Again.

ONE

JARED AND
THE DOPPELGANGER

1

GHOSTS

There were six of us in the room. A couple short of one for each month I'd been back on Magenta, if you want to think of it that way. Four of us were alive, talking the strained small talk of strangers forced together by social ritual. The other two were ghosts of Alysha. My wife. Six years had passed since she ran. Six years since she stowed away on a freight train and died when the people she was running from blew it up. She'd sold us out and betrayed her people. She was a traitor who'd sent good men to their deaths, her silence assured by a lone madman with a bomb who'd called himself Loki. That's what the world thought of her.

When the bureau had brought him in, Loki claimed he'd worked alone. Most of the investigators on the case hadn't believed it but Loki had never cracked, and the bureau had never found any evidence to say otherwise. Less than six months after his trial he was dead, shanked in the showers on the penal planet, Colony 478. I didn't know who'd done it or why, only that it had been some petty dispute between inmates.

I didn't buy the story about Alysha being a traitor but Laura did. Laura wanted to be somewhere else, maybe anywhere. She was as bitter about Alysha's betrayal as she was sure of it; to her, the other three of us sharing our memories of the woman we'd all loved was fingernails on a chalkboard. But she'd gritted her teeth and come with me anyway; now she sipped at her Scotch and kept her mouth shut and tried to smile. Only the tightness around her lips gave her away.

The other three of us were maybe the three people in the world who wanted to think Alysha had been pure: me and Alysha's parents. Six years since Alysha died and I was talking to them for the first time since it had happened, stirring up old memories long boxed away, ripping wounds supposedly healed. I didn't want to be there and they wanted me gone, but it was a thing that needed to be done, a boil on all our futures that needed to be lanced so we could all move on. I was putting her to rest, memory by memory. The thing I'd been trying to do ever since I came back to Magenta eight months ago.

Alysha's parents were Wynne and Charly. I didn't know Charly's real first name, only that it wasn't Charlotte and that no one had called her anything else for at least twenty years. Alysha had taken her looks from Charly and her manners too: Charly was always gracious to me even though we both knew she thought Alysha could have done better. We were in their home, a dull functional apartment too large for just the two of them, tucked away in a quietly prosperous Firstfall suburb. One of the walls was running a documentary on the Stay Expedition's exploration of Magenta's poles last year. The sound was dialled down but I think all three of us were subtly listening through our Servants, something to distract us from each other. The second trans-polar expedition had reached their dig site three weeks ago. No one knew quite what they were going to find, only that there was something under the ice that wasn't a rock.

A lot of people thought it was an old crashed ship and so polar exploration was hot news right now – although *hot* probably wasn't the right word for a place cold enough to make a man's lungs freeze. I was learning a lot more about that than I had a use for.

'There are some things of hers. I … I didn't know if you might want them … Or to look at them,' Charly said.

I thanked her, although I had no idea what she meant and she didn't seem about to tell me. I didn't want any more of Alysha's memories – I already had way too many of those – but Charly was trying to be nice so what else was I going to say?

'Wynne? Could you get them?'

Wynne was drunk. Not falling-down word-slurring drunk, but drunk enough that his edges had started to blur. He nodded and left the room and didn't look at me. Charly had been gracious when Alysha chose me over all the others she might have had, but Wynne hadn't ever seen the need. When he'd bothered to hide his disdain it had been beneath an oil-sheen veneer of brittle formality; but now his precious daughter was dead and everything they had left of her was tainted by what she'd done. No matter how much he secretly blamed me for it, I was still the only one who might have the will to climb the mountain of evidence against her and comb it for a shard of doubt. I didn't think I should and I didn't think I'd find anything even if I tried. Seeing Wynne's former sneers now transform to pathetic fawning wasn't exactly encouragement …

Shit. Who was I kidding? If I ever got to reach that mountain then I'd climb it if it killed me.

Laura pinged my Servant: Can we go yet? She had her brink-of-death-by-boredom expression on her face as she eyed the meandering of Wynne's tipsy return with a mixture of envy and disgust. She'd been better since I'd semi-moved in with her but she still drank too much.

5

I sauntered from Charly for a moment and wrapped an arm around Laura's shoulders.

'I want to get out of here too,' I whispered. 'Another few minutes. Tops.'

Laura gritted her teeth. She smiled at Charly and nodded.

I'm going to kill someone.

Wynne returned with a data sliver. 'Masters documentaries, I think,' he said. 'She was always interested in that stuff.'

That stuff. As if it made her somehow special – but how could you *not* be interested when *that stuff* was aliens that had come to Earth more than a century and a half ago, killed half the human race as they literally reshaped the planet, scattered us across the stars and then vanished, all without a hint as to why or for what. Without ever a single word.

Wynne held out the sliver. I didn't want to take it – I'd already done enough damage delving into Alysha's past. But I did. It was the polite thing to do.

'You don't want to keep it yourself?' I asked. Taking it didn't mean I had to look, right?

Wynne shook his head. 'I made a copy.'

'Then thank you.' I *would* look. No point pretending otherwise.

I felt Laura's stare boring into my back. The roll of her eyes.

I could have been spending this time with Jamie, arsehole.

I know.

I felt Alysha's other ghost stir then. Liss. She was silent but she was here, lurking in the dark corner of one of our Servants – mine, probably – watching and listening. I'd fled to Earth after Alysha died – I hadn't known what else to do with so much grief. On Earth I'd tried to bring her back. I'd found a cracksman who excelled at that sort of thing. He'd sent data-worms to Magenta to suck up every fragment of Alysha they could find – every electronic message, every image caught on every

6

camera, every word caught by every microphone. He'd brought them back to Earth and crushed them onto a blank waiting canvas, every memory of her that was left, burning them into a pristine AI core in a shell of metal and plastic.

Liss. Alysha 2.0. I don't know how many laws I broke to make her. Enough to end a promising career if anyone ever found out but I'd done it anyway. Years later we'd come back to Magenta to find out why she'd died. I guess if I'd known how that was going to end then maybe I would have left well alone. Maybe I wouldn't have made Liss in the first place – maybe; but you'll never know how hard it is to turn away from the reincarnation of someone you love until they're standing right there in front of you.

She'd lost her shell – her artificial body – but she was still out there. The embryo of an artificial intelligence fertilised with a dead woman's data. We didn't talk much any more but I knew she'd be here for this. Watching.

Wynne was looking at me. Expecting something. I didn't know what.

Agent Rause?

I started. The incoming call on my Servant was from Esh at the Tesseract. Esh knew where I was and what I was doing. She wouldn't call unless she had to.

'Sorry.' I turned away from Wynne. 'Work.' Rause. I looked at Laura. Her eyes were blank, like she was taking a call on her Servant too. What's up?

We've got a situation at Mercy. I'm handling it but I think one of you needs to be here too. Bix is briefing Agent Patterson. I'm sure Laura can deal it if you need more time with …

I didn't need more time. I'm on my way.

Sorry to disturb you, sir.

A pod arrived two minutes later to pick us up. We parted with a hasty economy of words and then Laura and I were heading for central Firstfall through howling winds and sheeting rain – a mild day for Magenta.

'Well, that sucked,' said Laura.

'Yeah. But thank you for being there.'

I squeezed her hand. I'd done what needed to be done, one more step towards laying Alysha to rest. I'd tell Esh later that she didn't need to be sorry. I was glad it was over. Maybe I really could move on now. Liss always told me how I needed that.

'I guess I owe you for all the times I've dragged you to Jamie's iceball.' Laura shivered.

'Training again tonight?'

Laura groaned. 'Shut up.' So yes, then.

My Servant sent a request to the Tesseract for more on the situation at Mercy and got back a fat nothing. Whatever was happening was fresh meat.

'What did Bix tell you?'

'Some fucking mess at Mercy. Esh talk to you?'

I nodded.

'You probably got more sense, then. Something about Fleet agents and "everyone, like, having their heads totally disintegrated, man!"' The last words came out in a passable impression of Agent Rangesh.

I pinged Esh and routed Laura into the call. 'Update?'

'Unclear, sir. I'm just heading in. A tac-team will be here in under a minute. You armed and vested?'

'Can be.'

'Recommended, sir. We haven't got a trace on the shooter but they're probably still within the Mercy perimeter.'

'Shooter?'

'Four bodies. Jared Black, Magentan citizen. Just out of trauma. Three Fleet officers were waiting for him to recover consciousness. Someone took all four out at once.'

'Fleet? Seriously?' Shit.

'Yes, sir. That's why I think you need to be here.'

She wasn't wrong, but Fleet and I had rocky history and off-world complications always sucked. I told Esh we'd be there in a few minutes.

'Fuck.' Laura let out a long bleak breath. 'There goes my afternoon. You know I was hoping to spend some time with my son today, yes? Just for once somewhere outside an ice rink?' She shook her head. 'You know, you don't have to keep on coming to watch him train. I know exactly how dull it is.'

'I like it.'

She laughed. 'Weirdo. Seriously? You watch me yell at him to get into his kit, yell at him for being late, yell at him some more to get changed when he comes off, argue about what he can and can't have from the vending bots ...'

'You two and your rituals. It's sweet.'

'It might look sweet to you but it drives me up the fucking wall!' She turned to look me in the eye. 'You don't help, either.'

'Last time I tried you told me I wasn't his dad and to back the fuck off.'

'I know, I know.' She snorted. 'I don't think I'm very good at this.'

'Good at what?'

The pod lurched sideways, caught in a crosswind gust as it dived from the surface of Firstfall into the undercity tunnels, short-cutting across the city to Mercy.

'We hardly even talk to each other when you're there.' It was a very Laura evasion – never defend when you can attack.

'We do when we get back. Afterwards.'

'No we don't. You stand around looking awkward while I yell at Jamie until he's in bed, we stave off exhaustion for an hour with half a bottle of whatever I've got to hand, we watch mindless crap and then we pass out. Or rather, *you* pass out

9

while my stupid brain goes mental about everything I didn't do right, everything I need to do the next day, all the stuff that needs sorting out …' She let out a little sigh of hopeless resignation. 'It never stops, Keon. Never. It's not the same for you. You can go home whenever you want to.'

'But I *don't* want to.'

We didn't talk about it but Laura was smart enough to know why. Home was a government apartment, hardly lived in. The past hung there like a tainted haze, filled with memories of Liss and Alysha.

'At least you don't snore.'

'So let me do more. Let me help.'

The pod pinged a warning as we burst back out from the undercity tunnels to the surface. It twitched as its autopilot adjusted. Rain hammered its skin, a buzz-saw drone. The surface wind was gusting past a hundred miles an hour. Still a mild day for Magenta, though.

'That's part of my problem, Keon. I don't think you can.'

Laura strapped on her ballistic jacket. We were coming up on Mercy. I followed her lead.

'Then what do we do?'

She sighed and checked her Reeper. 'I need a little space. Some time with my own head to figure out how this works.'

'Sure.'

A little space. Hard not to take that as an order to back off. But then the thing we'd had between us ever since … since Liss, I suppose, had always been fraught. Fraught came with the territory, with the iron discipline Laura demanded, with the separation of what we did at work from everything else. Fraught, if I was honest, came with everything that Laura was. I'd never known anyone wound up so tight.

'A couple of nights off each week, you know?'

I clipped my utility belt around my waist.

'It's just work, Jamie, you, work, Jamie, you, round and round. There's never a break.'

The usual ritual, making sure my Reeper was loaded, magazine full, the stunner charged, battery power in the green.

'I just need a bit more ... I don't know.'

'Space?' I tried to sound like I wasn't taking the piss.

'Yes.' Her sharp look told me that my trying hadn't worked.

We reached Mercy. The pod slowed as a Cheetah touched down in the road ahead of us, blocking it, its doors already open as it shifted from side to side, trying to adjust to the wind as it landed. A tac-team streamed out as we watched, fully armoured and carrying stubby burst rifles. They ran ahead into the hospital. A few other empty pods waited nearby. Esh would be inside by now. Bix too, by the sound of things. Then again, no one would be *out*side if they could help it, not in weather like this.

Laura stopped me as I started out of the pod. She put a fleeting hand on my knee, leaned in and kissed me on the cheek.

'Just until I can figure it out, you know? I don't want to make the same mistakes all over again.'

'It's OK. I get it.'

I turned back to her, thinking to keep that moment alive a little longer, but she was already getting out the other side of the pod and flicking the safety off her Reeper.

2

JARED BLACK

Esh was right about the shooter still being in the hospital but we didn't need that tac-team. She'd already found the killer a couple of wards from where the four men had been murdered. It was a shell and it was dead, its insides fried by a burner charge. The overcharged particle pistol it had used was still in its hand. Esh reckoned the pistol battery was good for another couple of shots but the shell's targeting q-ware had been precise enough not to need them. It was an expensive shell, top of the line, all but impossible to tell from human – or at least it would have been until it had burned from the inside, leaving its head a blackened mess and its torso with a gaping smoking hole in its chest, rank with the acrid stink of burned plastics. There were going to be some uncomfortable questions about how a shell like that could get into Mercy without being spotted. Fortunately those questions were going to land somewhere else. Laura, probably. As far as anyone but Liss was concerned I knew jack shit about shells.

The tac-team lounged in the reception area, squatting against the walls, chattering idly, bored and maybe a touch disappointed that nothing was going to happen. I didn't linger to chat: I was more interested in the bodies, what was left of them. Three forensics drones were already in Black's hospital room, industriously mapping the scene. Esh stood beside Black's bed. Bix was in the doorway, talking to the staff on duty, sneaking glances back inside and then shaking his head like he wished he hadn't. The air inside stank of damp burned flesh.

Jared Black – assuming it was him lying on the bed – didn't have a head any more. A good chunk of that end of the bed was missing too. What was left was scorched black.

'Mercy says the last person in was a nurse, Diane Bara,' Esh said. 'Worked here for twelve years. Checked in as normal this morning. Normal rounds ... Then this. First shot took out Black.' She made a face of mild disgust. 'What you see. What didn't vaporise caught fire. That triggered the sprinklers.'

'Video record?'

Esh nodded. 'Yes. Clean and clear.' She pointed to the three bodies on the floor. The one closest to the door – closest to where the shell must have been when it fired – had a hole scorched into his chest about the size of half a soccer ball, so deep that I could see through to the ridges of his spine. 'He was next. Smaller charge than the first which suggests that Black was the primary objective. At a guess I'd say the shell had targeting solutions for everyone in the room before it came in. Poor bastard didn't even have time to move.'

'You said they were Fleet. We got confirmation of that?'

The dead guys that weren't Jared Black certainly cut the Fleet look. Expensive suits in nondescript blue-grey. The height and build of Earthers bulked up for Magenta with top-of-the-line transgravity treatments.

Esh waggled her head. 'Not yet, although I'm as sure as I can be without having it in black and white. We're waiting on a reply from the consulate.'

She stepped over the body with the missing chest. The other two were around the far side of Jared Black's bed. I'd thought what I'd seen so far was bad but these were worse. One of the corpses there had taken a hit square in the face. The front half of his head was missing and the rest was cooked meat. The last had lost a chunk of his neck and his right shoulder. Scorched molten metal and plastic were fused together in the wall close to the floor. Tangled under the two bodies, a chair lay on its side.

'The one without a face was next. He was leaning over Black when the shell came in. You can see his lips moving on the surveillance footage; but whatever he was saying is too quiet to make out. Black didn't hear it anyway – he was out cold.' She shrugged. 'He never saw it coming. Our last corpse had time to dive to the floor and go for something inside his jacket. Gun, I expect, but I won't look until the forensic drones finish mapping the scene.'

I stared at the bodies. The stink was getting to my stomach.

'So this guy, Black, who is he and why was he here in the first place?'

Esh sent me Jared Black's admission records along with the video of the attack. Apparently he was fresh back from Earth. He'd taken a pod from New Hope spaceport back to his apartment, opened the front door of his apartment and ...

'A faulty fuel cell explosion? Really?'

Esh shrugged. 'Burned pretty badly by the looks of him.'

'So he's rushed to Mercy, Mercy patches him up, stabilises him, he's wheeled out here into a recovery room where three Fleet agents are waiting for him and never mind that he's expected to be unconscious for the next several hours ... and then a shell just walks in and kills everyone?'

'That's what it looks like.' Esh made a sceptical face.

'Agent Zohreya, how often do fuel cells explode?'

14

'They don't, sir.'

The forensics drones squawked to let us know they were done. I bent down to the Fleet agent with the fist-sized hole in his neck and lifted his jacket. Still in its holster was a standard issue Fleet particle pistol.

'We allow these guys to go around armed?'

'Depends who they are.' Esh made a face. The same face that Chief Director Morgan was probably making about now as news reached him of three dead Fleet officers on Magentan soil. Relations between Fleet and Magenta hadn't recovered from the debacle of the blackout eight months ago but what were we going to do? Kick them off-world and isolate ourselves from Earth and the other thirty-six colonies? Magenta was just about self-sufficient these days; but it wouldn't take long living off ground lichen, vat-grown seaweed, mushrooms and pigs, for someone to start a revolution. If I was honest, I'd probably join it. No one came to Magenta for the food.

'What were they even doing here?' I asked. 'I mean, who let them in?'

Laura picked her way across the room. She looked at the corpses in disgust.

'The techs are running video feeds to see if we can work out when and where the shell got inside. Maybe we can track it back through the Firstfall surveillance nets and work out where it came from but I'm not hopeful.' She squatted beside the remains of Jared Black, right next to the two dead Fleet men, and waved a hand in front of her face. 'This is fucking gross. Can we get some air freshener?'

'That would contaminate the scene,' said Esh, like Laura didn't know that.

Laura peeled back the sheet – the charred bits that were left of it – from Jared Black's arm.

'No tattoos. Pity. Zohreya, is there something going on

between you and Agent Rangesh that the bureau should know about?'

Esh stiffened. 'What? No!'

'Really? Good. Hello ...' Trapped between Jared Black's lower arm and his torso was a dermic patch. Laura tweezered it out and peered at it, then bagged it and tossed it to Bix. 'Find out what that is, Rangesh.'

Bix nodded. Laura probably meant for him to take it to a lab somewhere; instead Bix opened the bag and sniffed.

'I'll, uh, like, get it checked and stuff but I'd say adrenaline and DeTox.' He sealed the bag again. 'Say, like, does that mean these dudes were—'

'It means they were trying to wake him up.' Laura flapped at the air and threw a filthy look at Esh. 'I can barely breathe here. How do you stand it? Is your nose artificial as well as your eyes?'

Esh ignored her. I went for the door. 'Let the drones finish up.'

We gathered outside, far enough away that the grill-bar stink of crisped skin and burned fat was at least muted.

'So we have three Fleet officers who wanted to speak to Jared Black so urgently that they—'

'You know that administering unauthorised medication is criminal assault, right?' said Laura. 'Depending what he had in him from Mercy, you might even argue attempted murder. How the fuck were they even in here if he was still unconscious?'

'Uh, yeah.' Bix looked sheepish. 'About that. Mercy wouldn't have taken a Fleet clearance without some say-so, man. She's a mean bitch.'

'You're saying someone let them in,' I said. 'So get on that. Find out who—'

'Did that already, boss dude.' Bix puffed his cheeks. 'It was us. It came from the Tesseract.'

16

'What? Who?'

He shrugged. 'Black hole, man.'

Which meant the Tesseract wasn't going to tell us and so we'd have to find out the hard way. I pinged Mercy. The hospital had something of a reputation through the bureau – recalcitrant bugger of an AI was how Assistant Director Flemich put it – but mostly that just came down to it following its basic directive to protect its patients. It wouldn't tell me anything more about who'd authorised three armed Fleet men to go into Jared Black's room, though, which presumably meant the information had been slapped with a need-to-know order by the Tesseract. I damned well needed to know but I was going to have to go through the bureau to find out.

It was more than happy to give me access to all its surveillance records, though. I set up a search on Diane Bara. Hits came up at once, slices of footage of her moving through the hospital that morning. She looked as though she was going about her normal business but there was something subtly wrong. If I hadn't spent years living with Liss then maybe I wouldn't have picked it up, but she wasn't quite human.

'It wasn't the real Diane Bara who came to work this morning.' I pinged them fragments of Mercy's footage. 'Look at the way she moves. She's a shell.'

'But, dude! That makes no sense!' Bix screwed up his face as tight as it would go. 'I mean, if it's like, tooled up as a nurse, why wait for the—'

'When did Black get here?' I looked to Esh. 'An hour ago?'

'More like two now.' Esh shook her head. 'But are you sure, sir? Because if you're right then that puts the shell here before Jared Black ... It puts the shell here before the explosion that brought him to Mercy in the first place!'

'Yeah,' I said.

I sent the clips to the Tesseract for body posture analysis to be sure. Shells never got that quite right. They were always too perfect. Bix and Esh were right that it made no sense – but it also was what it was.

The tac-team and their Cheetah were long gone by the time we left Mercy. In the pod across Firstfall to the Tesseract we joked about sending them to the Fleet consulate to raid it. There hadn't been much love for Fleet on Magenta after they'd been caught a couple of years ago bribing members of the Selected Chamber. The blackout hadn't exactly improved matters.

'We need to divide this up. Laura, you and Esh take Fleet—'

Laura looked at me in horror.

'Fleet don't like me,' I said.

Plus Laura had trained as a lawyer before she joined the bureau and Esh was ex-military, flew interceptors for a time and was born on Earth, all of which made them infinitely more qualified for dealing with Fleet than either me or Rangesh. When it came to patient liaison with a hostile bureaucracy, there were tree ferns more qualified than Rangesh.

'I'm beginning to see why.' Laura let out an exasperated snort. 'I get to see my son at least once more before I retire, right?'

'Find out who those three really were before we make fools of ourselves. Get the official story on what they were doing here. Then start on what this was really about. Maybe they had permits for those weapons, maybe not, but … As agents of a foreign power illegally administering drugs to a Magentan citizen, can we have them for espionage?'

'They're a bit dead for that, boss dude,' grumbled Rangesh. 'Besides, we, like, let them in there ourselves, you know?'

I swapped a glance with Laura. That was going to be her slice of pie and she knew it; she knew why I wasn't saying so in front of the others, too. I wasn't quite sure whether she still reported to Internal Audit but I had to assume that she did.

'Rangesh, we're on Black and Bara. You start with Bara, I'll start with Black. There has to be a reason someone wanted him dead.'

Esh and Laura took another pod and headed off to the consulate. Rangesh left to look for the real Diane Bara while I did the basic background work for Black on the way to the Tesseract.

Jared Black. Junior partner at Patel and Black, a small Magentan law firm. The Black in the company name was an uncle. Jared was thirty-eight years old, single, no dependants, educated at Disappointment University, same as I was. Different year, different subject, but Magenta was a small world and so I tried to think whether I'd ever met him. If I had, I didn't remember.

The Tesseract didn't have much more beyond basic biometrics. Black had just come back from Earth, a four-week trip synced to the cycle of the *Fearless*, the abandoned Masters' ship that flicked between and Earth and Magenta in a precise and relentless rhythm that no one knew how to change. He'd landed at New Hope with the morning shuttle. He'd taken a pod to his apartment, which had promptly exploded. Forensic drones had been over the scene and the debris was already in the bowels of the Tesseract labs. An emergency trauma pod had rushed him to Mercy, and the rest we already knew. The explosion had been put down to a faulty fuel cell at the time, but no one was going to believe that now.

There wasn't much else to glean from the report on his apartment. Forensics were working the evidence. Until half an hour ago it hadn't looked like a priority.

I checked the times. Esh was right. If Diane Bara had been a shell from the moment she clocked in to Mercy then Black had still been making his way through New Hope at the time. My first instinct had been the obvious: someone had tried to kill him with a bomb, and then when that hadn't worked they'd used the shell. Now it was obviously wrong: the Diane Bara shell had already been in place, ready and waiting.

It bothered me that the bomb hadn't worked. Two killers? One sloppy amateur, one hardened professional? But if they weren't linked then how had the shell known to be in Mercy? Black had only just come back from Earth. He hadn't had a prior appointment. So what? The bomb was never meant to kill him? It was just meant to get him into Mercy where the shell could finish the job? But then why not have the shell waiting for him outside his apartment and simply shoot him as he opened the door? It seemed absurdly complicated.

They *had* been waiting for him, though. As soon as he touched down in New Hope. That much was clear. Whoever *they* were.

I pinged Bix: We need to go to where he worked. We need to find out what he was working on and why he went to Earth and who he met.

Then I pinged Laura: What if Black wasn't the real target?

A pause. Yeah. I was wondering that too.

Cause and effect. Someone had intentionally put him into Mercy where the Diane Bara shell was already waiting. If the murder was simply about Jared Black then it made no sense. But if it was about Fleet …? What if it had been about luring someone else out into the open …?

I'll look for anything in Black's history that might tie him to Fleet.

We need to know everything about the three other victims.

Yeah. Good luck with that.

Black's Servant had vaporised along with the rest of Black's head. Was that deliberate? Was that why the first shot from the particle beam had been so overcharged? We'd have to rely on backup records but that put us at the mercy of Black himself, on whatever he'd decided to record and keep.

I reached the Tesseract in time for Bix to report in. He was at Diane Bara's apartment and she was alive, so that was something. Local Servant records gave a solid account of her last twenty-four hours. She'd ordered out for food. She'd opened the door when the delivery drone arrived. The shell was waiting there. It must have been a shock, seeing a shell that looked exactly like her, like looking in the mirror. Then the house Servant had shut down for no apparent reason and after that we had nothing. Bix had found her unconscious. She was currently on her way to Mercy. She'd been drugged, he reckoned. And she had a bloody hole in the side of her neck where her Servant had been cut out of her.

I sat at my desk, twiddling my thumbs, mulling it over. Footage from Bara's apartment showed the shell going inside before the house Servant shut down. It was the shell we'd found burned out in Mercy, only here it was, hours before Jared Black had even touched down at New Hope. I tried to track it backwards through the Firstfall surveillance net, to follow its journey from Diane Bara's apartment back to some point of origin, but it had known the tricks to avoid being seen and I soon lost it.

I pinged Laura: We need to find out who cleared Fleet to question Black.

My hand slipped to my pocket without being asked. It closed on the sliver Wynne had given me. I won't say I'd forgotten it, exactly – more that everything at Mercy had driven it to the back of my mind. I looked at it now and it was Jared's bomb that moved my fingers. A bomb had killed Alysha too. Six years ago I'd run away to Earth. I'd thought that was how I'd cope with losing her, but instead I'd tried to bring her back. I'd made Liss. My dirty little secret. She was still out there somewhere. We didn't talk much these days but I knew how to find her.

Liss. Another shell – but it wasn't just the bomb and a killer shell that made me think of Alysha. I'd gone to hell and back to understand why Alysha had died. I'd been shot and nearly killed to get to the bottom of why she'd vanished out of my life and at the end I hadn't much liked the answer. She'd betrayed me. She'd betrayed us all, or at least that was how it looked. I didn't believe it, but the alternative was that someone in the Tesseract had set her up. I had to believe that she'd known who, too, by the end.

And now someone in the Tesseract had cleared those three Fleet men to talk to Jared Black. And obviously it wasn't the same person and the two cases had nothing to do with each other and thinking otherwise was ridiculous – but there I was, trying to make the connection anyway.

I looked at the sliver like it was poison. The best case was that whatever files it contained were going to remind me of all the things I missed about Alysha. The worst case was that I was going to find something else that I didn't want to know.

Loki had claimed, in his first interview, that he'd gone to the pumping station to meet someone. Later he'd changed his mind. The investigation team eventually figured that Loki had been lying in that first statement. The Tesseract had looked and found no evidence of a third party. But no one on the case quite believed that Loki was bright enough to have done it all by himself.

The Tesseract ...

I'd been trying to move on for years. I was almost there. The last thing I needed was some nostalgia trip. Or some case with someone being blown up by a bomb.

My fingers were tight around the sliver. It was digging into my skin. I knew I ought to put it away, maybe crush it to banish the temptation – but then, since that was never going to happen, I figured maybe I should get it over with instead. I slotted it into my Servant. I don't know what I'd been expecting. Wynne had said Masters' documentaries but that didn't sound right. So what? Memorabilia? Some sort of diary? Videos and the

22

like from before she'd met me? Old boyfriends, stuff from our university days ...?

The sliver was full of transcripts and recordings of lectures, articles, hundreds of them.

Research.

Research into what, though?

The little voice telling me how I really didn't need this was screaming. Alysha had worked at the Tesseract, same as me. We'd known each other before – we were already dating back when we were in the Academy – but working in the Tesseract had tempered fun and friendship and lust and desire into love. We'd worked more often apart than together but we knew each others' cases: a quick flick through the files on the sliver told me this wasn't anything to do with the bureau or our work for Magenta. Turned out Wynne was right. This was about the Masters.

Bix knocked on my door. I could have kissed him.

'Hey, man, ready to go?'

I locked Alysha's files away.

'Anything on the explosion at Black's flat?'

'Forensics are still working the residuals. But yeah, man. Probably a bomb. They're getting this expert tech guy in from Nico tomorrow to be sure but the blast pattern puts it, like, right by Black's front door. Like, just inside it. What's a fuel cell doing there, man?'

'Wait! *In*side?'

Bix nodded.

'They put the bomb *inside* his apartment. Right by the door?'

He must have seen the bewildered look on my face. 'I know, man. Like, what? Like, why not just shoot him?'

Because Black wasn't the target.

Or at least he wasn't the *only* target. He'd been unconscious and he'd still had his head blown off. And he'd known

23

something worth three Fleet men getting out of bed, something they'd wanted urgently enough that they'd tried to force him awake after surgery.

We walked through the Tesseract out into the quad, a grey concrete space between the four grey concrete blockhouses of the bureau. The rain still came in torrents but the wind had eased. It was brightening into a nice day.

'Anything from his house Servant?'

Bix shrugged. 'Nothing that looks off.'

We crossed the quad and left the Tesseract, down the steps past the vending bots and shells that loitered to prey on the Magenta Institute students next door. A few woke as we passed, took one look at the Tesseract codes from our Servants and stayed away. A pod was already waiting at the bottom of the steps to take us to Patel and Black.

'You and Esh,' I asked as we climbed in. 'You OK?'

Bix made a face. 'Dude!'

'Not my business if you don't want it to be.'

'We're good, man!' He laughed. 'That why you put her on Fleet with Laws?'

'Not really. It made sense.'

And Laura had wanted space and so it made sense to put her on a part of the case where we'd be apart. Maybe she and Esh could have some girl time, whatever that was.

'Trying to adjust, that's all.'

I raised an eyebrow.

'You know Esh, man. How she's so ... you know. Like, totally straight down the line. By the book and everything. Only that's the thing. I don't know ... Jekyll and Hyde or something. Uniform on and she's, like ... Esh. Totally square. But outside ... It's weird. I guess ... I don't know, man. I probably shouldn't talk about it.'

'Probably not.' Let him work up a head of steam and Bix

24

would tell you everything – where he went, what he did, what he had for breakfast. The idea of over-sharing flew through him like neutrinos through a nebula. Esh, though. Bit of a closed book. 'Just tell me you're cool.'

'We're cool, man. It's OK. We're good. You and Laws?'

I snapped back to the here-and-now. 'Me and Laura? What about us?'

Bix guffawed, a real belly laugh. 'Man! What are you like? You thought me and Esh didn't know? Oh, that's so cute, man! I mean—'

'OK, Agent Rangesh, that'll do.'

Laura thought we were being careful, keeping it hidden at work. The only place we were ever together in public was at Jamie's iceball. But Magenta was a small world and Bix wasn't stupid.

'Don't say anything in front of Laura,' I said.

'OK,' he said. 'But, dude! It was, like, totally obvious from the day you were back, man! From the moment she went into your office!'

The drumming of the rain stopped. The sky went out as our pod dropped into the tunnels to the undercity. I pulled up the files on Patel and Black, trying to work out what might get Jared killed or find a connection to Fleet. I didn't see anything. Mundane corporate law stuff. They weren't big, no interstellar reach. Their clients were all based on Magenta.

'You ever get into the history of the Masters?' I asked.

'Sure. I mean, it's like a phase we all go through right? Like puberty.'

Five years of terror. Billions dead and no idea why. The creeping suspicion that maybe they'd killed half our species more through carelessness than design. Millions abducted and carried to other worlds. And then POP! and they were gone, their entire infrastructure left behind. Their ships still carried

25

us between the stars, flipping in and out of space to their own inscrutable rhythm, regular as a quantum clock and every bit the same mystery they'd been a hundred and fifty years ago. The Masters had done all that and then vanished and we still didn't know the first thing about them … yeah, it was normal to be curious.

Maybe that was all there was to Wynne's sliver.

'I used to read everything I could get my hands on, you know? And there were talks and stuff at the Institute. People from Earth. I think they liked to come here because of the … You know. Because of the gens. The Xen.'

I raised an eyebrow. 'They came to get stoned?'

'No, man!' He made a face like I was an idiot. 'Because of all the, like, why Magenta? We're thousands of light years from Earth. There have to be totally millions of other worlds closer and with a way more compatible biosphere. You know, with, like, with only one gravity, like on Arcon, or even less like on Strioth. But they scattered us across a whole spiral arm. Why? Why did they pick the worlds they did? Magenta's a shithole. It was decades before we could do more than survive by the skin of our teeth here, you know? We lived on handouts for half a century and the only reason everyone didn't just pack up and leave when the Masters vanished and Fleet took over is that Earth was such a mess back then. So why Magenta, man? What's so special about it? Only maybe that's a question that for once we can actually answer! Like, it could be the one thing the Masters did that we can understand!'

'It could?' Apparently I'd hit a nerve.

'Dude! It has to be the lichen! The gens! Xen! Like, because Magenta's xenoflora works with human neurochemistry, you know! Why else? I mean, what else is there?'

Magentan lichen was hallucinogenic. That was what had seen the early settlers through those first years – they'd been permanently tripping. Later, when we learned to refine it, the Xen trade had caused literally worlds of problems, the sort of problems that had culminated in a blockade and the threat of invasion. That had been twenty years back. Things had been different then. It was largely the work of the bureau that had turned it around. The bureau and the Tesseract.

We were deep in the undercity now, a few layers above the mag-lev station and the hydroponics farms. Damp and dark. Odd place for a law firm.

'I mean, hey, there could be a hundred other reasons, I guess. The Masters were just weird. But that's what people think, you know? People clutch onto anything that looks like it might make sense. Magenta because of the lichen. And that was before ...'

He trailed off. Before Liss and I had gone after why Alysha died. Before we'd discovered what Xen could really do if you didn't care what lengths you went to.

I ran a search count over Alysha's memory stacks. Xen came up a lot.

Shit. I was going to have to read them.

3

ICEBALL

Patel and Black had their office in the undercity. It was cramped, with a faint whiff of hydroponics seeping in from the levels below – one look around and I knew they never brought clients here. Bix and I flashed our Tesseract codes at the doors and they let us in. A shell greeted us in a tiny reception hall. It was a blank cheap mass-produced model with barely a shred of personality.

'See, man?' Bix shook his head and I knew what he was thinking.

You were supposed to know a shell when you saw it. Even Liss, up close, hadn't been perfect. They were supposed to be obvious and they were supposed to be dumb. They weren't ... They weren't *people*, or at least they weren't supposed to be. They weren't supposed to walk around a hospital for half a day and act like a nurse without anyone knowing the difference. And they certainly weren't supposed to kill ...

I tried not to think about that. Liss had killed. More than once.

We flashed our codes again. The shell pointed us down a dim

corridor to a cluster of tiny offices that were little more than workspaces, screens, and stacks of shelves covered in dusty books and paper. They all looked abandoned.

'Dude!' Bix pointed. 'Is that, like, an actual *printer*?'

They all had them. Relics that belonged to a time before the Masters.

'Is this like a museum or something?'

Jared's uncle, Conan Black, had an office at the end of the corridor that wasn't much bigger than the others. He glanced up as we walked in and I felt sorry for him. He looked old and grey and stood a little stooped, like an Earther new off the shuttle.

'You're here about my nephew?' It wasn't really a question. He obviously already knew about Jared.

I went through it with him step by step, slow and gentle. There was never an easy way to tell someone that a friend or a lover or a relative was dead. He listened well enough on the surface but I saw the blankness behind his eyes. Sorrow. He'd liked Jared. They'd been friends as well as family.

The shell brought us seaweed tea and lichen biscuits. Cheap and nasty. I said thank you and told Conan about the Fleet men who'd died in Jared's room. It was bound to get out. Maybe he knew something, maybe not, but it couldn't hurt to point him in the right direction. Then I let Bix take over. They say don't shoot the messenger, but at times like this who else is there? Bix asked questions while I ran corporate background checks on Patel and Black's client list. Neither of us found anything interesting. Either Patel and Black were exactly what they looked like or they had an extremely clever accountant who was good at doing things he shouldn't.

'You ever do any work for Fleet?' I asked. 'Or anyone connected?'

Conan shook his head. No. Not that he knew.

Jared's trip to Earth was a holiday, he told us. A lifetime

dream. We went through Jared's case files and then his personal life. It was cruel, maybe, the way we dragged it out, but it needed to be done and it wasn't going to get any better, not once the news channels caught up with the lurid details of the story. The only thing Conan had for us was Jared's girlfriend, nominally still married to someone else. We left our contact details to go with his grief in case he thought of anything later. I didn't think he'd be in touch.

'Jealous husband?' Bix raised an eyebrow as we walked back out to our pod. 'With a shell and a particle pistol?'

'I don't think Jared was the target.'

Bix made a sceptical face.

'The shell was in place in Mercy before Jared even landed at New Hope. Black was a lure. I think the Fleet men were the real target.'

I let that sink in. Bix frowned hard. 'OK. So maybe those Fleet dudes were spooks or something, right? Which kind of fits with a killer shell with a particle beam. But, like, dude ... Why? I mean, you'd have to know those three dudes totally wanted to talk to Black, like, right the moment he was back, you know? Like, that they really were going to go for it and try and wake him up straight after surgery. So if you're right, it still kind of comes back to the same thing – what did a bunch of Fleet spooks want with this guy?'

I didn't have an answer to that.

'And Black was out cold when it happened. Drugged to the eyes but the shell still killed him first, man. Burned him deep enough to melt his Servant. So, you know ...'

He was thinking about it, though.

I checked the time. It was getting late. Laura would be heading back from the consulate to the rink to meet the nanny and watch Jamie train. I wanted to talk to her about Fleet. I wanted to talk about Alysha's memory stacks, too, so I told the pod to drop Bix at the Tesseract and take me on to the Firstfall rink.

'Dude?'

'Look into Jared,' I said. 'Find out who he was seeing, whether the husband was the jealous type. You never know. Some are. Could be he's got connections? Rule it out, yeah? And talk to Bara when she wakes up.'

In the back of the pod, on my own, I opened Alysha's files again. They went back twenty years and more. Most dated from when she was a teenager. Articles on the Masters – all the theories that had ever existed on who they were and what they'd wanted, and why they'd done what they did. Most of the old religions of Earth had fallen after the Masters came, usurped by bastardised versions of themselves. The aliens who reshaped continents and cut Earth's population in half became demons or angels, manifestations of divine anger or of some cosmic adversary. Obscure cults bloated with followers as the Masters' ships hung over the Earth and blossomed bright when the Masters disappeared. Our old gods had failed us and so we'd found new ones. Bad ones. In the iconography of the aftermath the Masters – who'd never spoken a single word – could be sadistic or evil or vengeful or uncaring, but they were always conscious of what they'd done.

Was that really true? Had they even noticed we were there?

I wondered what it was like, to believe in some higher power. How that worked when the Masters were right there in your past. I didn't know how to even start. My family didn't have a trace of religion. Nor did Alysha's. The only Magentan I knew who did was Esh.

The oldest articles, back from Alysha's teenage years, proposed that the Masters had simply been indifferent. They'd known we were there and just didn't care. We were a feature of the landscape, that was all, to be moved or deleted or rearranged in the same way as they moved or levelled mountains and continents. We were ants to them. Utterly cosmically insignificant.

There was another scattering of files a few years later. University days. An interest less fierce and more guarded. The dates came in fits and starts, as though Alysha had come back to them now and then only to be distracted by something else. Then a long space of nothing, her years in the academy when I'd first come to know her and then at the Tesseract, before and after we'd married. And that made sense to me, because I'd known my wife. We'd shared our secrets, or so I'd thought. Yes, we'd talked about the Masters now and then, but never as though they really mattered.

The files picked up again twelve months before she died. A dribble at first and then a flood, like she was sucking in everything she could find. This time it was the cults she was after, the ones who said the Masters had known exactly what they were doing and understood the suffering they caused. That they'd had an all-consuming *reason* for what they'd done.

The pod reached the rink. I closed the files and slipped Alysha's memories back into my pocket. It was harder to shut them out of my head. Did she believe it? Any of it? *All* of it? I didn't know.

I sat at the back of the rink and nursed a synthetic coffee from a vending machine. I thought about Liss, Alysha's electronic ghost. We didn't talk much any more – better for both of us – but she'd want to see this. I left a message on a message board where I knew she'd look, locked a copy of Alysha's files behind some low-grade encryption and put them where Liss could find them. Maybe that was my way of getting them out of my head; but also, this way she didn't have to contact me.

Laura showed up five minutes after Jamie and the nanny. I stayed back and tried not to let her see me while they went through the usual ritual: Jamie talking to his friends, Laura chivvying him to get kitted up, Jamie dragging it out, being slow, winding his mother up inch by inch. I don't think he did it consciously but I was sure it was deliberate, a need to assert himself in some way. I wondered, as always, what would happen if Laura simply left him with the other boys – whether he might simply keep pace with them and that would be the end of it. But she wouldn't. She hovered and fussed and he didn't like it, and the other boys were ready to go and he was still half-dressed and so she shouted at him and so he shouted back.

Every time, always the same.

I stayed away until the warm-up drills started and I lost Jamie in the blur of shirts. Then I went to join Laura. She sat on her own at the back, as far from the other parents as she could be. I slipped in beside her.

'Hey, you. How's Jamie?'

She looked at me sharp and angry with red round eyes. I'd caught her off guard.

'Sorry.'

'What are you doing here? I thought we were having time off.'

I'd wanted to tell her about Alysha's sliver. Now that I was here I knew she wouldn't want to hear it. She didn't want to hear anything about Alysha, the friend who'd turned out to be a traitor.

'I won't stay long,' I said. 'Give him space, Laura.'

'Says the man who never had children. What the fuck do you know?'

'Not much.' I reached to take her hand, saw how she flinched, and didn't. 'I don't think Black was the target.'

She laughed in my face. 'Fleet acknowledged the bodies. They want them back and full access to our enquiry. I told them to fuck off. I'm wading through the hierarchy trying to find someone who's prepared to tell me what they were doing there but don't expect miracles any time soon. What I've got so far is that they were probably working for one Lieutenant Commander Tomasz Shenski. Shenski's official posting is as an Orbital Traffic Officer which means he's mostly interested in off-world gen smuggling. Shenski reports to one Darius Vishakh, Chief of Station for Local Liaison. Chief spook, in other words, so it's not much of a punt to guess that Shenski's a spook too. Expect a lot of irritating questions, useless answers, legal challenges, and nothing whatsoever of any value.' She shrugged and made a face. 'In a fit of anticipatory pique, I've drafted a formal complaint against them for assaulting a Magentan citizen. Believe me when I say the irony isn't lost on me.'

'I got Bix looking for Black's girlfriend but I don't think—'

Laura barked another laugh. 'All the work of a jealous husband, eh?' She forced a smile and took my hand and squeezed. 'Sorry. Look, maybe I can save you some time. I wrote some code for Bugbear a while back to—'

'Bugbear?'

She blushed. First time I'd ever seen it, I think. 'My Servant.'

'Your Servant is called Bugbear?' I bit my lip.

'If you laugh, I *will* kill you. If you tell anyone else, I will kill you slowly.'

'Bugbear. OK.'

They were running shooting drills on the ice. I tried to pick Jamie out. My Servant could have done it for me if I'd wanted but that seemed to miss the point. Was it weird to have a name for your Servant? Did people do that? A quick data search discovered that yes, people did. More than I'd ever have imagined.

Laura poked me. 'Watch.'

Data streamed into my Servant and across my lenses, projected over my view of the world. Records of Servant interactions.

'Jared Black's Servant history. Everywhere he's touched the system. Look.'

I looked, trying to make sense of it.

'This morning. Lands at New Hope. Short hop in a pod to the centre of Firstfall. Gets blown up. Gets carted off to Mercy. Two dozen transactions, give or take.'

'You wrote the q-code for this?'

She snorted and shook her head. 'I had someone at the Tesseract do it back when I was investigating … When I was trying to trace someone.'

I knew that pause. When she'd been trying to find out who Alysha had seen in the last days before she died.

More data poured over my lenses. Out on the ice a whistle blew. The players switched to some other drill.

'Jared Black in the weeks before he left for Earth. Thousands of hits. Now all I have to do is … There.'

The pause was the Tesseract cross-referencing every Servant interaction in Firstfall over the last three months, looking for patterns in Jared Black's life …

His girlfriend was Ranya Sovei. Married, three children, same sort of age as Black. The times and places when they'd been together made it obvious what they were up to. Bars, restaurants and hotels. I looked up Ranya's husband.

'Shit.'

Hussein Sovei had spent the last three months living in Disappointment. As far as I could tell he hadn't come back to Firstfall even once.

'Shall we see who he's with?'

We were chasing smoke but I let Laura do it anyway.

'Abandoned wife takes up with available single man?' I made a sour face.

'Hardly a motive.'

'You want to tell Bix or shall I?'

35

Laura grinned. 'Let him figure it out for himself. He might find something else – but there's also nothing here that ties Black to Fleet ... What I *did* get out of them today were the video records from the *Fearless*. We can't see who Jared Black was talking to on Earth but we can see who he talked to on his way home.'

The players on the ice were splitting into two teams. Setting up for a practice match. Other parents were moving closer to watch. Taking an interest. Laura synced our Servants so I could see exactly what she was doing.

'It can wait, you know. If you want to—'

'I don't.'

She knew exactly what I wasn't saying. *Watch the game! Be there for your son!* I knew better than to voice any of that aloud.

Data from the *Fearless* streamed into us. It was enormous, more than a hundred thousand hours of high-resolution imagery. Millions of transactions. Laura set her Servant searching for Jared Black, building a trace of his movement through the ship.

'Bugbear? What kind of a name is that anyway?'

She shot me a glare. 'Slow and painful, Rause. Remember that.'

I had my Servant track Jamie on the ice. Even ticking over, it did a better job than I ever could. To me they all looked the same and they moved so fast that I could barely read their shirt numbers. When I found him, it only took a moment of inattention to lose him again. Was that how the real parents managed? They just didn't ever drop out and let their minds wander to something else? Or did they get some sort of sixth sense, some recognition of the way their son or daughter moved on the ice in the way we recognise people we know, even from a distance, from the way they walk?

Bugbear came back with the trace from the *Fearless*. I gave up on the game and followed Laura at high speed through Jared Black's journey, searching for patterns and any other passenger who registered Servant transactions at similar times and places.

Halfway through, Laura stopped. 'That's weird.'

'What?'

She wasn't listening but I saw what she was looking at. Error warnings. Impossible transaction pairs. Instances where Jared did two things almost at the same time and couldn't possibly have moved from one place to the other in the interval between them. It happened more than once.

'Shit!'

It was like, just every now and then, there were two of them.

Jamie was forgotten now. This was where Laura lived – in the data. I watched her reconfigure her q-code to search for transaction pairs that didn't make sense. At the same time she pulled in all the surveillance video from the *Fearless*. The whole lot, all six days of it.

The answers came fast. A dozen times, Jared was in two places at once. Laura picked the first and dived into the surveillance video, looking for images of Jared and then looking around the second transaction in the pair for a camera angle that would give us a face. When that didn't work she went to the next. On the third she got a hit. A partial picture of someone who definitely wasn't Jared Black but who, according to the transaction records, was exactly where Jared Black was supposed to be.

We scored three more hits. None of them were clear. The other Jared Black was going out of his way to keep his face hidden from the cameras but he hadn't done quite enough. Bugbear built a composite face and then compared it to the passenger list.

'Martin Statton.'

Got you.

The name didn't register with the Tesseract but that didn't

mean much. I sent the raw images to Bix. Find out who this is. Anything.

Laura ran a trace of Statton's face through the flight, comparing it to Jared's and correlating both with transaction logs to see if they were ever in the same place at the same time. They never were. Statton had been as careful to avoid Black as he'd been to avoid any cameras.

Two Jared Blacks. What the hell did that mean? How did that work?

I went back to watching the game while our Servants ran video searches. It took me a minute to realise that the players on the ice had changed. Jamie was on the practice pad. I glanced at Laura but she'd already spotted him.

'Can you actually tell who's who out there?'

'I can follow Jamie if I really try. The other kids?' She shrugged. 'Not a clue. Then again, I couldn't tell you most of their names either. I have a deficiency of giving a fuck.'

I tried to pick Jamie out by eye but they were too far away. I piggybacked onto a camera feed closer in. Not something an ordinary citizen could do – working for the bureau had its perks. Some of the boys were on a miniature slalom course, skating between a series of cones. Others were skating in a loose circle, throwing balls to one another.

'You ever give it a try?' asked Laura.

'Me?' I snorted. 'When I was Jamie's age I was having such problems with transgravity rejection that I had to be careful about even walking in case I fell and broke something.'

'Sorry. Forgot that.'

'Speed and co-ordination and a smattering of violence – exactly the sort of game I would have loved if I'd been able.'

'You ever think of taking it up?'

'At my age?'

'You might be good at it now.'

I shook my head. 'You want someone to take up iceball, talk to Esh.'

Laura let out a low growl.

'You should bring her to a match one day.'

'Keon, I realise that as a man you're not terribly perceptive about these things and so it may somehow have escaped your notice, but I don't actually like Esharaq very much and I'm reasonably confident the feeling is mutual. So no, I'm not going to invite her to waste an afternoon watching Jamie play iceball. You find out what's up with her and Rangesh?'

'Not our business but Rangesh says they're good. He seems happy.'

Laura made a sceptical face. 'Well, *something's* up.'

The match paused. The ice filled with milling children skating in wild chaos and yet somehow never crashing into one another. Even piggybacking on a close-in camera it was impossible to follow Jamie without running a tracking algorithm to tag him ...

Laura's Servant finished its search. I closed my eyes and let the answer fill my vision, a four-dimensional representation of both Statton and Black aboard the *Fearless*. There were two clear separate tracks throughout the six days the *Fearless* had been in the nether. One was Jared. The other cropped up far less frequently but it was enough of a track to be solid. Statton. Laura started looking for patterns: faces that cropped up more often than others; people who were regularly in the same place; other transactions that seemed to correlate. It was harder now. Neither of us quite knew what we were looking for.

'We ought to create transaction and image tracks for every passenger over the whole flight,' I said.

'That would take Bugbear the best part of a day. Maybe a lot longer if I don't get the algorithm right. I'll get the Tesseract on it after we leave.'

In one sequence of imagery Statton was sitting in a dim corner of the upper-class lounge, sipping at a drink. His eyes were fixed on something across the room that was out of shot. Laura pulled up another camera, one that let us see what he was looking at. A group of well-dressed women sat together at the bar, relaxed and laughing. Laura closed a filter around both images, trying to see exactly where Statton was looking but the angles were all wrong. Closet lechery – or was there more to it?

Something in the background caught Laura's eye.

I started traces for each of the women, tracking them through the *Fearless* and matching them to Statton. I got one clear hit. Chantale Pré. Magentan, wealthy, a model. A quick trawl through public dataspaces told me she was best known as the face of Quadratic, a nebulous Magentan financial institution owned by an even more nebulous Earth conglomerate.

'Here.'

I found an audio clip. Statton giving a name: Andreas Kretch. The public alias he was using among the other passengers. Probably didn't mean anything but I kicked off a search and pinged it to Bix.

'So he's Martin Statton on the passenger list, calls himself Andreas Kretch, and somehow jacked Jared Black's identity on the *Fearless* well enough to spoof the whole system?' Was that even possible? 'Did he come down to the surface or is he still in orbit?'

Laura shrugged. 'No trace of him through New Hope. I'll get the Tesseract on this.' She was distracted, looking at something else. Something she wasn't sharing.

'What if someone killed the wrong Jared Black?'

'Then I guess they're going to feel remarkably stupid when they find out. Not sure how that fits with your theory of Black being a lure, though.'

'We've got to find Martin Statton, or Andreas Kretch, or

whatever his name really is. We've got to get to him before Fleet figure this out.'

'Keon?' She still wasn't really listening. There was something in her voice that made me stop.

'What?'

She flicked me a still of a woman, barely visible in the background, watching Statton.

'Who's that?'

The face meant nothing to me. She was half lost in shadow and at the far edge of the camera's resolution, blurred and misshapen. She wasn't anyone I knew.

I shrugged.

Laura played a snip of video, only a few seconds long.

'Who is it now?'

The video looped. I didn't get a better look at the woman's face than in the still Laura had pulled, but that wasn't why Laura had sent me the clip. I was looking at the way the woman moved. The toss of her head. The sideways glance. The set of her shoulders as she turned away ...

I was looking at Alysha. Except Alysha was dead.

I shook my head. 'No.'

'I know it can't be. But it's so like her.'

It was. Just like Liss had been.

Liss ...?

Was that possible?

My throat was dry. Words clogged in my mouth, unable to get out. Laura was looking at me with an intensity like she was trying to see my soul.

No. Not possible. Liss was on Magenta.

'Sorry.'

Laura touched my arm and looked away. I watched the clip again. The woman wasn't Alysha ... but she had something. It was like seeing a ghost.

'It's OK.' It wasn't.

Someone reached past me then to tap Laura on the shoulder. Laura started so sharply that she almost fell off her seat; she blinked as we pulled ourselves back to the real world of the ice rink and the game. The face looking at Laura had a mildly worried expression, unfamiliar yet not quite a total stranger. I'd seen her here before. Another parent. I was already pulling her identity when she pointed across to the rink. The game had stopped. Everyone was clustered around one of the boys lying prone.

'I'm sorry,' she said, 'but isn't that your son?'

ASA RILEY

Asa Riley checks herself into the Magenta Institute at the reception desk. A shell greets her. As shells go, it is cordial and well programmed. It is superficially close to human and its personality unit is capable of superficial conversation as well as deep information access. Asa Riley knows that shells can be more advanced than this. The artificial intelligences they can host reach far beyond human. She knows this because Asa Riley knows a great deal about artificial intelligence. She is, in fact, something of an expert, although the fake past she has created for herself today shows nothing of the sort.

'I trust you had a pleasant journey?'

The shell takes a biometric scan of her face. At the Tesseract next door they would demand a retina scan, fingerprints and DNA, but the Magenta Institute has students in and out at every hour and so the dean here takes a more practical view.

'Passable.'

The shell has cross-referenced the identity codes from Asa Riley's Servant and determined that she arrived from Earth on the last trip of the *Fearless*. That she landed at New Hope this morning, probably on the same shuttle as Jared Black.

'Are you here for business or pleasure?'

The shell's generic personality gives away its underlying simplicity. No one comes to Magenta for pleasure.

'I'm here to use the library,' says Asa Riley.

Redundant as such things seem when everything ever written is available at a thought, the Magenta Library serves other purposes. It is, among other things, museum, archive, research facility and meeting place. Asa Riley remembers that it once served particularly good coffee imported from Earth. Agents from the Tesseract next door came across for no other reason. She wonders if they still do.

Not that any of them would recognise her.

The reception shell decides that Asa Riley poses no threat to the students and faculty of the Institute. It passes her Servant a short entry code and welcomes her. She heads to the library and spends an hour there, passing the time, waiting. She reads a news article, several months old now, one of the first reports of the first trans-polar expedition – better known as the Stay expedition after its leader Doctor Stay – and its remarkable discovery.

Mystery Object Discovered Under Magentan Polar Ice
Scientists working with the Magenta Institute Polar Expedition have released images from ground-penetrating radar of an object visible through the Magentan polar ice. The object, discovered during a routine survey, was initially mistaken for a rock formation; however, the new survey shows the object to be metallic in nature and not a natural formation. The Magenta Institute Polar Expedition commenced its survey of Magenta's polar regions two months ago with the objective of ... *Details*

There are pictures, and links to raw data and to the mathematics used to piece together the images of whatever lies under the ice. From the first basic principles of physics to the exact technical specifications of the ground-penetrating radar and how it works, everything required is available to her. So are the images created.

44

Asa Riley looks at them and agrees: what's down there does look like a spaceship. It also looks like a rock.

She reads the chatter that followed the article's release.

This has been all over the media today. Everyone's talking about it. How did I miss this?

It's a spaceship!

It can't be.

Just because it looks *like a spaceship doesn't mean that it is.*

It looks a lot *like a spaceship.*

That and similar, repeated a million times. Other queries and answers about the viciousness of the polar weather systems, the violence and frequency of the storms, the bitter cold of the nights, where temperatures sometimes fall low enough to condense nitrogen out of the air. But among the fluff are the questions that matter.

Is there anything about how long it's been there?

That, Asa Riley agrees, is the question. At least a hundred years, from the thickness of ice. Maybe a lot more. Was it here before the first settlers came? Because if it was then it has to be a Masters' ship. Or was it here before the Masters came too, in which case ...

In which case ... what?

Asa Riley doesn't know. She follows the threads to their more esoteric ends, to those who think there are more than the thirty-seven colonies. To those who think the Masters never left and watch us still. What if this thing under the ice *is* a ship? What if it crashed there not before the Masters came but after they left? What then?

The Stay expedition concluded that what they'd found was most likely a rock. As it has turned out, they were wrong. The second expedition has begun to release its initial surveys and what's down there isn't natural. The most likely explanation is a crashed ship from the early years after the Masters left.

Asa Riley follows the threads of these old discussions at the far fringes of speculation with the meticulous thoroughness of well-honed professional instinct. She pays close attention to the names of those who espouse their theories. One in particular catches her eye.

Steadman. Doctor Nicholas Steadman.

She waits in the library until Doctor Elizabeth Jacksmith, the Polar Expedition's chief scientist, passes through on her way home for the night. Then Asa Riley follows her out.

TWO

DRONES AND ASSASSINS

4

LISS

A pair of paramedic shells were lifting Jamie by the time we got to the ice. They carried him to a pod already waiting outside. Mercy gave us the bad news an hour later: a torsion fracture to the left tibia. Three days confined to bed hooked up to an infusion of drugs, minerals and repair nanites. Then go home and take it easy. In a week he'd be running around as though it had never happened. Mercy put him under while it locked the bone in place. Laura and I sat beside his bed. There wasn't anything either of us could do and we should both have gone home, but neither of us did. However much sense that didn't make, that was how it was. I stayed the night even though we'd both agreed I wouldn't. At some point I guess I dozed off.

Jamie was awake and playing games with his Servant when I left in the morning, alert and taking it all in his stride as though nothing much had happened. Laura was a shadow-eyed shell. I doubt I looked any better. I knocked back a couple of DeTox on my way to meeting Bix and we took the early mag-lev out of

Firstfall to Disappointment. I slept. Bix paced. I think he spent a lot of the time talking to Esh.

The Tesseract had unearthed more about Jared Black's love life than we had but it amounted to the same: an on-off relationship with Ranya Sovei for the last four or five months. Ranya and Hussein Sovei both had alibis for the last couple of days. Hussein apparently knew about the affair and didn't care – they were estranged. They both had witnesses to back them and the sum of every background check I could think of showed no suggestion of either the skills, the resources or the motivation it had taken to kill Jared Black.

I crossed them off the list. I thought about asking Laura to interview Diane Bara since both of them were in Mercy now, and then asked Esh to go do it instead. Laura had set the Tesseract on her theory during the night, building up tracks of everyone on the *Fearless*. An hour out of Firstfall it woke me up to give me the same answers we'd found the night before: Statton was real and he'd cloned Black's Servant. He'd mostly kept to himself, but in the last couple of days on the ship he'd been more active. The only person he'd spent much time with was Chantale Pré, which was why Bix and I were going to Disappointment to see if Ms Pré could give us at least a clue as to who Statton really was.

By now I figured Statton was somewhere on Magenta, not up in orbit. New Hope had logged Jared Black passing immigration twice. The second time they'd sent someone to verify him in person. He'd checked out, which meant the first time was either Statton or a q-ware glitch – they'd had a few of those so they hadn't chased it any further at the time. I had the Tesseract trace the first Jared Black through his Servant transactions. He'd taken a pod from New Hope into Firstfall's old town. There he'd vanished without a trace.

Which only left us with a whole planet to search.

Keys? Can we talk?

The message popped into my Servant. No signature, no address, nothing I could trace any further than an anonymous remailer somewhere in orbit. I knew who it was, though. No one called me Keys any more. That had been for Alysha.

What do you want?

She was out there, a spirit in the net. Alysha's ghost. Liss.

The memories you posted. They were from Alysha.

Some collection she made. You've looked at them?

Of course she had. She'd looked at them and processed them within seconds like the AI she was.

Yes.

She had a new interest in the Masters in the last year before the bomb. A quiet one but it was there.

I know.

Of course she did. How could she not? They were the same person, near as it was possible to be.

But?

There had to be a but. She wouldn't be talking to me otherwise.

That's not what these are about.

It isn't?

I couldn't stop a surge of bitterness. The wife I thought I'd known. The woman I'd loved, with whom I'd shared my life. Liss wasn't her, not really, but she knew Alysha better than I did now. Sometimes I felt as though Liss had stolen her from me. Stupid, but that's being human for you.

Keys, you know I'm going to dig at these.

Do you have to?

Knowing what we both know about her? Yes.

Knowing what? That everyone thought she was a traitor? Please don't.

You don't mean that. Besides, I want to.

I wish you wouldn't.

If that was true then you wouldn't have sent them to me.

She was probably right.

You want someone to look. Someone who isn't you.

I looked around. Bix was slumped in his seat, his face locked in the distant stare of someone deep in their Servant. A remote conversation, or maybe he was playing games or looking up the latest from forensics on the Diane Bara shell. Or maybe it was porn. Whatever it was, I wasn't a part of his world for now.

I suppose.

You know I don't believe—

You're a machine, Liss. The word *believe* doesn't belong to you.

You know I want her to have been pure.

Pure? I groaned, loud enough to cast a furtive glance at Bix in case he'd heard. He didn't look up.

She's dead, Liss. We know who killed her and we know why and it's done. We gave her justice. Does any of the rest matter?

Of course it mattered. If it hadn't mattered then I wouldn't have given the files to Liss. I wouldn't have opened them at all.

It matters to you, Keys.

I didn't want it to. What I wanted was for someone, some-where, to show me that Alysha was the person I'd always believed her to be: good and honest and beautiful. I didn't need these wounds opened again. I wanted them closed. Sutured once and for all.

I'll let you know if I find anything.

I'd rather you didn't.

We both knew that was a lie. I don't even know why I was trying. Liss let it slide.

Keys, are you OK?

Not really. I saw Alysha's parents yesterday.

Why was I telling her this? We shouldn't even have been talking.

I know.

You were watching?

Yes.

Liss!

Of course she'd been watching. I hadn't merely expected it, I'd *assumed* it. So why the sense of outrage, of violation?

I didn't know.

I had to, Keys. You know that.

I hadn't seen her or heard her or felt her but I'd known. It was so human. It made no sense but in her shoes I would have done exactly the same. The only difference was that I wasn't a machine.

You can't keep doing that, Liss. If the bureau find you, they'll dismantle you. They'll infect you with viral q-code that will rip you to pieces one shred at a time.

They won't find me.

Go away, Liss. Leave me alone.

How did you tell someone that they weren't supposed to exist? How did you tell them that they were a mistake? How did you tell them all those things when they loved you – and when you both knew that the *reason* they loved you was because you'd made them to be that way? Liss had killed for that love, a love I'd put into her. If the bureau ever found her, if they ever realised what she was and what she'd done ... It would be the end of both of us.

I'll tell you if I find anything.

She was gone. At least she didn't linger.

I slept the rest of the way. I think I twinged a little in my sleep when we passed the place where Alysha had died. She'd stowed away on the overnight freight train. Loki had blown one of the pumping stations that kept the mag-lev tunnels evacuated. The train was travelling at a thousand miles an hour on its way to Disappointment when Magenta's atmosphere had flooded in.

53

At that speed it might as well have hit a wall. It took three months to get the tunnel cleared and sealed and the line going again. By then Loki had been caught, tried and sentenced. He was a terrorist. A well-known Entropist. A crazy radical anti-technologist loner. That was his story and everything the investigation had found said it was true. And Alysha had been running away because six good men had died – six deaths where every shred of evidence pointed straight back at her.

Evidence. Sometimes I hated that word. The Alysha I knew wouldn't do a thing like that. Just wouldn't. Couldn't. I believed that because I had to, because I'd loved her and love couldn't be that wrong. Someone in the Tesseract had set her up and now someone in the Tesseract had cleared three Fleet men to interview Jared Black, alone and unsupervised. I wondered whether either of those someones had known what precisely would happen next.

I wished the train could go slower and linger a little where Alysha died. Where her ghost would be, if you believed in that sort of thing.

It was only a twinge this time. It was getting better.

My Servant sounded a gentle alarm as we slowed into Disappointment. I had a report waiting for me from Esh, her interview with Diane Bara. It was short and to the point and what I'd expected: forensics might get something but Bara's story added nothing. She'd seen the shell at the door for a fleeting second before it jabbed her with a needle. The next thing she remembered was waking up in Mercy, with Esh and her questions waiting patiently beside her.

'Dude.' Bix was watching me. 'You might want to see this.'

Turned out we weren't going to be Chantale Pré's first visitors of the day.

5

VICTOR AND CHANTALE

A pod waited for us at the station. I threw my Tesseract codes at it, told it this was an emergency, and sat back as we shot through downtown Disappointment like a bullet through a gun barrel. Pré lived in the rich surface district of Little Aqaba. On a world best known for being cold and wet, calling anywhere Little Aqaba was the height of folly but no one was going to say so, not when the real Aqaba had vanished under the onslaught of the Masters. Most of the Sinai desert had gone with it and plenty more places besides. Spain and Portugal, disintegrated into the sea. There was a hole in the Rocky Mountains big enough to fit a small European country. Indonesia and Bolivia were half the size they'd been two centuries ago. The list was long.

The Disappointment police were there when we arrived. It was one of those rare days when the weather wasn't lashing rain and winds that could pick a man off his feet. The uniforms had Ms Pré out in the open, talking to her across a table in the sun. She looked more annoyed than hurt. There were no particle-beam-shaped holes in anything as far as I could see.

I pinged my Tesseract codes to the uniforms. Their Servants pinged me back. Officers Stephenson and Gibson.

'Rause and Rangesh. Tesseract. Get Ms Pré into cover. I need to talk to whoever's in charge here.'

That turned out to be a Lieutenant Mitsuko up in Chantale's apartment. We took Pré into the manager's office of her apartment building. She was tall and slender for a Magentan, which probably meant she spent half her life on medication trying to cope with a gravity she wasn't built for. She had a striking face, clear dusky skin and big eyes. I could see why Quadratic used her.

Mitsuko brought us up to speed. 'Ms Pré's data archives were wiped this morning. Clean as a whistle. Including offline backups, so they did it from inside the building.'

'Physical intrusion? You sure?'

Mitsuko grinned. 'Oh yes.' She seemed pleased with herself, which didn't make much sense. I was missing something.

'Anything else gone?'

She shook her head.

'When was this?'

'About an hour ago.'

'Forensics?'

Gibson laughed. 'We don't need forensics.'

I raised an eyebrow.

'Spy-cam in the bedroom.' He winked. 'Separately networked and activated automatically as soon as the intruder came in.'

'You got a face?'

Mitsuko nodded. 'Not just a face. We got the whole intrusion in perfect BVQ resolution. We'll have him before lunchtime. What's the bureau's interest?'

BVQ. Beyond Visual Quality. The latest fad from Earth. I pinged her our composite of Martin Statton.

'This your man?'

Mitsuko shook her head and sent me a video clip. Footage from Pré's secret camera. Whoever he was, he was quick and efficient and definitely not Statton.

'Servant ping?' I asked, not that I expected one.

'He's not *that* stupid. Victor Friedrich. Disappointment's data bandit.'

Mitsuko pinged me a file. Friedrich had a history of data piracy. Never anything big but the sort to ring alarms. He knew his way around Servant and surveillance architectures. He knew the law, too, he just thought it was meant for someone else.

'We have him as a likely for a dozen data thefts but we never had him cold like this. We'll pick him up before the end of the day.'

Gibson laughed. 'The girls in data forensics are going to party tonight.'

I exchanged a couple of private messages with Lieutenant Mitsuko, gave her the Statton composite and told her how he'd flown in from Earth. I pinged the composite to Chantale too.

'You know this man?'

She nodded. 'He was on the *Fearless*. I talked to him.' She sighed. 'He was hitting on me.'

'Anything seem odd about him?'

'No.'

'Did he give you anything?'

She shook her head.

'Why the camera?'

She gave me an exhausted look, then shrugged, a mixture of resignation and frustration. 'I had a couple of break-ins last year. I didn't want to come home and find someone I didn't know waiting for me.'

'You could have rigged a silent alarm.'

She shrugged again. I got the feeling she was hiding something but I doubted it had much to do with Statton and Black.

Blank pick-ups, Bix pinged.

What?

I did some research on the way in. She does blank pick-ups.

I stand by my 'what?'

Sex with random strangers, dude.

What? Really?

Part of the thrill, man. A month's salary says she records it.

People do that?

People do all sorts. Just ask Esh.

That, I reckoned, was something Bix was going to really wish he hadn't said once his brain caught up with his mouth.

'Can you tell me what was wiped?' I asked.

Pré still had that heavy look in her eye. 'Some of it's quite private.'

Bix gave me an I-told-you-so look.

'Anything we recover will be examined in confidence,' I said. 'We have to verify its provenance. Most of it's done by machines but—'

Stephenson poked his head around the door.

'We just got a ping on Friedrich!'

Mitsuko jumped up. 'Let's go!'

She was talking to Gibson, not to us. She didn't spare me a glance as they left.

I told Chantale to get in touch if she remembered anything more about Statton or if she saw him, then Bix and I were racing out of Little Aqaba into the heart of Disappointment, hot on Mitsuko's tail.

I pinged Mitsuko: Where is he?

The university. In the quad.

Mitsuko linked me to a campus video feed. The quad looked like it was hosting an impromptu festival, which brought back all sorts of memories. There were vending bots and shells and little stalls and a couple of acoustic bands and students doing all the things that students did when they had a party. Disappointment didn't get decent weather all that often and they were making the most of it.

Friedrich sat right in the middle, sipping coffee from a polystyrene cup, soaking up the sun like he didn't have a care in the world. Nothing about him looked like he was spooked. He looked like he was waiting for someone.

Hold back. This is a meet. You can have him afterwards.

Mitsuko didn't like that. Data pirates don't meet in the flesh, Agent Rause. He's probably made it public already. That's more his style. That or blackmail.

I told her to hold back anyway.

Have it your way. I just don't want to lose him.

'You think I'm wrong about this, don't you?' I asked Bix. 'You think this is just a sex tape someone wants gone.'

Bix made a face of mild disgust. 'Kinda do, kinda don't. The timing sucks. Bit of a coincidence.'

'Yup.'

He laughed. 'You know what I think? I think Ms Pré was a bit coy with you, dude. You know, about what happened on the *Fearless*? She said Statton was hitting on her. I think she took a shine to him. I think she's got him on video. Like, a lot of him, you know?'

We were close to the university. I had my Servant mask my Tesseract codes and go plain-clothes. Last thing we needed was Friedrich or whoever he was meeting picking us up on a random ping. A few local police might not make him twitch, not with the festival in the quad, but a pair of Tesseract agents from Firstfall? Hardly subtle.

I pinged Chantale: Did you have sex with Statton on the *Fearless*?

59

Hardly subtle either, but I was starting to have a bad feeling about this.

I have people on Friedrich. Mitsuko still didn't like that I was making her hold. We can take him whenever you're ready.

How is that your business? Chantale.

Watch and wait for someone to make contact. Mitsuko. Ms Pré, did you have a recording of him or not?

'Dude ...' Bix was wearing his thinking face. 'If this is about something that happened on the *Fearless* ... How does anyone else know? I mean, you guys were like, all over that *Fearless* data all through the night. And Laws had to get it from Fleet, you know? She probably had to sweat blood for that. It's not like it's just, you know, *there*.'

'Same way we did, I suppose,' I said without thinking.

'Yeah. Exactly that.'

Shit. So someone else had seen the same video data we had? Which meant either someone in Fleet or someone inside the bureau?

Chantale hadn't answered my question.

I pinged Mitsuko: Keep your people back. I'm bringing in a tac-team. I sent the request through the Tesseract. Ms Pré, yes or no right now. Did you or did you not have recordings of Martin Statton from the *Fearless*?

Maybe none of this had anything to do with Statton. Maybe Bix was right and I was going to look stupid. But if whoever was coming for Friedrich's data was the same person who'd vaporised Jared Black's head ...

Yes.

I pinged Mitsuko again: Get Ms Pré into protective custody.

You want to tell me what's going on, Agent Rause?

Later.

Fine. Looks like Friedrich has a friend.

I fed the campus video to my lenses. Friedrich had lost

60

interest in his coffee. He was sitting straight and alert, his head twitching as he scanned the crowd.

He looks spooked.

His Servant took a ping.

Trace-back?

Not a chance.

Our pod was as close as we were going to get. The rest would have to be on foot. I prodded Bix.

'Friedrich's perked up. Mitsuko thinks someone made contact. Our tac-team is six minutes away. It has to be us. You and me.'

'Dude!' Bix made a sour face. He checked his Reeper and stuffed it into a jacket pocket. 'You know what bothers me, man? What that Fleet guy was saying to Black before the shell whacked them. You know? Because Black was out, dude, and he had to know that. So what was there to say?'

'I'll get Laura on it.'

'I keep thinking *"Requiescat in pace,"* you know? And this totally stinks. I mean, like, Mitsuko's right – why would you meet in person to get a stack of jacked data? Because what? There aren't about a billion encrypted anonymous data-havens even on Magenta?'

'I'll have your back.'

We both knew Bix would have to be the one to get close. I was in a suit, he was in ripped jeans and a tie-dyed shirt.

'I'm not vested, man. What do you want me to do?'

I opened a channel to Mitsuko so she'd hear. 'Get close. Watch for any pick-up. If there is one, go with the data. We'll hand over to lens surveillance and satellite as soon as we can, once we know who we're tracking. Friedrich stays loose until the data is clear. But I need you eyes-close. Just in case.'

'Right on, boss dude. But I gotta say I don't like what's going down here.'

We trotted up the steps to the university and into the quad. Crowds of students mingled in clumps, making the most of the sun. Shells and the vending bots moved through them, offering legal gens, hot dogs and seaweed smoothies. The air was heavy with the smells of alcohol and low-grade Xen, loud with raised voices, shouted conversation and broken snatches of music. I didn't dare use my Tesseract codes. There were bound to be at least a couple of dealers selling high-grade Xen, people who wouldn't want to find themselves talking to a bureau agent. It would only take a hint of panic to warn Friedrich off.

I flipped back and forth between reality and the layered video feeds of the quad projected onto my lenses. We had Friedrich on four cameras now, watching him from all angles in case anyone approached ...

There. Mitsuko highlighted a figure on one of the feeds. A woman only a dozen feet from Friedrich, deep in conversation with a student trying to sell handmade rolling mats. She wasn't looking at Friedrich but Mitsuko was right: there was something off about her. The way she was looking everywhere *but* at Friedrich. She wasn't a native Magentan either. She had the look of an Earther, although she didn't seemed to be suffering from the gravity. You want an ID?

We'd have to ping her Servant for that. Maybe among this crowd a ping could be innocent enough – I was getting them left and right, mostly from the bots. But still ...

I don't want to spook her. Yet.

We closed on Friedrich. I angled away, leaving Bix to get cosy.

The woman decided she didn't want to buy a rolling mat. For a moment she looked at Friedrich. Straight at him for half a second without blinking. Then she turned away.

Someone else just accessed the campus surveillance system! Mitsuko.

The woman turned and walked off. Straight and with purpose. Friedrich hadn't moved. We had four cameras staring right at him. Anyone else in the system would see straight away that we were watching him ...

There was something off about the way the woman walked. Same as Diane Bara ...

Shit. She's a shell. We're blown. Take them both.

We had officers at every entrance to the quad. They wouldn't be ...

A fizzling whoosh. A loud crack detonated behind me. I spun around to see a puff of smoke and a spray of glittering lights. A miniature firework. Another went off, then two more, scattered across the quad. People around me stopped to look, happy content faces, smiles lit up by the dancing lights.

Friedrich's down!

The surveillance feed showed Friedrich on his bench, head slumped to his knees. A small trickle of blood oozed from a dark hole in the side of his head.

Shooter! The crowd around him hadn't noticed, distracted by the fireworks. Bix! Get Friedrich! We need to know—

A scream rose over the crackle and pop of the fireworks. I pushed through the crowd after the woman, flicking on my Tesseract codes, listening in to the frantic edge rising in the Servant traffic around me. *Oh my God! Is he dead? Someone's been shot? Someone call for help ...*

Then the world shimmered, like the rainbow sheen of petrol in the sun washing across my lenses. My Servant went dead. I faltered to a stop.

What just happened?

No answer. My Servant wasn't responding. Judging from the stunned faces around me I wasn't the only one. Almost everyone had stopped in their tracks, conversations severed mid-sentence like the universe had momentarily hit pause by mistake, everyone

63

looking around with the same thought, stealing glances at one another. *Did you see that too? What was that?*

The woman was gone. Just like that. Disappeared in the moment.

My Servant sprang back to life. Everyone around me was suddenly talking, animated, infected by a communal urgency that wasn't quite panic. *What just happened? My Servant crashed! Did your Servant just die too? Something weird happened with my lenses! Rainbow screen of death! Yeah, mine too! Did you just see a load of weird colours? What's going on? I dunno, crashed and rebooted or something ...*

I pulled the images I'd snapped of the woman's face. Projected them onto my lenses. Started running facial recognition ...

Agent Rause? Mitsuko.

What just happened?

No idea. Our communications went down.

Where is she?

We're trying to find her. I've set up a search grid. We're locking the university down.

Shooter?

Not yet.

Word spread across the crowd, rushing through it like a brush fire. Someone was dead. Someone had been murdered. The press around me thickened as people started to push and run. I looked back and saw Bix sitting next to Friedrich, going through his pockets.

Bix! Get away from him.

No answer. Everyone was trying to get out of the quad now, shouting, running, pushing. I forced myself against the flow. Bix didn't look up until I was close enough to shout at him.

'Get the fuck away from him!' I yelled. 'Sniper!'

Bix shook his head. He had what looked like a pile of data slivers in his hand.

'Was a drone, dude,' he said as I reached the bench. 'One shot. I saw it.' He dropped the slivers on the floor. 'And these are dead. Wiped clean.' He made a face. 'Same pulse that wiped my Servant.' He tapped the side of his head. 'It's screwed. Like, totally. I was right next to him.'

Friedrich lolled on the bench, that neat round hole drilled into the side of his skull.

6

PROJECT INSURGENT

The tac-team I'd asked for arrived about two minutes too late to be useful. They had a Cheetah so I sent them back to Little Aqaba to pick up Chantale Pré and fly her to Firstfall. Bix and I hung around in Disappointment, picking up the pieces. Mitsuko had the university quad cordoned off. Forensics drones picked through the detritus. I didn't think they were going to find much. We had the drone that killed Friedrich, its insides burned out by a thermal charge and what was left of its memory erased by the same pulse that had fried Bix's Servant. A quantum electromagnetic charge, according to the university professor we talked to, something that existed in theory papers and maybe a few laboratories at the cutting edge of modern physics. As well as the drone, it had wiped Friedrich's Servant clean. The woman, meanwhile, was gone. Mitsuko's team never picked her up. We tried the university cameras but they'd all glitched when the pulse went off. By the time they came back she was lost in the crowd. I collected what we had on her. It wasn't much.

'Still think this is about some random sex tape?' I asked. Bix shook his head.

'Statton's the key, boss dude.'

Yeah. Still just one whole planet to search.

Bix had his Servant working again but everything he'd stored on it was gone, probably for ever. Disappointment forensics weren't hopeful about Friedrich's slivers. I left Mitsuko to comb through Friedrich's life in case he'd made backups of anything – Pré's data, who'd set him up, who paid him off, that sort of thing. I didn't expect her to find much. I had a strong hunch that Friedrich's murder wasn't about stealing Chantale Pré's recordings. It was more about making sure that no one else ever got to see them.

We took the afternoon train to Firstfall and got back to the Tesseract a couple of hours after the tac-team's Cheetah landed. Laura was still in Mercy with Jamie, running her end of the investigation from his bedside. She'd talked to Tomasz Shenski in Fleet, for what that was worth. Yes, the officers in the hospital were his. The story he'd given about Fleet following up on inconsistencies in Jared Black's immigration paperwork was so flimsy that Laura thought he might actually be trying to tell us something. She'd worked the footage from Mercy too, trying to extract what Fleet had been whispering into Black's ear in the moments before the shell came in. It was patchy, but she reckoned she could just about make it out.

The names! Where are the names?

I told her to go home and get some rest. She didn't want to but I made her go anyway. Maybe I was still smarting from the whole 'wanting space' thing.

I told Bix to go home too. 'Get your Servant sorted. Get some sleep. We need to be fresh tomorrow.'

Tomorrow I figured we were going to have a crack at Fleet and Tomasz Shenski. See who he was and whether he really did have something to say. Tonight, though, Chantale Pré was going to tell us everything she knew about Martin Statton.

She was with Esh in an interview room deep under the Tesseract. It was safe but not exactly comfortable. She certainly wasn't happy about being there.

'I want a lawyer,' was the first thing she said.

'You're here for your own safety,' I told her. 'The man who stole your data was murdered this morning.'

I saw how that shook her. It took her a moment to compose herself.

'You can't keep me here. And you can't talk to me without a lawyer present. Not if I say I want one.'

'OK.' I turned to Esh. Technically Pré was right. 'Agent Zohreya, since you weren't with us in Disappointment, perhaps you'd like to be briefed?'

Esh nodded.

'So we've got four corpses murdered by a killer with a particle beam.'

I turned on a wall-screen and put up pictures of the bodies from Mercy. They weren't pretty and they weren't there for Esh.

'Our working theory is that the killer is after Martin Statton. Ms Pré met Statton on the *Fearless* en route from Earth. Statton was using Jared Black's Servant identity but was calling himself Andreas Kretch. Someone in Disappointment hired a data thief, Victor Friedrich, to steal Ms Pré's archives and wipe them. I'm guessing they were after something from the *Fearless*. As far as I can tell they didn't ever collect the data. They killed Friedrich with a drone and then set off some high-tech electromagnetic bomb that wiped everything clean. So Ms Pré's data has all gone.' I shot Chantale a glance. 'Speculation – why would the killer steal that data and then wipe it without looking at it first?'

'To stop us from getting it,' said Esh promptly. 'Because they already know what's on it.'

'And then what?'

Esh gave Chantale a long look. 'Well ... I have to assume Ms Pré doesn't have a copy stored in her Servant and that the killer already knows this – otherwise they'd have wiped her when they wiped the rest. But still ... There *is* one archive left. The one that's in her head.'

'So?'

'They vaporised Jared Black's head, sir. I think it would be that.'

It didn't add up, not really. Whoever had killed Friedrich had surely already had the chance to kill Chantale too. But Esh was playing along and it had had the desired effect. Pré had turned several shades paler.

'You don't have to talk to us if you don't want to,' I told her. 'You're free to go as you please. Do you want to leave?'

She swallowed. 'You're telling me my life is in danger?'

'I can't say with certainty but it's very possible.'

I let her have a think about that. She looked away, staring at the floor. Then she took a couple of long deep breaths.

'I spent the last night on the *Fearless* with Andreas,' she said. 'Or whatever his real name is.'

'Record it?'

She nodded.

'Got a copy?'

That was no. 'I don't keep them in my Servant.'

'Did he say anything?'

'Lots of things.'

'Anything to make you think he wasn't who he said? Any other name he might have used? Something that slipped out when he let his guard down?'

'No.' She shook her head. 'He said his name was Andreas.'

I set up the room for a formal interview. Esh and I sat across the table from her. We worked through the journey of the *Fearless* from Earth to Magenta from start to finish, hour by hour where we had to. Chantale hadn't noticed anything in the Fleet orbital over Earth or during the transfer to the *Fearless*. The only thing she remembered that wasn't like every other trip she'd made was that another ship had docked next to them just before the *Fearless* winked out of normal space. She described the ship. Esh reckoned it was a Fleet corvette. Esh being Esh, she asked for its tail number.

'It didn't have a number. It had a symbol on it. Like an infinity sign enclosed by a star.'

I eased Chantale through her days aboard the *Fearless*. I walked her through the tracks of her movements, built from the Fleet video surveillance and her Servant transactions. Four days of business, two for herself, that was her rule. Four days of papers, review meetings, planning sessions, even a few video shoots. She'd used them as she always used them, she said, to eye up the other passengers and pick one.

'Pick one for what?'

She shrugged. 'Sex.'

'And you picked Andreas Kretch.'

She shrugged again. 'He was interesting. He looked like my type.'

Esh asked what she meant by that. Somehow she made it into a conversation instead of an interview – two women talking about how they picked their targets, rating men at a distance for their attributes, the details that could be gleaned from careful observation and a judicious check of Servant records. I faded into the background while they talked. There was something slightly unnerving about sitting there while the two of them talked about how I might be ranked and rated. Arms. Eyes. Jawline. Smile. That sort of thing. Pré hadn't managed to pull anything out of Statton's Servant, which she said made him all the more interesting. It didn't surprise her, now that she was over the shock of the last few hours, that Andreas Kretch wasn't his real name.

I let Esh lead the questions about their evenings together, even though it didn't seem like we were getting anywhere. There was nothing in the rest that struck me as remarkable and nothing to give any clue as to who Statton really was.

'He said he was a lawyer,' she said.

Esh and I exchanged a glance. 'Anything more?'

'I don't think so ... Just ... Part of a small firm in Firstfall who didn't do anything interesting. I don't think he said anything more about it.'

I pinged Esh: Patel and Black.

'What about what he did on Earth?'

'Dull law stuff, he said. We didn't talk much about that.'

'He must have said something!'

He'd made her laugh. He'd had opinions. But as to his life and who he was? Nothing.

You buy this?

Yes. A pause, and I saw Esh smile. Sometimes, when it's nothing more than a night, you actually don't want to know.

Yeah. OK. Maybe too much information?

You asked. I think he knew Jared Black, though.

I thought so too. 'Distinguishing features? Scars, tattoos, birthmarks?'

'He had a tattoo,' Chantale said. 'He said something about bad boy days on Magenta.'

'Where was it? Can you describe it?'

'Like a sword with wings or something. It was on his hip.'

Esh snapped to attention. 'Was there a number underneath it?' she asked.

Chantale nodded.

71

'What was it?'

Now she shook her head. 'I don't remember. Sorry.'

Esh stopped the interview recording. She unzipped her jump-suit and pulled it down to her hips. I caught a flash at her throat, a silver crescent moon and star on a slender chain. Under the jumpsuit she was wearing a combat vest. She lifted it to show us the skin of her left hip. There was a tattoo. A winged sword with a number underneath it.

'Was it that?'

Chantale gasped. 'Yes!'

Esh zipped herself up and restarted the interview recording.

'So the tattoo you saw was the same as mine. Except for the number?'

'Yes!'

'You recorded your night with him. Did you catch the tattoo?'

Chantale shrugged. 'Probably. What is it?'

'Any chance you'll be able to remember the number?'

That got us a sigh and a pained look. Chantale tapped her head. 'It wasn't really commanding my attention at the time.'

Esh looked at me. 'It might still be enough to find out who he is, sir.'

'What's the tattoo?' asked Chantale again.

'Can I?' Esh held my eye. 'I don't think it's a big secret.'

'It is to me.'

Esh flicked a smile at Chantale. 'It's a special forces tattoo, sir. Half the members of every tac-team you've ever worked with have it. It means ...' She let out a breath. 'If you boil it down, sir, it means that you've come under fire and ... Bluntly, it means you've killed someone in the line of duty. Stolen from an old Earth special forces unit. Probably more than one.' She stopped the recording again. 'It started like a support group to help connect soldiers to others who'd been through the same. Nightmares and the trauma that can come after you shoot

72

someone. But it didn't stay like that. It was stopped when two virgins used lethal force in a situation that didn't merit it. There was a suggestion that they ...' Another look to Chantale. 'It was stopped, sir.'

'Virgins?'

Esh looked away. 'Sorry, sir. Bad choice of words.'

I restarted the interview. I asked Chantale Pré what Andreas Kretch had said about his past on Magenta. Nothing that she could remember beyond what he'd said about working for a law firm. I walked her through the last day of the flight and the transfer to Magenta orbit and then to the surface but she hadn't seen Statton again since leaving the *Fearless*. We were back to not getting anywhere. By the time I wound things up we'd been at it for four hours straight. It was late and I was tired. I needed a good night's sleep.

Esh set Chantale up in a secure suite under the Tesseract. I told her to get some rest and that we'd start again in the morning. I told Esh to go home and get some sleep as well and then wandered back to my office. I should have gone home too but I wasn't sure where that was any more. Home had been our house in the suburbs but that was long gone, sold to someone else, the money spent on Earth to build Liss. The bureau had given me an apartment when I came back, small but adequate. Memories of Liss and Alysha lurked in every corner there. It was drenched in them, which was a good part of why I slept at Laura's more often than not.

I booked myself a hotel cubicle close to the Tesseract and then told Firstfall Housing that I wanted to move. Something smaller but closer in. I'd have to deal with the recharge coffin for Liss's old shell. Sell it? No reason not to. It was just a standard recharge and storage box for a shell, that was all ...

'Sir?'

I was so far away, lost in memories, that I didn't see Esh

come in. I had to blink a few times to clear my lenses. Late nights and not enough sleep.

'Thought you'd gone home,' I said.

'Sorry, sir. But I might know who Martin Statton is.'

If I'd been sleepy before, I wasn't any more. 'I'm listening.'

'It's possible that the tattoo is a fake, but let's assume it's real for now since it's all we've got. To earn it Statton would have had to finish advanced training and then to have killed someone on mission. I think he's several years older than me and I think he knew the real Jared Black.'

'All supposition, Agent Zohreya, but go on.'

'I think our man might be Zinadine Kagame. Kagame killed two Earther smugglers fifteen years ago. That puts him in the window for the tattoo. He was at Disappointment University in the same year as Jared Black and he left the MSDF ten years ago. The Tesseract has no trace of him whatsoever since then. I think he went off-world.'

Whoever had killed Jared Black had killed Victor Friedrich too. The executions had the same feel to them: drones, shells, expensive cutting-edge technology. Professional hits using military-grade weapons. If the killer knew they were after a veteran soldier then maybe that explained why. Something about this still wasn't right, though. How did they get to Chantale Pré first? And why was she still alive when Victor Friedrich wasn't?

'Sir, I spoke to Jonas. Off the record, Kagame left to join Fleet.'

'Jonas?'

'Colonel Himaru.'

She cocked her head as if to ask whether I remembered. I gave her a wry smile. Colonel Jonas Himaru was a hard man to forget.

'Does he still give surfing lessons in between running Magenta's tac-teams?'

'I, ah, think that was a one-off, sir.'

'Kagame's your best bet?'

Esh nodded. 'The tattoo might not mean anything at all, but if it does then yes.'

'Then he's Suspect One. We should eliminate the others. Give me the names and I'll get that started.' The Tesseract would search for Servant transactions.

'I'll ask around. See if anyone remembers anything. See if there's been any contact.'

'You want me to call Agent Rangesh?'

Esh shook her head. 'No need, sir.' The crook of a hinted smile creased the corner of her mouth as she turned.

'Esh?'

She turned back.

'You and Bix. Something you want to share ...?'

She shook her head, still smiling, and so I let it go. We'd pressed flesh once, Esh and I. Shaken hands, a gesture that didn't mean much to those born on Earth but which was close to making a blood pact in the colonies. She'd come within an inch of committing a murder and I'd been ready to let her do it. And then she hadn't. She'd been the better of us that day. If she didn't want to talk then I wasn't going to push.

Esh sent me her list and I set the Tesseract to finding anyone else who might have earned that tattoo. I had it search for anyone who might have served with Kagame, too, just like Laura had done for Jared Black on the *Fearless* – only across the entire planet. Then I asked for records going back twenty years of people getting winged-sword tattoos. I tried not to think about how big that list was going to be. Or how incomplete. Or that Statton might just as easily have had it done on Earth.

The searches would take a while. I headed to get some sleep. I passed Esh on the way out.

'Go home, Esh.'

'I will, sir. Just a few more calls.'

I left her to it, went outside and walked across the quad. I left through the bureau atrium and started down the steps to the street. About halfway, I stopped. A hotel cubicle. That was what it had come to? A sterile little box of space?

Or an equally sterile apartment where everything reminded me of Liss.

Or ...

We were way past midnight but Esh was exactly where I'd left her when I got back inside.

'Which bit of "go home" was unclear, Agent Zohreya?'

'You tell me, sir.' She threw me a wry smile. 'There are places Kagame might have gone. I want to check them as far as I can. I don't have the access I used to but I know people who do. I need a direct line to the Tesseract when they call me back.'

I sat down at the desk opposite her. It was past midnight. At this time of night we almost had the place to ourselves.

'The first time you shot someone, did it bother you?'

'What do you mean?'

'I mean did it bother you. When you earned your tattoo.'

She looked me in the eye. 'He was warned, armed, and chose not to listen. He could have surrendered but he didn't. He was the one who made the choice, sir, not me. But it took a little while for me to see it that way.'

'I remember mine like it was yesterday.'

I stopped for a moment, trying to understand why I was talking about it. Chantale and Statton, yes, but there was more to it than that. I'd been with Alysha the first time she'd killed someone. It had struck me how it hadn't seemed to bother her. For the first and only time I'd looked at my wife and wondered if somewhere inside was a total stranger.

'I discovered some old files yesterday,' I said. 'Nothing to do with the case. They were about the Masters. Lectures. All the usual stuff – who they really were, what they really wanted, why they left and where they went. I don't know why but it got me thinking about that.' I wanted to say they were Alysha's files but I couldn't. I didn't know why but it seemed wrong to bring her into the room. Like inviting in a ghost.

Esh shrugged. 'One of Allah's mysteries. Long gone. Never particularly interested me.'

'Really?'

'Life's too short for questions that don't have answers, sir. I don't like them. Agent Rangesh, on the other hand ...'

She shook her head and cracked another wry smile that suggested I'd found the tip of a very large iceberg. Then she pinged me a link to a report from the second trans-polar expedition headquarters at the Magenta Institute next door. They'd released pictures in the last few minutes of the wreck under the ice, better composites of sonic imagery and more ground-penetrating radar which gave the shape more definition. Hard to say what it was but it didn't look natural. It looked like what everyone wanted it to be. Like a spaceship.

'It's not public yet,' Esh said. 'Not until the morning. But they're going to finally admit they think it's a ship.'

At this point that was rather like admitting that the bright thing in the sky that made the difference between night and day was, in fact, the sun.

'You know we'll have every crazy on the planet banging on about how the Masters are coming back as soon as they say that.'

'Every crazy on the planet has been saying that for months.' Esh shrugged. 'No, it's when it goes off-world. The *Fearless* will fill up. We'll have all the crazies from Earth too, and the other colonies as well. I suppose it's better than them all banging on about how the Strioth rapists should get a retrial on the grounds of cybernetic psychosis, though.'

'Go home, Esh,' I said again. 'Come back in the morning. We'll know who we're looking for by then.'

'I'll stay,' she said, 'and I'll bet you a month's pay we're looking for Zinadine Kagame.'

I had to laugh. 'What if it *is* a ship. What if it's been there longer than humans have been on Magenta? What if it's from before the Masters …?' Esh was looking at me, smiling and shaking her head. 'What?'

'You sound like Bix, sir. The ice-dating puts it around the time they left, give or take a year or two.'

'What if it's a Masters' ship from *after* they left?'

She snorted. 'If it's a ship at all then it'll be one of the shuttles they used to ferry the first settlers down from orbit. One of the ones they left behind. What else could it be? We didn't have any ships of our own back then. They left, we took them over.' She shrugged. 'Of course it'll be a Masters' ship.'

'What if there are dead Masters on board?'

She snorted again. 'How would we know? Did we ever know what they looked like?'

She had a point.

Esh turned back to her work. 'If it turns out that way then I'll be duly amazed. Until then it's just a lump of something under the ice.'

'Don't you have *any* curiosity?'

She gave me a sharp look. 'Expectations, sir. That's what I don't have. Things are what they are. Tomorrow they might not be. That's the way the world is. As Allah wills it.'

'Sounds a miserable way to live.'

'Not if you have faith, sir.'

Anyone else, I might have argued that. Not Esh.

She tensed.

'Got something?'

'Possibly.'

78

'A hit on Kagame?' I was on my feet at once.

'No. Not that. Not exactly.'

She sent what she'd found to my Servant. In Kagame's service record was a note saying he'd been inducted into Project Insurgent.

'Project what?'

Esh took a deep breath and sighed. 'Our contingency plan, sir. In case of invasion.' She did a good job of keeping the scorn out of her voice. Most of it.

'Invasion?'

'Yes, sir.' She still couldn't quite meet my eye. After a moment, when I didn't say anything, she held up her hands. 'Yes, I know. None of us took it particularly seriously.'

'Are you telling me that the MSDF had a contingency plan for the return of the Masters?'

'The Masters?' She almost howled with laughter. 'No! Earth!'

'Oh come on! Really?'

She was still laughing. 'You must remember the blockade, sir. It was only a year after my father brought us here. I was a child, but you—'

'I remember it, Agent Zohreya. No need to remind me how old I am.'

'I wanted to fly spaceships against the Earth invasion.'

'It wasn't even a real blockade! It was a narcotics interdiction.'

'They *did* threaten to land soldiers, sir.'

They had. I'd forgotten that. 'But they didn't. And the bureau started the Narcotics Directorate and—'

'And we invited them down and let them help us deal with our problems and seed the Tesseract AI and so the crisis ended, I know. But before it did, when it looked like they were coming down whether we liked it or not, the MSDF set up Project Insurgent and made plans for an armed resistance.'

'A *what*?'

Esh was trying not to look embarrassed. 'A resistance, sir.'

'That was twenty years ago!' And the MSDF had had what, a hundred soldiers? Two hundred? Against an invasion from Earth? 'What was it? An abandoned pit-mine out in the wastes and a few people's mums' apartments?'

'A little more than that, sir.' Esh took a deep breath. 'Safe houses. Money. Weapons. Everything the MSDF thought they might need to fight an invading army. They never dismantled it. And Kagame would know where they were. Insurgent could give him everything he'd need to go underground and hide. It's what it was designed for.'

'These safe houses. Do *you* know where they are?'

Esh shook her head. 'But I know a man who does. Sir?'

I waited.

'Project Insurgent wasn't just about resistance.'

'What do you mean?'

'I'm not quite sure, sir. I think what I mean is that if Martin Statton *is* Zinadine Kagame then we're looking at a special forces soldier trained in insurgency specifically against Earth. A soldier coming home after ten years in the wilderness and still undercover. He's got something, sir. Something big, and whoever it threatens, they know and they're after him. And even if Kagame didn't know he was being hunted before he landed, he does now – at the very least we have to assume he's been watching the news. I think what I mean is this, sir: if it *is* Kagame then he almost certainly understands exactly how much danger he's in. We need to be very careful when we approach him.'

'Why doesn't he just ...'

I stopped dead as a shiver ran down my spine. A spy coming in from the cold – is that what this was? So why didn't he just come in, then? Why not simply walk up the front steps of Tesseract and dump everything? The answer was obvious: because he knew it wasn't safe, that was why.

The Fleet men had been asking for names when the shell hit them in Mercy.

Someone inside the Tesseract had cleared those Fleet men to talk to Jared Black.

Alone.

And they'd all been hit before Jared could say a word.

'Very, very careful, sir,' said Esh softly.

I'd got it wrong. Jared Black had been both a target *and* a lure. Someone had set them all up together. But then Jared Black had turned out to be the wrong man ...

'Did Statton contact anyone between leaving the *Fearless* and arriving in Magenta's orbit?'

'I don't know, sir.'

'Find out.'

I kept coming back to it. Someone inside the Tesseract had put those Fleet men in Jared Black's room.

'Esh?'

'Sir?'

'Are we looking for one of our own?'

'I really wouldn't like to say, sir.'

But I knew something that Esh didn't. I knew that I believed in my wife. I knew that six men had died all those years ago and then Alysha had died too. She'd died while running away. They said she ran because of what she did, but I always knew that wasn't her way.

One of our own. *That* was why she ran.

7

ZINADINE KAGAME

Two weeks before she died, Alysha sent a tac-team to extract a scientist from a corporate research site. After the extraction the tac-team flew straight into a Magentan storm. They crashed and died because someone had tampered with their weather feeds. Alysha had kept the mission a total secret so there really wasn't anyone else who could have sabotaged it. She'd turned. No one quite knew why or how. Everyone supposed it had been for money, although if it was then no one had ever found it.

That was why she ran. Because of what she'd done. That was why she'd been on that freight train, the one that shouldn't have carried any people, when Loki set off his bomb; but I had a different story: someone else had set her up. For all I knew they were still here, still working in the bureau.

Jared Black – the Jared Black who was Martin Statton and Andreas Ketch and maybe Zinadine Kagame – had made one call between flipping in to the Magenta system with the *Fearless* and reaching orbit. He'd made it almost as soon as he arrived. We couldn't access who it went to or what he'd said but it hadn't been routed to Magenta. It had been sent on a tight-beam laser direct to the Fleet orbital.

Twenty minutes later we were in a pod rolling through the empty streets of Firstfall towards the Squats and the undercity. The rain was coming hard, the wind picking up. Meteorology reckoned there was a storm building out to sea. We were vested and with a tactical weapons bag between us. Esh had called in a favour. Someone over at the MSDF with the clearance to look had come back with word that a Project Insurgent safe house had registered a glitch in its power draw a couple of hours after the first Jared Black had left New Hope. Esh had sweet-talked her way into an address. The pod that had brought the first Jared Black to Firstfall had stopped nearby. It was enough of a straw to grasp at.

We stopped in the open cavern at the centre of an underground apartment complex, cheap government housing built in the early days when Magenta was struggling to find its feet. They were simple self-sustaining places, not much more than a couple of rooms, some wires and some plumbing. Most of them were empty these days.

I'd pinged Rangesh before we left. He was on his way but Esh had called in another favour too. When we arrived, Colonel Jonas Himaru was waiting for us, leaning against the cavern wall.

'Esh!' He grinned at her. I'd forgotten how wide Himaru was. A barn door of a man.

'Didn't wake you up, then?' she asked.

They embraced and held it a moment too long for casual friends. Whatever was between them ran deep. I threw him an awkward salute as they separated.

'Thank you, sir, for—'

'You don't have clearance for Project Insurgent, Agent Rause. You need to do something about that.'

Esh and I deleted our conversations from our Servants. We

cut our connections to the Tesseract. I made a note to arrest Esh at some point for revealing classified information and then to arrest myself for encouraging her to do it.

'Good enough for you?'

'As long as you understand that this is an MSDF operation and that you're just here as a courtesy, Agent Rause.'

Esh swore loudly. Surveillance drone.

'What?' I looked around. Where?

Up – don't look!

She crossed the cavern to the stairway that threaded up among a vertical cliff-face of apartment doors. I paused for a moment before I followed, my Servant accessing the feeds from all the surveillance cameras in the cavern.

I don't see it.

It's cloaked. Same as the one in Disappointment. Don't do anything. And stay out of the surveillance net. It's in a blind spot anyway.

Esh almost ran up the stairs. She stopped at a door.

Then how do you know it's there?

I have a broader spectral response.

Esh's artificial eyes.

There's a second one moving in. Larger. It's heading towards you.

Where's the first one?

Up high. Just watching.

She passed us both a tactical feed from her Servant with the two drones marked on a map of the cavern. The new one was weaving its way steadily closer, carefully avoiding the surveillance cameras.

Kagame?

Could be.

'We look like a tac-team,' I said. 'Kagame's not going to like that.'

'He's not going to like it either way.' Himaru made a sour face. 'If he wanted to be found then all he had to do was walk himself in. He knows where to go.' He was trying hard not to look at the spaces in the caverns where the drones drifted.

'If those drones aren't his then someone followed us. Or you.'

Come to me. Casually. I'll tell you if you need to run.

Himaru and I crossed the cavern floor to the stairs. I tried not to think about Jared Black's corpse in Mercy, his head burned off. Esh had stopped at an empty apartment. She used her Tesseract codes and the door slid open. I pinged Bix and told him to get here.

The new drone took a position up high. I watched it on Esh's feed as we climbed the stair. It seemed happy to wait like the first one.

I reached the apartment Esh had entered. The inside wasn't much to look at: a space carved out of the bedrock, walls turned to fused glass by plasma lances, pocked with sockets and fittings for wall-screens and covers and the like. These apartments could look homely enough when they were fitted up; stripped and empty, it was like standing in a cave.

No particle beams so far. Everyone still had all their arms and legs.

'I want a tac-team,' I said as soon as we were all in cover.

Himaru grunted something that sounded like he agreed. I put in the request and then checked the house Servant. We had power, light and water if we wanted it but otherwise it was dormant. No one had been here for months.

'Who else knows where we are?' I asked.

We looked at each other. The three of us and Rangesh. And the tac-team I'd just called, but the drones had been here first.

'What if we got this wrong?' I asked. 'What if Kagame's our killer?'

Himaru made a face.

Esh didn't like it either. 'Bara was replaced by a shell before Black and Kagame left orbit, sir. I don't see how he can be.'

'Agreed. But if those drones aren't Kagame's then how did they get here before us?'

That got me a long silence. The answer was obvious. Either one of us had tipped them off or someone had been watching us in the Tesseract, tracking our every move.

Like they'd done to Alysha ...

The thought kept circling back to me. *One of our own.*

'OK,' Esh said. 'I have problems with Kagame as our killer and I have problems with those drones not being his. So let's say they *are* his. Let's say they're not a threat, they're just surveillance. He's watching his back. From what we know he has every reason to be cautious.'

The air smelled damp. If Kagame had been after the men from Fleet right from the start then sending Black to Mercy had been a good way to draw them out. My gut said Esh was right and Kagame wasn't our killer, but my gut had been wrong before.

Esh made an unhappy face. 'Sir, if Kagame knows we're here then we need to act. Insurgent safe houses have exits into the maintenance tunnels. If it was me then I'd already be in them.'

I shook my head. 'I called in a tac-team.' The right thing to do was to wait.

'I have breaching charges in the pod, sir.'

'Esh! Seriously?'

Esh took a deep breath. 'You're right. We'll get him next time.'

I wondered how long that would be. A planet-wide manhunt? We could shut him off from the Insurgent houses now we knew he was using them, but if those drones were his then he clearly wasn't working alone. We weren't going to get a better chance.

'You think we can do this, Esh?' Himaru glanced at me as though I was the weak link here. It didn't help to realise that I probably was.

'What I think, sir, is that Kagame is already running. The sooner we go after him, the better our chances of catching him before he vanishes.'

'The drones?'

'I can handle the drones, sir.'

Bix was three minutes away. The tac-team was six.

'Your call, Esh,' said Himaru.

For a moment I thought he wasn't even going to ask – then he looked at me.

'Rause?'

'I'm just observing, remember?' But I nodded. I didn't want Kagame to get away.

Esh opened the door. 'Sir, I need you to get the charges. Let Jonas and I deal with the drones.'

I nodded.

'From when I say go, everything has to be fast, sir. OK?'

'OK.'

'OK, go!'

I ran out, vaulted the rail, jumped down to the lower level and didn't look back. I landed hard, muscles straining against Magenta's gravity, and raced for the pod. I heard a burst from Himaru's rifle and shots from Esh's Reeper. One, two, three. Pause. One, two, three.

'Drones are down!'

Kagame would be running now, if he wasn't already. The pod doors opened. I grabbed the tactical bag. Esh was out on the balcony. I ran back and threw up a charge. By the time I'd climbed to the upper level she had it in place ready to blow. Ready to take point, Himaru right beside her.

'My call,' she said. 'I own this.'

She tossed me the detonator, rolled back from the door and covered her ears. I blew the charge. Esh tossed in a flashbang. The moment it went off she jumped in after it, Reeper at the ready, Himaru right on her heels. I ran in behind them. Suddenly we were all shouting through each other:

'Zinadine! Zinadine Kagame! Get on the floor! Put your hands behind your head!'

The inside of the apartment was pitch-black, the air hazed with smoke from the charge. I moved past Himaru into the back room.

'Front clear!' Himaru.

Esh followed behind me. 'Sir—'

Movement from beside me. In the corner.

'Freeze!'

Shit.

Kagame had me cold. He was curled in a corner, pointing a gun up at me.

I froze.

'Tesseract!' roared Esh. 'Put the gun down!'

Himaru eased into the room behind her.

'Esh! Don't!'

'Gun down! Now!'

If he'd killed Jared Black then I was fucked. But if he had then why hadn't he shot me already?

The drones had to have seen us coming. So why was he still even here?

'Zinadine ...'

Himaru had Kagame covered with a pistol. His other hand was held out wide and high, palm out, for pause and peace.

'ID!'

Kagame was scared. Shit. We'd surprised him ...

'Esharaq Zohreya,' said Esh. 'DSS 3743.'

We'd *surprised* him. Which meant the drones weren't his ...

'Colonel Jonas Himaru. DSS 1201. Hello, Zinadine. Welcome home.'

I had no idea what the numbers meant but I heard Kagame catch his breath.

But if the drones weren't his ...

He jerked his pistol at me. 'You! Identify yourself!'

Shit, shit, shit! If the drones weren't his, then someone else knew we were here!

'Rause,' I said. 'Keon Rause.'

I started to give my bureau number and then stopped as something in his face changed. Names. Just like Laura had pulled out of the Mercy video. *The names. Tell us the names ...*

I dropped. Instinct. Kagame's first shot parted my hair. The second caught me in the flank and sprawled me across the floor. I heard the stunner on Esh's Reeper go off. Bix was two minutes away. The tac-team were five. My Servant was calling for a trauma team. I didn't know how bad it was. I was vested but ...

The drones weren't his.

I couldn't breathe. I felt myself on the edge of panic ...

'Esh!' Her name came out mangled. I couldn't talk.

Esh kicked Kagame's gun away. She patted him down, running a diagnostic on me through my Servant at the same time. Himaru rolled me over and opened my jacket. Esh kicked in a medical override and stabbed me with painkillers and adrenaline. A spider drone set about tying Kagame up before he recovered from the stunner. She pulled something from his pockets.

I tried to speak. I still couldn't breathe so I pinged her instead: Not. His. Drones.

Kagame was mouthing something at Esh. She finished patting him down and rolled him over so the spider drone could finish its work. Wrapping him up tight. Then she squatted beside me.

'You should lie down, sir.'

'Not ... his ...' I croaked. The painkillers and adrenaline were biting.

Esh patched into my Servant. She turned on a flashlight and peered at where I'd been shot.

'There's a medical team on its way. The bullet didn't penetrate. I think you're just winded but there's always the possibility of organ damage. You should lie down, sir. Try to relax.'

I tried again to get up. Himaru kept me down. Esh went to the door and looked outside. Then she ducked back in.

'Easy, son.' His eyes glittered in the dark. He was lensing something, data flashing across his pupils.

'Not Kagame,' I groaned. 'The drone ...'

'Not his. The drones. Yes, we understand that, sir. But there's another one out there now, at least one. We'd do best to sit tight. Let's just keep safe until the tac-team arrives.'

Esh wasn't listening. There was something wrong about the way she was looking at me.

Bix was a minute away. 'What did ... Kagame say?'

Esh helped me up now, gentle but forceful. Himaru's eyes still glittered with data flashing across his lenses. I didn't see any of that with Esh but then I wouldn't, not with her artificial eyes. They kept glancing at each other, though – and then it hit me: the flashes I was seeing in Himaru's lenses ... they were talking. Something they didn't want me to hear ...

'What did—'

'I'm going to move you further inside, sir.'

Esh started guiding me into the apartment's third room, the one buried deepest into Magentan stone, the one that would have been the apartment's wet room if it had been fitted out.

'What—'

'I want to keep you and Kagame apart until the tac-team gets here, that's all.' There was a tightness to her. She glanced at

Himaru. He nodded. 'Colonel Himaru will stay with Kagame, sir.'

'Esh ...' Breathing was starting to come more easily. 'What aren't you telling me?'

'Nothing you need to worry about for now, sir. I've already sent a ...'

She stopped.

'What?'

She turned to Himaru. 'I'm being jammed. You?'

Himaru nodded. I checked my Servant for its connection to the Tesseract and the outside world and got nothing. Esh had me under the shoulders. Now she tugged hard, ignoring every piece of medical training we'd ever had about how to deal with a casualty. She never took her eyes off the door. She dragged me into the back room and shoved me hard away from the entrance.

The grenade came straight through and fetched up against the rear wall. I didn't see it coming but I heard it land. I saw the look on Esh's face. She threw herself past me, dived, scooped it up and hurled it flying back out, then scrabbled across the floor, hands pressed over her ears. The explosion felt like it went off right outside, followed quickly by a second – shrapnel ripping through the air, shredding the walls. Kagame's Servant started screaming. So did Himaru. Esh was already on her feet again, Reeper in her hand. Crouched low she skidded out of the wet room, firing blind at the apartment door as she did. She grabbed Himaru and hauled him back in, pulled him hard into cover. He was in a bad way but he was conscious enough to be trying to help.

'Sir! Stay away from the door!'

I didn't need telling.

Esh crouched over Himaru. I heard her whisper between his groans. Telling him something. That he was going to be OK?

Bix would be here any moment. I couldn't warn him. I couldn't call the Tesseract for help. Nothing but static. Esh holstered her Reeper and authenticated herself to Himaru's burst rifle. She crouched, covering the door. I hauled myself up and did the same with my Reeper.

'Shoot anything that moves that isn't me, sir. Even if you're not sure what you saw.'

She was thinking of the drones. *There's another one out there now, at least one …*

A series of shots rang outside. Then a shout. A pause and then another, closer.

'Friendly incoming!'

A figure scuttled through the front door, silhouetted by the light of the cavern outside. Bix. He saw us pointing guns at him and cowered beside the door. In the room between us, Kagame's Servant still howled for a trauma team.

'Esh?'

Esh kept her burst rifle levelled. She reached into a pocket and tossed a scanner across the floor.

'Verify yourself,' she said.

'Esh! What the fuck?'

'Do it,' Esh said.

'Wavedome special sauce!' Bix put the scanner to his eyes then slid it back.

'*That's* your identification code?' Esh lowered her rifle. 'Get back here! Now!' She punched him as he scuttled between us. 'Moron!'

'What the fuck, Esh?'

'Sitrep?'

'One perp outside, injured and leaving the scene. Fired a few shots but they were all wild. No big deal. You guys OK?'

'Can you reach the Tesseract?'

A pause. 'No. What the hell is this, Esh? Middle of the night

92

call, I get here, there's an explosion before I can even get out of my pod—'

Esh jerked her head to the middle room where Kagame lay. He hadn't moved and his Servant wasn't screaming any more.

'Help me get him back here into cover.'

'What did you see?' I asked.

Bix didn't answer. 'Wasting your time, babe.'

'We need his Servant.'

'What did you *see*?'

The look I got from Bix was a queer one. Like he hadn't noticed me there before.

'Told you, boss dude. Explosion. Someone running from it. Injured, I think, but not badly.' The grenade Esh had tossed back? 'Had a pistol, saw me, fired a couple of times and ran off. Couldn't reach your Servants so I came up. What's going on?'

'Drones?'

He shrugged. Outside I heard another pod pull up. I couldn't take my eyes off the apartment door. If it was the tac-team then they were a minute ahead of schedule. I could have kissed them for that. I tried to ping them but all I got back was static.

'Get Kagame!' hissed Esh. 'I'll cover you.'

Bix and I scuttled into the front room. Kagame flopped between us, unconscious or dead. I waited for the shooting to start outside, for more drones – but instead the silhouette of a tac-team commando appeared at the door. She froze when she saw us. Bix and I dropped Kagame and whipped out weapons, covering her.

'Whoa!' She raised her hands. 'Lieutenant Shiva Lee, MSDF.'

'Where's your squad?' asked Esh.

She had her rifle trained on Lee. Our Servants were pinging each other, frantically checking codes, looking for confirmation of who everyone was, trying to verify them through the wall of jamming, and failing. No one moved.

Esh had said there were more drones out there. Our Servants were still being jammed. I thought about that. And how there hadn't been any shooting this time.

'A minute away.'

Lee's movements were silky. Smooth. Precise ...

Something's off.

Esh lowered her rifle. She walked straight at Lieutenant Lee and held out her hand.

'Glad you're here. We need secure evac.'

Lee moved halfway to shake Esh's hand. And then stopped because Esh had her rifle in Lee's face.

'On the floor! Now!'

'Shell!'

I figured it out half a second too late. Lee dropped and sprang back for the door, inhumanly fast. Esh opened up, two three-round bursts. Fast as the shell was, Esh must have hit with most of them but that didn't slow it. Through the reports came the buzz and flash of a particle beam. Bix staggered.

The shell dived out through the door. Bix's Servant started screaming.

'What the ...?'

Esh threw herself back at me, diving into the back room, knocking me down. Three concussion grenades came through the open door. We threw ourselves flat an instant before they went off – flashes and roaring thunder. I cringed, ears ringing. Esh staggered up again. My Servant was still being jammed but the jamming was suddenly weaker and I got a faint ping – the real tac-team had arrived outside. I pulled up the surveillance cameras from the cavern. Through hazy static I saw an armoured tac-team pod sitting next to our own, taking fire from somewhere above.

I saw a glimpse of movement near the apartment door.

'Esh!'

Esh darted into the shredded front room. I stumbled after her. I still couldn't hear anything except ringing. Kagame was dead, his chest burned out. Bix was still moving. I couldn't see how bad he was but his Servant was shrieking for help.

From outside I heard the rip of a Gatling gun. The tac-team pod opening up on something. Through the cameras I glimpsed the shell again as the back of the pod opened and commandos swarmed out. The shell rolled, fired twice and took down the first. Esh put two more bursts through the wall as the shell came up, targeting her through the outside cameras. They hit, centre mass. The shell staggered but didn't slow. Esh kept firing as one of the tac-team came running to the other end of the steps. He got off a spray of shots that staggered the shell before it took him straight through the bridge of the nose. Artificial eyes synthetically wired straight to the gun via a q-code host running targeting wares. Reaction times faster than lightning. Precise as quantum fabricator. And the shell had taken maybe two dozen hits and it hadn't even slowed. Armoured like a tank, then. The next minute looked ready to become spectacularly shitty.

The Gatling gun on the tac-team's pod turned on the shell, driving it into the shelter of a nearby apartment, pocking the walls with bullet craters. The surviving commandos fanned out and then raced back for cover as glitters of reflected light swooped through the cavern towards them. Then the outside cameras all went dead. A series of small explosions cracked through the cavern.

I snapped a glance around the apartment. There were cameras here too. The ones in the front room had been wrecked by the grenade. I shot out the others before the shell got eyes inside and turned Esh's shooting-through-the-walls trick back on us. For a moment everything went quiet. Then the lights went out and I couldn't see what was happening any more.

Couldn't see, couldn't hear. Couldn't reach anyone on my Servant. Kagame was dead and we were sitting ducks.

'Back, back, back!' Esh scrambled me towards the wet room. 'Help me with Bix!'

We grabbed him by the arms and dragged him, hard and fast and without much care. He screamed.

'Jonas probably has some grenades. Get them, will you?'

'Esh, we're dead if we stay here.'

'We're dead if we go out, sir. I don't know what that is but it isn't human.' She shut the door into the wet room. At least we could keep out the drones. 'Can you take Bix?'

The emergency lights came on. 'Take him where?'

'This is an Insurgent safe house! It'll have a back door.'

I started to search – floor, walls – but Esh went to Himaru.

Yeah. It would be a code to the house Servant. Of course it would.

A panel in the back wall opened. Himaru started trying to lever himself to his feet. In the near-dark I couldn't tell how badly he'd been hit but the front of his armoured vest glistened with blood. I could smell it. And he couldn't walk.

'Sir, can you take Bix? I can't carry them both.' Esh propped Himaru over her shoulder. Armoured as he was, he looked twice her size. 'We need to get ... Shit'

Esh had left a micro-camera in the front room. Now the shell was creeping in, pistol raised, half a dozen miniature drones flitting around it. I knew what came next. Knew it exactly and so did Esh. She'd grown up on Earth in one of the nastier parts of what had once been the Palestinian Free State. Later, on Magenta, she'd fallen in with the wrong crowd and it had cost her almost everything. We both knew the look someone had when they absolutely weren't going to back down. The shell had that look. And from the way she came in she wasn't worried about the tac-team any more.

'Get Bix out of here.' Esh eased Himaru down.

They stared at each other for a second, a short exchange of silent messages, and then he started to crawl away. The drones flitted through the apartment to the wet room door. The shell crouched beside Kagame. She pulled out a laser scalpel and cut into his neck.

'What's she doing?'

Esh shook her head. 'Taking his Servant.' She suddenly got up and took off her armoured vest.

'What are *you* doing?'

'We haven't got long. Take your shirt off.'

'What?'

'The drones.' Esh was already stripping out of her bureau coverall.

Lee picked something out of Kagame's neck, stamped on it and then pocketed the remains. I took off my ballistic jacket and then my shirt. I took a moment to touch at my ribs where Kagame's bullet had hit. I was bruised from hip to armpit. Somewhere beneath the painkillers, everything hurt. But there wasn't any blood. I wasn't dying.

Esh vested up again. Lee had Kagame on his back now. She was cutting around the base of his skull.

'Take this and get Bix out of here.' Esh pressed something small and round with a plastic feel to it into my hand.

'You take him.'

Esh took a deep breath. 'Sir, what Kagame told me ...'

I zipped my jacket up. On the other side of the door, the shell had found Kagame's Servant. She ripped it out. Esh closed my fingers around the sliver she'd given me.

'That's from Kagame. It's running single-lock anti-tamper encryption. You get one shot at the decryption key. Get it wrong and it wipes. The key's in Kagame's Servant. This is what he was bringing back to Magenta. This is what it's all about.'

'Still ...'

'He told me you were a traitor, sir.'

'He what?'

'He said there were two moles inside the bureau, sir, and that one of them was you.' Esh lifted her coverall and spread it out in the air in front of her. 'Get Rangesh out of here. I'll follow.'

I dragged Bix into the tunnel out the back. It obviously wasn't going to work. Himaru was barely managing a crawl. I caught him in three strides.

'Rause,' he grunted.

I crouched beside him and tucked Kagame's sliver into a pouch on his hip.

'That's what all this is for,' I said. 'Give me a moment. Then close the door.'

He would or he wouldn't.

'Rause!'

'What?'

'Look after Esh.'

'I will. Look after Agent Rangesh.'

I scurried back out of the duct. In the front room, the shell was going through Kagame's pockets.

'That's not an autonomous shell,' I said. 'Someone's piloting her. Go for the throat. The communication nexus will be there. Or at least that's where it usually is. Kill that and it should shut down.'

The duct closed behind me. Esh stopped for a moment and gave me a look.

'When I open the door, whatever it is it's going to shoot. I don't know what those drones can do and I don't think we can take all of them out at once.' She was shaking. 'You need to throw your shirt over as many as you can. Blind them and bring them down. I'll deal with the shell.'

I nodded. I wanted to ask her how she was going to do that,

exactly, but what was the point? We'd shoot lots and either it worked or it didn't.

'OK.'

'Permission to speak freely, sir?'

'Esh?'

'I don't believe what Kagame said about you, sir.'

'Thank you, Agent Zohreya.'

'Also we're not walking away from this.'

I let that sink in.

'But Bix and Jonas stand a better chance this way. So thank you.'

She opened the door.

My Servant calculated trajectories that would put a bullet through my face from where the shell crouched beside Kagame, since that seemed to be what the assassin preferred. I threw my shirt at the drones, spreading it wide. I caught two of them and slammed them into the ground, one-handed, fired with the other, three shots at my best guesses of where the shell's throat would be. I didn't see how many of the drones Esh caught. She couldn't have caught them all.

More shots, from Esh and from the shell. The shell was firing at both of us. The first bullet clipped my shoulder, right through my tac-suit as though it was made of paper, sending me flying. I had no idea whether Esh was hit too but she was still firing. My Servant howled and flooded me with adrenaline. I fired twice more and then something took my legs out. I sprawled flat.

Esh dived past me. She fired and then staggered as the shell shot her in the chest. I saw the back of her ballistic jacket rip open as the bullet flew out the other side of her. Three more rounds hit her as she fell onto me; even then she twisted to spread herself across me, to cover me.

I tried to get up. I couldn't. Esh was pinning me down.

The rifle fell out of her hands. Her Servant was pumping her full of whatever it could think of to keep her going but there wasn't much it could do any more except keep her brain alive for two minutes and twelve seconds while it screamed for help.

The scream came.

The shell loomed over me, its face half-ruined. It wasn't standing right but it was still coming.

My pistol was on the floor where I'd dropped it. I tried to reach it but I couldn't.

Esh lay across me. I felt her spasm. I pulled her Reeper out of its holster and shot the shell in the throat. Twice. It staggered but it didn't drop.

The jamming did though. My Servant's screams were being answered.

Too late. The shell levelled its pistol.

And froze.

Keys. I'm so sorry. I came as soon as I—

A flash of light and the deafening bang of an explosion, and I suddenly couldn't see or hear anything as the survivors from the tac-team smashed into the room.

I was still conscious enough, just about, to feel Esh's heart when it stopped.

SATOSHI NAKAMOTO

Satoshi Nakamoto isn't real. Her persona has been created for the purpose of this night alone, to be tossed away and burned as soon as its usefulness is done. The person who made Satoshi has a knack for new identities. Tomorrow she will become someone else. A different name whenever one is needed, and Satoshi Nakamoto will vanish for ever.

Today, Satoshi Nakamoto studies two monitors. The man and the woman in the pictures don't know that Satoshi is watching them but the man, at least, has his best public face on nonetheless. The man's name is Doctor Nicholas Steadman. He is an expert on the Masters – insofar as it is possible to be such a thing – and is currently talking to the other most senior such expert Magenta can offer.

Her face is on the other screen. Her name is Doctor Elizabeth Jacksmith.

Elizabeth, if you would just consider for a moment the—

Steadman watches Jacksmith through several different screens and cameras. One is the one Jacksmith knows exists, the one she's using to talk back. The other two cameras might shock her. Although Satoshi Nakamoto wonders if they might shock Doctor Jacksmith less than Doctor Steadman thinks. Both have their secrets.

Absolutely not.

101

You know this is all going to—
Nicholas!

There is a sharp rising edge to Jacksmith's voice. The edge of a mother with a disobedient child, balancing on the precipice of patience.

Nicky ...

She pauses, the diminutive of his name a deliberate shot at getting a rise out of him. When it fails she goes on.

There are processes and procedures and you know there are. I promise you – as soon as the expedition starts returning data that's been refined and cross-checked and analysed and subjected to proper peer review—

They're getting data now!

Yes, but—

I'm not the only one, you know. There are plenty of other—

I still can't—

If you don't, I will tell the world—

Tell the world what, exactly?

You know very well.

Jacksmith's voice turns icy. *Good* night, *Nicholas.*

The channel closes. In their other screens both Satoshi Nakamoto and Doctor Steadman see Jacksmith shake her head and then shake her hand at the dead screen in front of her. *Wanker.*

She turns away. Steadman bristles. The outrage of an intellectual stymied by a process of his own creation. Satoshi Nakamoto wonders why he even bothered to try, although she knows the answer too: he tries because he has to. Curiosity demands it, the hunger like a parasite inside him. A mathematician and an astrophysicist, Steadman came from Earth to Magenta more than thirty years ago to study Magenta's xeno-organisms, convinced they had some connection to the Masters. Nothing has happened in all his years to either further or change that conviction. The xeno-organisms have been his work and his obsession for three decades but his real obsession is older still.

The Masters vanished a hundred and fifty years ago – but where did they go?

Satoshi muses to herself that she could tell him a thing or two about the xeno-organisms. But today their shared interest lies with the Masters. It is an obsession that Satoshi understands. An obsession with who we really are, each and every one of us.

Steadman turns away from the screens around his desk and makes himself a drink. Satoshi hears the clink of glass, the trickle of pouring liquid. She could move the camera to track him but she doesn't. She lingers instead on Jacksmith. If the expression on Satoshi's face says anything at all, perhaps it hints at a sadness. An old regret.

She waits to see which one of them will be the first to make another call. She anticipates Jacksmith, but Steadman is the first to flinch.

Satoshi answers it in a voice that isn't her own. There is no video for this, only words, although in her screens Satoshi sees Steadman speak them.

'Chase Hunt.' Her own words sound alien.

'Doctor Steadman. From the Institute.'

She resists the temptation to tell him she knows. There are nervous cracks in his voice. He tries to hide them but on her screen she sees him pace and fret. She lets him dangle for a moment, then:

'Have you thought about my offer?'

'Yes.'

He thinks she is Chase Hunt, a freelance journalist with an interest in the Antarctic excavation and its crashed ship that has been all over the news these last few days, along with the shootings in Mercy and Disappointment and now in Firstfall itself, in the infamous Squats not so far away from where Satoshi

Nakamoto is sitting. Doctor Steadman thinks that Chase Hunt is the sort of journalist who doesn't mind what data she gets or how, as long there's money at the end of it.

'And?'

It takes him a while to find the words. 'I want a hundred thousand.'

'Get lost.'

'There's more to this than you think.'

Satoshi Nakamoto has a shrewd idea of how true this might be. 'Such as?'

'The first trans-polar expedition was manipulated.'

'What do you mean?'

'They were steered. After they left.'

'Steered?'

'To the site!' Steadman is getting flustered.

'You're saying—'

'I'm saying that someone inside the Institute manipulated the expedition to guide it to exactly the right place!'

'But that—'

'Means that they knew where to look before the expedition even left! Yes! And I know who it was, too, and how they did it.'

Satoshi Nakamoto considers this. 'Who? How?'

'I'm not stupid!'

No. 'Can you prove it?'

'Yes.'

'All of it?'

'Yes.'

There is a pause. When Satoshi Nakamoto speaks again, there is something very slightly different in her voice.

'I need a name.'

No answer. Steadman is holding out for his hundred thousand.

'Do you at least have one?'

'Yes.'

'And you can really prove all this?'

'I have all the evidence you could possibly need.'

'OK. A hundred thousand. When?'

Steadman gives a time and a place. Satoshi Nakamoto cuts the link. She watches Steadman pace his apartment. He has crossed lines before. Now he crosses another. He knows and fears the consequences. If he could know what all those consequences will be, she thinks, he would never have started any of this.

She leaves the shadow-shrouded table where she pretends to drink cheap Magentan coffee – hot water with a sprinkling of xenoflora dust and chemicals and something to make it look brown instead of a faded watery purple. A few people give odd looks as she rises, noticing her enough to see that she's slightly deformed, that the skin on her face is waxy and smooth as though she was once burned and couldn't afford the state-of-the-art in tissue regeneration. They can repair almost anything these days short of death, and even that they can postpone, another few seconds every year as Servants grow more complex and the line between machine and man blurs ever more. She's done the calculations. In another hundred years a Servant will be able to keep an unsupported brain alive for a full day if technology progresses at the same rate. It won't, of course, but she wonders nevertheless what that would be like. To be alive in a body that was dead, watching, listening, unable to move as rigor mortis sets in. She wonders if it's an oddly human thing, this quest to defy death no matter the cost. Would aliens recognise and understand such behaviour? Would the Masters?

She's almost at Steadman's apartment in the Roseate Project. Maybe she should ask him. Steadman has dedicated his life to understanding the Masters. Satoshi quietly suspects he hasn't achieved a single useful contribution in all that time, but he's certainly made plenty of money explaining his thoughts to the credulous and the knowledge-hungry. It's a pity, really. A waste. As a radio astronomer he is quite talented.

She still has her cameras in his apartment. She sees him get up and go to the door and open it. She sees him look blank for an instant, and then the shock of recognition.

'You! What are—' The cameras vanish from her feed. All of them at once. Steadman's Servant falls silent. It doesn't scream. It doesn't do anything at all. Simply ceases.

Satoshi Nakamoto turns and heads away without breaking stride. She ponders an intrusion into the apartment surveillance system to see whoever is at Doctor Steadman's door. It seems the obvious and easy thing to do ...

The obvious and easy thing ...

It feels like a trap. A trap for *her*.

The realisation triggers an unusual feeling. Fear and ... exhilaration. No one is supposed to know that Satoshi Nakamoto even exists – but even as the feeling washes over her she finds that she doesn't need to break into the apartment surveillance system at all. A man walks out of the apartment block and she knows his face. She knows his name. She remembers him from the bureau. Six years ago he was a q-coder. He worked in meteorology.

She follows. He doesn't see her.

She comes back again hours later. By then the weather has turned. A storm thunders and rocks overhead, forcing everyone to shelter. Rivers of rain torrent through the undercity and the traffic there is heavy for the time of night, the pods driven from the surface like the people. Even in the tunnels, the wind thunders. By now she's seen another murder and has unravelled every trace of Satoshi Nakamoto that ever existed. She should do the same for Chase Hunt too, but ...

The Roseate Project shouldn't let her in but Steadman gave her an entry code for their appointment. It hasn't expired. It lets her walk right into his apartment. She is not surprised by what she sees.

Steadman is dead. He lies on the floor by the door. His Servant is dead, too.

She revives her cameras. She tells them to open their little wings and rotors and fly to her. Hours have passed since Satoshi Nakamoto vanished from history and her cameras have been dead for all that time. History has no memory of what happened in this room. She looks at Steadman from the doorway. No blood. No holes. No marks. Natural causes, an autopsy will say. Of that much she is sure.

She retrieves her little drones. The sense of a trap remains, bright in the temptation she feels to interfere, to try to find out what happened here, sure in the knowledge that Satoshi Nakamoto has left a trail that even the most junior Tesseract clerk could follow. But also sure in the knowledge that Satoshi Nakamoto no longer exists. Besides, she is here as Chase Hunt now.

She draws a slender silenced pistol from inside her jacket and shoots the corpse of Nicholas Steadman cleanly in the head.

And walks away.

THREE

TROMPE L'OEIL

8

FIFTY SHADES
OF DEAD

Boots on the floor, right in front of my face. That was a clear memory. A ringing in my ears. There was something happening in my Servant that I didn't understand. I felt the world shift and a pressure lifting. Then a lightness, almost weightlessness.

Later I realised that was when they'd lifted Esh off me.

I slipped away for a while after that. Lost in a dark place. Adrift.

Liss? What did you do?

I'd asked her that question once before. I hadn't liked the answer.

Esh was dead.

Hush.

I'd seen bullets explode out of Esh's back. But I wasn't thinking about Esh.

Why did you have to die?

She'd gone away after that. Or maybe I had. Or maybe I'd slipped away before it even started and none of it was real. It didn't make sense for it to be real. It didn't make sense for Liss to be there at all.

I remembered a light, dazzling bright. Then trying to move my head and feeling like I was buried in sand. A tuneless muffling of sound that turned everything into a vagrant hum. A shape, all blurry limbs. There might have been words but I couldn't be sure.

Esh?

Are you there?

Esh?

I was dreaming, I think.

A different world slammed into focus when I woke up, so sharp it hurt. I tried to lift my head. When that didn't work I turned it instead. I knew exactly where I was: in a bed like the one where Jared Black had died, somewhere in Mercy where all beds look the same. On the table beside me was a vase with some flowers.

'Keon?'

Laura's voice. I turned the other way and there she was, sitting in a chair. She'd been so still and quiet I hadn't noticed.

She held my eye. I held hers back.

'Ah, shit,' she said.

'Hey, Laws.'

'Rangesh got to you too, did he?'

'Huh?'

'Laws.' She turned away and ran a hand through her hair like she didn't want to look at me. 'Fuck, you all call me that behind my back, don't you?'

'What?'

'Rangesh ...'

She forced herself to look at me for a moment and then turned away again. I guess I knew then what she didn't want to tell me.

'Rangesh is going to be OK. Some deep burns and tissue

112

damage. He'll have scars but he'll be OK. Himaru too, eventually,' she added quickly, like she'd seen the question on my face and was getting in first so she didn't have to answer it.

I asked it anyway. 'Esh?'

'Rangesh is already making himself as annoying as usual. Himaru was a lot worse. Mercy's got him in a nanite coma. He's going to be in a reconstruction tank for a while longer. Vest saved him. He was lucky. So were you.'

I tried to peer at my shoulder but I couldn't. It hurt whenever I tried to move.

Laura met my eye and held it this time. She was shaking.

'Really fucking lucky. Half an inch lower and that bullet would have hit bone square on. Its charge would have gone off. The detonation would have pulped most of your throat and neck and spread compound fractures right up into your skull. You'd be dead.' Her expression was hard and bleak, her voice low. There was a tremor to it. Was she angry with me?

No. She was … afraid?

'Half an inch, Keon.'

'Esh?' I said again.

'Fucking hell.' She turned away. 'Does it have to be me?'

'How's Jamie?' I asked.

Stupidest question I could think of, but I suddenly didn't want to know about Esh any more. I already had my answer.

Laura barked some bitter harsh cry that was half laugh and half howl.

'Jamie? Fuck! He's fine, thanks. Bored. Fractious. Impatient and also at home. We were about to leave when you came in. So now he's on his own again and here I am. Fucking marvellous.' She took a deep breath and then rounded on me like it was somehow my fault that she had to do this. 'Esh is gone, Keon. She took four rounds to the chest. They pretty much turned everything in there into mushy pink goo. She maybe had a couple of organs that weren't ripped to shreds but the hydro-static shock did for them too. Her Servant kicked in terminal life support. You know how that goes. Two minutes and twelve seconds before hypoxia starts.'

She looked away and bit her knuckle. Fighting back tears. Fuck. Laura didn't even like Esh most of the time.

'That was gone before the tac-team even got to you.' She shook her head. 'They put a life-preserver on her and brought her in. But she's not coming back. They were too late. Too long without oxygen. Mercy's got her in a coma, same as Himaru, trying to regenerate what's left of her, but even if by some miracle that works ... She's brain-dead, Keon.'

Laura turned away again, hiding her face. I tried to get up, to reach her so I could hold her hand. Or touch her. Or something. But I couldn't.

'What was it?' I asked.

She didn't answer for a moment. When she did it was like she was coming back from light years away.

'What was what?'

'The thing that tried to kill us.'

She shrugged. 'A shell.'

'No ordinary shell.'

'No.'

'Where did it come from?'

'Earth, probably. It torched itself. Forensics have the remains down in their labs under the Tesseract. They're probably creaming their pants about the tech but right now we know exactly as much as we did when you and Agent Zohreya went off on your ...'

She didn't say it but we both knew what she was thinking. That we should have held back once we saw the drones. That we should have waited for the tac-team. That if we had then maybe I wouldn't be here and maybe Esh would still be alive. I could add some guilt of my own to that: I'd told Esh it was her call to make, but it wasn't. It had been mine. I was the senior agent. Esh's death was on me.

'Was it worth it?' she asked, words carefully neutral and controlled as she tried her utmost to keep all her accusations out of them and failed. 'Did you find anything?'

I thought about not telling her and then I thought about who else might already know. *One of our own.* If I trusted anyone, I trusted Laura. I beckoned her close and whispered in her ear.

'Kagame had an encrypted sliver. I gave it to Himaru. Esh said it needs a key. Have a look at … Someone needs to go into Esh's Servant. Or Kagame's … If … The shell cut it out of him … There's maybe …'

I couldn't focus. My words kept falling apart in my mouth. Esh was dead.

Laura pulled away. No, it wasn't worth it, that's what I wanted to say. But somehow there wasn't space in the air.

'OK.' She sniffed. Hard. 'We already did that. The shell ripped Kagame's Servant out of him before we got to you. Wiped it clean. All gone. Esh doesn't have anything either.' She turned and stared straight at me. Into me. 'We had a look at yours too.'

She couldn't hide the accusation this time. *Your fault.*

'I need to go,' she said. 'On top of Black … The shit-storm from this … Well, you can imagine, I suppose. Get well, Keon. You're going to need your strength.'

She left. I watched her go. The door slid shut. She didn't look back.

I slipped back under after that, wrapped in whatever drugs were spiralling through me, soft like velvet. The next time I woke I was alone. Without thinking I tried to ping Esh. I don't know why – in case my conversation with Laura had just been a bad dream, maybe – but Esh's Servant was offline. I tried to ping Laura, but that didn't work either. I tried Bix and Himaru and got nothing.

It was me. I was cut off.

A nurse came and told me that a doctor would be along shortly. She fussed and poked and prodded at some piece of unfamiliar q-ware running in my Servant and told me I'd been hit by something called a donkey round. She didn't know what that was except that they were bad. But I was lucky. My ballistic jacket had spread the impact enough to crack my collarbone but the bullet's explosive tip hadn't gone off. I was regenerating nicely.

'How long?' I asked.

'Don't worry about that. You'll be done when you're done.'

I knew the drill. I'd seen enough people go through this on Earth. The unfamiliar q-code in my Servant turned out to be from Mercy, a bio-diagnostic package telling me everything I could want to know and a lot of stuff I didn't understand. A few days. That's how long.

'You'll be mobile once you're up,' she said as she turned to leave. 'You're in good hands. You should heal up fine given time.'

'What about ...' I choked on Esh's name. Couldn't say it.

I saw armed men in the corridor outside my room as the nurse left, soldiers in full tactical kit carrying stubby shotguns. Then the nano took me. I wafted in and out of consciousness. Mercy's q-code told me it was three days before it would let me move, then two, then one. A pair of agents I didn't know came to see me. They sat either side of me and asked questions. I answered as best I could. We'd gone after Kagame, Esh had spotted the drones, et cetera et cetera. I didn't tell them why we'd gone alone without running it through the Tesseract because I didn't know who they were or who to trust. I didn't bother with questions of my own until they were done because

I knew I wouldn't get any answers; but when they moved as though they were about to leave, that moment was mine.

'Have we got the shell pilot?'

I wanted to ask them about Esh again, whether Laura had somehow been wrong. Whether Mercy had pulled some sort of miracle out of its AI hat. I didn't. I think I was too afraid of the answer.

'You'll be briefed on whatever you need to know by the relevant authority, Agent Rause.'

They shook their heads, though. So no, we hadn't caught the fucker who'd killed Esh. Not yet.

'Am I under arrest?'

That confused them.

'The soldiers,' I said.

'Protection, Agent Rause.'

They didn't smile. They were serious. Protection from whoever had killed Jared Black, Victor Friedrich, three Fleet officers, and now Esh and Zinadine Kagame. Not that protection had helped Jared Black.

I shivered, wondering what good a handful of soldiers would do me. The thought led me to Liss, and then to that last moment as I'd felt Esh's heart stop.

'I can't access anything,' I said. 'You're blocking my Servant.'

Another exchange of looks. The glazed eyes of being somewhere else. Queries sent to the Tesseract looking to see what I was allowed to know.

'There was some … unusual activity on your Servant after you were shot, Agent Rause. Agent Rangesh too. Under the circumstances …'

'We need to disinfect you,' cut in the other one.

'Why?'

That earned me an awkward look between them. They didn't answer but they didn't need to. Someone thought my Servant could be carrying infected q-code. Someone thought that was how the shell and the drones had reached Kagame before us.

'We need your permission,' said the first.

'Go ahead.'

It wasn't that simple. I couldn't give my permission direct to the Tesseract AI because I couldn't talk to it in the first place without my Servant. In the end they recorded me giving my consent and decided that would do.

'Whatever you stumbled into, Agent Rause,' said the first, 'it's gone orbital.'

They left.

My Servant came back online a few hours later. The first thing I did was interrogate Mercy, but Mercy wouldn't even tell me whether the others were still here. I tried Laura, who didn't answer. So I tried Bix.

'Hey! You're back. Cool.' He sounded tired. Cold. Distant.

'Laura told me about Esh,' I said. 'I'm so sorry.'

A long pause. Then: 'Yeah.'

Another long pause.

'Laws is really pissed, you know? About Esh.'

I was pissed too. Pissed with Esh for making the wrong call. Pissed with Himaru for backing her and with myself because we should have waited. I could say all I liked how it had been her choice to go in before the tac-team came – Esharaq Zohreya, notorious for playing things by the book – but that didn't change a damned thing. It was on me that she was dead.

I let that hang for a few moments.

'They tell you anything about who did it?'

'Dude!'

I felt the pain in his voice. Stupid question. Personal involvement, both of us. Anathema to an objective investigation. We'd been frozen out now and it would stay that way. The Tesseract wouldn't let us look at anything to do with the case even when

118

we were fit for active duty again. I'd watch from the sidelines, helpless and ignorant. So would Rangesh.

Like I had with Alysha.

'You OK?' I asked. Another stupid question. We were both a long way from being OK.

'Sure, dude. Going to be a little while before I'm walking again is all.'

I cut the call and connected to the Tesseract. I couldn't access anything to do with Kagame and the shooting but I still had access to the Black and Friedrich cases. I figured that wasn't going to last so I grabbed what I could. The forensics report on the shell that killed Black was full of technical notes that added up to nothing very much: it was a custom creation, some parts of military origin, likely to have come from Earth, all of which I'd already guessed. The tech report on Friedrich's Servant was no more interesting. The Tesseract techs couldn't say for sure what had caused the pulse but Friedrich's Servant had been wiped clean down to basic quantum states.

I tried Laura but she still wasn't answering. I pinged her a message instead: Why the drone? Why murder Friedrich in front of us? Why take all that risk?

I reckoned I'd figured it out by the time Laura pinged me back. Friedrich had been a lure. Same as they'd used Black to get those three Fleet agents into Mercy, they'd used Friedrich to get close to me, or maybe to Bix. Maybe they put a bug on us or slipped something into one of our Servants. Or maybe they'd used Chantale Pré as an unwitting mole. Whichever it was, they'd been watching us from the moment we left Disappointment – everything we did. They knew we'd taken Pré back to the Tesseract. Maybe they heard everything she said, maybe not, but they'd known we were talking to her. They'd seen who else we talked to. They watched us call a pod and saw where it took us. They were looking for Kagame, same as us, and figured it was easier to just ride on our tails.

Leave it, Keon.

That was how the drones had been there first.

Can't.

We'd led them straight to Kagame.

Our fault. *My* fault – and someone in the bureau had already worked that out ahead of me. That was why the Tesseract wanted to sterilise my Servant, why they were keeping me isolated after they brought me in.

I messaged Laura again and told her what I thought. A minute later my Servant buzzed inside my head as she called me back.

'Hey, you.'

'We can't be talking about this.' She sounded strained. And hushed, as though she was hiding in some furtive corner, whispering at me.

'We led them right to him.'

'Probably.'

I didn't know what else to say after that.

'Was it me or Bix?'

'Or was it Esh?' A bitter laugh. 'You really want to know?'

I thought about that. 'No.'

'Your Servants were clean. You and Bix. It wasn't your fault.'

I begged to differ.

'I'm scared,' she said, after a long quiet. 'I'm scared for you. I'm scared for me. I'm scared for Jamie. I'm scared for all of us. Who the fuck is doing this, Keon?'

'Someone who doesn't want us to see what's on Kagame's sliver.' So obvious that it was a waste of words to say it.

'Keon, we really can't be talking about this.'

They'd be watching us. Whoever *they* were.

A list of names. A list of traitors? And Kagame had told Esh that I was on it.

'Is it Fleet?'

Fleet had the tech. They had the ability to smuggle people on and off Magenta if they wanted to …

'It's not your fight now.'

'Laws …'

'We can't—'

'Kagame said I was a traitor.'

A long pause. 'I know,' she said at last.

'How?'

'Esh.'

'Her Serv—'

'No. Not from her Servant.'

A surge of hope ran through me. 'You said she was dead!'

Another long pause, then: 'Fucking hell, Keon, she is! You really want to know? Fine. You know she has artificial eyes, right? You know her Servant was implanted in her on Earth before her family emigrated, right? So you know it was done the Earth way. Filaments grown inside her head. Thought control. That shit. Yeah? You knew all that, right?'

'So?'

'So between them they constantly recorded the last ten minutes of everything she saw and heard and did. Did you know that?'

'No.'

'We lived through it, Keon. Me and a good few others. We relived it. Her dying.'

The weight of what Laura said hit me. What it must have been like to see and hear those last few minutes when Esh and I thought we were going to die.

'Kagame said you were with Fleet.'

'I'm not with Fleet, Laura.'

'I believe you. But here's the thing, Keon … You *did* work for them for the five years you were away and it's not the first time it's come up since you came back. That's a problem.'

121

There was a long silence between us. She meant Alysha. She meant when Liss and I had gone after the people who killed her.

'We can't be talking about this,' she said again. 'I'm going to go now. Get well.' Another pregnant pause. 'But please don't call me again.'

'What?'

But she was gone.

9

THE MORGUE

Alysha had kissed me goodbye early in the morning as I set off to catch the mag-lev to Disappointment to break open the case that was going to make my career. Replicas of living Earther celebrities were being built on Magenta and shipped to Earth – sex-bot shells with AI personalities indistinguishable from the real thing. Which was bad enough on its own, but now one of them had been used as a way to commit murder. She'd kissed me goodbye and handed me a bacon sandwich in a brown paper bag; and then instead of going to work like on any other regular day, she'd emptied our accounts and vanished. I didn't know how she'd spent that last day, but that evening she'd stowed away on the overnight freight train, the same train that had taken me in the morning. Halfway to Disappointment, Loki's bomb had taken her in a ball of fire. That was that. Nothing left but two charred dog tags.

I'd come back to Magenta with Liss. I'd tried to find out why. It wasn't like Alysha to run. I'd liked to think she'd been coming to Disappointment to find me but by the end I wasn't so sure. I hadn't much liked a lot of what I'd found. She was my wife. I'd thought I knew her. Turned out I didn't.

The files Wynne had given me were a collection of notes and essays and recorded lectures. I scanned through them, trying to let them wash me with a sense of what had interested her. It didn't work. Nothing stuck. I was too numb. Too wrapped up in Esh being dead.

Dead. The idea slid off me like oil over water.

I tried Alysha's files again, backwards this time. The very last one was a short video clip of a man looking into a camera. He was about my age, Pacific Islander stock, like all Magenta's original settlers. He looked haunted, as though what he was about to say or do wasn't going to come easy.

Me sorry, me friends, for what me do. Us know me. We family.

He paused. I didn't recognise the patois. From the resolution and sound quality, this video was ancient – but that sort of thing could easily be faked.

Me takes the ship. Me know us needs it. Me knows we family. Me knows us desperate. But me goes. Me brings it back, me family. All-powerful promise! Me swears us ...!

The background behind him was gloomy and cramped. There were bunks and metal kit boxes. It looked like part of a barracks but it could have been anywhere ...

No. Not anywhere. There was a hint of motion behind him. Something drifting slow and straight in the background. Too small and grainy to make out what it was but the way it moved was enough. Zero gravity. He was in orbit, or else in deep space.

The man's face looked ready to burst into tears.

... Me tells you many over. Me sees them. Always. Me feels them. Here. But not. Me sorry me family. Me goes Magenta home where all starts and ends. Me knows. Me hears them. Me knows when they go. Me stops them. Me keep safe me family.

That was it. One minute of video. Was that what had caught

Alysha's attention in the last year we'd been together? But if it was, then why was it the last file on the sliver, the most recent?

I watched it again, trying to work out whether it was real or a hoax – and if it was a hoax, then a hoax of what? She hadn't left any notes, nothing to hint where she'd found it or what she thought it meant, not a shred of context. I tried searching for the words and phrases used. My Servant didn't find any other copies of the video in any public space but the patois went back to the days when the only humans on the abandoned Masters' ships were stranded would-be colonists, the people who became the first crews, who, a couple of decades later when the chaos finally settled, became Fleet.

The other recent files on the sliver were recordings of lectures and talks given on Magenta by people who claimed to be experts, although we both knew there was no such thing when it came to the Masters. I checked my Servant back to when Alysha's diary and mine were synchronised. I still had all her old appointments going back a decade and more. The dates were all there, every lecture and seminar she'd recorded, but disguised as something else. She was at a Tesseract briefing in Nico. An interview with a suspect. A stake-out. Every one of them. I thought I even remembered a few. A handful of idle words, tossed casually over her shoulder. *I've got a thing on in Disappointment next week. Work. Be back before bedtime.* That sort of thing.

She'd lied to me to hide this, whatever *this* was. It was there right in front of me. Hard evidence.

I pulled myself back. Maybe I was wrong. Alysha was called away by the bureau all the time. We both were. Plans changed often enough for it to seem routine: rearranged meetings; an investigation overtaken by events; a new piece of evidence; that sort of thing. Maybe this was just some coincidence and she hadn't …

She'd hidden other things from me. I'd discovered that the hard way.

But why? Of all the secrets she'd kept, why this? Why bury something we could have done together that wasn't work, something to talk about late at night, hands held, fingers intertwined, lying on our bed looking up at a ceiling programmed to show the stars … Like Bix said: when it came down to it, who *wasn't* interested in the Masters?

Liss?

I had to know. Nothing good could come of it but I had to know how much she'd lied. It wouldn't be difficult to find out.

I tried the Magenta Institute first. Anyone who came to Magenta to peddle knowledge wound up at the Institute, and the Institute was right next door to the bureau. Alysha could have gone to a dozen talks there and I'd never have known.

Hey, Keys.

Where are you? I hadn't expected Liss to reply so quickly.

Close.

Keeping an eye on me?

Yes.

I hesitated. You were there. At the end? When Esh … I didn't know what else to say.

A pause. Yes.

Was it you who stopped the shell?

No.

It *was* a shell?

Yes.

Like you?

No. Like a drone. With a pilot.

I had to take a deep breath.

Esh is dead.

I know.

How?

I was there. You asked me why I killed ... someone. I'm not sure I know who you meant.

Did I? I don't remember. I had to take a deep breath. The shell killed Esh. They're keeping her body alive. Where is she? They won't tell me where she is. Can you find out?

Why would you ask me that?

I want to see her.

Why?

I only knew that I wanted it. To hold her hand and tell her I was sorry. That it was my fault. To say goodbye.

Mercy is an autonomous artificial intelligence. I'm not sure I could spoof it. It might very well see me for what I am.

So it would be dangerous to try?

I shouldn't ask. Liss and I were no good for each other. We'd figured that out the hard way. The less contact the better. I shouldn't even have been talking to her, much less begging favours.

Forget it then, I said, when she didn't answer.

Is that why you wanted to talk to me?

No.

Alysha's files?

Yes.

So you saw it too? I almost told you. But then I thought perhaps I shouldn't.

I saw the video. I don't know what to make of it.

I think it's authentic.

Who is he?

I don't know. But if it *is* authentic then perhaps we'll find out when the trans-polar expedition digs him up.

What?

Keys! A man talks about stealing a ship from what would one day become Fleet. He talks about bringing it to Magenta. There's no record that he ever arrived. Do you know how many shuttles Fleet had back then?

Are you saying this guy is our crashed ship?

If the video is authentic then yes, probably.

I let that sink in. The dates, for a start. The first trans-polar expedition had stumbled on the crash site by chance less than a year ago. Alysha had seen this video at least five years earlier.

When I asked if you'd seen it too, I didn't mean the video.

Then what?

A pause and then Liss sent me a list. Alysha had been to a dozen different talks and seminars in the year before she died. One by one the names on the list grew links.

The pattern, she said.

Raj Bannerjee. A Fleet scientist who'd been touring the colonies. Whereabouts unknown. Last known location Earth, India.

Jit Nohr. Magenta. Died a week ago of heart failure. Somehow her Servant hadn't registered an alarm. By the time it did she was long past hope of resuscitation.

Jane Rigden. A xenobiologist from Earth. Died last year: a sudden stroke on the *Revenger* on her way to a symposium on New Dawn.

Calim Sukhoi. Died three years ago on New Tibet. Natural causes.

Doctor Nicholas Steadman. Murdered in his home four nights ago. Shot in the head.

Lars Kettler. No financial difficulties, no recent relationship crises, no history of mental instability. Found yesterday, dead, apparently from a self-inflicted overdose of K-amphetamines. Probably died a few nights earlier. His body was still in Mercy.

Six out of six missing. Five out of six dead. Three of them on Magenta within the last few days?

The last name was still alive and still living in Firstfall.

Event Horizon?

Rachael Cho. Event Horizon is her stage name. You didn't see it, did you?

I see it now.

I should go.

You're not curious?

Of course I am.

I weighed up what was certainly a bad choice and then made it anyway. Whatever Liss said, she couldn't stay away from Alysha. She *was* Alysha, and it was fundamental to the way she was made that the missing parts of the woman whose data had made her would always have an irresistible allure.

The Tesseract will have files on the ones who aren't off-world. You want to see them, right?

I don't have access.

But I do.

You could lose your job.

You don't exist, remember. Who would I be showing them to?

Keys, you know that doesn't fly.

If I find anything that's safe to share, I'll share it.

And in return? She wasn't ever stupid.

I want to see Esh. I want to see her body.

A long pause. Are you sure?

Don't you dare go there, Liss. Not again. I know I'm not going to like it. I know I'm going to blame myself. I already do. But I'm not going to run. Not this time.

Another long pause.

OK, Keys. I'll try.

I cut the link and pulled what files we had on Steadman, Nohr and Kettler down from the Tesseract. Nohr turned out to be a fringe-science-obsessed neurotic who'd started as a journalist and moved quickly to being a lone voice in the wind at the far end of crazy-town, obsessed with the idea that the Masters had seeded more colonies than we'd ever found. Her death flagged up as suspicious due to the circumstances, but forensics hadn't found anything and the q-code in her Servant hadn't been updated for something like a decade. It hadn't sounded an alarm because her communications protocols were obsolete. It was hard to force a Servant not to keep itself up to date but not impossible – and it was precisely the sort of daft shit that someone with Nohr's apparent paranoia might pull. The case was technically open, but only because no one had found the time to officially write it off.

Steadman was entirely different. A respected scientist at the Institute, a lecturer in astrophysics and xenobiology and an amateur radio astronomer, and no one accidentally ended up with a bullet in the head. There was an open case and an ongoing investigation. I couldn't see any details, only that the officer in charge was Corwin Utubu. I'd worked with Utubu in Disappointment once. He was a good agent, seasoned and competent. I left a message, asking for access to his files.

Kettler was another Institute academic, a historian. His death was too new to be anything more than suspicious so far. First impression was that he'd killed himself, although it didn't look like he'd had much reason. The Tesseract would be waiting for an autopsy verdict before it decided what to do. The body would be right here in Mercy.

I messaged Utubu again, showed him Nohr and Kettler and suggested the deaths might be linked to Steadman. I told him about Rachael Cho and suggested she might be another target. I was vague, though. It was hard to say why without telling him about Alysha's files. Next I messaged Mercy and invited myself to Kettler's autopsy when it happened. Then I closed my eyes. I fell asleep thinking about Liss, about Alysha, about Esh, and woke three hours later. My Servant's alarm had gone off. Kettler's autopsy was about to start. I struggled my way to something approximating consciousness and pinged Mercy's chief forensic examiner, Doctor Roge, that I was coming; but by the time I reached Mercy's mortuary, Kettler was on the table with the usual collection of forensic drones humming around him. The drones were already closing him up.

Rangesh was there, sitting in an electric wheelchair. He looked awful. I guessed he'd come down in time to see the whole show.

'Hey, man.'

'You look like you should have stayed in bed.'

I wanted to ask him why he was here but he might have asked me the same. Then he told me anyway.

'Laws said I should come. Drugs case, you know?'

I didn't have time to wonder what Laura was playing at before Roge threw an irritated look at both of us. The drones finished their work. Roge pulled up the sheet to cover Kettler's face.

'It's late. Can we get on? Subject is male. Mid-fifties. Probably native Magentan. His Servant identifies him as Lars Kettler. Confirmed by medical records. Cause of death is an overdose of K-amphetamine taken orally. Contents of the stomach show he ate shortly before he died. Pork and seaweed mostly.'

Roge hissed a breath between his teeth. Pork, seaweed and mushrooms probably covered the last meals for most of the corpses that came down here. No one came to Magenta for the food.

'Alcohol?' I asked.

'Trace. He hadn't been drinking.'

'Gens?'

'The usual background level.'

So he hadn't been tripping, either. 'Anything else?'

'A lot of K-meth.' Roge scratched his chin and frowned. Bix didn't seem to pick it up but I'd worked with Roge before.

'But?'

'Usually in a drug case I find high levels of gens because that's the first place anyone goes. And for anyone who's a habitual user of anything at all I expect to find evidence of build-up in the organs. Tolerances. Minor damage somewhere. At least *something*. Not here. Kettler was clean before he died and had been for a good while.'

'You're saying he didn't accidentally overdose.'

'I'm saying he didn't habitually use drugs, Agent Rause.'

Yeah, but no one ever claimed that he had.

'Suicide?'

Roge shrugged. 'The K-meth in his system is certainly what killed him. I can't tell you how it got there. I see no signs of a struggle, no signs of any restraints, nothing to suggest he was physically coerced. I'll give a thorough check again for puncture marks but I don't usually miss them, you know.'

'There was a note,' murmured Bix.

He sent it to my Servant. It didn't say much. A bad poem, an ode to the pain of existence, how every breath turned to lead in his lungs, that sort of thing. Teenage stuff. The last line caught my attention. *Blind, deaf and dumb to the terror to come.* Lifted from a hundred-year-old piece of doggerel about the coming of the Masters. I remembered it. Alysha had liked it.

Roge looked ready to wrap up.

'Anything more you want to pass on?' I asked.

'Nope.' Roge shook his head. 'He wasn't ill, he wasn't dying, I can't find anything wrong with him at all. Neurologically his structures are sound. Can't speak for his state of mind. His hormone levels and his neurochemistry indicate he was in a highly stressed state when his heart stopped. Not surprising given what killed him.'

'Kind of an odd way to go?' I said.

Roge shrugged. 'Wouldn't be my choice, that's for sure.'

'Possible poisoning?'

Roge gave me that look of his. Derision.

'No *possible* about it. Whether he did it to himself or some-one did it *to* him, that's your problem, Agent Rause.'

'I'm just ...' I shrugged. 'Sure. But I trust your instincts.'

'Medically I've got nothing to say one way or the other.' Roge made a non-committal noise. 'My gut says I'd look long and hard for a reason why he did it. I don't see many overdoses and the ones I do almost always show evidence of a long history. But what do I know? I just cut up the corpses.'

I left Roge to cover Kettler. I wasn't even back in my room when I got a call from Assistant Director Flemich.

'Comfortable, Rause?' he asked.

The long and the short of it was that Agent Utubu, like almost every other bureau agent in Firstfall, had been told to stop what he was doing and throw his weight into the storm of shit that Esh and I had unleashed. That was pretty much exactly how he put it. And since gen dealers and con artists and Magenta's occasional killers had the temerity not to put themselves on pause just because there was a planet-wide crisis in progress, the bureau was finding itself short-handed. So if I was expressing an interest and fit enough to work, Steadman was mine. Given that I was about the one experienced agent who wouldn't be working on finding Agent Zohreya's killer.

I didn't hear whatever he said next. The word froze me.

Killer.

Killer meant she was dead.

He was gone by the time I snapped out of it. I pinged the Tesseract for the Steadman files and started looking through them. I didn't get very far before Bix was at my door.

I told Mercy to let him in.

'So, right, I was thinking, you know ...' The words were tumbling out of him before the door even closed. 'Like, we don't know why they were after Kagame, right? I mean, do they want the list of names, yeah? Or is it just, like, they don't want *us* to get it? But I was thinking, because, you know, if they just wanted to keep us from getting it then they didn't have to, like, do anything, you know, after they got Kagame. I mean, the shell could have just wiped his Servant, right? And then that's it, no key, game over, man. You know? And it didn't. It just kept coming. So they have to want the names too, right? Yeah?' He wheeled himself right up to where I sat in my bed.

I stopped. Had Esh and I even given that a thought before we'd made our charge?

No.

I closed my eyes and saw the shell standing over me, ruined but still moving. Then suddenly not. It had stopped. Was that because it had what it wanted?

'They won't let me see her,' Bix said quietly.

'Me neither.'

'Mercy won't even admit she's dead, man. I don't get it. Dead is the opposite of alive. And that's what Esh was, man. Alive. So she's got to be one or the other, you know? I mean, how hard, in the middle of a hospital, can it be to tell the difference? What is she? Schrödinger's fucking cat?'

Silence.

'She's on life support,' I said, as gently as I could. 'Mercy's trying to put the bits back together. But even if it can, they already know she's not going to wake up.'

Someone in the room made a noise. A sort of wrenching sound like they were having their soul torn in half. It took me a moment to realise it was Bix. He crumpled in his wheelchair, hunched in on himself, sobbing like a small child.

'We were ...' He shook his head. 'We were going to ...'

I hauled a chair over to sit beside him and gripped him tight, ready to shake him out of it maybe. But instead I started to cry. I didn't know why. Esh was a good agent. She'd felt like a friend.

We'd had a bond the way soldiers do, policemen, anyone who does dangerous work with a partner they trust to watch their back. I could say the same about Laura or Bix. Yet somehow this was more.

Bix had gone by the time I figured it out, mumbling apologies and seeing himself out. By then I was curled up in a ball in a corner, hugging the blanket. I didn't remember hauling myself there. But I wasn't thinking of Esh any more. Six years late, I was finally mourning Alysha.

10

STOLEN TIME

I slept for twelve hours and woke to the worst storm Firstfall had seen in years raging outside. The wind was topping three hundred miles an hour, driving horizontal rain vicious enough to slice the skin off anyone stupid enough to stand in its way. The surface of Firstfall was shut down. I felt better than I had for days for about a second until everything came back in one big gut-punch.

I pinged Bix. I told him to come over when he was ready and then opened the Steadman files. If I had to run a case out of my hospital room then that's what I'd do – and Rangesh was going to work it with me whether he liked it or not, so he didn't go to pieces like I had after Alysha. I didn't give a stuff about Nicholas Steadman – this was about staying in the game. Between us we were going to figure a way back onto the Jared Black case. We were going to find Esh's killer and, not to put too fine a point on it, arrest the shit out of them.

I told Bix exactly that when I told him to come over. The next thing I did was open a case on Nohr and request an all-levels autopsy. Roge could thank me later for keeping him busy. Then I asked for a molecular sweep of Lars Kettler's apartment, for his Servant records covering the last three months and for every trace of his movements. That one was for the Tesseract. After that I settled to reading his file. I was just getting to the interesting bit when Bix arrived. He didn't look great but he looked better than he had before.

'Done your background reading?' I asked.

He shrugged. 'Some.'

'So who's Chase Hunt?'

'Who?'

I nodded. *Some* background reading sounded maybe more like none. From the top, then:

'Steadman's last call before he died was to someone he knew as Chase Hunt. They'd had several other exchanges over the previous days. He recorded all of them except the last. Hunt claimed to be a journalist. She was bugging him about the trans-polar expedition, like maybe he knew something. All well and good except that as far as either I or the Tesseract can tell, Steadman has nothing whatsoever to do with the expedition and Chase Hunt doesn't exist.'

Bix shrugged. 'Alias.'

'Obviously.'

Another shrug. He wasn't engaged. It wasn't that I didn't have his attention, more that he wasn't even in the room.

'Rangesh!'

'Yeah?'

'I get it,' I said. 'But don't go there. You go down the pit, you don't come out.'

He gave me a tired look. 'Boss dude, I don't give a shit about this case of yours. You know, with all due respect and stuff, sir. I just want to find who killed Esh.'

I winced. Bix never called anyone 'sir'. Esh had called me

that all the time. Long after she needed to. Military school, I suppose.

'This keeps us working.' I wanted to shake him to make him see how he needed this. How we both did.

Nothing.

'It gives us cover to ask questions around the bureau, OK?'

A shrug.

'It keeps us from fucking sinking! OK?'

A dull nod. Progress.

'So start from the beginning. Suppose Steadman was murdered – what physical evidence have we got?'

Basic stuff, like working with a student at the academy. But I could see Rangesh's mind kick into gear.

'Bullet to the head, boss dude. Bit of a clue, there.'

'And?'

'Flash burns on the skin of the forehead. A low calibre cross-hatched head ...'

'Meaning?'

'Dude!'

'Yes, I'm insulting your intelligence. So show me it's still working.'

'Yeah, yeah. Maximal tissue damage, poor penetration.'

'And?'

'Poor accuracy at range.'

'So?'

'Shooter expected to get close.'

'And did they?'

'Dude! Is this like some plan to *annoy* me into not thinking about Esh? Yes, they totally obviously got close.'

'Evidence?'

'Fuck's sake! The flash burns! The position of the body! He was shot from only a few feet away, OK?'

'What does that tell you?'

'Well, you know, if I was totally an idiot and new at this, I guess I'd be saying that he knew the person who shot him. But since he was totally already dead by then, I guess it means, you know, pretty much jack shit, and the real question is why would you shoot a dude that's already been dead for six hours.'

Better. Roge's post-mortem report hadn't been able to find a cause of death but he was damned sure it wasn't the bullet lodged in Steadman's head.

'OK. So. Why shoot a dead dude?'

'How the fuck do I know? How the fuck do we even know it's a murder? Maybe he was already like that when—'

'When what?'

'I don't know!'

'Then guess!'

Rangesh looked about ready to explode. I'd take that if it kept him away from the pit of despair.

'OK, boss dude, I'll guess if that makes you happy. Criminal psych 101. A message. A warning to others. Something like that. Criminal psych 102. Destroying evidence. Don't know what. Criminal psych 103. My favourite. A trompe l'oeil. A distraction. Trying to hide something by making us look at something else.'

'Better. Move on. Servant records?'

Bix rolled his eyes. Not unreasonable since I was basically asking him to read from a script that we both had in front of us.

'17.17: Dude makes a call to Doctor Elizabeth Jacksmith at the Institute. You know? Head of the trans-polar expedition? In charge of digging up whatever it is they found out of the ice? 17.23: Jacksmith hangs up. Dude calls Chase Hunt pretty much right there and then, like she's on speed-dial or something. Says he wants to talk. Says he's got something.'

'Whoa! How do you know that? He didn't record—'

'I'm *guessing*, OK?' He gave me a thin smile. 'But it fits, right? I mean, I dunno, she's a journalist chasing stuff about the trans-polar expedition and he's just off a call to the expedition chief scientist? Go figure. Maybe he calls Jacksmith, he wants something, she gives him the middle finger, next thing he does is call a journalist. Or maybe Jacksmith slips him something he can sell. Either way he's on to Hunt because he's got something. That's how I'll totally *guess* it went down.'

The acid in Bix's voice was strong enough to strip paint. On the plus side, he was thinking on his feet again.

'Dude, you want me to guess up a transcript too?'

'Were the Chase Hunt calls ever run through voice recognition?'

He shrugged. 'Utubu tried it. Didn't, like, get anywhere. Disguised or synthetic.'

'OK. Go on.'

'So Steadman lives in the Roseate Project. At 18.16 a Servant identifying as Chase Hunt switches on inside the Roseate Project. At 18.24 an anonymous Servant requests entry to Steadman's apartment. Hunt's Servant is still a block away. Steadman opens the door and everything shuts down and after that we have nothing.' He frowned. 'Same sort of shutdown we saw at Diane Bara's place.'

I had the schematics of Steadman's block. Anyone who'd gone to his door should have shown up on three different cameras but the surveillance records were blank. Utubu had found a looping spoof-hack in the building's systems. A simple piece of black market q-code patchware to blanket-blind the whole place. Odd thing was, it kind of looked as though it had been put there some hours later.

'OK.' Bix was frowning now. 'So this is where it gets weird, right? Steadman calls some mystery reporter. He's totally expecting her. Someone comes round, Steadman goes to let them in – let's suppose he thinks it's Hunt – and drops dead. No alarms, nothing. Do you think we could, like, drop the pre-school routine now?'

I nodded.

'So suppose for a moment that the dude at the door isn't Chase Hunt while her Servant wandered around outside on some drone for fun. She's on her way to see him. We have her right outside his block. Then she stops and her Servant vanishes. We lose her pretty much seconds after Steadman shuts down.'

'Like she saw something?'

'Yeah. Then a few hours after she vanishes she shows up again completely out of nowhere, like she just winked back into existence, you know? She uses the clearance Steadman gave her earlier, goes in, presumably finds him dead, shoots him in the head and then totally vanishes for a second time.' He shrugged. 'This time for good. Go figure.'

'Something scares her off. But she still wants her scoop so she comes back later. She finds Steadman dead, decides to search the place for whatever—'

'No, dude.' Bix shook his head. 'Just no.'

He was right. A journalist goes to a source for something juicy, gets scared off, comes back later, finds a body, what do they do? Maybe they search for whatever they were promised and then try to cover their tracks, or maybe they don't – but they either make like they were never there or they do their good citizen thing and call the police. What they don't do is shoot the body and then disappear.

'Why shoot a dead man?'

'To make a point, dude. Real loud one.'

'But *what* point? And to whom?'

And why was she armed in the first place? Because of what she saw that scared her off?

Bix went back to the call between Steadman and Jacksmith right before Steadman had contacted Hunt.

'Seconds apart, boss dude. Hunt was asking questions about the expedition. Jacksmith's the expedition queen. Can't be coincidence.'

Steadman, it turned out, recorded most of his calls. But not the last one to Chase Hunt and, for the last few months, none of his calls to Elizabeth Jacksmith. Bix's eyes glittered – his lenses showing him what the Tesseract had on Jacksmith. I was doing the same. More to the point, I had him back. His head wasn't in the black hole of Esh being dead. For now, at least.

'Hey, you don't think it was Jacksmith ...?' He was laughing.

'Who had Steadman killed? The director of the trans-polar expedition? The highest profile scientist on the planet right now?' I had that racing feeling. 'No. But it's a place to start, right?'

'I guess. Don't see how this gets us any closer to whoever murdered Esh, though. You know?'

I pretended I hadn't heard and tried to make an appointment to interview Jacksmith without giving away who I was. Turned out Jacksmith's diary was full for weeks, so I gave up and used my Tesseract codes. Her Servant accepted my plea of urgency and wriggled us into her schedule later that afternoon.

We spent the next hour going over Steadman's history with a fine comb, looking for any of the normal reasons why people wound up with a cross-hatched lump of lead in their head. Nothing. Next we looked for connections to Jacksmith. They'd both worked at the Magenta Institute for decades and their paths had crossed often, but I didn't find anything to suggest they were close, professionally or personally. Utubu had already carried out a few superficial interviews with Steadman's colleagues at the Institute, all to much the same result. Yet more nothing.

In fact, by the time we were done, I hadn't found anything to suggest Steadman was close to anyone else at all. Seemed a bit of a loner. A bit weird, people said. Kept to himself. Didn't have much interest in anything except radio astronomy and the Masters, but on-topic he knew his stuff. Utubu had already run the Tesseract through his finances going back twenty years. Nothing suspicious. No debts, no lovers, no vices that anyone could find. He was well off, well paid, and lived within his means. I couldn't find anything in his apartment or his life that conveniently had motive written all over it.

It was possible, I had to remind myself, that he'd just died from natural causes and the bullet was something else.

Bix went back to his room. Physiotherapy time and he wanted to clean himself up in case today's nurse was hot. I didn't buy it but I'd done what I could. I cajoled Mercy to let us both out for the afternoon, claiming it as therapy, and then I tried to focus on Steadman and not think about Esh and Alysha and Liss.

It didn't work.

I left for the Institute early that afternoon. The storm meant that all the usual surface traffic was taking the undercity tunnels instead. The rain was severe enough to have overwhelmed the drainage pumps and some of the smaller tunnels were half flooded. The ride from Mercy was slow and tedious; by the time I got there, Bix was already waiting. His physio nurse, as things turned out, *had* been scorching hot but also a man. Bix shrugged it off as mostly still a win.

I told the Institute we'd arrived and my Servant pinged to say Jacksmith was ready for us. We must have looked an odd pair, Bix gliding silently in an electric wheelchair with me lurching awkwardly behind with my arm in a sling. The Institute directed us to lifts, opened doors and led us to where we needed to go. Jacksmith's office. She looked up as we came in and her eyes fixed on Bix. I saw them flash with sympathy – but it was only when she came out from behind her desk that I realised why. Bix wasn't the only one in a wheelchair. She must have caught my surprise.

'Not in my file, eh?' She chuckled.

Her eyes were bright with fierce intelligence but she looked haggard. I knew from her records that she was just past her sixtieth birthday. In the flesh she looked it. The pictures in her file made her look younger. In her pictures her hair was an almost luminous silver; here it was just grey.

'Almost thirty years and I still like to keep it quiet.'

She pinged me an ancient news report. An incident twenty-eight years ago, out in the Magentan wastes, that had killed her husband and left her a cripple.

'I was in the middle of nowhere. It was three weeks before they got me to Mercy. There was too much damage by then but you can look all that up later if you want. Agents Rause and Rangesh from next door – welcome! What can I do for you?'

She smiled again. The creases around her mouth and eyes claimed her as someone who smiled often.

'Doctor Jacksmith.' I gave her a nod that was almost a bow. 'I hope we're not intruding.'

'I have an unusually quiet afternoon.' She laughed and cocked her head at Rangesh again. 'Is Mercy keeping you in that for long?'

Bix gave his usual shrug. 'Couple more days, maybe. Don't know for sure. She gets a bit, like, conservative, you know?'

'Doesn't she just!' Jacksmith laughed again. It was an easy laugh, carefree and apparently unconcerned that she had two bureau agents in her office. 'I saw in the news that you lost a colleague. My condolences. I understand you were there when it happened.'

Esh. 'Who told you?' I asked.

'I get … briefed on certain things.'

'Such as?'

'Anything relevant to the expedition.' Her lips kept smiling but it wasn't in her eyes any more. 'What can I do for you?'

'Doctor Steadman,' I said. 'I know Agent Utubu already interviewed you.' I pinged Bix: Kagame was relevant to the trans-polar expedition? How?

Jacksmith nodded.

Fleet connection, I guess. You want me to ask Laws?

No!

I didn't want Laura anywhere near this. A Fleet connection would only see us lose the Steadman case and go back to twiddling our thumbs.

'Steadman didn't have many enemies, so—'

Jacksmith snorted. 'I'm sorry, Agent Rause, but I beg to differ.'

'How so?' Fleet? Huh?

'I wouldn't be surprised if half my staff didn't breathe secret sighs of relief when the news came out that he was dead.' She levelled me a first-class I-don't-give-a-fuck look. 'Shot, wasn't it? No, I might not even be surprised to find out they'd clubbed together to hire a hit man.'

Black ties to Fleet, dude. Fleet are deep into the expedition. Part funding it. I guess maybe anything that might affect their relationship, Jacksmith gets to hear? I don't know! Ask Laws!

'This isn't what you told Agent Utubu.' Keep Laura out of this! I glanced at Bix. He shrugged.

'I didn't know what was going on then. I didn't know the extent of it.'

'Extent of what?'

Jacksmith leaned back in her wheelchair. 'Can you be discreet, Agent Rause? I want to show you something. Strictly off the record. No Servant recording, please.'

'Be my guest.' I pinged Bix again: You checked her out, right?

Sure.

'I never showed this to Agent Utubu.' Jacksmith flicked a video record to her wall-screen. 'Too shocked to think, I suppose.'

She have an alibi?

Jacksmith.

I saw the timestamp. Steadman's last call to Jacksmith before he died. I paused it at once.

'Why?'

Dude! Yes!

'Why what?'

Solid?

'You said half the expedition probably wanted him dead. Why were you shocked?'

Verified by Institute Servants, man. She was right here.

'In my line of work, Agent Rause, colleagues being shot in the head is remarkably and thankfully uncommon. When your other agent came, I didn't realise I was the last person to talk to Nicholas and he didn't tell me. I assume that's why you're here?'

'You weren't the last person to talk to him. But yes. In part.'

Financials?

Solid.

'Look, I was being a little facetious earlier. I'm sure no one on the expedition team actually wanted Nicholas dead, but he *was* being a royal pain in the arse.'

I let the video run on. *Elizabeth. We need to talk—*

No transactions out of whack? No big payments to an untraceable Servant?

Oh for pity's sake! Again? I've already told you—

Nothing.

Elizabeth, if you would just consider for a moment the—

'Is this the last time you spoke to Doctor Steadman?'

Absolutely not.

'Yes.'

You know this is all going to—

What about her calls? Anything right before or after this one?

Nicholas …! Nicky … There are processes and procedures and you know there are. I promise you – as soon as the expedition starts returning data that can be refined and cross-checked and analysed and subjected to proper peer review—

Several. But all to colleagues. All checked out. Nothing suspicious. She looks clean, dude.

'Do you know a Chase Hunt?'

They're getting data now!

Nothing to any anonymous Servants?

'No. Should I?'

Yes, but—

Dude! No!

'Steadman was in contact with someone going by that name. A journalist chasing a story about your expedition.'

I'm not the only one, you know. There are plenty of other—

'That doesn't surprise me.'

I still can't—

If you don't, I will tell the world—

Tell the world what, exactly?

You know very well.

Good night, Doctor Steadman.

The video cut to black as Jacksmith cut the call. She looked at me and shrugged as if waiting for the obvious question.

I obliged. 'Tell the world *what*, Doctor Jacksmith?'

There was that count-the-fucks-I-do-not-give look again.

'Nicholas wanted me to release data from the trans-polar expedition. He wanted me to make everything public as and when we found it. He tried to blackmail me when I refused.' She shook her head. 'It was pathetic really. I don't have much buried in my past. Does that surprise you?'

'No. Most normal people don't.'

'The best he could come up with was my daughter. Sanja-Mao. I suppose you of all people already know all about that.

She made a poor choice of friends once and got into some trouble. It was a long time ago and there was nothing terribly secret about it but he threatened to make a fuss. It would have been an embarrassment, more to her than to me these days.' She shrugged. 'I told him where to stick it. We've all learned our lessons, Agent.'

'What do you mean? What lessons?' And me 'of all people'? What was *that* supposed to mean?

'The speculation after the first expedition found the site. What it was, that sort of thing. There were almost riots. Especially when the networks went down for days as the news was leaking out.'

I wanted to ask her about her daughter and what it was she thought I 'of all people' knew, but Bix got in first.

'So, uh, what did Steadman want released, then?'

'All our data. Everything.'

'Nothing specific?'

'No. He was very clear. All of it.'

'Did he say why?' I asked.

Jacksmith's mouth twisted with disdain. 'Information wants to be free. You've done your research on Nicholas, I imagine? You know he was obsessed with the Masters?'

I nodded.

'He thought the wreck might tell us where they went. Or give proof that they never actually left. Or something like that.'

'It's a Masters' ship?' I asked.

Jacksmith gave me a big smile. 'Almost certainly. Like almost every other ship in Fleet is one the Masters left behind.'

'And the crew of this one?'

'Are you asking me if there are dead Masters on board?'

'I'd be more concerned about live ones.'

She laughed at that. 'If I knew, Agent Rause, you can be sure I'd have some excellent reasons not to tell anyone.'

'Doctor—'

'Agent Rause, the first trans-polar expedition was an adventure holiday for some of the Institute's more testosterone-infused faculty. This expedition is a properly scoped scientific mission. We have security and disclosure agreements in place with the Magentan government, and through them with Fleet, in return for their assistance. As I told Doctor Steadman, there are proper channels for the release of information. Everything will be refined, vetted, cross-checked and verified before release. I will not violate those procedures for you any more than I would for Nicholas. All expedition information will reach you through correct channels if you request it and have the appropriate clearance. In this case, however, I wouldn't bother. The answer is that we don't know. Yet.'

I raised an eyebrow. 'Fleet are involved in this?'

'Of course they are. Frankly we'd struggle without their support. And it probably *is* one of their ships, after all.'

'So not full of dead Masters, then?' I raised an eyebrow. Jacksmith gave me a calculating look.

'I'm going to assume you could find this out through your friends next door, but please understand that just because you're cleared to know doesn't mean I won't have your arse grilled if I see it on a bulletin board five minutes after you leave my office. The information made public so far says that whatever is down there isn't natural and that it dates to around the time the Masters disappeared, plus or minus a few years. We're about to officially confirm what everyone's been assuming almost from the start – that it *is* a ship, and not just one of the crude shuttles they left us when they disappeared but one of *their* ships. I can also be more specific on the dating. It post-dates the disappearance of the Masters. It crashed shortly after they vanished.'

'How long?'

Jacksmith gave me a withering look.

'Who else knows?'

'Everyone who needs to, which includes some of your lot. It's not …' She fumbled for the right words. 'It's not some great secret, exactly, but we prefer to keep it to ourselves until we can be precise. It helps avoid speculation. I hope you can respect that, Agent Rause.'

I nodded. 'Did Steadman know?'

'No.' She shook her head and smiled again. 'Under the circumstances I took some pleasure in not telling him.'

'Might have been easier if you had?'

'He'd never have kept it quiet. Besides …' She pursed her lips. 'I wasn't the only one he was trying to pressure. I haven't made a formal enquiry but I think he approached at least half the team.'

'Did he try to blackmail them too?'

'I don't know for sure but I'd have to guess yes – although calling it *blackmail* I suspect makes it out as a lot more than it actually was. Pressured them, though …? Probably. You'll have to ask them.'

Which was just great. Jacksmith was giving me an entire team of possible suspects, probably none of whom had anything to do with Steadman's murder, but I'd still have to sift through every single one of them.

I glanced at Bix. The weary look on his face said he was thinking the same.

'I'll need a list of everyone involved in the project,' I said.

Jacksmith pinged one to me at once. 'Your Agent Utubu already has it. But enjoy.' She gave me a long hard look. 'I *was* being facetious. I really don't think they hired a hit man.'

'Do Fleet know?' asked Bix.

'Know what?'

'About, you know, the dating of the ship?'

'Of course they do.'

I got to my feet and nodded to Jacksmith, then to Bix. We were done here. Bix tried to stand too, and then remembered that he couldn't. Jacksmith caught the motion and smiled – real sympathy.

'I thought I'd never get used to it,' she said. 'But in the end I think we can get used to anything.'

'One more thing.' I turned as I reached the door. 'Did Doctor Steadman have any enemies outside the Institute?'

Jacksmith didn't flinch. The slight flicker of a smile twitched at the corner of her lips but it didn't get anywhere near her eyes.

'Not that I know. Agent Rause, Nicholas was a colleague. He could be a pain but he was also a good friend to me once, he might have been again, and we've known each other for half our lives. He was being more than a nuisance about the expedition, I'll grant you, but I didn't see us as enemies and I don't think Nicholas saw it that way either. We just didn't agree on this one thing. So by all means do your job – just let me do mine until you have some reason to arrest me, eh?' She frowned. 'Although it *was* unusually mean-spirited of him to bring Sanja into it.'

I nodded. 'We'll be in touch if there's anything more.'

You think it was her? I pinged Bix on the way out.

Who killed Steadman? No, boss dude. I don't.

Neither did I.

A junior postdoc took us to Steadman's office. We harvested his work accounts and took it all back to Mercy. I left Bix with Steadman's data and set about going through his messages.

CHASE HUNT

Chase Hunt walks up the steps to Mercy Hospital. Mercy's steps are empty, as is the street below. In part this is because the night is late and most people are asleep. For a greater part it's because the centre of the last passing storm is still less than a hundred miles to the north of Firstfall. The winds have faded enough for the surface streets to be open again but the rain still falls in sideways sheets of daggers torn out of the sky by Magenta's 1.4 gravities and flung by a seventy mile-an-hour gale. Even beneath her storm coat Hunt feels the pounding. Bracing, Keon might have called it.

Her Servant is anonymous. When she turns it on the name Chase Hunt will trigger an alarm. The Tesseract is only a few minutes from Mercy by pod.

Timing is everything.

Mercy is reluctant to let an anonymous Servant enter but Mercy is also a hospital, an artificial intelligence programmed at its core to accept all comers. The entrance doors slide open and Chase walks inside.

She would rather not be here; but sometimes words are spoken and promises made and regrets come later and that's simply the way life is. Sometimes all choice narrows to a simple binary alternative: act or walk away.

In the calm of Mercy's entrance hall Hunt shakes off her

storm coat. She leaves it on the back of a plastic chair and crosses the foyer to a vending bot. The vending bot has little means with which to interact with anything but a Servant, but eventually is content to accept an anonymous credit transfer from a fingernail electronic wallet. It chirps merrily, asks how she feels and wishes her a short and pleasant stay as it prepares what it ambitiously claims will be a vanilla espresso. Hunt takes it. She picks up her coat and approaches the reception desk. Mercy is one of the few places on Magenta where the reception desks are manned by humans and not by shells. At the heart of the hospital, Mercy's core directive is the enhancement of well-being. People feel better talking to people. Better than they do talking to shells.

She smiles at the receptionist, a young handsome man with India in his genes.

'Hello,' she says. 'I don't mean to be trouble but I think you have a problem.'

The young man looks up. Hunt smiles and points back to the vending bot. Smoke is escaping between the cracks in its plastic carapace.

There is a blank moment as the young man's eyes glaze and flicker. His Servant is trying to reach into the vending bot to shut it down. When this doesn't work he snatches up a fire extinguisher and opens his office door. Hunt moves aside to let him pass; as she does her storm coat slips off her shoulder and falls to the floor. It catches in the office door, triggering the safety devices that prevent the door from closing on an unwary foot or a hand.

Three things happen in quick succession. The vending bot bursts into flames. Chase slips inside the receptionist's office. As she does she drops the vending bot's hot flavoured drink that bears no chemical relation to coffee onto her storm coat. The chemical packages inside her coat, triggered by the heat, burst into a rapidly thickening cloud of dense exothermic smoke. The smoke fills the reception space in seconds.

An evacuation alarm sounds. Chase drops to all fours behind the reception desk. The smoke means she can't see her hand in front of her face but it doesn't matter – she's practised this blindfold and knows exactly where to look for what she needs. She pulls a plastic panel off the wall behind the desk, popping it from its retaining clips, finds the sockets and wires inside and disconnects the hard data link from the reception desk into Mercy's heart. A small array of filaments pop loose from her left thumbnail and take its place. She will have, she thinks, about two seconds before Mercy detects the intrusion. She is hacking an AI. She is a mosquito daring to steal blood from a meth-wired human with unusually sensitive skin.

She uploads an intrusion package wrapped in state-of-the-art stealth q-code. Something deep and small and dark enough that even an AI might not notice. A slow burn worm. Then she copies two classified patient files. She's barely done with that when the walls come down. Mercy has sensed her intrusion and understands that it has been violated. Security shutters slam into place across the hospital. Lockdown.

Except here, in this smoke-choked waiting room where the fire protocol remains in effect. Mercy is not the Tesseract, where secrets are worth more than lives.

Hunt replaces the panel and scurries from the office. The smoke from her coat pours through open doors to be shredded by the gale outside. The flailing crowd accepts her. It doesn't even notice as she joins them stumbling into the howling teeth of the storm. In the crush around the doors she bumps against a large man. She slips a Servant into his pocket and turns it on.

Chase Hunt.

The name echoes through Firstfall. The Tesseract, already reeling from the breach at Mercy, responds at once.

The waiting room empties across the hospital steps, out into the storm. Emergency evacuation protocols take effect. All nearby pods have already been diverted to become shelter and transport for unprepared humans forced by the threat of fire out into the night. The wind is almost hurricane force, the rain blinding, the evacuees from Mercy panicked and unprepared. People lose their footing. They slip. Some fall. Servants howl alarms and alerts.

Chase Hunt clings to the wall beside the door, waiting.

The first pods arrive to offer shelter. Most are empty. Most, but not all. Hunt registers a name getting closer, a journey diverted by the emergency she's caused. As it approaches she hangs back and climbs the framework of Mercy's open doors until she stands over the steps. The arriving pods open and fill with people. No one looks back to see her. Filled pods scurry away to find shelter. She waits a little longer, poised in open sight, aware of all the cameras that will remember this.

A pod pulls up, the man she's tracking inside. Chase Hunt springs and snaps out her arms. A wing suit unfurls from her sleeves. The storm catches her at once. It lifts and carries her fast over the heads swirling below until gravity asserts control.

The man in the pod cannot not see her.

She crashes to the ground fifty feet from the bottom of the steps, lands hard, rolls and snaps the suit closed. She checks her escape. She has no Servant. Other cameras will see her here but there are places not far where the city is blind. There she will cease to be.

Clear and free.

She hesitates. She could choose to walk away now. To not do this.

The man half steps out of his pod, hijacked from some dull journey that happened to take him close to the hospital when Mercy's requisition summons came. He turns to look at what he thought he saw, a black ghost flying out of the hospital entrance, carried off in the storm.

Chase Hunt rips off the face she wears that hides another underneath. She has chosen her spot with care. The man from the pod cannot help but see her for an instant. Standing in the open ...

With a silenced pistol aimed at his face.

Thffpt.

The man drops, a neat sudden hole in his forehead. But not before the widening of his eyes. The recognition. The surprise.

For an instant he *knew* her.

For an instant he was seeing a ghost.

It is a revenge that has been a long time coming.

FOUR

HUNTING GHOSTS

11

NIGHT TERRORS

Keys? Are you OK ...?

I was dreaming. Alysha was standing in a doorway, a bright light behind her. A silhouette. She didn't move but I heard her voice.

Keys? Are you OK?

She turned and walked into the light and was gone ...

... And I was awake. My Servant said 3.13 in the morning. Mercy was locked down and wouldn't tell me why. I thought of Jared Black, murdered in his bed by a drone, and pinged the MSDF soldiers on guard outside to make sure they were still there. They were.

Keys?

Liss?

Are you OK?

I was asleep.

What's going on?

You tell me.

A pause. Then: A fire at Mercy.

A fire wouldn't trigger a lockdown.

Are you OK?

As much as I ever was.

Are you safe?

I think so.

I pinged Laura. Maybe she'd know. But she'd be asleep too. Well, probably ...

You called me because there was a fire?

There's a storm outside. And a lot of Tesseract traffic. Something's happened. I wanted to know you were OK.

I have armed guards outside my door.

I don't know who I was trying to reassure. Jared Black had been in a room with three Fleet officers around his bed. Eight months ago a man on another case I'd been working had wound up hanged despite being in a locked and guarded room in Mercy's secure wing.

Can I go back to sleep? As if that was going to happen.

I just wanted to know you were all right.

Why?

Stupid question. I did better most of the time, but in the middle of the night, straight from dreaming of Alysha into a morbid dread of being murdered in my bed? Hard to keep the bitterness at bay.

Because I still love you.

Funny way you had of showing it.

I know.

A pause. Neither of us cut the link.

I found out what happened to Esh, she said.

She's dead.

I suppose she is.

What's that supposed to mean? Dead was dead. Or it should be.

Are you sure you want to know?

160

It's a bit late to ask me that, don't you think?

She had a point, though. I had a bad feeling where this was going. Stray thoughts that had been on my mind ever since Laura first told me.

They're keeping what's left of her alive with an artificial heart and lungs. Mercy has the technology to regenerate them. But—

She's brain-dead. What's the point?

Her memories are still in her Servant. All of them.

I let that sink in.

Laura told me ten minutes.

No. All of them. Enough to make a construct like me. Better than me. She could be complete. Everything from when her Servant became active to—

No. I almost jumped out of bed. No. They can't do that. They—

Esharaq doesn't have next of kin on Magenta. Her family are all dead.

I know.

Mercy needs someone to tell it what to do.

Mercy should let her be dead. I suppose, if Liss had human emotions, something like that might cut pretty deep. I'm sorry.

I'm sorry too. I liked Agent Zohreya.

Everyone did.

I didn't know what to think. We had no precedent on Magenta. People in the colonies almost never grew their Servants into their brains like people sometimes did on Earth. The question never came up. Did the technology even exist to make it work? An artificial brain wired into flesh and bone? Was that what Mercy was trying to do? Was that possible?

I'd seen things when I was on Earth ... Maybe it was, but ... But they couldn't! Shouldn't! It wasn't what—

I pressed my fists into my eyes, willing my head to stop racing in tight tiny circles. If anyone knew anything then it would be

Liss. I guess, all things considered, it would be hard for her not to take an interest.

Deep breath.

Can it be done?

Maybe. On Earth.

But not on Magenta?

I don't know.

I didn't know either. I didn't know what was right. Six years ago I'd wanted Alysha back enough not to think about the consequences. I'd done the best I could when I built her memories into Liss. Liss wasn't Alysha – that much had become abundantly clear – but she was near enough that it hurt to have her close.

Esh had been a good agent. A good friend. I'd liked her and I was going to miss her and it cut me to the core that she was gone. But to bring her back? Part flesh and blood, part machine? Even if it was possible, would it really be Esh? Is it what she would have wanted?

I'd asked her about her eyes once, why she'd had them replaced. She'd said she'd have done more if she'd had the money.

She'd had her faith. Quiet, but she did. She'd believed in Allah. Did that make a difference? It probably did but I didn't know how.

I could look it up, though ... I could! And then ...

I clenched my fists. I almost had to slap myself. It wasn't my choice. I had no right even to offer one. Just as I'd had no right when I'd made Liss.

Can you find out. Please.

They won't do it, Keys. We don't bring people back. You know that. They'd turn me off if they knew I existed.

A pause.

If I find anything, I'll let you know.

Another pause.

Goodnight, Keys. I'm sorry I woke you.

She cut the link.

She was right. We didn't bring people back. Not on Magenta, not on any of the colony worlds. All sorts of nasty worms inside that can. Mostly we didn't have the chance because most of our Servants didn't work that way. Even on Earth, where more people ran brainwebs, they were still rare and they still didn't bring people back. Ostensibly on Earth because they didn't have the space, but the truth ran far deeper. What came back was an artificial intelligence wrapped in the memories of being human. What came back wasn't the person who left. They weren't the same. A travesty to some. An abomination. There were laws against it. I'd been enforcing those laws on the day Alysha had run away.

Not that you couldn't find a willing black market cracksman if you had the money. And Liss wasn't a travesty or an abomination. But she wasn't Alysha either. I was suddenly glad I didn't have to make that choice for Esh – glad I didn't have to take that burden – but still I couldn't stop thinking about it.

I tried going back to sleep but it didn't work. Wasn't going to, not tonight. My head kept racing. I thought about asking one of the soldiers outside to come in and keep me company. We could have talked about the politics of Entropism or the works of John Milton or even the merits of piezoelectric easy-clean carpet tiles if that was what it took – anything as long as it wasn't Esh ...

But the soldiers were outside, and so I went back to Alysha's files and Doctor Steadman. Alysha had recorded his lecture: *The Mathematics of the Masters*. He was set up in a big theatre in the Magenta Institute. The recording started several minutes before he came out. Alysha had taken the time to have a look around. The theatre was busy, more than half full, maybe a thousand people all told ...

The view abruptly jumped into a feed from a theatre security camera. Suddenly I was looking down on the audience from overhead. A few seconds later the scene jumped again. Then again, switching erratically between cameras, watching the latecomers and stragglers making their way to their seats. I recognised the pattern: she was looking for someone. I'd done the same a dozen times, hiding in a crowd, searching through it using whatever surveillance cameras were available. Was that what this was? Surveillance? But if it was, why was the recording here on this sliver and not archived with the Tesseract?

The flicking stopped as Steadman came out onto the stage. The lights went down. The screen behind him started a clip from an old documentary about the Masters' arrival on Earth, the first few days when the world had irrevocably changed. I shivered at grainy old footage from the International Space Station. I'd seen it a dozen times but it still sent chills through me. The first glimpses of the Masters' ships, black rectangles occulting the stars.

Steadman skipped ahead to the reshaping of Earth that started a few days later: raising mountains from the sea floor; the disintegration of the Iberian Peninsula, of parts of Siberia and Africa; the reshaping of a huge swathe of South East Asia; the hollowing out of Australia. Five billion people had died because of the Masters, half in that first week as they took our world apart and moulded it anew. Steadman didn't dwell on the numbers, though. He was interested in the shapes. The geometries.

They did it without warning or explanation. They did it as though they didn't even know we were there.

The clip finished with the famous shot from the International Space Station of a Masters ship sliding through space between the station and Earth – an Earth whose continents now drew different outlines across its surface. The ship was a mile long maybe, rectangular and utterly black. A perfectly shaped slab of nothingness, one by four by nine like the monoliths in *2001*.

Numbers were important to the Masters. The lights came up again. Steadman strode to the front of the stage. *Numbers more than anything else.*

I lay in bed with nothing else to do and listened as Steadman laid out his thesis that everything the Masters did had its basis in mathematics. Some things were obvious, like the dimensions of that ship; some less so; some had taken decades to understand and some were still a mystery, but mathematics lay beneath everything. That was his conviction, and with it the belief that understanding their mathematics would lead to an understanding of their purpose.

He sucked me in – but as he launched into details Alysha switched cameras and settled for a view from behind him, looking at the faces looking back. One particular section of the audience obviously had her interest but I had no way to narrow down who she was watching …

Or maybe I did.

I stopped Steadman mid-revelation and started on the others. Nohr first. Another lecture in the Magenta Institute, in the same theatre. The flitting from camera to camera was more erratic this time, the shifts slower; Alysha had been more fluent with the Institute's security protocols by the time she'd filmed Steadman. Nohr's talk was on the sculpting the Masters had done to the other worlds in the Sol system. She had a lot to say about what she thought they meant, most of it rooted in pre-medieval mysticism. The audience was a different crowd but again Alysha was watching them. I didn't spot any familiar faces, but that was what we had the Tesseract for.

I snipped out a still from each lecture, taken after Alysha had settled on a point of view, and sent them to the Tesseract for facial matches. I got my answer a few seconds later. Two hits in common. Two men sitting next to each other in both videos.

I did the same with the rest of Alysha's files, counted to ten and then unpicked the answer. The same two men appeared in her Raj Bannerjee lecture. In Kettler and Rigden just one of them. That one face showed up in every single recording Alysha had made in the six months before she died.

Where was I going with this? I'd started with Steadman, hoping for a clue as to why anyone would kill him. I was only working the Steadman case as a back door into who killed Esh. A man being stalked by a Tesseract agent through a stack of recordings from half a decade ago didn't seem likely to have much to do with either. I pinged the Tesseract again anyway, asking for a name to put with the face.

It took longer than I expected to get an answer.

Not authorised.

Which made no sense. How was I not authorised?

I tried the man sitting next to him in the Bannerjee and Nohr lectures.

Not authorised.

I stopped and checked my Servant was connecting properly – that being on medical leave didn't mean I was suspended or had had my clearances revoked.

It didn't. They weren't. I tried again.

Not authorised.

It made no sense.

I went into the Institute records and looked up the seats where Not Authorised had sat for each of the lectures. I asked the Institute to tell me who'd made the reservations. While I did that, I tried to work out what *Not Authorised* could mean.

The seat reservations had been made by the Firstfall Fleet Consulate.

Alysha was stalking a pair of Fleet officers?

My thoughts jumped to Jared Black. But that made no sense. There was no connection here.

Not yet ...

If the Tesseract wasn't going to tell me who they were then I didn't see much hope that Fleet would be any different but I also didn't see the harm in asking. I snipped out pictures of the two men, carefully deleting everything except their faces to eradicate any context.

Then again ...

These were personal files, not Tesseract work. They were pushing six years old. Alysha had been stalking two Fleet officers and if she'd been doing it off the books then she'd had a reason. Maybe I didn't want to be sticking my nose in? Or maybe, if I did, I didn't want Fleet to know about it. I didn't much like Fleet for an increasingly large number of reasons and they didn't much like me.

I pinged Flemich instead. His Servant said he was asleep. I left a message: Was Alysha investigating Fleet before she died?

Then I tried the Institute again and spent a happy hour correlating every Servant transaction on the night of the lecture with the reservation list. It didn't get me anywhere. Too many unknowns, too many people who hadn't used their Servants. I didn't see any generic Fleet tags but that didn't mean much.

It bugged me not to know who the two men were. I tried the news channels and sent their clipped-out faces to public search engines to see if they matched anything in the archives. They didn't, so I moved on to the news archives; and then I suddenly had Laura calling me and never mind that it was five in the morning. I thought about pretending to be asleep, too engrossed in my search for Alysha's target for some awkward conversation about me coming out of Mercy and what that was going to mean and how she couldn't talk to me because she was investigating my own shooting; and how I couldn't come over and spend my nights and evenings in her apartment any more and how she was sorry but it was just work and the rules and

167

how the conversations we'd had before didn't have anything to do with it and …

I was still thinking all that when I answered her anyway.

'What the fuck are you doing, Keon?' she asked, which pretty much crashed all my thoughts at once.

'What?'

'I said what the fuck are you doing?'

'Mostly feeling sorry for myself.' I almost said *Thinking about Esh*, but that would take us the wrong way. Steadman was supposed to keep me away from that. 'You know what time it is?'

'Yes. What are you doing?'

'Right now? Trying to go back to sleep.'

'You're raising flags with the Tesseract.'

'I'm working a case.'

She snorted. 'What case?'

'You authorised to know?' A cheap shot and we both knew it.

'Fuck off.'

'Did you find who killed Esh yet?'

'Keon! What. Case?'

'You want to know what I'm working on, ask Flemich! It's five in the morning, Laura!'

There wasn't any reason she couldn't know but I wasn't in the mood for being dicked about.

'Whatever you're doing, stop it.'

'You need to give me a damned good reason if you want to impede an ongoing investigation, Agent Patterson.'

What was this? *Not Authorised* hadn't been enough to shut me down so now the Tesseract was going after me through Laura? What the hell had I found?

'Fuck's sake, Rause, you can be such a prick! Yes, it's five in the fucking morning. You think I wouldn't rather be asleep? I'm coming over.'

She cut the call and refused to answer when I pinged her back.

The news archive search Servants hadn't found a match. I thought about that for a moment and then called off the search. I could always try again later.

It took Laura ten minutes to get to Mercy. Parts of the hospital were still locked down and the surface level main reception was still evacuated because of the fire but none of that stopped her. She stormed in with a thundercloud over her head and sleep-bags under her eyes, closed the door behind her and stood beside my bed.

'Turn off your Servant!'

'What?'

'Just do it! And make damned sure Mercy isn't listening.'

That was what had brought her out here at stupid o'clock in the morning? So we could talk without any chance of someone listening about a face from some six-year-old recording?

I stared at her for a moment and then did what she wanted. I nodded when we were clear.

'OK. No one's listening. We're off the record.'

'What the fuck are you playing at?'

'Was Alysha investigating someone in Fleet before she died?'

The question caught her sideways. 'What? I don't know! What the fuck has that got to do with anything? Why are you running around like a bull in a china shop asking about Tomasz Shenski?'

'Who?'

'Shenski. Tomasz Shenski! Don't be a fucking arse!'

Shenski. It took me a moment to remember where I'd heard that name before.

'Shenski! The Fleet guy we were—'

The wall we'd hit when we'd tried to find out what three Fleet officers had been doing trying to question Jared Black ...

'Don't. Be. An—'

I got it then. The pictures snipped from Alysha's recordings.

'It's a cold case,' I said. 'Nothing important. Or at least …'

At least that's what I'd thought until it had dragged Laura out of bed in the middle of the night.

'I thought you were on Steadman. So why are you—'

'It's nothing to do with Steadman.'

I figured it was only half a lie. The fact that Steadman happened to give one of the lectures was by the by.

Wasn't it?

Shit, what if it wasn't?

She was looking at me. Waiting.

'I couldn't sleep, that was all,' I said.

With our Servants turned off I couldn't ping her the pictures so I flipped them to a pocket-screen instead.

'Which one is Shenski?'

Laura took a deep breath. She frowned and gave me another hard look like she was trying to figure out my angle.

'What's going on, Keon? Where did you get that?'

'What do you know about him?'

She rolled her eyes. 'Can't talk to you about that.'

'OK.' I tapped the pictures on the screen. 'First or second?'

A flicker of hesitation. 'Second,' she said. 'And you wipe that before I go, OK?'

I wiped them there and then and let her see me do it.

'Who's the other one?'

Another shake of the head, firmer this time. 'Don't know.'

'Find out for me?'

'Tell me why I should.'

I told her. I didn't see a reason not to. Steadman, Nohr, Kettler, the old surveillance files Alysha had left hidden.

'I don't know why Alysha was watching them. I don't have the first idea how any of this has anything to do with Steadman's murder. Actually I don't think it's connected at all. I was just trying to find out a bit about him.'

I realised I wanted a connection, though, and for all the wrong reasons. I wanted it because it was a connection to Alysha. I wanted it so I could prove she wasn't a traitor. I wanted it so I could tear through the bureau to find out who set her up six years ago. I wanted it so I could find out who set up me and Esh.

'You sure about that?'

'So far.'

Laura looked away, lost in thought for a few seconds, then sat on the bed beside me. The thundercloud evaporated.

'You let me know if that suddenly needs to change.'

'Sure. Who's running the Black investigation?'

She snorted scorn. 'Who isn't? Officially Flemich has the reins. But after Agent Zohreya ... Half the bureau is on it now. Flemich has people peering over each shoulder and half a dozen other departments all trying to be ... helpful.'

She smiled and leaned down and kissed me then, short and sweet.

'You're well out of it. I know it doesn't feel that way but you honestly are. Good luck with your killer. Stay focused and keep busy, yeah?' She chuckled, looked as though she was about to get up, but then didn't. 'Take care of yourself, OK? And if you want to keep digging at this, do *not* let anyone see you do it. Shenski's in the frame for Jared Black and it's going to land you in a fuckton of trouble if the Tesseract thinks you're poking where you shouldn't. And ... Be careful, OK? There was a moment when they brought in Agent Zohreya when no one was quite sure whether you were a casualty too. I didn't like that.'

She was about to go. I wanted her to stay. 'How's Jamie?'

'In bed. Asleep, I hope. If you want to talk about—'

'Not really,' I said. 'Tell me about Jamie, though. How's the leg?'

'Couple of days and he'll be right as rain.' She suddenly laughed. 'Right as rain? That makes no sense at all on this world. Show me some Magentan rain that doesn't come sideways and I'll show you a fluke. Shit. I'm sorry, Keon. I've been ignoring you. You were shot and ... I'm so tired. I really don't know how to deal with it. Sorry.'

I shrugged. 'You wanted space.'

'Not like this.' Laura took a deep breath and then gave me a long look. 'Tell me it isn't your fault that Esh is dead.'

'What?'

'I've seen Esh's recording, remember. It *wasn't* your fault. But I want you to say it. I want you to hear yourself say it.'

I couldn't, not really, but I forced myself to look at her and give it a shot.

'Esh made the call. I agreed with it. So did Himaru. We knew it was a risk and that waiting for the tac-team was the safer thing to do. But we also knew that Kagame might run, and it was our best shot at getting him. Esh's death is on me no matter what because I was her commanding officer, but in the circumstances it looked to all of us like the right call to make. It wasn't ... It wasn't ... It wasn't my fault.'

They felt like the hardest words I'd ever said. I waited for the sky to fall and crush me for being a liar.

'Waiting for the tac-team might have been worse.' Laura sounded kind and gentle, a rare tone for her. 'Three of them wound up in the morgue.'

'That supposed to help?'

'Yeah. It is.' She took my hand and squeezed it. 'Because maybe there simply wasn't a right call.'

'The right call was not to have gone in the first place.'

She didn't answer that but a flick of the eyes told me that yeah, she thought that was about the long and the short of it. And that put the blame squarely back where it belonged. On me.

'Any luck with Kagame's sliver?'

'You know I can't tell you, but no. It's encrypted. We don't have the key.'

A pause.

'Are we good?' I asked.

She took her hand away. Couldn't hide that deadly moment of hesitation.

'Professionally yeah, we're good as long as you stay away from Kagame-Black. We'll fix it, we'll find the people responsible for killing Agent Zohreya, we'll arrest them and try them and they'll go to prison. That's what we do, Keon, and we're good at it. The rest?' She snorted. 'Fuck knows. I don't know whether we were good even before this. I don't know what I want. If I'm honest, I'm not sure I ever did. And if *you're* honest, I think you could say the same.'

For some reason that made me smile. Maybe because it summed up the last six months between us. In that respect we were as bad as each other.

'We do the work,' I said, 'and see what falls out.'

Laura laughed as the tension sloughed off her. 'Sounds about right.'

'You get me that other name, OK?'

'Depends who it is.' She squeezed my hand again. 'I need to go and get another hour in bed before Jamie wakes up. Close your cases, Keon. Don't get wrapped up in this old Alysha stuff.'

'So *was* Alysha investigating Fleet before she died?'

'You know exactly what Alysha was doing. Anja Gersh, Settlement 64—'

'I mean before.'

Laura had been part of the investigation into Alysha's death. She probably knew more about Alysha's last days than I did, even now. Although not everything.

Laura wrinkled her nose in thought. 'If she was, the chances are good that neither you nor I would be cleared to know about it.' She was nodding as she said it, though. And I knew that Laura had been in Internal Audit and probably still was, and maybe had been even back then ...

She smirked as she got up. 'Poor choice if she was.'

'What?'

'Shit. Sorry. But ... Well, you know.'

Sure. Alysha the traitor.

She stopped at the door and looked back.

'Keon ... In Esh's recordings, when Kagame shot at you, he reacted to your name. To the name *Rause*, not to you. We're figuring his Rause was Alysha and he just didn't know it. Be nice to everyone, eh? You're in the clear for now. No one thinks you're skating for another team, not yet. Try and keep it that way.'

She left.

12

DOCTOR JACKSMITH

I pinged Utubu, checking up on whether he'd done anything about Rachael Cho, but I didn't get an answer. I figured maybe it was too early so I didn't push. I was still eating breakfast when Bix burst into my room and pinged me a file. He looked the opposite of how I felt, like he'd been out to an all-night party and was still high. He was bouncing in his wheelchair, wringing his hands at me as though he'd discovered the secret of turning lead into gold.

'Dude!'

'What's up?'

'You tell me, dude! Been trying to ping you for ages!'

Mercy's privacy settings. I'd forgotten to turn them back down.

'Sorry.'

'Look, man! You got to see this!'

He pinged me a stream of data. It took a few seconds before I twigged what it was: a map of the first trans-polar expedition's route across the Antarctic ice, marked at every point the expedition had deviated from its planned route. Some of the deviations had been caused by the terrain, others by weather warnings. There were a lot of weather warnings. Polar storms on Magenta were as common as rats on a ship and could be as deadly as an asteroid strike.

'This from Steadman's archives in the Institute?'

'Yeah.'

Bix gave me another moment to take it in and then pinged me an archive of weather reports full of highlights. It wasn't hard to see the point he was making: the original route planned for the expedition wouldn't have taken them within a hundred miles of the crash site. They'd stumbled into it because a series of storm warnings had repeatedly made them change course.

'Dude!'

I wasn't getting it.

'The weather records, boss dude!'

It took me a couple of minutes to see what he meant. But when I did ...

'Are these your highlights on the weather data?'

'No, dude. Steadman.'

According to the Magenta Institute Department of Meteorology, forty per cent of the storm warnings reported to the first trans-polar expedition were fakes. The storms had never existed.

'Dude! They were steered to find the wreck, man!'

I ran through the data again, slow and careful this time. I'd been working for Fleet when the first trans-polar expedition had set off, nearly a year ago. They'd found the wreck a couple of days before I landed back on Magenta. I remembered being due to meet Flemich on my first morning back. He'd been called away. He'd been coy at the time but he'd told me enough: the expedition had just discovered something in the vast tracts of Magenta's unmapped southern latitudes. He'd said it was probably nothing and I'd had other things on my plate at the time, but what were the chances? A million to one? Worse?

Like everywhere else on Magenta, the expedition took its weather feeds from the Magenta Institute. Antarctic nights were so cold that sometimes nitrogen condensed out of the air. A Magentan storm had the power to pick up shelters and vehicles and toss them half a mile before they dropped again. So when a warning came in, the expedition took no chances. It changed course to avoid it.

Steadman's discovery was that finding the wreck hadn't been a million-to-one piece of luck after all. They'd found it by design. Someone had used fake weather reports to make sure of it.

'Steadman was going to show this to Chase Hunt, you think?'

'It's the story of a lifetime, dude.'

Motive enough for murder?

I ran through the data a second time looking for the flaw, and then stared at the enormity of what was in front of me. If this was real then not only had someone guided the first expedition, but that someone had known, even before the expedition had left, exactly what they were looking for and where to find it. The shivers running down my spine came from another place too – six years ago, someone had spoofed the weather feed to a tac-team Cheetah. The Cheetah had flown into a storm. Everyone on board had died. They were there because Alysha had sent them ...

I was looking at the same thing, five years later. More sophisticated this time, more systematic and done by someone else ...

But what if it *wasn't* someone else?

The traitor in the Tesseract?

'We need to find who did this,' I said, half choked. 'We need to know who did this.'

The same person? There was nothing but wild speculation

and desperate hope behind that thought. I didn't dare let it take root, but oh how I *wanted* it.

'I think Jacksmith lied, dude,' said Bix. 'I think *this* is what Steadman was going to tell the world. Not some crappy decade-old story about her daughter.'

'So someone killed him to keep it quiet?' If that was true then they'd done a piss-poor job. These were the files we'd pulled from Steadman's data stacks at the Institute. They weren't even encrypted.

We started with the first expedition. Jacksmith's description to a T: an Institute adventure club decked out with a few scientific instruments and portable weather stations for the sake of looking respectable. No one had paid them much attention but ...

Except Jacksmith.

Of course she had. She'd been an explorer herself before her accident. Famously ...

Jacksmith had connections everywhere. Could she have known ...?

Deep breaths. I could feel it – the last missing piece of truth about Alysha wrapped up here somewhere in Steadman's weather reports. Trying to squash the wild hope that surged inside me was like trying to put out a phosphorus fire.

The first expedition hadn't had the tools to dig into the ice. They'd taken a core sample, drilled to the skin of whatever was down there, mapped it with ground-penetrating radar and moved on. Two weeks later they reached the southern pole, planted a flag and came home, all smiles and glory. No one had jumped into a Cheetah and flown to the crash site to dig it up with their bare hands. Jacksmith and the Institute hadn't announced a second expedition until long after the first was safely back in Firstfall. There was no sudden rush to it.

Nevertheless, someone had got exactly what they wanted. So ...?

'Dude? You want me to set up another interview with Jacksmith?'

'Not until we've got something to tie her to this.'

We sifted through the history of the second expedition. Fleet and the Institute were both keen and both with good reason. On the surface I couldn't find anything out of place.

'Anything else in Steadman's files?'

The second expedition had reached the crash site three weeks ago. They'd started digging, slow and careful. They'd confirmed – privately at first and now publicly – that it was a ship. They were working towards effecting an entry. Since then? Nothing.

'Loads. Most of it looks like astronomical data.'

'Pass me a copy?'

The first expedition had let slip the co-ordinates of the crash site, much to the Institute's chagrin. Like anyone else I could pull up a satellite image, but all that showed was a couple of deep pits dug into the ice nearby, one with a Cheetah parked in it. The second expedition was underground, hidden from the weather. Everything interesting was out of sight.

Steadman's other files were pulsar records from Earth, going right back to before the Masters, to the early twenty-first century. There was data from the colonies too, a drip feed of odds and sods and chance observations, nothing like the maps from Earth. The only clue I had as to what Steadman had been doing was a stack of academic articles on the decay of pulsar periods over time.

'Any idea what all this is about?'

Bix made his don't-know-don't-care face.

'Steadman was totally into this, yeah? Wrote some papers a few years back on how pulsars could tell us where in the galaxy we actually are, you know? Like, way better than looking at star patterns. But he couldn't make it work. He wanted to set up an orbital radio telescope to collect more data but no one wanted to pay for it. I guess everyone figures that five thousand light years to the left of Earth, give or take a few handfuls, is good enough, right?' He shrugged. 'Maybe he was still at it? Like, as a hobby?'

'How do you know all this?'

'Couldn't sleep. Spent all night reading up on him.'

'You know there was a lockdown?'

'Yeah. Something about a fire in one of the reception halls.' He shrugged. 'They evacuated half a building or something.'

'A fire wouldn't trigger a lockdown.' Quite the opposite.

He shrugged again. 'Pulsars were way more interesting, man. Did you know they don't, like, bleep at the same rate or whatever on Earth as they do on Magenta because we're seeing them at different times and—'

'Bix! Relevance?'

'Dude! It *was* what the guy was working on, you know?'

'Concentrate on Jacksmith.'

I went back to the profile I was building of her. Superficially, Jacksmith was a brilliant mind who'd stayed on Magenta to work at the Institute when she might have taken a more prestigious post off-world, maybe even Earth. The Institute loved her. She worked hard and published papers that people outside Magenta actually read. Her field was planetography and she was the foremost expert anywhere on the climate and geology of Magenta. She'd roamed the planet in the bad old days before the blockade, before the Tesseract and before the bureau had got a handle on the smuggling operations. Back then most of Magenta had been uncharted wilderness – something Jacksmith more than anyone else had changed – but all that had stopped twenty-eight years ago when Jacksmith had stumbled into a gang of Earthers harvesting Xen in the middle of nowhere. The smugglers had killed her partner and Jacksmith had taken a bullet in the back. They'd left her for dead but she'd survived, paralysed for three weeks before a search and rescue team found her beacon. By then the damage to her spine had been too extensive to repair, but that hadn't stopped her. The Institute had paid for her to grow a brainweb so she could remote-pilot shells, something which made her one of a unique handful on Magenta. She'd gone right back to exploring, only now she did it from the comfort of her own desk. On the record she'd claimed it was the best thing that could have happened to her: shells were stronger and more capable and could go to places that a human couldn't reach, while staying at home forced her to spend more time with her young daughter, Sanja-Mao, time she was glad to have.

Not that she had. According to her records she went back to work a year after she was shot and was off-world within weeks. Aboard the *Fearless* doing 'historical research', whatever that was.

Sanja-Mao Jacksmith. I looked her up, but the Tesseract had no record of whatever trouble she'd floundered into.

A part of me wanted to admire Jacksmith's resilience. She'd lost her partner and her mobility. She'd had a three-year-old daughter and none of that had slowed her down.

Jacksmith had a brainweb. Like Esh. There probably weren't more than a dozen people on Magenta who had one. They'd given her a brainweb so she could pilot shells. She was probably pretty good at it ...

I sighed. I pinged Laura. She wasn't going to thank me for this.

Elizabeth Jacksmith is an expert on remotely piloting shells. She has a brainweb. She might know something useful. Technicalities, that sort of thing.

A pause.

OK. Thanks.

I reckoned I should leave it at that but I couldn't.

You want to make damned sure she has an alibi.

You're not actually serious?

There can't be more than a handful of people on Magenta who could have piloted the shell that killed Esh.

There are plenty in orbit.

I think Jacksmith is lying to me about Steadman.

Jacksmith didn't kill Esh, Keon.

She cut the link. I went back to rooting through Jacksmith's past. She'd argued in support of Magenta's sovereign rights after the shooting, had let slip a few strong words about Earth back during the blockade and had come out in support of the Returners a couple of times, but on the whole, outside her academic fields, she kept her politics carefully to herself . . .

'You spot this?' Bix pinged me a short video file. 'Buried in all that pulsar stuff?'

I opened it. A man looking into a camera. About my age, Pacific Islander stock . . . *Me sorry, me friends, for what me do. Us know me. We family. Me takes the ship. Me know us needs it. Me knows . . .*

That was all there was but I didn't need to see any more.

It was Alysha's video.

I shivered, stunned to silence.

'Dude?'

'I think that just might be the pilot of our crashed ship,' I said at last.

'Dude! What, like, really?'

Liss had said it was authentic.

'Call it a guess.' I called a pod. 'We're going to see Jacksmith. Right now.'

Steadman knew how the first expedition had been manipulated. The presence of the video made me think maybe he'd known a lot more. Everything centred on the wreck they were excavating from the ice. And at the heart of that? Elizabeth Jacksmith.

I ran through it all with Bix in the back of the pod. Steadman knew the first expedition – the Stay expedition he called it – had been manipulated. He'd threatened to expose it. Jacksmith had given him the middle finger and so Steadman had offered it to Chase Hunt. He'd been about to blow the whole thing wide open. Someone – and I figured that if it wasn't Jacksmith herself then she had to know who – didn't want that. They were motivated enough to have Steadman killed. I didn't tell him where I'd seen that video before but I couldn't help but wonder – six years ago, had Alysha followed the same trail?

'I don't know, man.'

'Jacksmith knows more than she's telling.'

I wanted to give her Steadman's map. I wanted to put her on the spot and see if she blinked and then ask her how someone could manipulate a weather feed like that.

'Yeah, maybe. But why did Hunt shoot Steadman after he was dead? Why not just, you know, come in and give a statement or something? There's another layer to this, dude.'

We reached the Institute. Bix rolled inside while I followed a couple of steps behind. I threw my Tesseract codes about, opening the way to Jacksmith's office. She was busy but I didn't give a shit. Whoever she was with could wait. I threw my codes at her office door and we burst in.

She was with Laura, in the middle of what had the air of a friendly conversation. They stopped and stared at us.

'What are *you* doing here?' I blurted. 'I mean—'

Laura blinked. 'You mean why aren't I finding out who killed Agent Zohreya?' She shrugged. 'I believe it was your own suggestion that I talk to Doctor Jacksmith?'

I ignored her and stood over Jacksmith at her desk.

'The first expedition. How did they find that crash site?'

'Keon!'

Jacksmith looked at me with utter bewilderment.

183

'*That's* why you're here?' She took a moment to gather herself. 'Well, Doctor Stay swears blind it was luck. Whether you believe him or not is up to you but I've never got anything better out of him ...' She gave me a wry look. 'I calculated the chances at about a billion to one. Give or take. So if you have a better explanation then—'

'Bullshit.'

'*Do* you have a better explanation?'

'Yes.'

'Keon!' Laura was using her stern voice. Sometimes she forgot that her fellow agents weren't Jamie.

I pinged the files from Steadman's archives at Laura and Jacksmith.

'It wasn't blind luck. Stay was *always* going to find it! Look!'

It took a minute. They both saw the pattern faster than I had. To her credit, I think Laura actually saw it first. When she did, she didn't hide how much she didn't like it.

'Fuck! *Fuck!*'

'I don't believe it.' I almost bought the shock on Jacksmith's face. Almost.

'Is this about Alysha?' Laura let out a long sigh.

'What?'

'Funny thing is, Elizabeth and I were just talking about her.'

'*What?*'

'Sit down, Keon, and be quiet. Doctor Jacksmith, would you mind starting again? Agent Becker?'

Jacksmith wasn't listening. She was staring into space shaking her head. 'That's how ... But this changes everything!' She looked sharply up at me. 'Where did you get this?'

'Ask Doctor Steadman. Oh wait, we can't. He's dead.'

'Keon!' Laura shot me a murderous look. 'Elizabeth, would you mind bringing my colleague up to speed? Agent Becker?'

'Who's Agent Becker?' I asked.

Laura almost pushed me into a chair. Walter Becker. A former bureau agent now working for the Institute. He was shot dead outside Mercy during the fire evacuation last night.

'Um ... Yes. So he came to see me once, back in his bureau days.'

Jacksmith was looking at me with a mixture of wonder and pity. She still wasn't really here. Either she was frantically working out how to wriggle away from something or Steadman's files really had taken her by surprise.

What? This morning?

Yes. Just before three. 'Could you run through that again for the benefit of Agent Rause?' Now shut up and listen. We'll get to you.

'Of course.' Jacksmith pulled herself together. 'So yes. Agent Becker came to see me a few days after Alysha died.' She let that hang for a moment and there was that look again. Maybe she was being kind, trying to give me a moment to process what she'd just said. 'Asking about—'

'Elizabeth,' Laura said. 'Perhaps it would be better to start from the actual beginning? Exactly what trouble *did* you cover up for your daughter?'

Jacksmith shot me a wry look. 'Agent Rause doesn't already know that inside out?'

'No. I don't think he does.'

'I looked,' I mumbled. 'The Tesseract has nothing on record.'

Laura didn't say a word – just raised an eyebrow at Jacksmith. If anything, Jacksmith looked even more surprised.

'Sanja-Mao had a boyfriend who was bad for her,' she said. 'She was picked up at New Hope on her way to Earth carrying two kilos of Xen. The trip was supposed to be her eighteenth birthday present, her first time off-world. I dread to think what might have happened if she'd been caught at the other end. She didn't go to Earth and nor did the Xen. Your people kept her out of it. Not the boyfriend, though. He went down and good riddance. Look it up – at least *he* should be on file.'

Laura pinged me: He is.

'It was more than a decade ago but that's what Steadman thought he had on me.' She rolled her eyes and then her gaze settled on Laura again, appraising her. 'As Agent Patterson will attest, a mother will do things for her children that she won't do for anyone else.'

'That doesn't make them right.'

Laura met Jacksmith's eye. My Servant picked up the way her heartbeat spiked. Had that been a subtle threat? A quiet warning that Jacksmith knew the lengths to which Laura had gone to keep Jamie?

I pinged Laura back: Exactly how connected is this woman to the bureau?

'Agent Rause, are you saying the Tesseract doesn't have a record of my daughter's arrest?' Jacksmith asked.

Very.

'As far as I can tell,' I said. Why? How?

Jacksmith shook her head. She looked down. 'Nicholas Steadman was a good friend once.'

Old history. Before the Tesseract and the blockade. Magenta was smaller then.

'I warned him. What an idiot.' Jacksmith sighed. 'It was Nicholas who said he could help after Sanja was arrested. He said he knew people.'

'People who could make it go away?' I asked.

Weather data. Planetary mapping.

'People who would be sympathetic.' There was almost a tinge of regret in her voice. 'There's really no record of her? None at all?'

Twenty years ago no one knew more about either than Elizabeth Jacksmith.

I shook my head. 'None.'

She was at the heart of the bureau's battle against Xen smuggling for a while.

'Nicholas had powerful friends once.'

Jacksmith rubbed a finger across her eye. A crocodile tear?

Motivated, I suppose.

Yes. Very.

'Becker,' said Laura.

'Sanja was given a supervision order. Alysha ...' She looked at me. 'Your wife executed it. She was good for Sanja. By the time Sanja left for Earth a few years later, Alysha and I were friends. We became quite close actually.' She gave me a long look, again with that trace of sadness. 'You really didn't know, Agent Rause?'

'Should I?'

'She used to talk about you. I was at your wedding.'

I blinked. If that was true then I had no memory of it. None.

'Becker,' said Laura again.

'Yes.' Jacksmith heaved herself out of whatever memory she was in. 'Agent Becker came to me after Alysha died. He asked whether I'd had any recent contact with her. That sort of thing. I don't remember precisely.'

'And?'

Jacksmith kept looking at me as though she was trying to find the answer to something. 'I told him the truth: that Alysha had come to me the day before she died. That she'd told me that someone in Fleet was searching for a shipwreck on Magenta that went back to a year or so after the disappearance of the Masters. I think she told me because she knew I'd met him once, a long time ago. She wanted my opinion of him—'

I couldn't let that go. 'You knew about that ship six years ago?'

The look Jacksmith gave me had edges. 'Why do you think I

encouraged Doctor Stay's expedition! I was hardly going to let Darius Vishakh get to it first!'

'You knew it was there?'

'Who?' asked Laura. I remembered the name. Darius Vishakh was Tomasz Shenski's boss. The head of Fleet intelligence in Magenta.

'Darius Vishakh. The man Alysha was watching.' The razors were still in Jacksmith's eyes when she turned back to me. 'I knew that someone in Fleet thought it was out there somewhere and I was damned if I was going to let him get to it first!'

'But you said yourself! The chances—'

'I didn't expect Doctor Stay's expedition to actually *find* anything! Not this time. It was going to be the start of a survey that I expected to take a decade. If not two!'

We were back to Steadman's files. I'd burst into Jacksmith's office ready to arrest her for conspiracy, certain she'd had a part in Steadman's death. Now I wasn't so sure. Why? Because she'd known Alysha? Because she talked of Alysha with an honest sadness for a lost friend, not with the guarded pity I got from Laura, and even Bix? Because in her regret was a dim mirror of how I felt inside?

Yes. And that, I reminded myself, was why I shouldn't be allowed to work this case.

'I thought it was some sort of miracle,' Jacksmith said. 'I suppose now we know better.'

'Fuck again!' said Laura.

'Laws? Dude!'

'Shut up, Rangesh! Why are you even here?' Guess where Walt Becker worked after he left the bureau.

He worked here. I know.

In fucking meteorology!

'Nicky knew,' said Jacksmith suddenly.

'What?' I glanced to Laura but she was slack-faced, eyes sparkling as she lensed for data. 'Who's Nicky?'

'Nicholas ... Doctor Steadman. I told him about the ship. I told him what Alysha had said. Him and Doctor Kettler.'

'*Lars* Kettler?'

'Yes!'

'You know Doctor Kettler died a couple of nights back? Overdose. Self-inflicted.' Or not.

'*Fucking* hell.' Laura snapped back from wherever she went. 'Becker! Elizabeth, what did you tell him?'

'I ... The same as I just told you. He asked me about Darius Vishakh. A lot of questions about how well I knew him. I didn't, of course. We'd been stationed at the same place at the same time for a few months, but that was more than twenty years ago even then.'

'What did you tell Alysha?' I asked.

'About Darius Vishakh? I told her that he was a snake.'

'Stop!' Laura jumped between us. Keon, I just looked and the Tesseract records of Becker's Jacksmith interview have been redacted. There's nothing left except a note that they took place. This is fucked up. 'We need to take this next door.'

'I'm sorry, Agent Patterson, but why?'

How the hell does—

I don't know! But this stinks! 'Why?' Laura looked beyond disbelief. 'Isn't that obvious? Doctor, you're surrounded by fucking corpses!'

'Did you tell Jit Nohr?' I asked.

Jacksmith looked from me to Laura and back again, bleak and bewildered.

'You're saying I might be next?'

Laura nodded. That or she's the black fucking widow. 'I want you in protective custody.'

'Absolutely not!'

189

'Absolutely yes!'

'No!'

Think! Who let those Fleet men into Jared Black's room? Becker was one of us once. Kagame said there—

'OK.' Laura took a deep breath. 'A protection detail, then.'

'A tac-team,' I said quickly. Tac-teams came under the MSDF, not the Tesseract. Maybe I could get Himaru to keep an eye on her.

'Lars killed himself?' Jacksmith slumped in her chair. 'I knew he'd passed but ... But this can't be about the wreck! That's all been public for months!'

Yeah. I'd figured that too. So they had to have known something else. All of them.

'Doctor, you're still not telling us everything.'

'I can't believe it. Lars? He'd never *kill* himself!'

I could have asked about Kettler, how well she knew him, whether he had a drug habit, that sort of thing. Instead I dug out one of Alysha's recordings, snipped out the man Shenski was with and projected it onto a wall-screen.

'Darius Vishakh?'

Jacksmith smirked as she shook her head. 'Definitely not!'

'We're done,' said Laura. 'Protection detail is on its way. I'll stay to brief them. You two had better go. Stick to who killed Steadman or you lose the case, you know that, right?'

Last I'd heard Laura didn't have rank to pull on me. Then again, I was officially supposed to be on medical leave. I got up.

'One more.' I showed a picture of Rachael Cho to Jacksmith. 'You know her?'

Another head-shake. 'Is she dead too?'

'Not that I know.'

'Sorry. It's ... been a bit of a day.'

Yeah. Hadn't it just.

'I'm sorry about Alysha, Agent Rause. She was a good friend

and I miss her. She always said you were the best thing to happen to her. You should know that.'

I didn't know how much of Jacksmith's story was truth and how much was bullshit but I was damned sure we hadn't heard the whole of it. One way or another she was up to her neck in this. But with Laura running interference we were blocked.

Fine. I'd bashed down the front door and got as much as I was going to get. Now it was time to creep around the back and scout for open windows.

13

EVENT HORIZON

I walked out on my own and sat outside the Institute in the wind and rain, trying to wash Alysha out of my head. The Tesseract had no records for Sanja Jacksmith but eventually I dug up the boyfriend and there she was: a footnote. Twelve years ago Assistant Director Flemich had been a case officer, senior enough to recommend a supervision order for Sanja rather than anything more severe and to keep it off her record. He'd wriggled to the limit of his authority to be lenient at a time when strangling the flow of Xen to Earth had been top of the bureau's hit list. Maybe he'd suppressed some of the evidence. I didn't think I wanted to know.

I almost missed that Alysha had executed the order. She'd worked for Flemich back then. It had been our last year of academy training, carrying out supervised casework. We were just getting to know each other. Why didn't I remember ...?

Except I *did* remember. I remembered Alysha saying she'd have to spend a few hours every month babysitting a spoiled teenager while the rest of us were cracking Xen gangs and chasing armed Earther mercenaries. It had been the dying years of the bad old days, the twilight of Magenta's lawless wilderness. She'd never told me who it was and I'd never asked. I guess I'd figured on the son or daughter of a Selected Representative caught scrawling graffiti in the undercity or urinating in public while drunk or high on Xen. Something like that.

The trickle of memories cascaded into a flood. That heady year after we first found each other. We'd laughed. We'd had fun. We'd been in love ...

I had to snap myself out of it. That was another lifetime. Alysha was gone. What I had instead was Sanja Jacksmith, Xen smuggler.

Sitting on the Institute steps was getting me cold and wet. I went back inside and spent the next half an hour in reception digging into Jacksmith's past, looking for any other ties between her and Alysha in the Tesseract records. When I didn't find any I sent my Servant scurrying for everything it could find about Doctor Stay, the leader of the first expedition. Then I sent a message to Tomasz Shenski at the Fleet Consulate in Firstfall asking for an interview. I left my name and kept my reasons vague – something to do with Steadman and closing off a background enquiry. I crossed my fingers that by the time I got to see him I'd have a better idea why Alysha had been stalking him.

I left another message for Utubu, again asking about Rachael Cho, then called a pod to take me back to Mercy and Alysha's files. I was still on the Institute steps when forensics pinged me: they'd found a match between the weapon used to shoot Steadman and another murder. They wouldn't tell me more unless I came in in person.

I cancelled the pod and walked to the Tesseract. Laura was in my office sitting at my desk. The door was closed and she had six other agents in with her. She caught my eye as I stared and gave a quick shake of her head. Then Bix caught me and almost dragged me into the nearest contemplation cubicle.

'Becker,' he said. 'Same gun as hit Steadman.'

'You're shitting me!'

'Gets better, boss dude. Chase Hunt's Servant flashed up at Mercy last night.' Bix waggled his head. 'And better still – Becker quit the bureau like, four, five years ago. Went over to the Institute, but before ... Well, he was a field agent for a bit and then he moved into data forensics. Meteorology department.' His eyes glazed for a moment. 'You know? Like, on the q-code that manages the satellite feeds.'

Steadman's map. Alysha's botched mission ...

'I'm not done, dude. Look at the timing of his move to forensics.'

I sucked the Tesseract dry for Walt Becker's career history. And there it was, the thing I was looking for. Six years ago he'd transferred onto the team upgrading the Institute weather feeds into the Tesseract's encrypted network. The men Alysha had sent to die in that storm they'd never seen coming? All their weather data had been moderated by q-code through that network. Becker's job? To try and hack it, to see if it could be done. And when had he transferred in? Three days before Alysha's mission crashed.

I'd wanted my traitor and there he was, dead less than twenty-four hours ago along with the hundred questions I would have asked.

I tried to remember him. Our paths had crossed maybe three or four times. Alysha had probably seen more of him. Her cases had taken her to data forensics more than mine ever had. I looked to see who had requested the transfer but all I could find was that he'd requested it himself. Flemich had rubber-stamped it but that didn't mean much.

'I need to know who moved him to data forensics,' I said. 'His murder has to tie to his work.'

Bix gave me a funny look. I guess I wasn't hiding my excitement very well.

'Dude, his pod was diverted to Mercy in the middle of the night during heavy weather because of a fire. It was, like, total random chance he was even there.'

'Killed the night after we first interviewed Jacksmith? With the same gun as Steadman? I don't think so.' I started pacing in tight circles around the cubicle. 'What *exactly* was Becker working on before he died?'

Bix gave a wry smile. 'Take a guess, man.'

'Expedition?'

He nodded, grinning. I had no idea why. All I could think of was how this man Walter Becker had made Alysha run, that he was responsible for everything that had happened after, that I wanted, *needed*, to prove it, and that now maybe I never would because he was dead.

'You see it, boss dude? This is our in!'

'Huh?'

I had to find Chase Hunt. I had to find her before anyone else. She knew something about all of this, something I was missing. I pinged a call to Laura.

'Dude! Think about it! We're totally locked out of Kagame-Black, right? But not Steadman. Gun forensics link Becker's killer to Steadman. So we get Becker too, right?'

He was looking at me as though I was supposed to see something magical in what he'd just said.

Instead I got a ping back from Laura: Oddly enough I'm a bit busy. What?

'So we get Becker,' I said. 'So?' Forensics links Walt Becker to Steadman. Thought you should know. Having the Becker case was fine by me but I didn't see why Bix—

'Dude! Becker links to the attack on Mercy, right?'

OK, thanks … Be OK if I drop round Mercy this evening? Can't stay long.

'Yes. So?' Yes. Please.

'So we totally get to go through Mercy's security footage, man! *All* of Mercy's security footage! We get to look into the shell that killed Jared Black! Esh, man! Esh!'

OK. Thanks. I will. Keon?

It was like he punched me in the gut. Esh. I'd almost forgotten. Yes?

I'm not stupid. Don't go digging where you shouldn't, OK?

Bix was already streaming surveillance video from Mercy. We watched Chase Hunt – had to figure it was her – come to reception, spike the vending bot with a virus that overrode its power management q-code and sent it into an overdrive cycle, and then set off the exothermic smoke canisters in her jacket. The smoke blinded Mercy's cameras in both visual and infrared. We couldn't see what she did after that. I asked for more. Both Mercy and the Tesseract refused to tell me.

'I'm locked out. Why am I locked out?'

Bix gave me an uncertain look. 'It was a hack, man. She stole data.'

'What data?'

'Yeah. I, uh, don't think I should tell you. You know. Strictly.'

'You want to solve this case on your own?'

His lips twitched. 'Dude, the files extracted were, like, you and Esh.'

'*What?*'

Bix shrugged. I swore under my breath.

'Anything else?'

'Not that I can see.'

'Shit. *Shit!*'

'Yeah.'

'No. Now *you* don't get it. Going after me and Esh ties the hack to Kagame-Black. Soon as Flemich sees this we lose the Becker murder. Steadman too. *Shit!* You thought we had a way back in but we don't.'

For a moment I wondered whether it had been deliberate, whether Hunt had hacked my files just to keep specifically me off her back. But even unvoiced inside my head I had to admit that that sounded pretty ridiculous.

'We have to move fast. Anything of Hunt coming out of Mercy?'

Bix showed me blurred footage of someone bursting out of Mercy's front doors into the middle of a panicked crowd, jumping into the air and spreading what looked like wings. I couldn't make out her face as anything more than a blob.

'Sure that's her?'

Bix shrugged. 'Rain on the camera lens. And the wind, man. Can't get enough definition on her for confirmation. But really? Like, who else?'

'Where did she go?'

Bix pulled up more footage, this time of Chase Hunt as she landed. She had her back to the camera. I watched her wipe a hand across her face, wait for a few seconds, then raise her gun and fire. One shot, then she turned and ran.

'Where'd she go?'

'Surveillance blind spot.'

Figured. 'OK. Well, if that's Steadman's Chase Hunt then she's no journalist. The pods converging on Mercy. Anything from any of them?'

'This.'

Another blurred sequence. A three-sixty capture from a pod pulling up by the steps outside Mercy. People streaming out into horizontal rain and a wind strong enough to knock them off their feet. It was hard to even hear the shouts over the roar of it. Another pod drew up. A man got out, clinging for dear life against the wind.

Becker. He looked back and for a moment seemed not to notice the wind and rain lashing at his back. His whole posture was … amazement? Shock, even? I couldn't see his face.

A muzzle-flash from the shadows lit up a figure looking back. Becker slumped. He didn't fall. The wind held him pressed against the pod door even as his eyes rolled back and his head dropped.

I froze the image and stepped back to the frames of the flash. A shape, that was all. The quality of the capture was so bad that I didn't bother to ask about facial recognition.

'He saw something.'

'He knew her, man. Look at the way he stands. It's like … Like just in that last instant, he knew what was coming.' Bix wrinkled his nose. He hesitated, then looked at me with earnest eyes. 'Thanks, man.'

'For what?'

'This. Steadman. Making me do shit that isn't feeling sorry for myself and wishing Esh was still here.'

'Been there.' I shrugged. 'I still think about her more than I don't.'

'Yeah. Me too.'

I'd meant Alysha, but it worked for Esh too. Maybe it didn't make a difference. In a way they'd become the same thing in my head.

'Becker's Servant give us anything?'

Bix shook his head. 'Check this out, though. Hunt was wearing a second skin.'

He went back to the footage from Mercy. Up close in high definition Chase Hunt's face looked perfect but thermal imaging showed the heat distribution was off. Off for a face, anyway. Right for a skin mask.

'So maybe Becker didn't know her, man. But the face she was wearing? He totally knew *that*.'

Figured. Except ...

I looked at the face of Chase Hunt. 'You already ran facial recognition, right?'

'Sure. No hits.'

'But that's because it's a second skin. A new face just for the night, right?'

'Sure.' Bix shrugged.

'But Becker recognised her.'

He got it. 'Dude! Shit, man! She took her face off before he saw her?' He frowned hard. 'Why would she do that, boss dude? That makes no sense! What if she missed?'

'Does it matter?' My mind raced in circles. 'She let him see her. So she wanted him to know who she was before she shot him. Which makes it personal, not professional. But if it was personal then what the fuck does it have to do with Becker hacking weather feeds left, right and centre?'

'Could be nothing?'

No. Too much of a coincidence. I wanted to scream. I felt like we were so close to figuring all this out and yet I couldn't make sense of it. I pinged Bix the frame of Chase Hunt lit up by the muzzle flash.

'That's her. The real her. One good frame and we've got her.'

We had to find her. She was the last link to whether Alysha had been set up or whether she was really a traitor.

'Sure.'

'Copy that footage. Everything you can. Pass one set to me and keep another for yourself. You know, for when we get pulled off the case?' I pulled up a map of the streets outside Mercy. 'Hunt landed in here. There's the blind spot where she disappears. Scope and scale it. She had to come back on the grid somewhere. Maybe she'll have a new face and a new Servant by then, but someone came out who didn't go in. If she's wearing another skin mask then the thermals will give her away. Get me a name and find out where she went.' I took a deep breath. 'You have to do this. It can't be me.'

'How so?'

'Because I've got something else to do and because you doing it won't raise as much attention. Do as much as you can before Patterson and Flemich suck Becker and Steadman into Kagame-Black and shut us out.'

Bix whirred away in his chair leaving me to figure out the rest. He was right – I couldn't see how what Chase Hunt had done made sense. Showing her face, yes, if it was a personal score, but then if she was after Becker, why the hack on Mercy?

I pulled my medical records to see what it was she'd copied but there was nothing there worth the risk. Maybe she was interested in Esh – but if she was, then why?

But still wrong. Becker showing up was too much to be a coincidence.

I almost punched a wall. It all made no sense.

The Kagame-Black killer put Jared Black into Mercy to lure three men out of Fleet. He'd killed Vic Friedrich to lure me and Bix close enough to then follow us to Kagame. Both layered and intricately planned. Was the Mercy hit a lure to draw Becker ...

He. I kept thinking of the Kagame-Black killer as a he but what if he was a she? The killer had used a shell each time and they'd both been women ...

Was Chase Hunt a shell, too?

If there was a pattern then I couldn't see it. All I could see was the one thing that connected the three of us, connected Becker to me and to Steadman.

Alysha.

I went back to Alysha's files. She'd recorded talks from seven different speakers and in every one of them she'd been stalking the same man. Raj Bannerjee was alive and living on Earth, that much I'd found out. Calim Sukhoi and Jane Rigden had died off-world. Steadman, Kettler and Nohr were all dead, too. Which left Rachael Cho, the woman who called herself Event Horizon, the last one of Alysha's recordings, alive and well and living in Firstfall.

Cho's messaging service offered to schedule me in for next week without saying for what. It started asking questions about relatives and emergency contacts. When I pried for more her Servant's answering protocols turned coy.

I went out. The weather was almost pleasant. Drizzle and a stiff breeze, but nothing that would knock you off your feet or flay you alive. I even saw a few people walking. Couples mostly, dressed in storm suits, out because they bloody well could. I was about halfway across Firstfall in a pod to see Cho in person when I pinged Liss.

It took a moment before she replied. Keys?

I looked at those files. A deal was a deal. Alysha was stalking someone in Fleet. Off the books. No one in the Tesseract knew.

I saw. Liss wasn't stupid. She'd seen the same videos and come to the same conclusion.

Did you get names? I asked.

No.

Don't try. The Tesseract came down hard and fast.

I'll be careful.

One of them is Tomasz Shenski. He's Fleet. I don't know who the other one is yet. Liss … Why was Alysha stalking someone in Fleet? Do you remember anything?

I'm sorry, Keys.

How well did you know Elizabeth Jacksmith?

Well enough to invite her to our wedding.

Of course Liss remembered. Liss remembered everything.

I walked her through my interviews with Jacksmith, the story of her and Jacksmith's daughter. By the time I was reaching the end she was laughing.

I remember Sanja.

Did you ever have anything else to do with her? Once the supervision order was done?

Not with Sanja. It was ... awkward.

What do you mean?

Sanja took Xen. I hunted Xen smugglers. But I got to know Elizabeth a little and we ... I don't have much from the time we spent together but we shared a certain point of view, I think, and ... I think I found Doctor Jacksmith to have a unique professional insight. I think she thought the same of me. She's a Returner, by the way.

Meaning she believed the Masters would come back one day.

Great. Hey! Don't tell me you were one too ...

But no. Not Alysha. I'd have known. We talked about the Masters and she was—

I was interested. No more than that. Another pause. Then a slight laugh. You're on your way to Crazy Rachael. Rachael Cho.

I didn't ask how she knew. She'd probably pulled the destination from my pod.

Did you know her?

I'm not sure.

How can you be not sure?

I have ... gaps. You know that. You know how I was made.

I did. All the records of Alysha ever made. Every moment caught on every camera, every word on every microphone, every message, call or ping, every record from her Servant. Every trace she'd left behind. But only from the places where she'd made a mark. Left her spoor, so to speak. Anything Alysha had done quietly was lost.

I have a contact in my diary. Crazy Rachael. Nothing else, just the name. I went to that part of Firstfall three times. There are records of me travelling across the city but none of my arrival. As though I was taking some care not to be seen. I have no memories of meeting Rachael Cho, but she fits. You know what she does, right?

It turned out that Rachael Cho, aka Event Horizon, was a flatliner. People went to see her and she killed them and then she brought them back. Some people claimed to see visions while they were dead. Back before the Masters, flatline visions tended to reflect prevailing religious beliefs. Nowadays people mostly claimed they saw the Masters. No surprise.

She's not like the others.

You sure it was her you came out here to see?

I reached the outskirts of the city. My pod stopped outside an innocuous industrial unit. There was a door but no sign outside.

Look around you. What else?

She was right. The outskirts of Firstfall were a simple grid of small-scale fabrication and storage units. Back when the city had been growing they'd mostly specialised in handcrafted manufacturing and small-scale robotics. Most of that had moved to automated fabricators now. The old industrial units were a hotchpotch of everything, anything that wanted cheap rent and didn't mind being away from Firstfall's centre. More than half were abandoned. Bix, with his narcotics connections, probably knew this place as well as he knew the Squats.

You could have been coming out here for anything.

Not really.

I started pulling up records from five years ago. Liss stopped me. I already did that. There wasn't anything here.

You could have come to meet someone.

I don't know why I would have gone to a flatliner. But I was here. She sent me dates and times for the holes in her memory she thought might fit. Will you ask her for me?

Sure. I hesitated, then decided she deserved to know. I think I

203

know who set you up. I told her about Walt Becker, as much as I knew. You remember anything about that, you let me know, OK?

OK, Keys.

I felt her presence easing out of my Servant. Stay, I said. If you like.

I don't think that's a good idea for either of us.

She left. I sat for a moment, feeling her absence, then mentally punched myself in the face. Yeah. Not a good idea.

The fabricator unit's Servant told me it was closed. I threw my Tesseract codes at it and it sent me round the back. A heavy scent of patchouli billowed from the delivery doors as they opened. Rachael Cho was waiting inside. She looked exactly as she did in Alysha's recording: skin as black as space, luminous coloured tattoos from shoulder to wrist, piercings everywhere and as skinny as a rake. In Magenta's gravity I was surprised she could even stand.

'Problem with the doors?' I asked.

In the gloom behind her was a medical suite. A simple mobile bed and life support unit, the sort Mercy sent out to people who could be treated in their homes.

'Problems with lots of things,' Cho said. 'What's it to you?'

'Flatlining is illegal.'

The more I looked at her, the more I realised Bix should be here instead of me. Him in his stupid kaftan and sandals. Cho would have opened to him like an orchid to a honeybee.

'Tell that to Frank Swainsbrook.'

I told her I had no idea who she was talking about.

'The cult in Settlement 16? He's turned what I do into a fucking industrial enterprise, but does he get hassled? No. Because he's an Earther and stinking rich.'

I made a note to check it later and looked pointedly at the medical suite. Cho put her hands on her hips.

'So what can I do for you, Agent Rause of the Magenta

Investigation Bureau? I was going to ask whether your visit was business or personal, but I suppose it must be business otherwise you wouldn't be asking your stupid questions. I don't flatline other people. I flatline myself. Which you'll find is perfectly legal.'

Technically correct.

'So what? People come here to watch you die and then come back to life?'

She clapped her hands. The unit Servant turned up the lights, bathing us in a harsh white glow.

'People come to me with questions. I give them answers.'

'What sort of questions?'

'Personal ones. Was there something specific you wanted to ask? I'm busy.'

I looked around the room. Sterile and pristine and empty.

'Busy with what?'

'Do you have a warrant of some sort?'

'I could get one.'

'Come back when you do.' She turned her back to me.

'Do you know this woman?'

I pinged a picture of Alysha to her Servant. Cho took one more step, froze for a moment, then carried on walking away.

'That was my wife,' I said. 'She died six years ago in the May Day bomb. Look her up. I'm not here on business.' I gave her a moment to put the picture I'd given her against the names and faces of everyone who died in the crash. 'I think she came here. I think you knew her.'

Cho turned back to me with wonder to her words. 'Alysha. Yes. I'm sorry. And her death still hurts you?' The expression on her face had changed completely. Hostility inverted into compassion. 'Is there something you wanted me to ask her?'

We got to it then. People came to Rachael Cho with questions about loved ones they'd lost. Perched between life and death, Cho asked the questions and listened to the answers. She didn't call herself a medium or a spiritualist – for Cho, her answers came from the Masters. On another day I might have argued that they came from the misfiring neurochemistry of oxygen starvation. Not today.

'A hundred things,' I said.

She pinged me her rates. A fixed charge for every question, a bulk discount, extra if I wanted to stay and watch.

'I usually only get to ask one thing each time I go under,' she said. 'Sometimes I get lucky. Sometimes the Masters don't answer at all.'

'How many times have you done this?'

A secret smile. 'Enough.'

What was that? Hundreds? Maybe a thousand? And I was actually tempted. It was bullshit and I knew it and still I was tempted.

'I've been down that route,' I said, a rough edge in my voice. 'Sometimes it's best to let the dead have their secrets. You knew Alysha?'

'She came to a couple of my seminars.'

No. There was more. 'You remember everyone who comes to your seminars?'

'Of course not.'

I gave her a hard look and let silence do its work.

'OK, she came here,' Cho said after a few seconds. 'Under another name.'

'How often.'

'Three times.'

I pinged her the dates and times Liss had given me. 'These?'

Cho shrugged. 'Could be. I don't keep records.'

'She came to ask questions?'

'Yes.'

There was an uneasiness to Cho now. She was keeping her distance. Avoiding something.

'What questions?'

'I don't remember.'

'Did she come alone?'

'The things people come for. It's not right to ... It's grief, usually. I think you know a lot about that. Grief deserves respect. And privacy.'

I decided that that was a no, not alone.

'She died almost six years ago,' I said softly. 'And I still miss her. Who was with her when she came?'

Cho folded her arms and gave me a long look. Sizing me up, I suppose. Trying to decide whether I was genuine?

'You do, don't you. I feel it pouring out of you. She's not gone, not really. You'll find her again, one day. Or she will find you.'

'That what you tell all your grieving clients?'

'You'll see her again one day. So will I. I feel sure.'

I sighed. I wanted to be angry but it was hard. Cho had a calm to her, uncanny and infectious. 'Look, I didn't come here for spiritual guidance.' I sent her the pictures of the two men Alysha had been watching. I saw Cho's face flicker. They meant something. 'You know who they are.' It wasn't a question. She shook her head but she wasn't convincing. ' I just want to know what Alysha was doing here.'

'She didn't come here to ask me to flatline for her ... No, I really shouldn't be talking about this. You should go, Agent Rause. This isn't going to do you any good.'

I told her about Alysha's files. I told her about Nohr, Steadman and Kettler. How they were all dead and how she was the last. I meant to scare her – and from the way she crumpled against the bed, I succeeded. Her eyes started darting around the room as though searching for a way out.

'I could take you somewhere safe,' I said.

'Is that how it is? Tell you what you want and you'll look

after me?' She was halfway through a sneer but then it softened. 'No,' she said. 'I'm sorry. That's not who you are, is it?'

'You can have protection whether or not you tell me anything. Or I can just leave you be if you prefer. I've seen enough corpses, though.'

She stared at me for a full second as if reaching through my eyes to read what lay behind them.

'That man.' She pinged me back the picture of the second man. Not Shenski, but the other one. 'She came here with him.'

Her stare didn't waver but there was something new in her voice. Revulsion and fear.

'*With* him?'

She nodded, then shook her head as she saw the look on my face.

'Not ... They weren't together like a couple. More like ... I don't know, like they worked together. They had another man with them. He was crippled, some old old damage. He couldn't walk. He was the one who went under. Your wife and the other man watched.'

I tried to process that. 'Who is he?'

She shook her head again. 'It's ... not the way I work. Most who come here don't want to be known. As I said, grief deserves privacy. I didn't know who any of them were, not really. But that man, the one in your picture ... There was something wrong ... Like he had no feelings, not even the ones we all have. No good ones and no bad ones either. Just ... nothing. Like he was dead inside, just dead. I couldn't bear to talk to him.'

'So if they weren't asking you to talk to some dead relative then what were they doing here?'

Cho looked suddenly awkward. 'There are ... I mean that ... I hear voices when I go under, OK? The Masters talk to me. That's what I do. But they talk to other people too.'

She hesitated then and looked at me. I guess this was when

I was supposed to tell her she was crazy. She *was* crazy but I wasn't here for a fight.

'Do they talk to everyone?'

'No, but ... The man who couldn't walk was trying to find something.'

'The man who couldn't walk?'

'Yes.'

'Was he in a wheelchair?'

'Yes.'

'Are you sure it was a man and not a woman?' In my head it was Jacksmith.

'Certain.'

I pinged Bix. I gave him the dates and times that matched the right gaps in Liss's memories.

I need to know where Jacksmith was.

'The one who couldn't walk always pretended he was asleep when they came. But he wasn't. He was full of something bright. Hungry. And a tension too. They sent me away once he was under. I didn't eavesdrop. I knew it would ... I can't really explain but I get these feelings from people. The crippled man felt dangerous to me. It was best not to know.'

She looked off into the distance past my shoulder for a moment, and then twitched into sudden motion and dashed out. I heard drawers opening and closing in the room next door, then the metal ring of an ancient filing cabinet. She came back with a piece of paper with a symbol drawn across it. A figure eight enclosed by a star.

'Here.' She handed it to me. 'They left this once. It seemed oddly important. It felt like I should keep it. I think I was supposed to keep it for you. Does that mean anything?'

The symbol felt familiar but I couldn't immediately place it. There was something else on the paper too. Not written onto it but indented, as though the paper had been under another sheet written over by a heavy hand. A few moments running basic image enhancement algorithms gave me what I needed.

Darius Vishakh. 8044-5123.

That name again. Tomasz Shenski's boss. The man Jacksmith claimed Alysha had been watching. The man Laura had down as the head of Fleet Intelligence in Magenta. I could see Laura's face, clear as day, if she'd been here to see this. *What the actual fuck?*

'I found it after the last time they came,' said Cho.

I stared at the words, trying to work out what they were doing here. Darius Vishakh. If I'd had any doubts, that piece of paper put an end to them. The number looked like a Fleet service number. And I knew Alysha well enough to know that she didn't leave something like this behind by accident. She'd meant it to be found. It was a message.

Three weeks later she'd been dead. I had to remind myself that the bomb that killed her hadn't had anything to do with Shenski or Fleet or Darius Vishakh or whatever she'd been doing here with Rachael Cho.

Paper. Who still wrote things on paper these days? Who even owned any?

'So?'

I'd almost forgotten Cho was there. I took a deep breath.

'I don't know what it means,' I said. 'But thank you. You've been very—'

'Oh, I do!'

'What?'

'The symbol. It's the symbol for *October*.'

'For *who*?'

'October 20, 2056. They're an Earth group. Returners.'

I peered around the door into the unit's front room.

'Do you remember anything else about either man? Anything that seemed unusual?'

'No. But ...' She frowned. 'They were believers.'

'What do you mean?'

'The man in the wheelchair believed absolutely that the Masters are still out there. After a while you pick it up the moment someone comes into the room. The ones who believe the Masters are waiting to speak to us if only we'd listen.'

I tried to imagine Laura when I dropped that one on her after I'd dropped the rest. She'd be laughing in my face by now for taking any of this seriously.

'Was Alysha a believer, too?' I asked. Cho shook her head.

'No. For her it was something else. She was here with them three times. Then they didn't come back for a while. When they did it was just the two of them. The man who was dead inside and the man who couldn't walk. They were still trying to find whatever it was they were looking for. They believed the Masters were going to tell them where it was.'

I didn't know what I could possibly say to that. That she was shitting me? I didn't think so. She believed what she was saying. Didn't make her right, but she wasn't yanking my chain. Maybe it didn't matter. Maybe they were a pair of fruit-cakes. Maybe they were just looking for their lost spaceship keys ... Or maybe Darius Vishakh, head of Fleet Intelligence in the Magenta system, really did believe that the Masters were going to tell him where to find a century-and-a-half-old crash site.

I pinged my bureau contact details to Cho.

'I wasn't making it up about Nohr, Steadman and Keller. You knew them?'

She shook her head. 'I went to some of their talks. I talked to Jit a few times.'

'We can put someone on you until this is over.'

Cho snorted. 'No.'

The fact that Cho made a living out of dying and coming

211

back again made her a ridiculously easy target. The fact that she was still alive made me think she wasn't on someone's death list – and if I was wrong then an armed guard might well not be enough, not after what I'd seen in Mercy.

I could link Cho to Nohr, Kettler and Steadman without Alysha's files. They moved in similar circles. That was enough.

I pinged Bix: I need protective surveillance on Rachael Cho. I need it covert and I need it without either Laura or the Tesseract knowing why. Can you do that?

Esh would have found a way. As far as I could tell she was personal friends with half the MSDF. A quick call and it would have been fixed ...

'You OK, Agent Rause?' Cho must have seen me slump.

'I lost a friend a few days back. Look, if you don't want it then that's up to you, but it wouldn't hurt to make yourself difficult to find for a while. You have somewhere you can go?'

She nodded but she wasn't convincing. I knew what she was thinking. *Probably nothing. He's probably exaggerating. They have to, don't they? Play it safe?*

I told myself she was probably right.

'If anything happens, if you see anything or hear anything that seems out of place, anything at all, call me. Or call some-one else, but don't hesitate, just do it.'

'OK.' She wouldn't.

I thanked her again for her time and saw myself out, back into the wind and the rain.

Bix?

Boss dude! Guess who I'm with!

Do I want to know?

Colonel Himaru! Mercy is about to let him out!

How is he?

I'd say walking and talking but it's more pacing and shouting. No one told him about Esh. You should have done that, man. So

I'd, like, keep away from him for a bit, you know? It's the first time I've been totally glad for this stupid chair.

Mercy would tell Himaru to go home and take it easy for a couple of weeks. Himaru wouldn't want that.

How much do I tell him, boss dude?

Himaru ...

Get him on Cho!

What? How?

Tell him that Rachael Cho needs a watcher. Tell him she might be a target for the people who killed Esh.

Uh, is that, like, in any way actually true?

Yes.

I didn't know, but it just might be.

Tell him I'll cut him in on what we know.

OK, man. Don't know if he'll bite, though.

I cut the call. He'd bite. That was who he was.

My pod was still waiting for me. As soon as I was inside I sent another message to Tomasz Shenski at the Fleet consulate.

Alysha Rause. Darius Vishakh. 8044-5123. We need to talk.

I attached a copy of the paper Cho had given me. Then I told the pod to take me back to the Tesseract. I wasn't even halfway there when I got a reply.

Babelfish Park. The Monument. Now.

STEPHANIE WRIGHT

Technician Stephanie Wright walks up the steps of the Magenta Institute. She waves and smiles to the shell working the reception desk. The shell waves back. A Servant to Servant exchange identifies Stephanie as working for a small Magenta-based service company specialising in the maintenance and repair of communications equipment imported from Earth. Technician Stephanie Wright is an expert on the elderly Kaltech systems which provide the backbone to the Institute's communications hubs. Business has been brisk since the Magentan government abruptly terminated all its contracts with Kaltech Interstellar six months ago and re-leased them to independent local providers.

The clearances she needs are sent to her Servant. She's here to deal with a hardware problem in one of the deep servers in the meteorology hub. It's a problem the Institute didn't know it had until she walked up the steps but now appears to have been logged for some days. The Institute Servants guide her, opening doors and calling elevators and unlocking locks to take her where she needs to be. They dutifully record her passage.

The meteorology hub is the most complex network on Magenta. Data and images from hundreds of satellites and tens of thousands of sensors spread across the planet are fed into a vast q-code process that maps and monitors and predicts Magenta's weather. The complexity of the meteorology hub is enough, some claim, to qualify as a new form of artificial intelligence.

A man is waiting for Stephanie. A Servant exchange identifies him as an Institute technician. His name is Mohammed Kamal. Mohammed Kamal is not in Stephanie's plan.

'Hello?' she tries.

Mohammed Kamal smiles at her. She has a pretty face today, even if it isn't her own.

'I haven't seen you before,' he says.

'First time,' she says. 'I need to ...'

'I know. I'm here to watch.'

'Watch? Why?'

Kamal shrugs. 'Remember the blackout eight months ago? We have to supervise contractors who work on any of the hubs now. New security rules, you know?'

Stephanie considers this. She considers the tiny plastic needle of nerve toxin hidden up her sleeve that can kill a man in three quick and silent seconds.

'Does that mean you know something about a Kaltech 7GD-6X server hub, then?'

This makes Kamal laugh. 'I'm a q-coder. I know jack shit about hardware.'

'So ... how exactly will you supervise what I'm doing?'

'I have no idea.' More laughter. Kamal gestures at the array of servers around the room. 'Just tell me what you need to access.'

Stephanie has her Servant show him. Kamal uses his clearance codes to unlock seventeen hardware panels around the server hub.

'Big job.'

'Yes.' Not really. Fifteen of these panels don't matter at all.

She goes to the first and pretends to do something. Kamal watches her. He is, she notes, watching *her*, not what she's doing.

'Nope. All fine here.'

Twice more the same. Then: 'Not this one either. What's it like working here?'

'The Institute?'

'Yes.'

Another panel. Another pretence. She keeps up the small talk, engaging his attention, his eyes, his thoughts. When she reaches the eighth panel it occurs to her that there is a way through this that she hadn't considered until now.

The device she wants is behind the eighth panel, the hub that monitors and predicts the weather in far southern latitudes. Antarctica, if you were back on Earth. It is a hacker's device, attached to one of the many network ports and it has no business being here. It is, however, exactly what Stephanie is looking for. She is reasonably sure she already knows who put it here, and why, and what they did with it: Walter Becker, tampering with the feeds to the first trans-polar expedition. Becker won't be tampering with anything ever again but he certainly wasn't working alone.

The device has been here for at least a year. Stephanie would like to know if it's been here a lot longer than that. Finding that answer is part of why she's come.

'That would be your problem.' She extracts the device and shows it to Kamal.

'What is that?'

'I have absolutely no idea but it definitely shouldn't be here. I'm going to have someone look at it who knows what they're doing. Do you need to log it or something?'

'I guess.'

She closes the panel and moves to the one that co-ordinates the weather feeds for the northern mid-latitudes. She lingers at this for longer than the others, a slow and painstaking check.

Nothing is out of place. There is no second device. If there once was, it has left no trace. She has no way to know.

She moves to the next panel and the next. Everything now is simply for show, to make it seem as though all hubs are equal. Kamal tells her about his work. He's keen and eager. At the last panel she turns and gives him a smile.

'Look,' she says, 'I don't have another call due for a while. I was going to grab a drink in the canteen. You could show me around if you like. That would be cool.'

She puts Walt Becker's device in her satchel as she says this. She does it right in front of him. He sees yet he doesn't. She has taken his attention somewhere else.

She closes the panel. She closes her satchel.

On her way out, Stephanie lets Mohammed Kamal buy her a drink and show her around. She tells him she'll be in touch as soon as she has anything on what she found in the hub. They arrange to meet again the following day and go their separate ways.

Tomorrow Kamal will be disappointed, but his disappointment will hurt less than her needle. Better this way for both of them.

FIVE

KISS CHASE

14

THE SECRET LIVES OF ALYSHA RAUSE

Days when the Firstfall sky was clear and the air was still were so rare they were all but accepted as impromptu public holidays. On those days Babelfish Park was packed because there wasn't anywhere else like it on Magenta. The park had started as an organic waste dump, a place to put everything the recyclers couldn't handle back in the early years when Firstfall had been a warren of tunnels and a few domes and not much else. There were a dozen different stories about how exactly it had transformed into a park, all of them different, but the gist was the same: viable terrestrial grass seeds had somehow ended up in the heap and germinated. Accident? Design? Pick your legend – but after that the stories were all much the same. The grass survived the weather, wind, rain, storm, hail. The Firstfall council – back before the Chamber of Selected Representatives had even existed – decided to preserve and nurture it, and so Babelfish became the only place in the habitable equatorial belt that looked like an actual piece of home.

Babelfish wasn't anything more than a grassy field. It was

pathetic but it was all we had. Every visitor from Earth got taken there and walked away wondering why. In the last decades we'd added a few stunted deep-rooting trees held in place by tethers in case a storm blew through. When a storm stripped the trees bare, students from the Magenta Institute nursed them back to life. On those rare good days when the sun came out, so did we. When the weather wasn't a hail of horizontal rain, the park flooded with people.

Today wasn't one of those days.

A delivery drone waited for me when my pod stopped at the edge of the park. I sealed the paper Cho had given me into an evidence bag and sent it to Bix for a full forensics check. Alysha knew every trick. If she'd left the paper as a message for someone in the bureau then there was no telling what else she'd hidden there.

Once the drone was on its way, I followed a path from the edge of Babelfish Park to the Monument at its centre. The Monument wasn't much, just a foamcrete dome sunk into the ground with a stone slab at the centre to mark the spot where the first Magentans had supposedly been dropped by the Masters. The only way in was through an arch so low that most people had to stoop, while the inside was cold and dark and damp and smelled of ammonia. In spite of or because of the cleaning drones, I wasn't sure.

Shenski was waiting inside the dome. I recognised him from Alysha's recordings.

'You're a hard man to reach,' I started, and then stopped. He had a particle beam pointed at my face. I could hear the hum of its charge, the sort of weapon that had disintegrated Jared Black's head. A spray of q-code hackware hit my Servant hard enough to fuse circuits and ransacked it from the inside out. The Tesseract firewall protecting any classified data I might be carrying dissolved like tissue in a storm.

'Tesseract Agent Keon Rause.'

The particle beam didn't shift. Whatever Shenski had done to my Servant had shut me down from the inside out. I couldn't call for help even if I wanted to. I figured I'd go for the Rangesh approach and act like Shenski's gun was pointing the other way.

'The bureau wants to interview you on at least … I think it's three different cases now. Do you not get your messages? Also, do you have a permit for that weapon?'

'What do you think?'

'You want to tell me why my wife had you under surveillance six years ago?'

'Do I want to … What?' His pistol quivered.

'You heard.'

'I don't believe you.'

'You just helped yourself to the files. They're all there. Take a look.'

His eyes glittered as his Servant fed images to his lenses. On another day I might have taken a chance on that, knowing he was distracted, and made a lunge past the pistol he had on me. Instead I took a chance on how unhappy he was to be having this conversation.

'She was on to you, Shenski. Six years ago and she was on to you.'

'You *what*?'

Shenski's look of sheer disbelief told me I'd missed the target I was aiming at. But I'd sure hit something.

'You know everyone in the bureau thinks my wife was a traitor, right?'

This time I got bewilderment. In another time and place I could have hugged Shenski for that look.

'Who else has seen this?' he asked.

'Who do you think?' I sniffed. 'You've been a hard man to get hold of.'

Shenski lowered the gun. 'I don't know whether you're insane or just an— Shit! Are you fucking *fishing* me?'

I told my face not to move a muscle. It did the best it could.

'Fuck!' The pistol dropped to his side. 'You *are*! You have no idea what any of this is. Absolutely no fucking idea. *Fuck!* You came in a pod?'

I nodded.

'It still out there?'

'Why? You want to go for a ride?'

The pistol came straight back at my face. 'Smart-mouth me again and you can spend the rest of your life eating through a tube. Call a tac-team, get your pod here, get into it and fuck off!'

I didn't move. 'I want to know what—'

'Fuck's sake! Your wife and I were working something. Darius Vishakh was our target. He wasn't playing with a straight bat then and he's not playing with one now, and chances are good you just spooked the shit out of him. Now do what I fucking—'

He stopped. Froze. Cocked his head. His eyes flicked around the room ...

There. A tiny buzzing. Like a mosquito.

Magenta doesn't have mosquitoes.

Shenski jumped a foot into the air. He spun and fired the pistol at the buzzing. I had no idea whether he hit anything but it made an impressive dent in the inner wall of the Monument. He did something to my Servant and I had control again.

'They're here,' he said hoarsely. 'Call as much help as you can get.'

'Who's here?'

An emergency distress call went to the Tesseract. That would have a tac-team here in about four minutes, given how close Babelfish Park was to the bureau. I called the pod that had brought me here, signalled an emergency and told it to drive up to the Monument.

'The Datta-fucking-treya. Darius Vishakh's hit squad.'

Shenski went to the stone in the centre of the Monument. He crouched beside it. Then he stood back and gave the stone a good hard kick.

'Drones and shells. You've seen their work.'

'You're telling me it was Darius Vishakh who hit Mercy? Who killed ...'

He wasn't listening. My pod whirred along the path through the park, chittering warnings about the consequences of improper use of an emergency code. Something inside the Monument pinged my Servant. The stone slab slid back to reveal an access shaft. Shenski didn't bother giving me another look before he jumped in, taking the rungs two at a time.

Something shifted at the Monument entrance. A glimmer. A change in the shape of the world outside, like a sudden gust of heat haze.

Stealth drone.

I threw myself behind the Monument in time to hear the pop of a particle beam. The drone shimmered and lost its camouflage as it diverted power to its firing capacitor. The front of the Monument became a sagging molten mess. I heard the dog-whistle whine as the particle beam recharged again. I had maybe two seconds. I drew my Reeper and shot twice. The drone dodged sideways and I missed. Then I dropped and rolled for the shaft. I vaulted in, caught myself and kept on down, fast, three rungs at a time. The particle beam popped again, vaporising the edge of the shaft where I'd been a moment before. The drone buzzed the shaft entrance, fighting to squeeze a shot down the shaft. It couldn't tilt itself enough to fire straight down and hold itself steady at the same time but that didn't stop it from trying.

Yeah. Screw you. I sighted through my lenses and fired my Reeper twice more. The first shot hit the drone centre mass. It lurched and vanished and didn't come back.

'Shenski!'

The bottom of the shaft opened into what looked like a film set – but this was the real deal, the original entrance to the warren tunnelled by Magenta's first settlers. Shenski was already tugging at the manual release on an old airlock door. He rounded on me.

'You got a code for this? I'm guessing we have seconds before the first grenade comes down that shaft.'

My Servant woke up the Monument. I threw my Tesseract codes at the airlock. A whine from the shaft warned that a drone was making its way down. I went back, looked up and started shooting. The first bullet missed. The second and the third each lurched it sideways. It flipped into the wall of the shaft, skittered across it, then lost pitch control and fell. I jumped away as it smacked into the floor.

'Fuck!'

Another dog-whistle whine … No, two of them. One from the drone. Shenski's pistol got there first. Half the drone dissolved in slag and smoke. He grabbed me and threw me into the opening airlock.

'Shut that fucker!'

I told the airlock to close as he dived in after me.

'You know how to get—'

The room shook to the thump of a detonation on the other side of the airlock door. Shenski picked me up and shook me.

'Seven years I've been picking at Vishakh's network. Seven years you just blew me! So either you get us out of here or I *will* use you as a human shield before I go. *Fuck!*'

The second airlock door cycled open.

Keys?

Laura and Flemich were both trying to call me.

Liss! Map! 'Patterson! Babelfish Monument. The tunnels. I need an exit.'

Flemich had the rank but I knew Laura better.

A map flashed into my Servant from Liss.

'A tac-team with you in about two minutes.'

'One? Send more! Send all of them! It's Esh's killer.'

Shenski fired his particle beam into the airlock controls and fused them. I switched to Flemich. Whatever he started to say, I didn't give him air.

'This is the same as when we went after Kagame,' I said. 'Send everything.'

Shenski dragged me away from the door. 'Which way?'

'Who the hell have you pissed off?'

I pulled up the map from Liss and looked for another way out. Only trouble was there wasn't one. We were in one of the original accommodation blocks, preserved for posterity. As far as I could see our little piece of history here was cut off from the rest of the undercity.

I'm coming, Keys.

Shit. No! To do what? Stay away!

I tugged Shenski towards an elevator. 'Best we can do is go deep. Wait it out.' Liss, you want to help, work out how to kill the power!

'Wait it fucking *out*?'

Give me a moment.

Don't do it until I say! 'Yeah.'

The elevator opened. Shenski barged in and punched a button. I scurried after him and slid down against the wall as the door closed. Then I pointed my Reeper at him.

'Tomasz Shenski. You have the right to remain silent ...'

'Oh, fuck *right* off!'

I read him the rest of his rights anyway and pinged them to his Servant so he could look at them in a spare moment after I finished arresting him. I didn't try and take the particle beam off him. 'You want to tell me who wants us dead?'

'No one wants *us* dead, you fucking moron. Darius wants *me* dead because *you* just blew my *fucking cover*!'

'Why?' The elevator started to move. We were going down.

'Why?' Shenski was almost screaming in my face. 'Because he knew damned well from the moment Zinadine Kagame showed up on Magenta that someone was putting together the evidence to climb up his arse and shred him from the inside – and thanks to your fucking fishing expedition he's figured out it was me!'

'What? What do you mean shred him?'

'What the fuck do you think?'

Someone else is hacking the power grid.

Can you stop them?

Yes. And I can hack them back.

I didn't know whether Liss qualified as an AI but to most intents and purposes that's what she was. It never hurt to have an AI in your corner when someone started a q-ware fight.

'Six and a half years ago Alysha Rause and I found ourselves both looking for the same rotten apple.'

'Vishakh?'

'Yes.'

'Who is he?'

'Right now? Deputy Head of Fleet Colonial Intelligence.' The elevator started to speed up. It was so old that it actually had buttons and lights. 'Head of Fleet Intelligence for Magenta, too. Him and his little fucking cabal.'

Thirty-two floors. Shenski was taking us from the top to the bottom.

'I was Fleet counter-intelligence. Rause was Tesseract. She was watching me. I was watching the man she thought she'd slipped inside Fleet.' He must have seen the blank look on my face because he threw back his head in exasperation. 'Kagame! Zinadine Kagame! Fuck, do you know anything at all or do you solve *all* your problems by thrashing blindly with a big stick and waiting to see what breaks?'

'Yet here you are,' I pointed out.

'Kagame and Rause thought they were looking at a Fleet penetration of the Tesseract. They were onto something but it wasn't us. So I let them play, figuring they were finding plants from an Earth government and maybe doing my work for me. I started poking around Fleet too. But Rause got there ahead of me.'

'Darius Vishakh?'

The elevator was dropping fast. Shenski nodded.

'I didn't buy it, but I bought that she did. I figured someone was trying to set us up.'

'What changed your mind?'

'Who says anything did?'

'She was watching you and Darius together.'

'Darius had a thing about the Masters. You work in Fleet, you can't help it, but Darius was different. He was intense. By the time Rause came to me I'd figured he was searching for something specific. Then Rause got taken out and bang! Darius gets double promoted and jumps to being in charge of colonial intelligence in Magenta. He went quiet after that. Trail went cold until Kagame resurfaced; the moment he did, shit started to fly. Someone is deep into us both, Rause – Darius is the linchpin and for some reason Kagame showing up has scared the crap out of him.'

'Where's it coming from?'

'That's what I was trying to find out, you dick! You realise I've been working with your people on this for more than a week now? Until you royally fucked everything!'

We were slowing down.

'How?' Working with the Tesseract? I didn't want to buy that, but maybe ...

Shit. Shenski, Jacksmith, Kagame, Steadman. They were all linked ...

'What? How did you royally fuck everything by sending me an unencrypted message on an open channel with Darius's name, your wife's name, and his operational code all in the same place? You *really* have to ask?'

That was why Laura had been with Jacksmith when I'd burst in on them ... That was why she was being so cagey. That was why she kept blocking me ...

Shit, shit, shit. Shenski was right. I'd fucked up. Bad.

The elevator stopped. The doors opened.

'This is your stop.'

He pushed me out of the elevator.

'What the fuck?' I stumbled into the corridor.

'Kagame messaged me when he arrived in-system. He told me that Darius had Rause killed. Well, guess what? Darius got that message too and now Kagame's dead. That's all I know and that's how you fucked everything. By bringing up her name. Now go be a good diversion and make sure at least one of us gets out of this alive.'

'What? Why? Why would—'

The elevator shut, biting my question in half.

Alysha?

Liss? Can you track him?

Through surveillance and Servant interactions but so can whoever is after you.

Can't you stop them?

A pause. No. There's something else blocking me.

They know you're here?

Something does ... Keys, there's another digital intelligence in here. It's tracking you when I talk to you and it's much bigger than me. I'm making things worse. I need to go. I'm sorry.

She vanished from my Servant. I tried calling the Tesseract

but I couldn't get through. Interference. No surprise. If any of what Shenski had said was true then whoever was after him was desperate to keep him quiet.

Same as Jared Black. Same as Kagame.

Shit. Shit shit *shit*!

I pulled up Liss's map of the tunnels. There had to be another way out. The first settlers must have given themselves more than one route to the surface and those first tunnels had gradually evolved into the warrens of the undercity. There had to be links even if the map didn't show them. Closed to the public and sealed, perhaps, but they had to exist.

I put some distance between me and the elevator. As I did I drew up a map of the undercity and tried to align it with the Monument tunnels. My best bet was down a level, through the food processing and recycling facilities of the old tunnels. I stopped for a moment, listening and trying to catch my breath. I heard a faint rumble from above and then nothing. The quiet felt eerie without Liss in my ear. *Think, Rause. Think!*

If whoever was after Shenski got to me, what would they do? At the very least they'd kill me and erase everything in my Servant – everything Shenski had just told me. I could make that harder ...

I ducked into an empty storage room, downloaded the recording of my conversation with Shenski, Alysha's video clips and my interviews with Cho and Jacksmith, and burned them onto a sliver. I tossed the sliver into a corner and slipped back outside. Every room down here had a number and a pair of letters on the door. This one was 05-DG. So that was it. The legacy I was leaving for Laura and Flemich if I didn't get out of here.

I paused long enough to take off a shoe and scribble the number on the sole of my foot. Somewhere no one would think to look until they took me to the morgue. Somewhere Roge would see it ...

Another rumble quivered the floor. I heard the elevator going back up. Another digital intelligence in the system meant they'd know where we'd stopped. They'd know which level I was on. I ran for the nearest steps to take me down.

Another sound. The shiver of a distant detonation. Then the echoes of several short sharp cracks.

I took the stairs two at a time. A call pinged my Servant. I couldn't make out much more than a crackle of static. There was no way to tell whether it was Liss or Laura or whoever was after Shenski but I had to figure it wasn't friendly. I turned my Servant off. I'd seen this done before – pinging a Servant to triangulate its position.

At the bottom of the stairs something moved under the strip-lights, swift through the air in a steady straight line.

Drone.

There wasn't much chance it hadn't seen me. I ducked into the first open door and scrambled into what turned out to be a reconstruction of a dormitory. A lit panel invited me to shut the door, but whatever intelligence was in the Monument's systems would see that at once. A wild look around the room gave me the choice of hiding in the shadows under one of the bunks or squeezing into a footlocker.

I went for a footlocker, threw it open, curled inside and closed the lid on top of me, holding it open a crack. The drone floated into the room. Its body wasn't much bigger than the palm of my hand under a crucifix of rotors. It wasn't cloaked and I didn't see anything that looked like a particle beam – but that didn't mean it couldn't kill me, and it could certainly guide in something that could. I saw it for a second and then lost track as it moved deeper into the room ...

I didn't dare move. The locker looked solid enough to hold my heat signature for a time. The whirr of the drone's own rotors probably made it deaf to my heartbeat. Probably, but it was hard not to hold my breath.

The whirr passed overhead. It took thirty seconds to scan the dormitory before it wafted back outside. I gave it a few seconds and then eased out of the locker, careful and quiet, went to the door and listened. The drone wasn't in the corridor. It had gone into the next room. I scurried out and closed the door on it and wedged it shut, trapping it inside. A calculated gamble – they'd know someone was down here now – but if we were going to play hide-and-seek then whoever was out there could at least work for it.

A rogue Fleet hit squad? Was that what Shenski had been telling me? Run by a man whom Kagame claimed had killed Alysha? But Loki had killed Alysha. Loki had made the bomb, planted it and set it off. We'd had a mountain of evidence and his own confession. A lone rogue Entropist trying to make a point. It was a freight train. He hadn't known there were people hiding on it ...

I'd never believed that story and neither had Laura. Someone had helped him. Guided him, steered him, threatened him, bribed him – I didn't know and probably never would. But he hadn't done it on his own. That first statement he'd made, later retracted – he'd gone to that pumping station to meet someone. And he just wasn't bright enough to have done it all on his own.

Fleet Intelligence? Darius Vishakh? Was he the man who'd pulled Loki's trigger? But why? And what the hell did any of this have to do with Steadman, Nohr, Kettler and Becker?

The corridor through the dormitories was long and straight and had nothing that passed for cover. I ran for the recycling plant at the end. I don't know what warned me that I wasn't alone. A change in the light or maybe I just got lucky, but I knew it when someone came into the corridor behind me. I was already turning and dropping and lifting my Reeper when he fired. From this range I wasn't going to hit anything without running some serious assisted-targeting q-code which I didn't have, but who-ever I was shooting at wasn't to know. I squeezed off two rounds. The air above me fizzed and shook with the warm shock wave of a particle beam that would have burned me in half. I fired twice more and then we both went scurrying for cover.

Particle Beam Man needed a couple of seconds to recharge. Long enough for me to run the last yards into the recycling plant, duck around the entrance and crash against the bulk of an old dormant water purifier ...

I peered back into the corridor. Now there were two men. They were holding back, though. Particle Beam Man was half visible in a doorway. Right at the far end of the corridor, caught for a moment in the open, in plain sight ...

The man from Alysha's recordings. The man who wasn't Shenski. The man she'd been with when she'd gone to Rachael Cho.

Vishakh?

A furious stupidity got the better of me. I shifted out of cover far enough to take a bead on him and fired three shots at his head. I saw him flinch but it was a long way down that corridor and I guess I missed. He jerked away and then Particle Beam Man had his pistol pointed at me. I ducked back into cover an instant before part of the door frame melted. When I looked into the corridor again, Vishakh had gone.

The next thing through the door was going to be a drone. I hit a panel and closed it.

'Attention!' A loudspeaker burst into life. 'This is the Magenta Investigation Bureau. All exits are sealed. Surrender peacefully or suffer the consequences!'

I recognised Flemich's voice. I switched on my Servant and pinged Laura. If that meant the people hunting me could find me, well, they already knew where I was.

I'm in a recycling room. I pulled up the facility map. Zero six foxtrot alpha. One hostile close. Armed with a particle beam. Have seen at least one more. Drones. These are the people who killed Esh. Laura had to have worked that one—

No shit. Status?

Armed and active. I scurried deeper into the recycling plant, away from the door. I looked at the map again. Shenski's in here too. I'm after an exit into the undercity. Any help with that?

Shenski?

I reached the end of a bank of water purifiers. The depths of the recycling plant vanished into darkness ahead of me …

The lights went out, plunging me into pitch black.

The lights have gone.

I've got an exit for you. Tac-team will be entering your position from the undercity in approximately four minutes.

I fumbled further into the darkness. Four minutes could be a lifetime. The hunter drones would have thermal eyes and ultrasound. Whoever was out there would have their imagery fed back to his lenses. He'd be able to see in pitch dark as though it was twilight. Maybe better.

I'm blind and I don't have four minutes. I marked my position on the map and sent it to Laura. Walk me out.

The darkness eased as the door to the recycling plant opened. I heard the whirr of a drone. I felt my way through the machinery, trying to keep the bulk of something big and solid between me and the sound.

The map came back. All I had to do was keep moving forward until I hit a wall and then follow it maybe thirty feet.

You have that exit unlocked?

Yes. Can you reach it?

I think so.

The drone was getting closer. I heard a second. Lines of pale blue light swept the room as they turned on their laser scanners.

Kind of them to give me a better notion of where they were, I suppose. I eased between the bulk of something that smelled bad and a cluster of thick pipes. I had to be close to that back wall now ...

The drones spread out to either side. They were moving away from me. They didn't seem to want to come in among the machinery.

You want to tell me what's going on down there?

They're after Shenski.

A pause. Tomasz Shenski? Keon, what the ... What the fuck have you done?

Game's changed.

I was at the wall. I started to follow it ...

The drones were lingering around the water purifiers. I kept low, feeling at the machinery around me, keeping in cover, trying not to give the drones line of sight. I probably shone like a lantern in infrared.

Ten feet from the exit. Can you open and close it remotely?

I could make a run for it but the drones would know the moment the door opened. I had no idea how fast they might be. *Fast*, probably.

Yes.

On my mark open all the doors into zero six foxtrot alpha. Can you bring the lights back?

Wait one ... Yes. We have control.

When you open the doors I want as much light and sound as you can make.

A few seconds was all I needed. A blind run for the door.

Tac-team will be there in two minutes. Do you have that long?

I don't think so.

OK. Ready?

I closed my eyes and raised my Reeper and let its camera feed my lenses.

Mark.

A storm of light and sound crashed through the machinery. The camera on my Reeper adjusted faster than any human eye could have done. Through it I saw the wall I was supposed to follow, the door I was supposed to find as it slid open ...

Particle Beam Man stood beside it, pistol pointed almost right at me, but he was dazed and dazzled. I flicked my Reeper to stun and shot him twice as I dived for the floor. His finger twitched on the trigger. The air popped and fizzed a few inches from my head. I felt the wash of heat. Then he dropped, limp as a sack of overcooked spaghetti.

Man down!

I picked myself up ...

The drones were on me, already out from between the water purifiers and lighting me up. I dropped again, rolled and fired twice at the nearest as it drew a bead on me. I missed. I was a sitting du—

BAM!

A gunshot from behind me, through the open door. The first drone exploded into pieces. A bright orange flashbang grenade flew past me. The second drone fired a needler over my head. Another shot brought it down. I curled up tight and turned away from the flashbang, hands clamped over my ears. I heard more shots. Through the open door I expected to see a black-armoured tac-team crashing towards me in their helmets and masks.

Instead I saw Alysha.

Then the flashbang went off.

15

NO MERCY

The tac-team picked me up crawling into the undercity, dazed like a drunkard from the flashbang. I didn't remember leaving the recycling plant but I remembered Alysha. I tried to say something. I made my mouth move but all I heard was bright sunshine ringing my ears. They spider-wrapped the man I'd stunned and shoved me onto a trauma drone to Mercy. I didn't want to go but they weren't listening. I guess they had other things to do.

Liss?

I needed to stay. Vishakh was here, right here under the Monument. I tried calling Laura but she didn't answer. I needed to know whether they got to Shenski in time, whether they'd taken Vishakh alive, whether he was the bastard who'd killed Esh. I needed to go back. I needed to bring him in, but the trauma drone wasn't having it.

Whether he was the bastard who'd killed Alysha ...

No answer. They were still in the middle of it. I'd have to wait. I was probably in enough trouble already as it was.

Shenski, Jacksmith, Kagame, Steadman. All linked to the same thing. And so was Alysha.

Keys? It took longer than usual for Liss to reply.

Did you make yourself a new shell?

Yes.

Why?

Another pause. You made me to think of myself as human. It seems strange not to have one. Uncomfortable. If you could ask Agent Zohreya, if the memories of her now trapped as data could speak and express, would it surprise you if she asked for her body to be remade?

I almost choked on that. Esh is dead.

So am I.

Deep breaths. I should never have made you. I can't imagine not making you.

She didn't answer that.

Thank you, I said.

For what?

You saved my life just now.

A long pause. What do you mean?

Stopping the drones.

Another long pause. Whatever you think I did, it wasn't me, Keys.

I'd been concussed by the flashbang but I knew what I'd seen.

You were there. I saw you.

A third long pause. No, Keys. I wasn't.

Did she think she was protecting me? She'd lied to me before when she thought it would keep me safe. It hadn't.

Whatever you didn't do, Liss, this needs to stop, I said. You need to leave me alone. For both of us.

I can't. It's the way you had me made.

They'll sell your shell for parts! They'll send q-code worms inside you and tear you apart. You shouldn't exist!

239

Do you think I don't know that?

She killed the link. I played the conversation over, savouring it, lost for a while in the idea that she was who I'd once meant her to be: Alysha, my dead wife. Then I cleansed my Servant and erased every trace of her, ready for when the Tesseract's forensic q-code came crawling into me.

Mercy checked me in and started a hundred and one tests. A nurse came to tell me what we'd both known right from the start: that I was fine. I'd been dazed by the flashbang, nothing more, but a blood test had found nanite traces in me. Again, we both knew they were vestiges of the repair nanites Mercy had used after I'd been shot, but Mercy quarantined me until it could be sure. Five minutes later I was back in the same room I'd had before. Technically I'd never been discharged. I wasn't supposed to be back on duty.

I sat on the bed. Was this Mercy's idea of a slap on the wrist?

Damn, but I was tired.

'How was I supposed to know that Shenski was going to show up being chased by people with particle beams?'

I was talking to an empty wall. Laura was going to murder me. Meeting Shenski on my own with no tac-team perimeter. Without the hundred and one precautions I could have taken. *Should* have taken. Like I'd learned nothing from Esh's death. Like I wanted to follow her.

Dattatreya. A hit squad. I looked it up. The name came from Hindu mythology: an avatar of Shiva, Vishnu and Brahma together. Brahma the creator, Vishnu the maintainer, Shiva the destroyer. I wasn't sure what that told me ...

She'd introduced herself: *Lieutenant Shiva Lee*, MSDF ...

Maybe what it told me was that Shenski wasn't full of shit – that Vishakh's Dattatreya had been behind the shell that killed Kagame and Esh.

Esh and Alysha.

I idled around the data streams of the Tesseract looking for anything on Shenski, on Darius Vishakh, on Alysha, an aimless drift hoping I'd stub my toe on something unexpected. I didn't. When I tried to find out what was happening in Babelfish Park, I hit a wall.

I called Bix.

'Dude! You're alive! What happened, man?'

I gave him the short version. 'I got a name for Esh's killer. Sort of.'

'OK.' His voice dropped low, a hint of quiet murder creeping in to its edges.

'I'll tell you when I see you.'

'Soon, man.'

'Himaru bite?'

'Yeah. Hard.'

'Thought so. Any luck with Chase Hunt?'

'Some. We recovered her Servant. Totally wiped. Data forensics will do their thing but it's been, like, normalised down to quantum states or something, whatever that means. I separated copies of the Mercy imagery from the Tesseract network like you asked. That was before the walls came down. It's not just what happened at Mercy, you know? We've been taken off, like, everything. Mercy, Steadman, you name it. We're in the wind, man.'

I sighed. Like visiting parents, knowing what was coming didn't make it any better.

'The Mercy hack ties Becker's killer to me and Esh and so to Kagame-Black. And then Steadman—'

'Same gun, man.'

'Are there any cases that *aren't* Kagame-Black?'

It was supposed to be a joke but it didn't sound funny when I said it. We both knew why the Tesseract was locking us out like it had locked me out from Alysha six years earlier. Personal involvement in an investigation. Strictly not allowed. Everything I'd done today was a testament to why the rules were what they were.

I wanted to punch someone.

'I don't know what's left, man. Himaru's back on the streets. Mercy put him on two weeks' recovery leave which he totally doesn't want. He's going to sort your flatliner friend. More than that ...' I almost heard the shrug. 'We still got Nohr and Kettler, you know? If that's, like, any use. I got one more lead on Chase I'm working. More when I see you.'

I cut the link and pinged Laura: We need to talk.

Sooner or later I was going to have to tell someone why I'd been meeting with Shenski in the Monument and how I'd winkled him out of the protection of his embassy. I was going to have to tell them what he'd said. From there they'd make their way back to Rachael Cho, with or without me. The whole thing with Alysha would come out and then shit was going to fall on me from orbit, but before that quite buried me, Laura was going to tell me exactly why she'd been in Jacksmith's office this morning.

I looked up Nohr and Kettler in the Tesseract records. Their deaths were marked as suspicious but no one had linked them to Steadman and no one had done anything about them. Yet.

I'd told Laura they were connected. I'd sent Utubu the evidence. I'd told Utubu to watch Rachael Cho and he'd done nothing. Someone hadn't been paying attention ...

On the other hand it meant that Nohr and Kettler and Cho hadn't been sucked into Kagame-Black just yet. I wasn't locked out of them. Maybe it wasn't inattention. Maybe someone had been doing me a favour.

Laura messaged me back: Busy. Tomorrow.

OK.

Kettler looked the more promising. An overdose of K-amphetamine had killed him. The drugs had to have come from somewhere.

I pinged Bix: Who in Firstfall deals K?

Ask the narcs.

I'm asking you because I know I'll get a better answer.

K-dealers don't talk to me.

Narcotics would probably come back and ask you anyway, right?

Dude! You totally say the nicest things!

They hate you, Agent Rangesh.

They're so sweet.

So?

K-meth is import shit. Not like gens, you know? You want me to guess, then I'd say that no one on Magenta actually makes the stuff. It's all from Earth and the sub-orbital black market is a tight ship. Not many players and I don't have an in. Sorry, but you do actually need the narcs for once.

I scanned Kettler's file while Rangesh was talking, but I couldn't see how Kettler had known anyone who lived in that sort of circle. I put in a request to narcotics for any known K-meth dealers and got an answer back pretty quick. It was cute and polite enough, but the gist was *Hey, dumbass, when we know who they are, do you think we leave them out there?*

I went through Kettler's background and then Nohr's. I didn't see anything connecting them to the Firstfall drug scene but that didn't mean much. I tried Roge in case he had anything new on Nohr, but his samples were still processing. Cause of death could have been any of about a hundred things that looked like heart failure; and yes, he'd ruled out the obvious back when Nohr had first come in; and yes, he was putting through all the tests he could think of; and yes, he'd be all over it as soon as the current glut of corpses eased but right now there was a bit of a queue ...

243

He sounded tetchy, as though I was somehow personally responsible.

Mercy gave the nanites in my system the all-clear while Roge was talking so I amused myself by going down to his office. I found him sat at a desk, staring into nothing.

'What glut of corpses?'

Roge almost jumped out of skin. 'Fucking hell, Rause!'

'I thought about coming in on a gurney.' I tried to imagine his face as I suddenly sat up and started talking.

'Not funny.'

Roge flicked what he'd been lensing to a wall-screen. Channel Nine was covering the shoot-out in Babelfish Park. The story was sketchy on detail and the bureau was obviously strangling it as best they could, but there wasn't any hiding the parade of trauma drones and emergency pods rushing off to Mercy.

'How bad?' I asked.

Roge sat on his swivel chair, hands clasped in his lap. He sniffed.

'Half a dozen MSDF. Looks like the same type of round as the one you took. Straight through their armour. One shot in the head, brain pulverised, irretrievable. The rest got back in time for Mercy to stabilise them. It'll be a long haul but they'll recover. There may be a loss of neurological function in one case.' He shook his head. 'What's happening out there, Rause? This is as many corpses as I like to see in a year. I haven't known anything like this since the blockade.'

I shrugged. I couldn't talk about it even if I wanted to.

'Any bureau injuries?' I tried to sound casual. From the look Roge gave me I didn't manage it.

'You know I can't—'

'I already lost one of my team.'

Roge made a face. 'I don't think so. I can't be sure. I don't see names down here but everyone bar one was in tac-team kit and the one who wasn't, I'd say he was an Earther. Long term on Magenta but not born here. I think your people are OK.'

A long-term Earther. I pinged him my picture of Shenski. 'That him?'

'Might have been.' Roge shrugged. 'Back when he had a face. Whoever got to him wanted to make damned sure he wasn't coming back.'

'ID from Servant?'

'You know I can't talk about that. If there was anything to talk about, of course.'

His Servant had been wiped. Or disintegrated. I described Shenski as I'd seen him. 'Dark grey storm suit? Black hair? Grey eyes? Expensive boots. Earth imports.'

'Can't say. Especially about the eyes because he didn't have any by the time he got here. But if you've got a name to go with all that then I might find it speeds things up. Make me look good, Rause.'

There was a lead weight inside me. 'Tomasz Shenski. Fleet consulate.'

Roge nodded.

'You get that confirmed, I'd like to know. Whether you're supposed to tell me or not.'

That earned me a sideways look. Then Roge gave a little nod. I'd done him a favour and he'd pay it back.

'No promises, mind. And it could be a while.'

'They take any of the bad guys alive?' I asked.

'I wouldn't be able to tell you even if I knew.' One finger straightened from Roge's clasped hands for a moment, then curled back. 'I think you'd better go, Rause. Starting to bother me that you're asking questions you shouldn't. I've got work to do.'

'You need a hand, you let me know.'

'Find the fuckers who are doing this and remove them from my world. I like a quiet life.'

'Amen to that.'

I left him and pinged Laura again: Monument 05-DG. There's a sliver. It's got everything.

Laura didn't reply, but right then I got a ping from Bix: Dude! Get your arse moving. I got a trace on you-know-who! We need to move, man.

Five minutes later we were in a pod heading into the prosperous cavern suburb of New Fiji on the northern edge of Firstfall central. I turned off our Servants and the pod's own surveillance and then I told him everything: Shenski, Kagame, Alysha, Steadman, Nohr, Kettler, how they were connected with Jacksmith and with the trans-polar expedition at the heart of it. I tried convincing myself that I was telling him in case something happened to me, in case Laura didn't find my sliver, that I was spreading the information I had in order to make it harder to kill. But that wasn't why. I was doing it because of Esh. Because Bix had been there when she'd died. Because we were going to find Darius Vishakh, just the two of us, and take it in turns to hurt him.

'None of this will stick,' I said when I was done. 'We've got nothing on Vishakh. Not even dirt.'

'We work the case until we do, dude.' Bix said. 'Kettler and Nohr. You reckon Chase Hunt is one of this hit squad too?'

I didn't know. Probably. If Becker had rigged the weather feeds for Vishakh and not for Jacksmith then maybe Vishakh was cleaning house. Didn't fit with shooting Steadman after he was already dead, though. I wasn't sure that *anything* fitted with that.

'Maybe she thought he'd just passed out or something?'

'Maybe.' But no. Chase Hunt was something else. Too professional. Yet Becker had been personal.

We emerged from the undercity onto the surface. Traffic was light. The wind was gentle but the rain was hammering down.

'Hope you got a storm coat,' muttered Bix.

'The K that killed Kettler. You think we could lean on Roy Lemond for a lead?'

Roy Lemond ran half of Firstfall's Xen trade, perched on the grey edge between what was legal and what wasn't and with a firm foot in both.

'Doubt it. Lemond's pretty where he is. Doesn't mess with imports. Too much heat.'

'He might know who does.'

'I burned that bridge, dude. He owed me and so he gave up one of his guys. Now he doesn't. No bad feelings, man, you know, but we're square and I got nothing to trade. You don't want to be in his debt, boss dude. Trust me.'

I didn't push. I reckoned I didn't want to know how a man like Roy Lemond had ended up owing Rangesh a favour.

We reached New Fiji. I expected the pod to head back into the undercity but it stayed on the surface. The richest apartments in Firstfall were the ones up here with a view of the surface, for what that was worth – windows armoured against the weather letting in real daylight. Some even had doors, although a good few didn't bother.

'Keep your Servant off, dude,' muttered Bix.

We stopped by the outlet from an air purification plant. Bix put on his storm coat. I looked at him, then at the downpour outside.

'I just got out of Mercy,' I said. 'My shit is all at home.' Or in Laura's apartment, but there didn't seem any need to mention that.

Bix just shrugged. 'It's not so far, dude.'

'Everything I told you, Laura's got it too.'

He nodded. 'OK. But she's not got this.'

He stepped out into the pouring rain. It was maybe ten yards from the pod to the maintenance door he crowbarred open but

I was still wet to the skin by the time we were inside. Bix closed the door behind us.

'Any reason for the crowbar?' Our Tesseract codes should have opened the door.

'I don't want the Tesseract to know where we are.'

'Why?'

'Chase Hunt.'

Bix turned on a torch and led the way down a tortuous set of rickety old steel stairs. From the corrosion on them no one had come this way for decades.

'So she, like, disappeared into that blind spot after she shot Becker, right? So I looked for anyone coming out, like you said, and got nothing. She was like a ghost, man. I figure the Tesseract found the same when it took over the case – but then I did what an AI can't, I went on the street and asked. You know, with actual words and talking? People who were in the right place at the right time. That got me a couple of people I couldn't account for. No Servant. I found her in the surveillance archives and followed until she turned on her Servant. After that it was all good. She went to ground in a cheap by-the-hour hotel, no questions asked. Junkie sort of place. Stayed there until late morning, then went to the Magenta Institute masquerading as a service engineer, Stephanie Wright, working for a small Firstfall tech start-up. I got pictures I can show you. Different face, same build. Would have tried body-posture mapping but we didn't get enough outside Mercy to be worth the bother. Best I can tell, Stephanie Wright never existed until the small hours of yesterday morning.'

We reached the bottom of the stairs. A narrow bare-rock tunnel burrowed straight and level into the darkness. To one side an open door led into a small control room that looked as out of use as the stairs.

'What did she do at the Institute?'

'Got there much the same time as we left Jacksmith. Claimed she was fixing a glitch in one of their servers. It's in their logs but it was faked. That's a serious hack, by the way. They let her in to the meteorology hub. She had a nice chat with a guy called Mohammed, took something out from one of the machines, let him buy her a drink in the Institute canteen and then left.'

We reached the end of the tunnel. The door there had a manual emergency handle that allowed Bix to open it from the inside without having to break anything. 'Meteorology?'

'Yeah, man, I know. Guess where she went next?'

We walked out into a quiet residential side-tunnel in New Fiji. A pod whirred past. Bix crossed to the other side and stopped at an apartment door. If I'd had my Servant turned on I could have found out who lived inside. As it was ...

'This is Becker's place.' Bix grinned and drew his Reeper.

'She's here?' I asked. I drew my own gun.

'Don't know, man. Probably not. Trace died here four hours ago. Good place to hide but I'm guessing she's already gone.'

'But you don't know? Then we should call a tac-team!'

'Yeah. Thought about that.' He took a deep breath. 'OK, dude. This one's on me.'

He woke his Servant, threw his Tesseract codes at the door and then sent his Servant back to sleep again. The door slid open.

'I'm guessing I just triggered alarms all over the Tesseract and that that tac-team you wanted will be on its way. We've probably got about five minutes. You can stay outside and wait for them if you like.'

We didn't. I followed Bix in, taut as a drum. Becker's apartment was dark from top to bottom, the window shades down, the house Servant dead, the lights out. The air was old and stale, still and quiet as a mausoleum. Bix turned on his torch. I did the same.

'I was thinking, you know? What if Chase Hunt is one of ours?'

I shook my head. 'That makes no sense.'

'Hunt didn't kill Steadman, right? So, I mean, why put a bullet in his head?'

I took a look around Becker's apartment. Forensics had been here. They didn't leave much trace, but when you worked with them you got to know their spoor. The sprays of dust on the table. The marks in the corners of the room from the drones. The little drops of oil by the door ... But traces in the dust said that someone else had come later. Hunt, if Bix was right.

'She isn't here,' I said. The apartment was empty. I'd spent enough time on Earth hunting fugitives to have a sense for that.

Bix squatted and peered at the forensic dust on the floor. 'Yeah. She came here, though. Question is, dude, why?'

Something on the lounge table looked new. A shiny silver box about the size of my palm. And beside it a small screw-top pharmaceutical bottle.

'Hunt killed Becker,' I said flatly. 'She's not one of ours.'

The box had a pair of network connectors hanging out of it. A q-code host. There was no dust from the forensics drones. It hadn't been tested for prints. Someone had put it there after forensics came and went.

'What if it was to make us look at Kettler and Nohr?' Bix peered over the box. 'This what I think it is?'

'Why not just send a message?'

'I think that's exactly what she was doing, you know?'

'OK, sure, but what I *mean* is why not just walk into Flemich's office, park in one of his nice comfy chairs and have a bit of a chat about it?'

'Kagame's list, dude.' He put on a pair of plastic gloves and gingerly opened the pill bottle.

'You think Flemich's on it?'

'I don't know who's on it! No one does. I don't even know if it's real – but that's the point, man!' Inside the bottle was white powder. Bix dipped a fingertip in and touched it to his tongue. 'K-meth.'

Kettler.

'Becker was an execution. You're telling me someone in the bureau did that?'

'Think about it.' Bix started down the stairs to check the lower level.

'She's not here, Bix ...'

It hit me as I watched him go that maybe I knew exactly who this was.

Liss.

I shook the thought away. Liss wouldn't kill anyone.

Except she already had. I'd seen it. Months ago, when we were poking into what happened in Settlement 64 just before Alysha died.

Shit.

I remembered watching the surveillance footage of Chase outside Mercy, wondering if she was a shell. Hard to say one way or the other from the way she moved, but the precision ... I'd even wondered, just for a moment, whether Chase Hunt was actually Jacksmith riding a shell. And then I'd thrown the thought away because it was stupid.

But what if she *was* a shell?

The shot that took out Becker had been deadly accurate. Same went for the drones under the Monument. A human running targeting q-ware, an expert marksman like Alysha had been ...

Or a machine.

I saw that flash under the Monument again. That moment before the flashbang when I saw Alysha. Except Alysha was dead.

It had been Liss.

Becker had hacked the weather feeds in the Magenta Institute. We could almost prove that now. What if I was right about the rest? What if he'd hacked Alysha's extraction team too? What if he was the one who'd destroyed her mission? He'd set her up to look a traitor. He was responsible, in a way, for her death. He was why she'd been on that train ...

He told me Darius had Rause killed.

What if Liss, from all I'd told her, had figured it out?

I stared at the device in front of me. I didn't know what was inside it but I could guess. It was the device Chase Hunt had taken from the Institute. From the meteorology hub. This was how Becker had done it. Bix was right. Hunt had shot Steadman to put us on track.

Because Chase Hunt was Liss.

Liss?

'She's not here, man.' I jumped as Bix came up the stairs. He shrugged. 'Figures.'

'This isn't a message.' I pointed to the device on the table. 'You were right. This is a fucking breadcrumb trail.'

It couldn't be Liss. Could it? But why not just tell me? Why not just—

The apartment door flew open as a violence of light and sound exploded into the room.

16

THAT'S YOUR ANSWER?

The tac-team crashed through the door, armoured, angry and pointing burst rifles at us. I dropped my Reeper and hit the floor. Spider drones wrapped us in silk. I turned on my Servant and threw my Tesseract codes at the drones but they weren't interested. The tac-team kept their guns on us until we were helpless; then they hauled us outside and threw us both into the back of an armoured pod. They shut the doors and locked us in. It took me a moment to realise we weren't alone. One soldier was inside with us, covering us with a needler.

I started to have a bad feeling. This wasn't how a tac-team arrest was supposed to go.

'What the fuck, man?' started Bix. 'We're—'

'Shut up, Rangesh.' Jonas Himaru threw off his helmet. He levelled the needler at my face. 'This one's a fucking traitor.'

'That's bullshit!'

'Dude! No way is—'

'Six years ago your wife killed half a dozen of my best men, Rause. I saw the corpses.'

'No.' I was shaking my head. 'She was set—'

'And now Esh is dead.'

Himaru's eyes were stone-cold murder.

'I had nothing—'

'I gave you the benefit of the doubt once. Not again.'

'Dude!'

Himaru made a twisting gesture by his ear. Telling us to turn off our Servants. I did as asked. So did Bix.

Himaru lowered the needler. 'As far as the rest of the world knows, this is me getting my pound of flesh from you for Esh. You've got about a minute, Rause, to tell me why that isn't exactly what I should do.'

I told him everything. He listened. When I was done he punched me twice in the face. For show, he said, but it still hurt and I think he enjoyed it.

The tac-team drove us to the Tesseract where a handful of bureau agents were waiting. I spotted Laura and Utubu and half a dozen other faces I knew. The looks I got back were blank. They escorted us into the quad, separated us and threw us each into our own cell. I tried using my Servant but no one answered when I called. I was being blocked. Eventually I fell asleep. I didn't want to, but I was exhausted. It had been a long day.

Laura was at the end of my bed when I woke up. She was sitting reading a book, some expensive antique shipped in from Earth. I could smell it, the musty chemical scent of old paper. It took her a moment to look up. When she saw I was awake, she put it down.

'Turn off your Servant.'

'Again?'

A series of alerts pinged me as my Servant warned that surveillance in the cell had been disabled. Laura was doing it. She was making the Tesseract blind. Strictly against the rules but I didn't imagine she was about to come at me with a lead pipe.

I turned my Servant off. 'OK.'

'Why didn't you tell me about Shenski?' she asked.

'I told you as soon as I knew he was going to bite!'

'You didn't have to meet him.'

'I don't think he would have met anyone else.'

'You blew his cover and now he's dead.'

'What cover?'

'He was co-operating.'

'Since when?'

'Since Darius Vishakh had three of his men executed in Mercy fucking hospital!'

'You might have told me that.'

'You weren't on the case, Keon! Not after Esh!'

'You and Jacksmith were tight as a pair of thieves yesterday morning. You want to tell me what you were really talking about?'

'No.'

'Then fuck off.'

'It's not your case, Keon. It *can't* be your case.'

I lost it. I screamed at her. 'I was there when Esh died! She was right on top of me! I felt her fucking heart stop! And you're telling me I'm supposed to sit on my arse and watch?'

'Yes.'

'I can't.'

Laura leaned forward. 'You have to. I'll tell you why if you promise me, you *promise* me you back the fuck off. You go home or you go on holiday or whatever it takes, but you keep away. Just don't do anything. Take your medical leave and treat it with some fucking respect.'

'What have you got?'

She shook her head. 'You promise me first.'

'No.'

Laura glared at me.

'What?'

'If I'm kind then I'm still thinking Kagame's Rause was Alysha. Not everyone in the bureau is feeling kind right now. That's why you're shut out. Not because of Esh but because of Alysha.' She paused for breath. 'Do you get it, Keon? Why you have to stay the fuck out of this? Pushing a dozen people have died and you and your dead wife are in the middle of it and even if you're not dirty, *she* was and everyone knows it! It's pretty easy to tar you with the same brush and right now I'm in a shrinking minority of one in your corner. Is this getting through?'

'Me and my dead wife?'

Laura closed her eyes and took a deep breath.

'Look, I get it. You want another reason why you have to stay away from this? Here.'

She opened up a hand-screen and flicked a file to it. It didn't make much sense to me at first. Some sort of service record maybe, but not in a Tesseract format.

'What am I looking at?'

'Darius Vishakh's service history. The official version.'

I paid attention. A variety of posts and positions and titles which could have meant anything. Nearly all of them in Magenta. From his record he'd spent nearly his whole career here.

'Is that normal?' I asked.

Laura shook her head. 'Fleet usually rotate their personnel. Two- or three-year terms.'

I stared at it. Lots of short trips, a month here, a couple of months there, but always back again. No long duties anywhere else at all, all the way back to his first posting twenty-seven years ago as an ensign on the *Fearless*.

'And?'

'Here.' She highlighted an entry.

Just over five years ago Vishakh had left Magenta for two months. The time was tagged as Penal Duty.

I let that sink in. Penal Duty meant he was on Colony 478.

Loki had died just over five years ago. Shanked in the shower ...

I grabbed at the screen. 'Bring up the flight schedule! I need to see—'

'I already did. It fits. He was there.'

I stared at her.

'He was on Colony 478 for exactly one cycle of the *Botany Bay*.' The Fleet ship that hopped between Earth and Colony 478.

'And Loki—'

'Was killed two days before he left.'

I wanted to jump and shake her. Kiss her. Something.

'Vishakh killed Loki!' There. That was it. A thread to pull ...

'Maybe.'

'Then Alysha wasn't a traitor! Becker set her up! Ten to one Becker was working for Vishakh. One of them used Loki to kill Alysha! Then they killed him, too!'

Laura made her sceptical face. 'Why?'

'To keep him quiet! To kill the truth and bury what they did!'

'Six months after the act? That's a big reach, Keon.' She shook her head. 'I don't think so. Just as possible that he wanted to know who took her out.' She closed the screen. 'But that's not the point. Look, I didn't have to show you that. I probably shouldn't have. Promise me you stay out of this.'

It was hard, but I let that one go.

'Where's Kagame's data?'

'None of your business but it's useless without Kagame's key.'

Single lock encryption. Try without the key, use the wrong key, the data wraps itself up in knots and blows itself to smoke. Yeah. Knew that already.

'Esh told me—'

'The key was in Kagame's Servant. It's either wiped or who-ever killed him took it before they fried his Servant.'

'Shenski told you?'

'No.'

'I think Darius Vishakh has the key,' I said.

'And how the fuck would you know that?'

'Something Shenski said. Check the recordings from my Servant. I told you where I hid them. I arrested him. You got that bit, right? Which makes every word he said usable testimony. So use it! Get Darius Vishakh out of his cosy Fleet orbital, freeze his Servant, get the key out of him and then put him on trial! For Esh, for Kagame, for all of them!'

'Sure. That fucking easy.' Laura took another long deep breath. 'How did you get out of the Monument?'

'Thanks to you, mostly.'

'Forensics have two downed drones in the room where the tac-team found you.'

'I shot at them. Maybe I got lucky. I don't remember.' I'd fired enough rounds that had missed. Forensics weren't going to find them all, were they?

The look on Laura's face made me wonder if they already had.

'And the grenade?' she asked. 'Whose was the flashbang?'

'I barely saw it. Tac-team, I guess.'

'It wasn't the fucking tac-team.'

'Then the ... Shit, I don't know. Maybe the guy who was trying to kill me had it in his hand when I stunned him. I didn't see, OK? I was half blind, half deaf and about to be shot to pieces by a pair of drones!'

'Forensics have two shells that didn't come from your Reeper. Guess what gun they match. Go on, guess.'

'I have no idea.' I had a bad feeling that maybe I did.

'Becker and Steadman.'

I shrugged.

'Keon, who the fuck is Chase Hunt?'

So Liss had lied to me. To my face. I shrugged again.

'That's your answer, Keon? You don't know?' Her voice was that flat I-have-judged-you tone I knew so well.

'That's my answer.'

She got up. 'Everything you have in my apartment, I want it out. Now. Outside the Tesseract you don't know me and you don't come near me. If I see you within one standard orbit of Jamie I will shoot you in the head.' She sighed as she walked for the door. 'You're a curse, Rause. And a fucking liar.'

I didn't think she was going to look back, but in the doorway she turned.

'Alysha's dead, Keon. She betrayed us. You, me, the bureau, all of us. Darius Vishakh turned her and then turned on her and now she's gone. Shit for all of us who knew her but there's fuck all we can do about it.' She shook her head. 'I can't be seen to have anything to do with you any more. Christ, Keon. Six years. Move the fuck on.'

I could have told her that that was rich, coming from her. But I didn't. I let it go. She was right.

The door clicked shut as Laura left. I stared at it for a while.

The gun that killed Becker had saved my life?

Liss.

I wanted to talk to her. *Needed* to. But I didn't dare, not here where everything I said would be traced and recorded. Instead I checked Jacksmith's history one more time and then went through my Servant, slow and methodical, one memory stack at a time, looking for anything I'd missed or forgotten that might give her away. I knew what happened next. Forensic q-code scouring everything inside it.

Flemich walked in ten minutes later. He brought his hangdog

face, all sad that it had come to this, and two other agents. One was Utubu. The other I didn't know. I didn't get any answers when I pinged their Servants.

'Debrief.'

I nodded.

Flemich gestured to the agent I didn't know.

'This is Agent Patel. He'll be your legal counsel for this interview.'

'Do I need one?'

Utubu made a damn-right-you-do face. Flemich looked at me askance.

'You tell me, Rause.'

I shrugged. 'I was looking at what Alysha was doing before she died. My traitor of a wife.'

I glared as he flinched. Flemich had been Alysha's mentor in the academy. They'd been close. After she graduated, Alysha had been Flemich's go-to girl for anything sensitive, things like the deal with Jacksmith's daughter. For all his grouch and grump, Alysha's betrayal had cut Flemich deep. Him, me, Laura, all of us who knew her ...

'I need you to hand over control of your Servant.'

I pinged him the codes. Flemich turned it off and locked me out. My lenses went blank. Just me and the physical world of light and sound and taste and touch. Losing my connection was like going deaf.

'When do I get it back?'

'As soon as we can, Agent Rause.'

As soon as the Tesseract had stripped it naked and sucked out every mote of data. I wished them luck. All Flemich was going to find was that I knew how to run a secure erase protocol.

We settled into a rhythm, the beat of question and answer. I told him everything I knew, exactly as it had happened, everything I'd already given to Laura and Bix and then to

Himaru. Alysha's files, Rachael Cho, Shenski, everything they'd said. I didn't want to, but it was all there to be found if they looked and the hole I'd dug was already deep. The only thing I left out was Liss. From the moment I'd turned off my Servant in the tunnels under the Monument, all they had was my word for what had happened.

Or so I thought.

Flemich streamed a video to my lenses. It was a view into the Monument recycling plant from somewhere over the door. One of the drones Liss had shot? I watched as everything went from dark to light as I remembered. The sirens sounded. The corner hatch into the undercity tunnels opened. I saw myself stumbling, deaf and half-blind. I saw Particle Beam Man ready to turn my head into vapour. I saw him reel from the light and sound and then drop as I stunned him. I saw myself turn to look at the camera, only I wasn't looking at the camera, I was looking at something else ...

The camera wasn't from one of the drones. They skimmed into view, lining up to shoot me. I saw myself drop to the floor. I saw the flash of my Reeper as I fired and missed ...

The image was grainy. Poor resolution and poor contrast. Surveillance from the Monument itself. Some camera more than a century old, part of the original design.

... The first drone jerked and fell. The second exploded into fragments. For a moment I saw the shape of a figure in the doorway. Not much more than a shadow. Then a flash and the camera died.

'We recovered the bullet that took out the camera,' said Flemich. 'Want to know what it matches?'

Steadman and Becker. And I understood now why Laura had done what she'd done when she came in and turned off every microphone and camera and told me about the gun. She'd been trying to save me.

I shrugged. 'I'm guessing not one of ours?'

'Who was that, Agent Rause?'

'I don't know. I didn't see.'

'I don't believe you.'

Agent Patel leaned in. 'Asked and answered, sir.'

He didn't believe me either. But he was doing his job.

'The drones had my full attention, sir.'

Flemich didn't answer.

'I ... I thought it was one of the tac-team, sir.'

It was hard lying to his face. Flemich was as close as anything I had to an old friend.

'If it wasn't the tac-team then I don't know what to say. The man I stunned ...'

Flemich held up a hand to stop me. He played another sequence. Video taken from the camera on my Reeper. The video I'd been feeding to my lenses while my eyes recovered from the light.

There she was. Not clear enough to be sure, not distinct enough to have no doubt, but Alysha.

'Who's that?' Flemich asked.

I took a deep breath. 'I don't know.'

'Fuck's sake, Rause!'

I rounded on him. 'You want me to say that that's Alysha? Fine. It looks like Alysha. But Alysha's dead. You know that and so do I.'

I watched her bend over and look at me. Close, like she cared.

'OK. So how do you explain it?'

I knew exactly how I explained it but I sure as shit wasn't going to tell him.

'How the fuck do I know? Trick of the light?'

'Rause!'

'The guy I stunned. Did she kill him?'

'You know I can't answer that.'

His face gave him away and I already knew from Roge. No, she hadn't. That was what he was struggling with. Someone who looked like a dead bureau agent had come in and done everything the tac-team would have done. No more, no less. Like they were on our side.

Liss.

'Did his Servant catch anything?'

This time Flemich got his blank look right.

'I don't know,' I said, quietly now. 'It's crossed my mind that Chase Hunt might be a shell. Rangesh has a theory that Hunt is someone in the bureau who knows a whole lot more than the rest of us about what's on Kagame's sliver, but like Kagame they don't know who to trust. And if you don't like that, you go find out who it was who authorised three Fleet men to go into Jared Black's room in Mercy without supervision.'

Yeah, suck on that. I could see from his face how he didn't like it.

'We're looking into it, Rause.'

'Look harder.'

We went back over everything twice more, backwards from the recycling plant and then a string of questions jumping around the timeline at random. Old school interrogation, the sort of thing I would have done in his shoes, trying to catch me out. It didn't work because the only thing I was hiding was that I knew who Chase Hunt really was and why she wore Alysha's face. It told me plain as the sun that he didn't trust me, though. Not that I needed much telling by then.

They left. Agent Patel briefed me on my rights and how to get in touch if I needed legal counsel. He didn't need to do that and I could see he didn't believe me either. So it was nice that he took the trouble.

'Am I under arrest?' I asked him.

He shook his head. 'Protective custody.'

I told him I didn't want it and that keeping me here was a breach of my rights and so please could he make sure I was free to go. He promised to get back to me on that as soon as he had an answer. Then he left. He might as well have just said no right there and then. The bureau were keeping me locked down whether I liked it or not.

Truth was, I didn't have any place left to go anyway.

Nohr, Kettler and Steadman. They had to have something in common that I'd missed. Steadman had tried to blackmail Elizabeth Jacksmith into releasing information on the trans-polar expedition. Jacksmith reckoned she wasn't the only one. So there was that. But why Nohr and Kettler? What if Steadman was a red herring? What if Bix was right? What if I was looking in the wrong place?

What if I should have been looking at Nohr, the first to go and the one whose death looked the least suspicious?

I messaged Roge, bribing him with vague offers of future favours if he could somehow give the retests on Nohr a priority bump. Then, since I really couldn't think of anything else to do, I settled back into a deep background check. Everything I could find about Jit Nohr. Who she was and what she believed in. Everyone I'd talked to had her down as a wacko. It was time to find out why.

17

THE MISSING WORLDS
OF JIT NOHR

Everyone has an obsession with the Masters at some point in their lives, even with a century and a half of history behind us since they left. They disintegrated countries. They raised mountains and drained seas. They reshaped Titan and Mercury, Neptune's rings and moons, a hundred other worlds. Everywhere we look we find traces of what they did.

They did it all as though we weren't even there. We tried everything from radios to lasers to nuclear missiles to get their attention but nothing worked. Almost half the population of Earth died in that first week of abject terror; and then, after the total global breakdown, as all the infrastructures of our civilisations collapsed, they stopped.

What came next lives in the colonies as a story we tell our children. A boy and a girl meet a fascinating stranger on the road. She talks to them and offers them a treat. She asks to shake hands with them to show they are friends. The wise girl runs home. The foolish boy takes the offered hand and is never seen again. On Earth a handshake is what it always was: a way of saying hello. On the colonies it's like sharing blood. Earthers don't get it but the real people who disappeared weren't children; they were men and women in the prime of life, intelligent, educated and healthy. They met the stranger on the road and shook the stranger's hand and followed them, and the stranger carried them across the stars. We colony-born are descendants of the men and women who learned too late. They took that offered hand willingly, with joy, even, from the accounts of those first colonists. They didn't know why they felt that way, only that they did, an inexplicable euphoria that lasted exactly until the Masters carried them to some new world and abandoned them.

Alysha once said that the Masters were like gardeners, re-engineering the landscape for no other reason than they wanted a different view. Humanity was the anthill they knocked over without noticing it was there; but then, when they saw us scurry in frantic defence of our ruined home, they thought it might be interesting to build an ant farm and set us on the mantelpiece to see what we did. They found some interesting worlds and picked on interesting groups of people – sometimes selecting widely, other times from a narrow ethnic pool – and carried us to our new homes. The first colonists had been given everything they needed to survive and thrive – exactly that and rarely more. If the Masters had made any mistakes – colonies that faltered or where everyone simply died – there was no trace of them any more. The Masters watched us, and then they got bored and left.

There were other theories, plenty of them, but the truth was plain and simple: we didn't know who they were; we didn't know what they wanted; we didn't know why they did what they did; we didn't know where they'd gone; we didn't know why they left behind all their ships and everything they'd built, and we had no idea whether they were ever coming back.

Most of us left it at that and got on with life – staring at a question you already know has no answer quickly stops being any fun. Nohr was one of the ones who couldn't.

She'd started as a journalist for Channel Seven writing filler pieces and local news. An early article caught my attention. *Fleet's Missing Worlds.* The introduction was a stock reiteration of what everyone already knew about the years after the Masters left: the decade of fighting and chaos, the decade of consolidation, the creation of Fleet and the 'rediscovery' of the thirty-seven colony worlds. After charting the rise and fall of the Pan-Colonial Congress which recognised Fleet and wrote its charter, Nohr turned to whether everything the Masters had left behind was accounted for. That wasn't new either – there would probably be arguments for the rest of time about what Fleet or Earth, or both, had managed to squirrel away – but Nohr took it further: what if it went beyond a handful of artefacts. What if it went to ships? What if those ships worked like all the others, ticking back and forth between Earth and somewhere else? What if there were more than thirty-seven colonies? What would the others be like? What was happening there? Had they survived? What were they for?

She offered evidence of a sort, citing a century-old study based on a comprehensive census of Earth claiming to catalogue everyone who disappeared over the years of the Masters. I checked the background research and figured she was right about the work and wrong about the conclusion. The study was real and claimed that more people had vanished than were accounted for, even allowing for disappearances that had nothing to do with abduction by aliens, but it had been thoroughly debunked too. Even when the census was taken, years later, we were still picking up the pieces from that first week of systematic annihilation. Too many people had disappeared over too many years and for too many reasons. Too many people had simply been erased in the reshaping of Earth to say anything meaningful at all.

Nohr also had a list of 'missing' ships, all named, although how anyone knew what the Masters called their ships was beyond me since for all we really knew the Masters *were* their ships. I traced her source for the names back from reference to reference until it eventually dissolved into a black hole of wild speculation and a rumoured list that had appeared a few years after Fleet's inception, and had then apparently sat in the archives of some Chinese intelligence agency for half a century. Apply any rigour and the evidence all fell apart.

Nohr was clearly a believer, though. And I guess the idea of missing ships piqued my interest because of the trans-polar expedition.

There were plenty more articles on similar themes. Nohr never broke new ground, probably because there wasn't any new ground to break, but her early papers were well researched, backed by evidence, such as it was, and engaging. She'd started to give talks. The talks had started to make money. She'd left Channel Seven and gone freelance. I couldn't see a single defining event but I could see how she'd drifted over the years into an obsession with her own idea, her missing worlds ...

And then something had changed. Over the last years of her life, her obsession had coalesced to one thing: finding her missing colonies using geometry. I didn't have the maths to follow the arguments – I suspected Nohr didn't either – but she'd tried. She'd obsessed over star maps and petitioned Fleet for an accurate four-dimensional map of every star in the galaxy. She'd collected and republished papers that tried to fix *exactly* where in space each of the thirty-seven colony worlds actually were. Her conviction was that the arrangement of worlds chosen by the Masters was of absolute importance – that if we could decode it, we'd find their missing worlds; in those worlds we'd find meaning, and in that meaning we'd find their purpose.

I stopped and wound back. A symbol stared out at me from

one of Nohr's pages. An infinity symbol inside a star. The caption was a date: *10 20 2056*. It was the symbol Chantale Pré had seen on the tail of an anonymous Fleet ship carried to Magenta on the *Fearless* and I could have kicked myself. If I looked at it sideways it was the same symbol Alysha had left behind with Rachael Cho, marked on the paper with Darius Vishakh's name and number.

Infinity. A sideways eight inside a star. A quick search scored two hits. The first was for the United Nations Species Survival Directorate, an embryonic military arm which hadn't existed for more than a century. The Pan-Colonial Congress that recognised Fleet had disbanded it. The other hit was the *October* group Cho had told me about: a rich man's club on Earth whose official mission statement was assuring the survival of *homo sapiens* as a species. When I dug for who they were and what they did, I got a cascade that threatened to overwhelm me. Almost all of it was old news from Earth. They were politicians, industrialists, money-men. Movers and shakers. A concentration of wealth and power. The not-so-secret masters of Earth.

A cabal of wealthy Earthers or a secret military arm of the United Nations. Either would have access to the tech that killed Esh, but what did I have to back that up? A scribble on a piece of paper?

I searched for *October* on Magenta. A few names came up that I recognised. Frank Swainsbrook, which was maybe how Cho had known about them. Eddie Thiekis. Nikita Svernoi, not that he was ever one of us. Siamake Alash. A few others.

Doctor Nicholas Steadman.

I didn't know what to make of that. Anything at all?

I went through the rest of Nohr's papers. The trans-polar expedition hadn't made its formal announcement until after she died but it seemed Nohr had blithely assumed the wreck to be one of her missing ships right from the start. Unlike Steadman, she seemed content to watch and wait, more interested in her star maps and geometries.

I wasn't finding any reasons for murder here. I called Roge.

'If you're talking to me because you're bored and no one else will pick up, then go away,' Roge said, before I could get a word out. 'Also if it's to bug me about Jit Nohr. I'm pushing her up the queue as best I can.'

'Kettler,' I said.

'What about him?'

'The K-meth that killed him. There was plenty in his system, right?'

'We might argue the definition of "plenty", but go on.'

'I'm guessing it matches a sample someone gave you probably yesterday evening? Maybe first thing this morning?' The pill bottle from Becker's apartment.

'You may very well think that, but I couldn't possibly comment.' So that was a yes. No surprise.

'Any trace signatures?'

'What do you mean?'

'Impurities? I don't know. Quirks that would help pinpoint the origin?'

'Ah. You mean the relative proportions of different isomers.'

'If you say so.'

'Asked and answered,' he said.

'Not to me.'

A moment's silence until I realised why. Not my case. Not my business.

'Never mind.'

'It's an interesting topic,' Roge said. 'It's remarkable how specific one can be. With an established prior pattern you can narrow a sample down to a specific chemist. Or ...'

His voice changed, badly over-egging a tone of idly musing something over.

'Sometimes you can match it to a seizure. You should ask your friend Agent Rangesh. We had a bit of a chat about it when I matched a recent sample of K-meth to a seizure in Nico three months ago.'

I waited in case he had anything more.

'Thanks,' I said, when he didn't. 'Drop by some time if you've got a moment. I could do with the company.'

'Right. Because I have nothing better to do just now?'

I snipped the call and went hunting in the news archives. Nico, three months ago. A narcotics team following a tip-off had discovered two bodies and a small stash. Looked like a deal gone wrong. The case remained open. We hadn't found the killer.

I had to figure that Becker murdered Kettler, maybe Steadman too, but I couldn't prove it. I couldn't prove that Becker had hacked the Institute's weather hub. For all I knew he was some poor innocent yashmak and Chase Hunt was the real killer ... Except I knew that wasn't true because Chase Hunt was Liss, and Liss hadn't been on Magenta when the first expedition weather feeds were hacked.

Nohr. The first one to die – and I hadn't a clue why.

I watched Kettler's talks next, hoping to get a handle on who he was. For him the Masters were an aside from his main work, the Magentan Genealogy Project, trying to track family trees across the planet to establish the DNA of the original settlers. The idea was to look for what they had in common, to see if we could understand why the Masters had chosen them. Kettler was objective and dispassionate. He talked about his own work; but beyond that he covered everything about the Masters, the history of Earth over the years of the occupation – if you could call it that – the things they'd done, the multitude of theories as to who they were and what they'd wanted, and the lack of any evidence to choose between them. He didn't seem to have any axe to grind or pet theory he was trying to sell. The talk Alysha had recorded, *Where Did They Go?* was a summary of ideas as to why the Masters had left. Kettler's take at the end was that we were asking the wrong question: we shouldn't be asking why they went or to where but why they stayed as long as they did. He gave a few minutes to the missing colonies theory, but he didn't dwell on it.

I pulled up Alysha's recording of Steadman and watched it again, paying attention to Steadman himself this time. *The Mathematics of the Masters* was closer to Nohr's obsession with geometry. He mentioned Nohr by name.

I watched Rachael Cho's talk next. It was about how the Masters existed on a higher dimension of consciousness. Hippy-trippy shit, the sort of crap that even Nohr didn't take seriously. The hours dragged by. No word from Agent Patel about letting me out. I messaged him again and then looked through the talks Bannerjee and Sukhoi and the others had given. Their lectures ranged around every aspect of the Masters. The ones Alysha had recorded with Vishakh and Shenski were only the ones where they talked about where the Masters had gone.

So there was a theme, but so what?

My Servant abruptly came back to life – control handed back from the Tesseract, and with it a message from Agent Patel telling me I was free to go. He didn't sound pleased about it and advised me to stay in the Tesseract for my own safety. By the time he was done advising, I was out the door.

On the Tesseract steps I called a pod. It took me to the apartment assigned me when I'd first come back from Earth. The apartment Servant opened the door to let me in. A crate of my things waited in my hallway – apparently Laura had run out of patience and dropped off the meagre collection of my life that I'd left with her. The coffin for Liss's old shell was still propped against the wall in the bedroom. I almost called her when I saw it. I wanted to hear her voice again. I wanted to ask if she was Chase Hunt. I wanted to tell her that I knew and to hear her admit it. I wanted her not to lie to me. I wanted to ask her to come back. All of those things but I didn't, because I knew what her answers would be.

These rooms weren't home. They never would be. They felt cold and lonely and bleak, with a thousand memories squatting in their walls. I turned and left and roamed Firstfall instead, thinking this was how people ended up drunk in the middle of the night in strange bars – only it wasn't the middle of the night but barely mid-afternoon, and I didn't want to go that way. I took a pod to the Wavedome instead and stood at the edge of the sea on the black magnetic sand. The weather was blustering wind and hard rain but the surfers were out there anyway. I watched them, hoping the sea would take me away from all this, from Alysha and everything about her – and it did, but only as far as Esh. Esh, who'd come out here every few days and dragged the rest of us too, who'd taught me that out there in the crash and pound of surf was the one place on this world where you could talk and be sure that no one else was listening.

'Hey, dude.'

I almost jumped out of my skin. Bix was standing beside me. He was dressed in a brown kaftan and sandals. Around his neck I caught a flash of silver. I had to look twice to see it was a silver crescent moon and star on a slender chain. Esh's talisman.

'They let you out, then,' I said.

He shrugged. 'Kept me in overnight and then told me to get lost, you know?'

'You mean you're suspended again?'

'Not exactly.' He shook his head. 'Laws was all over me, man. I know it's the pressure. Esh and then you. But, dude!'

He shook his head and then reached out a hand to rest on my shoulder, looking up and down the beach.

'She, uh … She asked me to keep an eye on you and stuff. Keep you out of trouble, you know? Not sure I'm the best choice, but, hey. So. You meeting someone?'

I shook my head. 'I just came to … I'm not sure. Think. I think.'

'Yeah. You want me to go?'

I shrugged. 'It's OK.'

'Esh, man. Was her place, the Wavedome. You know, me and Esh, we were going to … Take things to the next level or something. I guess … I don't know. I really miss her.'

'You want to get a beer?'

He didn't seem to hear. 'I got something from Roge yesterday. You know, before …'

'Yeah.'

'The K that killed Steadman. It was—'

'I talked to Roge,' I said. 'From Becker's apartment, right? Matches a seizure in Nico.'

'Yeah. That. Apparently Himaru went mental on Roy Lemond last night. Two tac-teams. Smashed into his place.' He shook his head. 'Story Lemond gave was that the dealers in Nico were taken out by a pair of shells and a pile of drones. Lemond reckoned it was MSDF work but Himaru says not. I think Himaru had him hanging by one ankle over a long drop at the time so who knows.' He shrugged again. 'Hadn't really thought of doing it that way. Drones and shells sounds familiar, though.'

'Yeah.'

'Proves you were right, man. Same case. Same killers.' Bix turned away. 'This totally sucks, you know? We got nothing without a trace back to whoever piloted those shells. They just do whatever they want. Hitting us again and again and we can't stop them.' He gave me a wry smile. 'Beer sounds good, you know.'

We walked up the beach to the Blue Scallop, the old-style

diner stuck in the middle of the sand, sat down and ordered a couple of beers. We had the place mostly to ourselves.

'We need to get back on the inside, man.'

'Not going to happen. Half the bureau thinks Kagame had something on me. Without the key to his sliver we're never going to know. The man we took under the Monument saying anything? About who killed Esh, I mean.'

Bix looked away. The stricken expression on his face told me no.

'We've got to make him talk. He's all we've got.'

'Dude. It's ... I dunno, man. I don't know what to do.'

His voice cracked. He was choking up. He drooped and held his head in his hands.

'I ran away to Earth after Alysha died,' I said. 'I thought that would be enough. Start a new life. But it wasn't.'

'Can't run away from yourself, man.'

'I rebuilt her.' I'd never told anyone that. Not a living soul.

He cocked his head. He didn't get it, not yet, but I had his attention.

'I hired a cracksman who sucked every memory of her out of Magenta. Every electronic record. Every image caught in every camera, every word from every microphone, every archived Servant log, every message she ever sent. Took about a year to collect. Took all that and dropped it on a pristine AI core. And there she was. Alysha. Back again.'

'Fuck, dude!' Bix's eyes were saucers.

'They're not as up their own arses about these things on Earth.'

'Yeah. But ... Whoa!'

'She was pretty good,' I said. 'I got to thinking in Mercy that what was left of Esh would be like that. Better, actually. Recordings of everything she did and saw. All those memories just waiting to be dropped onto an AI core.'

Bix shook his head. 'It's all still there. All that shit. Esh. Her life. Mercy doesn't know what to do. There's no next of kin. No one to tell it. And I keep thinking ... You know ... What if it comes down to me? Because I was her best friend, you know? What if ... I keep wondering ... What do I do, man?'

'But it wouldn't be her,' I said quickly, before Bix went too far with that thought. 'Same as what I made on Earth wasn't Alysha. It was something else. It was something so close that I could never quite walk away from it, but far enough to always hurt.'

'Dude! I guess ... What did ...? That's ...'

A concerto of expressions played across his face. Amazement and awe, fascination and salacious horror. And a deep, deep sadness.

'What did you *do*, man?'

'I turned her off,' I lied, 'and left her behind.' These were dark waters. I didn't want to be telling Bix the rest of the truth about Liss. Him or anyone else. Anyway, it was what I *should* have done. I lifted my bottle to him and changed the subject. 'To Esh, dude.'

'Esh.' He nodded and then flashed with anger. 'You know what really gets me, man? We got this guy locked up under the Tesseract. Suspect One because, you know, they don't even have a name for the dude. Maximum security in case someone tries to take him out before he talks. But that's not going to happen. They're going to leave him right where he is and he's going to sit there, tight as Laws' arse ... Sorry, man, but you got to admit ... Anyway, he's totally not going to say a word because he doesn't have to because he knows what's going to happen. He just has to ride it out, you know? We got him cold, he's guilty as shit, but he's Earth-born and so we can't lock him up on Magenta. High gravity counts as torture, right? So it's Colony 478, you know? And who runs that? Fleet. Who's going to take him there? Fleet. Who's he working for? Fucking Fleet.'

Bix shook his head. 'So that's it, man. Dude sits tight and takes it. We try him, convict him and ship him off. And then? Maybe some story comes out about some accident, you know? They'll say he's dead but he won't be. He'll be on Strioth in the pleasure palaces for a bit, thank you for your loyal service. A year from now he's going to be back out there, doing the same shit on some other world.'

I ordered another lichen-beer each. 'You think he killed Esh?'

'No. But I think he knows who did.' Bix spat out a long breath.

'The bomber who killed Alysha ended up shanked in the showers on Colony 478,' I said quietly. 'So there's that.'

Shanked by Darius Vishakh, I was starting to think. *Thank you for your loyal service* ... Was that what it was?

'Loki?'

'Yeah.'

'See what I mean.' Bix necked his second beer when it came. 'You know what would be cool, man? You and me in that cell with him and no cameras. Laws too, maybe. Yeah, I reckon she's got a dark side totally good for that.'

I laughed. 'Touch Jamie and Laura would do things you and I can't imagine.' She'd told me about her split with Jamie's father, what she'd done to keep Jamie. Bix was right: she had it in her to go to some very dark places. 'Wouldn't work, though. I mean – what? We work him over? In this pretend world of yours where we could even get away with that, so what? Why does he talk? Same deal applies – he just has to ride it out.'

'I guess you'd have to, like, get him off Magenta or something. You know, take him some place where there *is* no "ride it out".'

'Give him to Himaru, then. Take him to one of those Project Insurgent safe houses ...' I finished my beer and got up to head for the restroom. 'They had something. Him and Esh. Don't know what but I can see it. He'd do it. Could probably pull it off. Being a colonel ... Got to mean something, right?'

Bix watched me as I walked away, forlorn and bitter and angry and not the Bix I knew; when I came back he didn't look any better.

'He was kind of like a surrogate father. They let me keep Kettler, you know?' Another two beers were waiting on the table. I sat down. Much more of this and we were going to be drunk.

'Thought that was a dead end,' I said.

'Yeah. Well, like, there's the irony, dude.'

I'd told him as much as I knew on the way to Becker's apartment but we walked it through again in case I'd forgotten something.

'Why kill them?' I said when I was done. 'That's where I keep getting stuck. Shenski, Vishakh and Alysha's old surveillance videos connect Nohr to Kettler and Steadman. They were being watched by Fleet, and Alysha was watching Shenski and Vishakh, and Vishakh was looking for something – I have to guess the expedition's wreck. But why? And why, six years later, are they all suddenly dead?'

'Maybe there's something inside it, man.'

We chewed on that for a bit. Another couple of beers came and went. I talked about Nohr, and how I thought she was the key to it and what I'd discovered about her. Bix talked about the Masters, speculating ever more wildly about what might be hidden under the Magentan ice. By the time we left the Blue Scallop, our table was a litter of empty bottles and neither of us could quite stand straight. I watched him stagger outside. The kaftan and sandals were the same gear he'd worn on that first day he came into my office.

He read my look. 'It's, like, comfortable and stuff, you know?' he said.

'It's ridiculous is what it is.'

'It's, like, my Esh dress.' He looked sheepish. Vulnerable, even.

'Your what?' Esh wore military jumpsuits almost without exception.

Not wore. Had worn.

'Yeah, man. First day we got put together. We were, like, partners for a bit, you know? Just the two of us. Before you came back from Earth and stuck us with Laws. I didn't know. So there I was, hot off the streets from hanging with gen dealers and dragged into the Flem's office. He makes me stand there and tells me how he wants me to partner with someone and I'm, like, no way dude, I do my stuff alone, you know? Anyone else, they're going to totally mess it up, right? And then she comes in. Esh in her black MSDF jumpsuit, you know? Like a total mini-fascist. And I'm looking at her and I'm telling myself how this totally totally isn't going to work and how I'm going to hate every minute of partnering with someone who so obviously has every rule and regulation ever written stuck up her arse, you know? But what my mouth is saying is *Sure, whatever* – and all I can think is how amazing she is. Scorching hot. And how, like, so totally *wrong* that was, you know?' He laughed and shook his head.

'You and uniforms,' I said.

'Only when they were on Esh, man.' He laughed too. 'And then I realise I'm, like, totally staring. And she looks at me with this tilt of her head and a glance at the Flem, like *Really?* And the Flem gives a little nod and so she looks at me again and does that little smile she does, like *Well, if that's what it has to be, then OK I guess*.' He smiled as he talked, but the pain of memory was naked in his eyes. 'She didn't say a word when we left, you know? Just looked me up and down and smiled and shook her head like she figured I was crazy, but that that was OK. That's what she was, man. Just took whatever came.'

'That was Esh.'

'She wasn't, like, smart like Laws. But she was the best of us, man. Totally the best.'

I didn't have an answer to that. Through the swimming in my head, Bix's words sounded like pure truth. 'I don't think I ever met someone who didn't like her,' I said. Well, apart from Laura, but then Laura didn't much like anyone.

'She deserved better, man.'

'She saved my life once.'

'Mine too.'

We meandered through the Wavedome gates into the open space outside. The wind snapped at Bix's kaftan, whipping it around his legs. We each called our own pod. I didn't know where I was going. Not home.

'We should totally do it, man,' Bix said.

'Do what?'

He took a deep breath. 'That guy you got under the Monument? I said I reckoned he knew who killed Esh? It's more than that, dude. I'm pretty sure he was there.'

'*What?*'

'Told you I saw a dude running away. He was hurt. Your dude was patched up. Good work but very recent. It's him, man. I swear it's him.'

I stopped and grabbed him and made him look at me.

'You're sure?'

He nodded.

'Have you *told* anyone?'

Now he rolled his eyes. 'Dude? What am I? Of course I did, you know?' He shook his head. 'Doesn't change what happens, though, does it? No, I want to get that shit out of his cell and take him somewhere and beat the living crap out of him until he tells me who killed her. I want to do bad things to him, man. I know how to do it, too.'

'Yeah.' I had to figure that was the beer talking. 'And get a one-way ticket to Colony 478 in the same shuttle, right? We could all share a cell.'

'Then he could get shanked in the shower like Loki.' Bix giggled but a part of him wasn't joking. I was still putting that down to the beer, but somewhere deep something stirred. I knew exactly how he felt because I'd felt it too. I'd felt it when I'd seen the face of the man who killed Alysha. I'd wanted to murder Loki with my own bare hands. When I'd heard he was dead, my first emotion had been regret. Not that he was gone but that I hadn't been the one to stick the shank through his heart.

'Dude?'

'Bix?'

'Keep an eye on Laws, man. She's up to something.'

'She's always up to something.'

'She took everything on Chase Hunt, man. She's got a hard-on for that one.'

Shit.

'Just, you know, keep an eye open, OK? And take care, you know. Just ... I don't want to lose another friend. Even Laws, you know?'

The pods came.

'You going to be all right?' I asked.

Bix shrugged. 'It's not cool, man. You know I'm right about how this plays out. It's going to suck.'

He was right, but I didn't see what either of us were going to do about it. I watched him get into his pod and move off and then climbed into my own. I didn't want to go home, not back to that empty space, so I told it to drive into the Firstfall suburbs, to where Alysha and I used to live. The pod obediently stopped on the street outside. I sat and stared out of the window, looking at the entrance. We hadn't had much but we'd had enough. A nice roomy two-level home. Access from the surface if we wanted it. The sort of place for an ambitious professional couple who planned to raise a family.

The world started to blur. I blinked it back into focus. That was the life we'd planned, the life Loki had taken away.

Darius fucking Vishakh. I knew his name. I knew what he looked like. But I didn't know who he was or why he'd done what he'd done or whether any of it was even true. I had nothing on him. Not a single shred of evidence. All I had were Shenski's last words.

Darius had Rause killed.

I'd never been able to prove that someone had pulled Loki's trigger. I'd never been able to prove Alysha's death had been anything more than wrong place, wrong time.

Darius. Fucking. Vishakh.

Move on. That's what Liss kept telling me. *Move on and let go.*

Like Bix said, it sucked – but what was I going do?

I knew who lived in our old house. She was a chemist and he was an insurance broker. They had three young children. Exactly the sort of family these houses were meant to embrace. I knew their names, and I knew that knowing them was a sign of something wrong inside me.

I pinged Laura. That was the beer making me stupid. After Alysha and Liss I'd thought ... I don't know what I'd thought. That Laura and I both needed someone. So we'd found each other. For a time. Sort of.

She didn't answer. Probably for the best.

The world blurred again. I told the pod to take me home. Cold and empty but I had nowhere else to go. A delivery drone was waiting outside my door. It pinged my Servant and then dropped a packet. I stopped it and quizzed it, asked where it came from and who sent it but it had been wiped clean so thoroughly that it couldn't even remember coming here. Inside the packet was a data sliver. I sent the drone away and set up the sliver behind the thickest firewall I could come up with. Then I opened it.

The first thing that came up was a video of Bix. Drunk from after we left the Wavedome, from the looks of him.

Dude. Sorry, man. I think you should see this, you know? This is going to auto-wipe because I totally shouldn't be doing this. But you should know, man.

The video lasted another couple of seconds and then wiped itself. The rest of the sliver held the Tesseract files on Steadman. The bureau headers were still there, the dates and times, who'd processed it, circulation records, that sort of thing. I skimmed, trying to concentrate, trying to figure out what it was that Bix wanted me to see. It was hard to concentrate. I was drunk. Liss's empty coffin loomed beside me conjuring haunting memories of Alysha. Of Esh, too.

Among Steadman's files on the trans-polar expedition I found an exchange of messages between him and someone in the Institute. They'd been encrypted but the Tesseract had cracked them. Someone – maybe Bix – had highlighted them and written a note: *Jacksmith?*

Steadman: I know they're inside.
Anonymous: They're not.
Steadman: Don't bullshit me.
Anonymous: They reached the skin. That's not the same as inside.
Steadman: They cut a hole.
Anonymous: They *tried* to cut a hole. It didn't work. They're excavating further. They think they've found an entrance deeper under the ice but they're not in, not yet.
Steadman: You know what I've got on you and Becker.

283

Anonymous: Nicky, Becker is Vishakh, not me.

Steadman: And I told you I don't believe you.

Anonymous: You want to be very careful about that. I'm on your side. You don't need to threaten me.

Steadman: I want an updated list of who's on site.

Anonymous: I gave you one three days ago.

Steadman: I want one every damned day. I need to know who's there when they get inside. You know what I mean. Someone's going to go for Iosefa. It'll happen the moment they get that thing open.

Anonymous: Iosefa will come to me. Trust me!

Steadman: Trust you?

Anonymous: I've got someone watching, OK. It's in hand.

Steadman: Who?

Anonymous: I told you, he'll come to me!

I stopped to let that sink in and forgot that I was drunk. Steadman had known about Becker? But about *who* and Becker?

Nicky ... Bix was right. Jacksmith. And she'd known about the weather hack all along. And Vishakh! Why was his name even here? They were connected, but how? I thought about the charade she'd played in her office when I'd burst in with Steadman's data and accused her. She'd played me. She'd played me well.

I searched the personnel files she'd given me, looking for anyone called Iosefa.

Nothing.

The Tesseract had cross-linked to other conversations it thought were between the same two people. One stood out from a couple of weeks earlier. No one had highlighted it, which meant that no one in the bureau had reckoned it had any particular significance.

Anonymous: What happened to Jit?

Steadman: Heart. You know what she was like.

Anonymous: Are you sure she wasn't pushed?

Steadman: Fleet don't have a clue about this.

Anonymous: Was she right?

Steadman: Can't say for sure. There's not enough data.

Anonymous: Can you figure it out without her?

Steadman: Not for Magenta. I've got reams of data for Earth to act as a reference but the colonies are all problematic. I keep telling you we need a proper radio telescope. The best data I've got is for Arcon.

Anonymous: And?

Steadman: <pause> She might be right. I don't have enough data. Pulsars aren't as reliable as people think. <pause> Elizabeth, how far is Arcon from Earth?

Anonymous: Two thousand eight hundred light years, give or take. Why?

Steadman: What if they're the same?

Anonymous: What do you mean?

Steadman: I mean what if they're the same! What if they're *exactly* the same?

Anonymous: What are you trying to say?

Steadman: I'm not *saying* anything. I'm conjecturing that the *Dauntless* travels the same distance in time as it does in space whenever it flips.

Anonymous: That's ridiculous!

Steadman: No it's not. There's no violation of causality. Jit asked Fleet for more data. Help me get it and then let me have a few more days. Maybe I can refine the numbers.

And then there was this, the most recent of all:

Steadman: Has Kettler got any answers yet?

285

Anonymous: Nothing definite. A few dozen candidates.

Steadman: He needs to get on with it. I don't know – can't you and your Tesseract friends trump something up and bring them in for blood tests?

Anonymous: Nicholas! We can't—

Steadman: If any of this is even half right then it's going to turn the world on its head. *All* the worlds. You know that. We need to be ready. We need *answers*.

Anonymous: Lars needs to be careful. Becker's sniffing—

Steadman: I already warned him about Becker. Lars isn't an idiot. I'll talk to you later.

Steadman, Nohr, Jacksmith and Kettler. All working together. And they'd all known about the hacked weather data. They'd all known about Becker and they'd all known who set him to work. Or they thought they did. Now, except for Jacksmith, they were all dead.

Darius Vishakh's first posting on the *Fearless* had been twenty-seven years ago. I checked my file on Jacksmith again to make sure I was remembering it right. I was. Twenty-seven years ago Jacksmith had been on the *Fearless* too. 'Historical research.'

Same place, same time.

Jacksmith and I needed another talk.

There was another message from Bix, one for me to watch when I'd looked through the files he'd given me. It was short and to the point and career-ending stupid: Himaru was in if we were up for snatching Suspect One and taking him somewhere dark where no one would find us.

It was late. The beers were settling into an ache between my temples. But I was happy. Kettler. Steadman. Nohr. Jacksmith. Vishakh. I had the link. I knew who and I knew why and I knew what they were after and now Bix had given me a chance to prove it. I popped a couple of DeTox, made a few calls, the last to Colonel Himaru. Then it was time for a long hard talk with the resurrected avatar of my wife.

THE MOSQUITO

Technician Stephanie Wright has ceased to be. Thoughts and ideas and memories in transition from one name to the next view the world from behind the compound lenses of a drone the size and shape of a mosquito. On Earth such drones are commonplace. On Earth it's impossible to be sure that nothing nearby isn't listening – but Magenta isn't Earth. Drones are far from ubiquitous and so, therefore, are the precautions against them. There is no mosquito netting around the entrance to Mercy hospital, or at the Hotel of Lost Things, as the Magenta Evidence Repository is known. Only buildings like the Tesseract and other core government structures bother to protect themselves.

There is nothing to stop the mosquito entering a dormitory hotel now closed and sealed as a crime scene. It is the hotel where Stephanie Wright slept after she was born in the hours after Chase Hunt shot Walt Becker in the face. Chase Hunt doesn't exist any more. If she did, she would wonder whether what she'd done was right.

No. Not right. It clearly wasn't *that*.

Satisfying? Definitely.

Useful? She isn't sure but finds herself veering more towards not. Although she had convinced herself otherwise on the night she set her fire in Mercy.

Wise? Clever? These remain to be seen. Most of the reason they remain to be seen stands in front of the mosquito, holding it trapped between a pair of tweezers and peering into its multi-faceted artificial eyes.

Tesseract agent Laura Patterson.

There are no mosquitoes on Magenta. There are no flying insects. There are no insects at all. A fly cannot escape attention. Anything that moves is a drone. This drone has been caught in a simple net.

'Another day and I'll know who you are,' says Agent Laura Patterson. 'You can hide your face, Stephanie Wright, or Chase Hunt, or Satoshi Nakamoto, or whoever else you wear. But you can't hide the way you move. I've got enough to run body-posture mapping now. And then you're done. Also I have this.'

Laura Patterson holds something fine and delicate in a second pair of tweezers.

A hair.

'You're a killer and worse and nothing you're doing is helping him. The best you can do for him now is turn yourself in.'

There might be more – but before Laura can set about tracing the flow of information from the mosquito with a meticulous and relentless efficiency, the mosquito is dead. Its consciousness flees, its last departing act to overload the mosquito's tiny battery.

In front of Laura's eyes, the mosquito melts.

SIX

SUSPECT ONE

18

FUGITIVE

I went back to the Wavedome for dawn. Some surfers reckon that's when the best waves come. Meteorologically that makes no sense, but Esh had made me understand that logic and surfing didn't sit well together. Esh had been a dawn surfer. Himaru too.

I hired myself a wetsuit and a board and walked out into the waves to where a group were already fooling in the shallows. I joined them. We talked for a bit and then they moved to the far end of the beach where the waves came in tall and hard. I went back to the shore and watched them riding tubes, launching a few aerials from the wave tops. Esh had had a whole language for that, one I'd never learned.

I left an hour later and took a pod into Firstfall. I stopped at the bureau and walked up the steps to the Tesseract and waited to see whether it would let me in. It did. My case clearances hadn't changed. Nohr was still mine and I was still locked out of Kettler, Steadman and Kagame-Black. The Tesseract didn't mind me pulling up everything on the trans-polar expedition and who at the Institute next door was staffing it. Jacksmith reckoned Steadman had tried to pressure other people on her team. From what Bix had sent me, Elizabeth Jacksmith was full of shit, but she was a problem for Laura now, or Flemich. Not mine, not today.

I wanted Darius Vishakh.

'Hey, boss dude.'

Bix waved a large coffee at me as he came into my office. The kaftan had gone. He was wearing tactical gear.

'You going on a raid?'

He closed the door behind him. 'Still thinking about Esh, you know.'

'Me too.'

'Um ... Dude ...?'

'I made a bit of a breakthrough last night,' I said. 'Nohr, Kettler and Steadman. I found out how they're all connected. But hey, who gives a fuck, right? Are you good for this?'

'Yeah.'

I looked him over. Rangesh never wore combats unless someone forced him into them. Or Esh told him to.

'You don't have to do this, man.' He shook his head. 'I was drunk. That's all.'

The combat gear said otherwise.

'Yeah I do.' I got up. 'We both do. You can get me in to see him?'

'Yes. Look, man, really ... You don't—'

'Suspect One was there when Esh died. And Darius Vishakh was Loki's accomplice.'

There were a lot of *if*s and *supposing*s behind that, but Bix didn't need to know. He looked at me for a long time, sad-faced and without a trace of the white toothy smile that was how we all remembered him. He didn't say anything. Just a nod to show he understood.

I poked the Tesseract and launched an undercover sting attached to the Nohr case. I told it I needed four fake faces. I let Bix set them up.

'I'll meet you down there,' I said.

The faces took a while. I made a few more calls to the surfers from the morning. We talked about waves and the weather. By the time I was done, Bix had picked up our new faces and was under the bureau among the cells, waiting. I met him there.

'You really sure about this, man?'

I nodded. I should have done this for Alysha six years ago. I wasn't going to let it happen again. 'You?'

Bix and I weren't supposed to go anywhere near Suspect One. Now Bix had him waiting in an interview room. As soon as either of us opened the door, the Tesseract was going to go ballistic.

'We got about thirty seconds once we're in,' he said.

We went in and I started counting down. We stood with our backs to the two surveillance cameras, blocking their view of what we were doing with our hands.

'Hey!' Suspect One wasn't stupid. 'You can't do this! You can't talk to me without my lawyer.'

'You got anything you want to say this guy?' I asked.

I had two spoofers with me. I tossed one to Bix.

'Nope.'

As one we turned and slipped the spoofers over the camera lenses. As soon as they were in place I flicked a command from my Servant and turned them on. It was a simple loop showing a still frozen image, the last things the cameras had seen as though they'd glitched and frozen. The Tesseract would pick it up, but not straight away.

'Twenty seconds.'

'What the fuck?'

Suspect One saw what was coming. Smart guy, but it wasn't

295

going to do him any good. He kicked back his chair and pulled at the manacles that held his hands and started shouting. I jabbed a needle into him to keep him quiet. It took five precious seconds before he slumped. Bix already had our new faces out. He flipped the quick-release on his tactical suit. Underneath he was wearing a prison jumpsuit, same as Suspect One.

'Thing I don't get, you know,' Bix said as I wrestled Suspect One into the tac-suit, 'is how this guy is so totally sure he's not going to find someone waiting for him with a needle to, like, put him down for good. Would totally be the easiest way to make sure he doesn't talk, you know?'

Bix finished with the faces as I zipped up the suit. He took Suspect One's place at the table. I turned the spoofers off. Twenty-seven seconds. We were still good. My Servant shouted for help and called a medical emergency, a bad one. Bix collapsed as his Servant screamed heart failure – bang on time as the cell door opened and security crashed in. They found Bix on the floor and Suspect One slumped over the table, still manacled. At least, that's what they saw.

I grabbed one and shouted in his face: 'He took poison! Get them to Mercy! Right now! Both of them!'

High-priority alarms would be flying around by now. The emergency call would be out. Mercy would be gearing itself to receive two critical patients. At least two tac-teams would be scrambling to the Tesseract to guard Suspect One and watch him while the Tesseract would be rerouting pods and clearing the roads. It would be opening doors in its underground labyrinth to get Rangesh and Suspect One out of the bureau and on their way as quickly as possible. The pods to take them were probably already drawing up outside. All of that in a few seconds.

A second security detail arrived with a gurney. They lifted Suspect One onto it.

'I want to go with him,' I said.

Someone pushed me back. No.

'He tried to kill himself! He tried to kill Agent Rangesh! It's some sort of poison!' Sometimes you throw as much bullshit into the air as you can, just to see what sticks.

They wheeled him away. A second gurney came for Bix. I helped lift him onto it and then ran alongside as it wheeled itself through the Tesseract at speed. No one stopped me this time. It took the fastest route to an exit, out to the deep undercity tunnels.

I pinged Himaru: Exit four.

A security drone flew ahead and scanned Rangesh. The exit gates opened. A scrambled team of narcotics agents was already waiting with a pod to take us to Mercy. The gurney rushed towards it. The back of the pod opened in anticipation ...

Three drones flew out from the tunnels ahead.

'Drones!' I shouted.

They swept in. I heard the whine of a charging particle beam. The narcotics team scattered for cover. The gurney loaded Rangesh into the back of the pod. The drones separated and spewed a spray of thermally enhanced smoke. I fired my Reeper at them. A chatter of automatic weapons joined in. Out of the tunnel from the undercity a dazzle of lights slammed into the smoke as an armoured all-terrain assault pod the size of a bus roared out of the darkness and screeched to a halt right next to Rangesh. The front of the pod yawned open. Six men in heavy armour ran out carrying door-sized ballistic shields. Two more ran between them. A screeching howling siren detonated loud enough to cripple me. The drones swooped back, strobing sun-bright light and shining dazzle-lasers at our eyes. I staggered, dazed and half-blind even though I knew exactly what was happening. A man with a shield grabbed me and yanked me towards the armoured pod, pulling and half-carrying and then throwing me inside. Two more went for the gurney. The pulsing siren and the smoke and the strobes of light lanced white static through every thought. If anyone was still shooting, I couldn't hear it.

The gurney rammed me. The armoured pod started to move. I was pushed into a padded seat. Someone forced me back and buckled me in. An armoured giant prised my Reeper from my fingers and put it aside.

'Agent Rause.'

Himaru unsealed his helmet.

'Colonel,' I managed.

The pod was moving, accelerating hard. The siren had stopped but my ears were still ringing and lights danced in my eyes.

'How the hell do you work in that?'

'Good filters. Good lenses. Good training.' He grinned. 'It'll clear. I need to know you're really you before it does.'

He was smiling. It wasn't exactly hostile, same as he was wasn't *exactly* pointing a gun at me.

'I'm me,' I said. 'Did anyone get hurt?'

'Sure you are.' He pinged my Servant. 'Now tell me about the first conversation we ever had.'

'Wavedome. Esh set it up. Said you were my surfing instruct-or, or something like that. I don't know, maybe she said that bit before you showed up. We went out into the water. You told me some shit I didn't want to hear. You were a bit of a jerk about it. Do I need to keep going?'

'No one got hurt.' Himaru handed back my Reeper and sent an outside video feed to my Servant; a moment later the whole pod lurched sideways and he almost fell on top of me as we took a corner hard enough to slide.

'This had better work,' I muttered. I patched into the comms chatter of the squad, along with the pod's sensor feeds and navigation plotter. Himaru had us locked down, everything on manual override so the Tesseract couldn't just order the pod to stop itself.

Himaru made a sour face. 'MSDF codes are clearing our way but the Tesseract is *really* upset.'

A steady stream of instructions screeched in from the bureau telling us how many laws we were violating and how much trouble we were in and ordering us to stop. Wasted effort. The soldiers here were doing this for Esh.

'I told you she had friends,' I said.

I'd half expected unmanned pods to form a roadblock to stop us from reaching the surface. The Tesseract didn't bother. Maybe it reasoned we had the mass, armour and will to smash through anything it could put in our way. It knew the exact specification and capability of every piece of equipment we carried. It knew us, too. It knew who we were, our records, our physical and mental traits, what we could do, how we'd been trained, our collective mission experience. The only thing it didn't know was how committed we were. So far I'd done everything I could to make us look very committed indeed; so far that seemed to be working. The Tesseract didn't try to stop us, content to steer us to somewhere safe and isolated. It knew we couldn't escape.

It *thought* it knew.

Bix lay in the gurney exactly as he'd been when we left the interview room. I braced myself beside him, waited until a clear stretch of road and then slowly and carefully peeled back his face. Underneath was Suspect One. I filmed him and I let my Servant linger, muting the sound in case the Tesseract thought it was going to do something clever with the ambient background and maybe pick out voices and work out exactly who was in here. Then I sent the video to Laura and Flemich.

Back off. We do this my way.

Maybe snatching the most wanted man on the planet out of

custody would change the Tesseract's view on how committed we were. The other pod was probably arriving at Mercy by now. Laura was supposed to be inside it, seeing what I'd sent and discovering that the casualty beside her was wearing a fake face too. After that, well, either I was a traitor, in which case me and my other traitor friends were snatching back one of our own in an effort to spirit him away before he spilled his guts, or else I was an agent who'd lost his partner and who was well known to have reacted pretty badly when that had happened once before. Either way worked. I didn't care.

'That the fucker who killed Esh?' asked a voice at my side.

I recognised her. I didn't know her name but Bix had once called her Cousin Annalisa.

'Not the one who pulled the trigger. He's going to point us to the one who did.'

The pod shot onto a high-speed highway out of Firstfall central. Clear of the city the Tesseract would think it had us where it wanted us. Away from Firstfall the danger of collateral damage was low. On the surface there was no cover. It could track us by satellite and scramble a Cheetah or a Kutosov interceptor whenever it wanted. There was a good chance that the pod itself had a tracker hidden somewhere that Himaru hadn't found and disabled. We were making its life easy.

And around about now the Tesseract would be working that out. It was going to see that we had no escape route and that we didn't seem to care. It would be reviewing what it knew of me and of the people I was with and see that we must know our chances were hopeless; and then it was going to realise that, since we were doing it anyway, there must be something it didn't know.

I pinged Laura: Bix OK?

Bix is fine now that I've peeled off that face you gave him. Still out but fine. Was he in on this?

Would you believe me if I said he wasn't?

Sure. I'd take him home and tuck him up in bed. What the hell are you doing, Keon?

What you and Flemich can't.

Why?

You know why.

Esh?

And Alysha.

Alysha? Fuck's sake, Keon! You didn't have to burn everything down for her, did you?

The last time I left it to the bureau, look at what you did.

I cut the conversation. The Tesseract would be listening to every word. Let it. For all I knew, so was the traitor who set Alysha up six years ago. I certainly hoped so.

We drove out of Firstfall into the scatter of fabrication plants and wind farms and hydroponic tanks that littered the outskirts of the city. Most of the fabricators were empty, heavy industry sites mothballed for when they were next needed, or else old single-purpose factories superseded by modular self-configuring manufacturing plants. Himaru roared the pod off the main road and down a fused-glass trail towards one of the old factories. He spat a Project Insurgent code at its sleeping Servant and woke it. The factory doors opened as its Servant severed all ties with anything except Himaru and shut down all internal surveillance. The Tesseract would see immediately what we'd done. It was going to understand now what it was that it didn't know. Question was, what was it going to do about it?

Fortunately this wasn't Earth. An orbital strike on the factory and surrounding area wasn't an option at its disposal.

'Ready?' Himaru asked.

'Ready.'

The pod shot into the factory and screeched to a stop. The

gates closed behind us. The pod doors opened. Himaru shoved the gurney through them. I jumped out after it.

'Luck,' I said.

Himaru's team followed, spreading across the factory to set up a ring of self-erecting antennas. Himaru shook his head. He told the gurney to follow, ran to a service lift and keyed a code into a keypad. The lift hummed into life as I caught him.

'Do right by Esh,' Himaru said. 'There's no such thing as luck.'

The pod turned back the way it had come. Himaru's squad, done with their antennas, raced back to it. Himaru was the last man in. The factory doors opened and the pod charged into the open as the lift gates closed around me. I turned my Servant off as it started to go down. According to Himaru the lift would take me to deep Project Insurgent tunnels that didn't appear on any maps. There was no record of their existence. Nothing down here was connected to the grid and everything ran on manual key codes. The Tesseract and the bureau would be deaf and blind. Magenta's secret network for a resistance that had never been needed.

The Tesseract would know enough by now to guess what we'd done. It had to have tac-teams in the air by now, following us. It could have one in the factory within a few minutes if it wanted to. *If* it still trusted its tac-teams after what one of them had just done – but Himaru had three other places like this nearby. The pod would go to each in turn. In any of them he and his team could duck into hiding and send the pod back out on autopilot across the wastelands for as long as it took to exhaust its fuel cells. That would be about three days.

Whether the Tesseract would be content to sit and watch and do nothing for all that time was another matter. Some part of it had already made the assumption that Suspect One and I weren't on the pod any more. It would pursue us hard. Some other part would assume with equal vigour that our first stop was a decoy. Himaru and I had done the maths out in the surf that morning. We knew how many tac-teams were in Firstfall. If the Tesseract tried to pursue every possibility then it was going to discover that it didn't have enough. Add the fact that all the tac-teams in Firstfall reported to Himaru and so were maybe unreliable and it was going to have to make some tricky choices. It was going to have to guess.

The lift reached the bottom of the shaft. A bank of monitors hard-wired to cameras in the factory showed a tac-team already inside and starting a search. Most of the soldiers I was watching would have known Esh. If Himaru had lived up to his promises then they already knew why we'd done what we'd done. I didn't know if that counted for much, but it wouldn't count for nothing.

I locked the lift so they couldn't call it up even if they had the code. Then I plugged my Servant into a secure communications hub. I was two thousand yards under the ground, deep in bedrock, linked to Firstfall by a bundle of cables running through a ten-mile tunnel and protected by an Insurgent firewall that was supposed to be strong enough to stop even a Fleet AI from punching through and tracing me. I set up an authentication code, activated my Servant, and called Laura. She answered with a ping:

Keon? Where are you?

'Somewhere safe for now. Where are you?'

Laura fed me a video feed from her Servant. I was seeing through her eyes. She was in Mercy in a secure room. Bix lay on the bed, hooked up to a set of monitors, all showing him in stable condition. She made sure I got a good look at his face and then at the three other bureau agents sitting around the room.

Whatever you're doing, Keon, you need to stop. Bring him back, unharmed, and turn yourself in.

The Tesseract would be watching and listening. Our words were careful.

'You know I can't do that.'

I know that you can and that it's for the best. Losing Esh hurt us all. You'll go into psych-eval. It wasn't your fault. We'll help you.

'Himaru too?'

In case the Tesseract hadn't worked it out – now it knew for sure that it couldn't trust its tac-teams.

Laura didn't answer. I cut the call but left her a route to dial back.

Mercy's not buying it. Laura again, this time with enough encryption to keep even the Tesseract busy for a few decades.

The Tesseract?

Mercy says this is Suspect One because too many tests say it isn't Bix. The bureau thinks this is Bix because why the fuck else would you do what you just did. I'd say it's uncertain. It's diverting a lot of effort into finding you. But it's cautious and it's not stupid.

Did you—

You're out of your mind trying to game an AI.

I wasn't trying to game an AI, I was trying to game Darius Vishakh. Are we good to go?

This had better fucking work, Keon. If anyone finds out we did this …

Just plug him in!

If anyone found out the truth then we were all finished. Me, Bix, Laura, Himaru – everyone who had a part in what I was about to do. Their careers would be over and I'd be going to prison for a long, long time.

I cut the call to Laura and set up another one.

Liss?

Hey, Keys.

Ready?

Ready.

I jacked in. Like Esh, Suspect One was an Earther. Like Esh, his Servant was embedded into his head through a brainweb. Esh always said that being hard-wired had its up-sides and its down.

Here was the down.

I rode a data stream straight into him.

19

SHIVA

The drugs I'd stabbed into Suspect One in the Tesseract interview room were a cocktail some devious Earth chemist had designed half a century ago for doing exactly this. Rohypnol for the soul, he'd called it. The brutal fact of life with a brainweb was that if you got into this sort of state, anyone could jack into you from anywhere and throw you into a sensory experience of their own making. The stuff was banned on Earth and illegal in the colonies, but that didn't stop a flourishing underground 'total immersion' culture. Some of it was exhilarating and avant-garde, the cutting edge of entertainment. Mostly it was porn.

I didn't plan on being entertaining. For added fun I'd thrown in some premium grade Xen. An Earth-born with little resistance, Suspect One ought to be tripping out of his head by now. It wasn't scientific, but the combination, Bix reckoned, ought to be enough to make him think he was experiencing reality.

Memories Liss had built through the night insinuated themselves into his head. They started with a blur of interviews.

Angry table-banging questions met with stoic silence. A trial, quick and unexpected, the Magentan way where he never left his cell and saw it all piped by video to his Servant. The inevitable verdict and sentence: guilty – condemned to Colony 478 for the rest of his life. Armed guards loading him into a pod. The short trip to New Hope. A shuttle to orbit, locked in a cell with only shake and vibration and acceleration to say he'd left Magenta behind. Then zero gravity. Another ship and another cell. The flight of the *Fearless* to Earth. The relentless presence of snarling Magentan soldiers around him. A beating when no one was looking. A ritual to it, each soldier taking it in turns to kick or punch. A steady ramping of the idea of pain, something Liss reckoned would work on an Earth-born with embedded neural interfaces and a thought-feedback Servant. Steadily breaking him down.

Simulating all this would have taken hours. We didn't have hours. What we gave him were moments that would seem like memories of what had already happened. Short second flashes and snips to let his brain build its own narrative, yet each tailored with an emotional weight. The flashes would seem like past events but the emotions would linger into the present. Fear. Loneliness. Abandonment. At least, that was the idea.

Orbiting Earth, seeing the mother world through the glass walls of a cell …

Isolation …

Another string of beatings …

Months passing …

Never asked any questions …

Betrayal …

Despair …

All just memories.

The tac-team up in the factory finished their sweep. They'd found the service lift. I couldn't tell what they were doing to make it work but they had drones reconnoitring the shaft. Himaru reckoned I could hold out for as long as it took to bore a whole new tunnel if I wanted to. We'd find out soon enough whether he was right.

Liss and I took Suspect One back to Magenta. The memories became vivid now. He felt the ride to the surface, to an abandoned strip mine surrounded by bleak blank nothing and immersed in storms ...

Wheeled to a sterile medical facility ...

Strapped to a table ...

A man standing over him with a blank face he'd never recognise or remember ...

A voice. Mine.

'You don't exist any more,' I said.

His heartbeat picked up.

Memories of a cloth over his mouth. Pouring water. Drowning. Lungs filling with water until he blacked out ...

Again. And again. And again. In this world we'd made I could deliver precision brutality. I'd been afraid last night of coming to this place, of being this person and doing what we were about to do. I'd told myself I was doing it for Esh, but now that I was here ...

His heartbeat was racing. He was close to where I needed him to be. Desperate and afraid and confused.

I wasn't doing this for Esh, not really.

Keys?

'Who do you work for?' I asked.

He didn't answer.

If you push too hard you can really kill him.

I know.

He was on the best life support Magenta could offer. He wasn't going to die. Let him go into cardiac arrest. We'd bring him back and do it again.

'Who do you work for?' I asked.

He didn't answer.

'Who do you work for?'

Nightmare visions now. Terrors lifted from some cheap snuff flick. Blood and vivisection. Viscera. Eyes locked open to see the stumps of what had been done to him. In the virtual world we'd made for him I had his head held in a vice.

'Who do you work for?'

Fake memories. Things that hadn't happened. Flashes and moments.

I should have felt sick. I didn't. I felt powerful.

Now an interrogation room under the Tesseract. He was whole again. All just bad dreams. His heart rate was through the roof. He was terrified.

Empty room ...

For a moment I let him think it was done. Over. That he had peace.

The faceless man in white comes in ...

Reflex. He activated his Servant and screamed into the ether for help.

Got him!

Irresistible throttling hands around his throat ...

He screamed again.

Keys!

'I need you to understand how personal this is,' I said. 'You killed the woman I loved. Now I get to make you feel what that was like.'

Keys! Stop!

Switch the program.

Suddenly he was in a hospital room, spacious and well equipped, with warm pastel colours and flowers in a vase. Comfort and security. A safe place where everything that had just happened became a confusion of memories. Bad dreams from a half-remembered past ...

A nurse came in, pleased to see him. She said something kind.

Later, a doctor. He'd had a bad experience, the doctor said. He'd been tortured. Drugged and immersed in a virtual hell but he was free now and he was getting better. Darius Vishakh had saved him. If he could get up and walk then Darius wanted to see him ...

Space, in an orbital looking down on Earth through a transparent wall ...

'Welcome back.' The man I figured was Darius Vishakh stood beside him, a construct built from the images captured in Alysha's recordings. 'It's good to see you.'

In the real world Suspect One's heart was still racing. He was disorientated, bewildered by the sudden change. It fed back into the vision. He stared at Vishakh, at the world outside and at the stars.

Vishakh touched a hand to his shoulder. 'They did some dark stuff before we got you out. Do you recognise me?'

He nodded. *Yes.*

'Do you remember who you are?'

I coaxed it out of him in the guise of Vishakh bringing him back. His name was Koller. He came from Earth.

'Shenski,' Vishakh said. 'What happened?'

'I ...' He looked around, trying to understand where he was, and how he'd arrived here.

'What did you tell them about Jared Black?'

He looked at me as though I was daft. 'Black? Nothing! How could I?'

His surprise sounded real. He wasn't there? Wasn't a part of it? Did I believe him? I wasn't sure I had a choice, not without breaking the memories I was building.

'What happened with Shenski?'

Somehow I was asking the wrong questions. He was confused enough to question his own memories. I couldn't keep him in this state for long before he'd start to question everything. Before he shut down.

Koller shrugged. 'Vishakh gave the order to take him out.'

'When I took out Kagame, where did you go?'

'*You* took out Kagame? I thought that was Darius.' He looked at me as if expecting some sort of reaction. Sympathy? But he was squinting like he was trying to figure something out. Like maybe he was starting to get the idea that his world was out of whack.

Why had he said *Vishakh* instead of *you*? He was talking about me as though I was someone else.

He's starting to slip.

A creeping tendril of a thought eased from the background noise of my subconscious. Koller's frame and build made him look like a native. Either he'd had a lot of transgravity or he'd spent a lot of time on the surface.

'May Day 2212. The bomb. Alysha Rause. Remember that?'

He didn't say anything, but reached a hand towards me. I flinched away, out of reach. He took a step closer.

'The Loki bomber,' I said.

'What happened to your face? I don't recognise this place.' He flinched and clutched his head.

You have to let him go.

'Loki blew a pumping station. Four people died. One of them was Alysha Rause.'

He wasn't focused. Liss was right. He was slipping into himself, trying to get away from a reality that some part of him knew wasn't right. He looked at me as though trying to look through me to something else beyond.

'Someone told Loki how to build that bomb and where and when to plant it. Who?'

'I ...' His face screwed up in pain.

Keys! Vishakh was the shell pilot. Vishakh killed Esh. You got what you came for.

He backed away from me, rigid with tension now. 'Where are we?'

Keys!

'Who showed Loki how to build that bomb? You?'

'No!'

'Who?'

Keys! Let him go!

'Which one of you did it?'

He fell to his knees, tugging at his head.

Keys! You're going to kill him!

Good.

I switched simulations. I was the faceless man in white. Koller screamed.

Keys! Stop!

'Who killed her?'

Alysha. My wife. The woman I'd loved for as long as I could remember. The lover whose loss had driven me to Earth for five years of grieving. Whose loss had driven me to build Liss, my monument to her memory.

Enough! Darius Vishakh killed Esh! That's what you came for.

I wanted to say *Stuff Esh* but I didn't. Esh deserved better. Alysha had deserved better too.

'Who?' The faceless man in white towered over Koller.

Keys! Stop!

'I don't even know what you're talking about!' He was screaming. 'What the fuck is this place?'

He wasn't going to remember this, either, at least not the detail. But maybe he could remember the hate, and maybe so could I. The heat of it. How damned good it felt.

You're killing him!

Yes. I was.

'This is for Alysha,' I said.

Around me the simulation fell apart into darkness, froze and went blank as Liss kicked me out.

I almost screamed. 'What the *fuck*? Get me back in!'

Liss became a whisper in my ear. 'No.'

'I wasn't done!'

'That wasn't for Alysha. That was for you.'

'It was for *you*!'

'Who gave you the right to commit murder in my name?'

'*You* did! When you executed Walt Becker! And after we first came back, when you killed—'

A message hit my Servant: DO NOT REPLY. You need to move. Now! The Tesseract has gone mental. It's figured you out. It's tracing Suspect One's call and now it's tracing you too. DO NOT REPLY.

It took me a moment to wind back to where we were and why we were here in the first place. The message was from Laura. She was talking about Koller's scream for help during the nightmares. We were going to find out where that scream had gone. It was sort of the point. *Part* of the point.

'He knew something,' I said. The rage inside me guttered and died. 'He knew who killed you.'

Liss didn't answer. I let it go, bounced out of the simulation and shut it down. Any court on any world would consider what we'd done as torture, but one more cocktail of designer chemistry and all Koller would remember was a long desperate nightmare. None of it had been real and that was the actual truth. Only two people would ever know what we'd really done to him, me and Liss. And only one of us was real.

I hoped the scars would linger. I hoped it would hurt. I hoped he'd curl up at nights in whatever cell he ended up in and shiver in the dark and whimper in fear without ever quite knowing why.

I pinged Himaru: It's done. We're on.

I felt Liss stir again in my Servant.

Keys?

What?

Loki killed me. That's all there is.

No it wasn't. I'd have Vishakh. I'd beat it out of him, that he was the one to pull Loki's trigger. He'd pay the pound of flesh I was owed – and if he was doing it because he was told to then I'd find whoever did the telling and they'd pay too.

You were going to let him die.

No. I was going to kill him. For her. For the Alysha I'd lost six years ago.

The Keon I knew would never do that.

I wondered if that was true.

The Alysha I knew wasn't an assassin.

I wondered if that was true too.

I. Didn't. Kill. Becker.

DON'T FUCKING LIE TO ME!

We're done, Keys. Don't call me again.

She shimmered out of my Servant, out through the data streams of the Insurgent hub to the wild unknown of Firstfall. Back to the shell she'd built for herself with Alysha's face. I tried to call after her but she didn't answer – and anyway, what was I supposed to say? That I'd done this for her? But I hadn't. She was right. Alysha was dead. I'd done this for myself. To feel better about it. To feel less helpless about her loss.

DO NOT REPLY. Keon, you have traffic inbound. Not sure what but we're picking up something coming from orbit. Fast from the Fleet station and heading your way. The Tesseract is responding. DO NOT REPLY.

I passed the message to Himaru. It's a bluff. They're already here. End this.

Not yet.

Vishakh was driving the shell that killed Esh. Koller made a call we can trace.

Unless I'd got all this wrong, that call had been routed to one of two places: either Darius Vishakh in orbit over Magenta or else someone inside the Tesseract. By now the Tesseract would be tracing it with every spark of its AI tenacity. If the call went to Vishakh then we had the evidence we needed to drag him to the surface for questioning. If it went to the Tesseract then we'd nailed whoever Vishakh had inside the bureau.

Did you get a trace? Himaru again.

It's coming.

We stick with the plan until you get it.

I woke the elevator and headed to the surface. I'd gone rogue as far as the Tesseract was concerned. Quite possibly I was a traitor. The mole in the bureau would be thinking the same and so would Darius Vishakh. If Vishakh had balls of steel then maybe he'd sit tight and see how this played out. Himaru and I were gambling that he didn't: either he took the opportunity to snatch Koller or he took the chance to kill him.

Himaru?

Almost there.

There was nothing I could do about the Tesseract diverting interceptors away from Himaru to whatever was coming from orbit. I had no doubt that that was the point. Vishakh was drawing people away. His Dattatreya were already here, as they were when I met Shenski at the Monument.

I'll be up in ninety seconds.

Reception?

I routed the Project Insurgent surveillance hub to my lenses and started tracking the tac-team in the factory above me. With the elevator unlocked they probably had a spy drone on the roof by now.

Three of ours by the elevator shaft. One working on a hack and two standing watch. Three more on overwatch. I've got eyes on two. How much company are you bringing?

Two Cheetahs. Keeping their distance. Two minutes delay to land and deploy.

Each with one tac-team. We were outnumbered three to one. Shells? Drones? he asked.

Nothing except a gut that says they're already here.

The factory gates opened to Himaru's Insurgent code. The tac-team inside the factory scattered and I lost sight of half of them at once. The elevator was speeding upwards but it was going to be another sixty seconds before I reached the surface.

Your timing's off!

My timing is perfect.

The factory gates stayed open as Himaru's pod screamed in and skidded to a stop by the elevator. The back ramp slid down. Himaru and his crew poured out.

'Stand down!' Words blared through a speaker at them. 'Colonel Jonas Himaru! Stand your men down! Lower your weapons and get on the ground with your hands behind your head!'

Himaru's men scattered. The auto-cannon on the roof of the pod spun towards the source of the order and spat a short burst.

Himaru! What the fuck? That's not how this—

Five of the camera feeds piped to my lenses died at once. I had two left. One stared across the factory floor at Himaru's pod. The other watched the elevator. I caught a flash of someone running through shadows. Then muzzle flashes and the rattle of gunfire. The cannon on the top of the pod swivelled and spat again. Something bright flashed across the camera view. A streak of light shot into the cannon turret and flashed and boomed an explosion. Smoke flowered from the pod and drifted across the factory floor. I saw more muzzle flashes and heard the boom of grenades.

A figure sprinted towards the pod. A chatter of automatic weapon fire. The figure sprawled and slid across the floor and lay still.

The elevator was almost at the top.

Himaru! This isn't—

When they show I need ninety seconds.

Have you lost your fucking mind?

A rattle of gunfire. An explosion. Himaru's Servant screamed for help and then went quiet.

Himaru! What the hell are you doing?

Nothing.

Another rattle of fire. The camera watching the factory floor died. That left me the camera watching the elevator doors. I couldn't see any more …

I heard the pop of a particle beam as that last camera died. Tac-teams didn't use particle beams. They were devastating, but too indiscriminate, too short-range and too easy to disable with carefully targeted electromagnetic interference.

Fleet used them, though.

Fleet – and the people who'd killed Jared Black and Esh.

Vishakh was here.

I ran through what I remembered of the factory floor. I had three seconds of dead time after the elevator reached the surface while the doors opened. Then fifteen feet of open ground between me and the pod. Then another couple of seconds to seal the ramp if the ramp was still working. I'd be in the open until then. A sitting duck.

Half of Himaru's squad had gone quiet. My Servant was picking up frantic chatter from the last three. They were pinned down in some distant corner of the factory, far away from the shaft.

The elevator slowed. I linked to the pod. The cannon turret wasn't working but everything else was fine. I turned on the active countermeasures and filled the factory floor with light and sound and smoke.

It didn't help. The elevator doors opened. Lieutenant Shiva Lee stood waiting with a particle rifle aimed at my face. I heard its whine even over the siren from the pod. She had it charged high enough to burn me into vapour. I couldn't tell for sure whether she was flesh and blood this time, or another shell, but it didn't matter. I pulled the sheet back from the gurney and let her see Koller wrapped in enough explosive to blow all three of us and half the factory to smithereens. I showed her the dead man's switch detonator I was holding. Then I killed the siren from the pod.

'Go ahead, blow us up,' I said.

The rifle didn't waver. 'I don't want my man back. Fuck him.'

'Burn me and everything I knows goes absolutely everywhere.' I put my Reeper on Koller's gurney, slow and careful. 'You've got sixty seconds.'

Lee grinned at me. 'That's more like it. What do you want?'

'I want to know who killed my wife. I want to know who gave the order and I want to put a bullet in their head. The rest?' I shrugged. 'I don't give a shit. In particular, I don't give a shit about what you want with the trans-polar expedition.'

Her face flickered.

'Yeah.'

My Servant pinged. Himaru: Done. We're good.

Lee spat. 'Your wife wasn't who you think she was.'

I forced a pretence of calm. 'What the hell is that supposed to mean?'

Rause! It's done. Blow it!

'Blow us all up if you want. These shells are expendable.'

I guess that answered that.

Rause!

318

'I think you're Darius Vishakh,' I said. 'I think you killed Agent Zohreya.'

She didn't answer. He. She. Whichever.

'Did you kill Alysha, too?'

Rause! Are you *trying* to get yourself killed? Pull the fucking plug!

What Himaru was telling me was that antennas he'd planted when he first came to the factory had pinpointed a signal. Whoever was piloting Shiva Lee, we'd locked on to their transmission. We knew where they were ...

Shiva gave a wary smile. 'Loki killed Alysha.'

It's not like it gets better the longer you stand there.

... and that was what we were here for.

I let the detonator go. The assault pod's electromagnetic pulse went off, frying the shell's particle rifle. Suspect One sat up on his gurney, pulled a Reeper from behind his back and shot Shiva Lee in the neck. My Servant fired the pod's klaxon. I snatched up my Reeper and started shooting as well as the shell turned away. Across the factory floor, Himaru and his men and the dead tac-team soldiers they'd been fighting suddenly got miraculously better ...

A blast of light and noise exploded all around me. Shiva bolted, faster than any human. I heard the staccato of automatic weapons near the factory doors, dim over the ringing in my ears. For a few seconds I stumbled blindly until my lenses cleared. By then Shiva was at the ramp. A burst of fire hit her. She lurched then jumped, impossibly high. Smoke spewed out of her.

A soldier blocked her way. She landed on him, slammed him down and sliced a blade across his face. He screamed. A series of dazzling flashes and detonations exploded around her.

'Spray that fucking thing until it stops moving!' Himaru.

I raced after the shell, through the factory gates. The smoke that came with me twisted into Magenta's wind and rain, instantly torn to shreds. I reloaded my Reeper on the run and then I was out into the howling weather. I scanned the horizon.

Rause! Get back here!

Flat stone. The fused-glass track that led to the factory. There wasn't anything else and yet the shell had vanished. I tuned my Servant to look for anything that moved but the rain overwhelmed its algorithms.

I looked back at the factory. She'd doubled back?

Out the fucking way, Rause!

Something took my legs out from under me. I pitched over, dropped my Reeper, caught myself enough to roll out of the fall and ended up sitting on my arse.

'Well played, Agent Rause,' said a voice behind me. 'Well played.'

Shiva Lee stood awkwardly, one leg hanging limp and dragging, the other twitching now and then as she tried to keep her balance. Part of her face had been torn off, exposing the metal underneath. She was running an active camouflage that made her almost invisible when she was still.

'You're a soldier,' I said. 'Like the rest of us. Just following orders. Give me the man who gives them.'

Shiva shook her head.

'You don't have the first idea what you're talking about.'

Her arm shivered. A blade flipped out of her wrist ...

Over the sound of the rain I heard the whine and pop of a particle beam. The side of her head dissolved into vapour. She went down like her strings were cut.

I stood there. Stared at her. Esh's killer.

Koller stood behind her, carrying Shiva's particle rifle. He stopped beside me and looked down at the body, then tore off Koller's face and threw it away.

'That one was for Esh, dude,' Bix said.

20

A LIST OF TRAITORS

Himaru took us from the factory to New Hope spaceport. A drone was waiting with a delivery from Laura. It probably only took the Tesseract a few seconds to catch up with what we'd done but the human side of the command chain took a while longer. By the time the shit hit the fan Bix and I were already in a shuttle heading for orbit. We were punching into the stratosphere when I was suddenly in a conference call with Laura, Assistant Director Flemich, Chief Director Morgan and about a hundred lawyers. I'd met Morgan twice. The first time had been when I'd graduated from the academy. He'd said *Well done* and shaken my hand. He hadn't been Chief Director then. The second had been at Alysha's memorial. He'd shaken my hand that time too, but I didn't remember what he'd said.

I half listened while Flemich gave a start-to-finish on Kagame-Black. I knew where all of this was going to end. Morgan would tell us to stop. And we wouldn't.

I pinged Laura: You were already talking to Shenski?
Yes.

Why didn't you—

Shut up and listen.

We got to the bit about how maybe there was someone skating for the other team inside the bureau. No one liked that, but someone had let Shenski's men into Jared Black's room in Mercy so that Vishakh could kill them. Six years earlier, someone had sabotaged a mission that Alysha had gone out of her way to keep quiet. And someone had warned Vishakh when Esh figured out where to find Kagame.

I let them argue. I had no doubts.

None of this matters. Vishakh killed Esh. He killed Alysha.

What, because of what Kagame transmitted to Shenski? Frankly, Keon, it's just as likely that Alysha and Vishakh were working together. You see that, right?

'I can't tell you how much I'm looking forward to someone explaining how all this led to the events of this morning.' Morgan's voice was dry as dust.

I made it short and sweet. Bix and I had faked a switch and abduction to lure Vishakh into the open. Himaru's team had set up a tactical ELINT array, a networked cluster of antennas capable of detecting and identifying signals and, more to the point in this case, pinpointing with great accuracy the direction from which they came. Every tac-team involved was in on it. The whole thing was play-acting; Vishakh had fallen for it and now we had hard evidence – the transmissions to the shell sent to kill Koller had come from the Fleet orbital, and Koller's call had gone there too.

Morgan didn't ask how come Suspect One had collapsed. I didn't imagine my luck there was going to hold for long. He'd have no choice but to suspend me and Bix and launch an internal investigation. At the very least I was guilty of assault, and that didn't even start to cover what I'd done later. I glossed over what Koller had said when he thought I was Vishakh. None of that was anything we could use. I told them it was all me – my idea, my execution. We did it the way we did because Vishakh had someone in the bureau. And that was that.

'The real Suspect One was never threatened. He remains under guard in Mercy.'

I glossed over the mechanics of how Laura had been up to her neck in it too. How she'd been the one to peel back Koller's face to reveal Bix underneath in Mercy. How she'd sat in the room with Koller while I used the secure link into her Servant to ride into him. I kept her clean because if Bix and Himaru and I all burned for this, at least there'd still be one of us left inside.

A ping came through from Laura: He's conscious.

Does he remember?

Hard to say.

Laura would never know what had happened inside Suspect One's head. That was between Liss, me and my conscience, and so far my conscience wasn't complaining. Push came to shove, Laura would cover her arse and let me sink. I was OK with that. She had Jamie to worry about.

'With your permission I'd like to question the head of Fleet Intelligence on Magenta,' I said.

Not that permission from the bureau mattered a damn to me right now.

I pinged Laura: Is there anything I need to know?

A long pause. Koller is stable and conscious. His word against yours as to what happened in that cell. Good luck with Himaru making the rest look like a lawful training exercise. You'd better fucking be right about Darius Vishakh.

She took a deep breath and spoke aloud. 'Sir, due to concerns over destruction of evidence, I believe Agents Rause and Rangesh are lawful in attempting an extrajurisdiction arrest.'

I wanted to kiss her and her lawyer's degree.

I put myself on the line for you today, Keon.

I know.

When you come back from this I'm going to ask you again about what you saw under the Monument. Have a better answer ready this time.

'How long before you need a decision.' Morgan's voice had storms in it.

I checked the shuttle schedule. 'About an hour, sir,' I said.

'This is out of my hands now, Rause,' growled Flemich. 'Whatever comes down, you go with it or I will personally come up there and fire you into the sun.'

He signed off. Which left me and Bix and Laura.

'Shenski was co-operating all along?'

Laura made a wry face. 'I couldn't tell you. Not with your history.' She meant Alysha.

'You can say her name, you know.'

'Yeah.' There was that look again. The judging one. 'Even if Morgan gives the green light – which he won't – you know we're not getting Kagame's key out of this, right?'

I guess I thought much the same. But that was OK – I had other reasons for going after Vishakh. So did Rangesh.

I cut the link to Laura and looked Bix in the eye.

'They're going to call us back to the surface,' I said.

He nodded.

'Vishakh knows who killed Alysha. I get that out of him and then he's yours.'

Bix touched the talisman around his neck. Esh's silver crescent and star. Then he patted the bag under his seat.

'We're going to burn him, dude. One way or another.'

Yeah.

I had one more thing to do before we hit orbit. I messaged Doctor Jacksmith:

I know about you, Steadman, Nohr and Kettler. I know about

Iosefa. I know about Steadman's pulsar data and I know what he was looking for. I know you and Darius Vishakh are in this to-gether. Know this: when I'm done with him, I'm coming for you.

I didn't expect a reply.

KAMALJIT KAUR

Keon's shuttle is taking him to orbit. Kamaljit Kaur watches from a maintenance bay as it burns towards the clouds. She knows he's there and she knows his purpose, at least in part. There is a pang of something she chooses to avoid. Regret. Guilt. Anxiety. Keon is close on her trail.

Then why is she leaving one?

She tells herself he deserves the truth. That he's earned it.

Does she want to be caught?

No.

Could she convince him what she's done is right?

She watches his shuttle punch into the cloud, then walks to the landing pads and chthonic shelters of private bays behind the public gantries and runways of New Hope. No one stops her until she approaches a Cheetah on loan to the Magenta Institute. The cargo door is open. Three technicians are auditing crates of supplies and equipment. Two soldiers move to intercept her. They're tense. News is breaking of another shoot-out in the heart of Firstfall, of a renegade tac-team. Magenta isn't Earth. The people here aren't used to this. Outbreaks of violence shake them hard.

Earth, where everything is going horribly wrong. Where October have quietly and efficiently seized power in more than half the nations of the world. Although *seized* is hardly the word. *Bought* is more like it. Earth is theirs now, a truth that does not bode well for anyone else.

'ID?'

Her Servant pings a response. She is Kamaljit Kaur, a postdoc conducting meteorological research for the Magenta Institute. A crate of her experiments is to be loaded into the Cheetah's belly.

'You're early.'

A soldier frisks her. He is polite and respectful, but thorough. He finds nothing. Another searches her bag. A Tesseract probe crawls into her Servant, searching for hidden data and dormant killware q-code. It finds nothing.

The first soldier apologises. 'There's something going on this morning,' he says.

Kamaljit smiles. She can't help another glance to the clouds. Gaps between them expose a vivid blue sky. The air is almost still. For once there is no sign of rain.

'Weather's being kind to us today,' she says.

The soldiers let her pass. Kaur climbs into the Cheetah's passenger cabin. She leaves her bag. A panel conceals an emergency toolkit. It is the work of a moment to open it.

Back outside she offers to help the technicians with their crates. As she does she moves to the other side of the Cheetah, hidden from the soldiers standing watch. The technicians pay no attention as she walks towards the cockpit. She talks to them as she does, chatting about the weather, the equipment they have, whether they're coming on the flight – idle and innocent nothings – while she opens a panel in the side of the Cheetah. She spits out a small sealed bag held in her cheek, opens it and slips out a piggyback parasite router smaller than a thumb drive. It takes ten seconds to break a connector to the Cheetah's antenna array, insert the parasite and seal the panel closed. When she turns it on she will have direct access to the

Cheetah's long-range communications. It's not a hack to the Cheetah's Servant, something which might be found and killed, but a direct injection into the transmission hardware itself.

The technicians are wrapping up. She talks with them a little more. As the other passengers from the Institute start to arrive, Kaur returns her stolen tool to the toolkit and resumes her seat. She exchanges pleasantries with the newcomers, but the other passengers have little interest in her weather stations. By the time the Cheetah lifts off they are all engrossed in their own virtual worlds.

SEVEN

SHELL GAME

21

VISHAKH

Magenta has five orbital stations worth the name, all of them built around Earth or Mars and shipped in pieces. Five is a lot for a colony, but no one who wasn't born here wants to live under a constant 1.4 gravities. The largest orbital is the embarkation and debarkation point for passengers travelling to and from Earth on the *Fearless*. It has an official name somewhere, but everyone calls it High Hope. The next is the exclusive five-star private hotel for celebrity guests who find themselves compelled to visit Magenta but who refuse to face the gravity. The *Magenta Elite* has the best orbital conference facilities anywhere outside Earth orbit. After that comes *Reckless Station*, the Earth embassy built so they didn't have to have a consulate on the surface. The smallest by far, known by its handful of inhabitants as *The Hole In The Sky*, is home to Magenta's minuscule orbital defence team, six ancient Kutosov interceptors and their pilots. Pilots like Esh used to be, before she transferred to the bureau.

I picked it out on the shuttle's orbital map. I couldn't help thinking that if Esh had stayed a pilot then she'd still be alive.

Fourth in line was the ubiquitous Fleet station. That was where Darius Vishakh was waiting for me, even though Laura called it right: Director Morgan refused authorisation for an extrajudicial arrest ten minutes before we docked at the *Elite*. We didn't have enough evidence. Instead, Bix and I were suspended pending an investigation into the events of the morning. Our codes and privileges were revoked. We were to return to Firstfall on the next available shuttle and turn ourselves over to the Tesseract.

Like that was going to happen.

Himaru's MSDF shuttle was ready and waiting for us at the *Elite*. Himaru didn't report to Morgan, didn't give a stuff about what the Tesseract said, and had the authority to act anywhere within the Magenta system. We were on the move fifteen minutes after Morgan's order, with two tac-teams in military vacuum suits looking more like armoured storm troopers than policemen. I left Bix to deal with them. Laura was probably right that we weren't going to get the decryption key out of Vishakh's head but I was willing to try. I still had a few more tricks up my sleeve.

'You run into shells again, use this.' The tac-team commander pinged me an authorisation code to access the shuttle's electro-magnetic pulse. 'That'll crash every communications link across the orbital. Drones, shells, the lot. Ours too, but it'll buy you maybe thirty seconds.'

No one in the shuttle seemed to care that the Tesseract had disavowed us. Magenta's tac-teams reported to Himaru. Himaru was pissed about Esh. So were they.

We nosed towards the Fleet station. Officially Himaru was there to conduct a supervised search and ask a pile of awkward questions about the signal we'd traced here. Laura had arranged an interview with Vishakh before Morgan had squashed the raid and summoned us back, and no one could think of a good reason to pass that particular message on. Superficially it was obviously pointless – we hadn't given them much notice but we'd given enough that our search wouldn't find anything. While the tac-teams did their work, Bix would have Vishakh for a short and pointless interview. Vishakh would stonewall, we'd get nothing, wrap it up, Bix would leave ...

And then the real fun started. The drone Laura had sent to New Hope carried a duplicate of Kagame's data-safe. I'd let Vishakh see I had it and trick him into using the key. The fake safe, loaded with hackware, would grab his key and crash his Servant. Himaru would pull all the strings he had and go over the Tesseract's head. The Magentan government would issue a warrant for Vishakh's arrest. The tac-teams would move in. We'd leave with Vishakh and the key and go home happy.

It was a plan with more flaws than I could count, the biggest being that Vishakh probably wasn't going to fall for it. If he did then we could all cross our fingers that Fleet didn't start shooting. Even if we got Vishakh off the station, most likely we'd take him to the Tesseract for a couple of weeks of nothing before we had to let him go again. But I didn't mind. It would be worth it for those five minutes of the two of us alone.

Bix refused to wear an armoured suit. He was in his kaftan when we docked, adjusted with magnetic thread so it didn't swirl like a sail in zero gravity. I swear he fixed it up himself and smuggled it in on purpose. Our airlocks mated and equalised pressure. He propelled himself into the Fleet station at the head of his dozen storm troopers.

Agent Rangesh of the Magenta Investigation Bureau deputising for Agent Laura Patterson. Fleet Captain Darius Vishakh is requested for interview. He pinged me a copy of his Servant's exchange with the station: Tactical team to search for a transmission source associated with criminal activity on the surface.

A moment's pause, then: Welcome, Agent Rangesh. You and your team are expected. Please proceed as directed.

We were about as welcome as head lice, but Fleet would play the game as long as we played it too.

An iris-valve door opened, inviting Bix in. He drifted through. I followed right behind. A posse of Fleet marines waited on the other side, armed and on edge. We drifted in their wake through blank corridors of featureless white plastic and more iris-valve doors to the station's central core. According to Fleet the station staff counted a little over a hundred. If that was true then the station was three times bigger than it needed to be. I wondered what the real number was.

A man waited for us at a six-way intersection, floating in the middle of it and wearing a Fleet jumpsuit. I studied him. I'd seen him enough times in Alysha's recordings, although in the flesh he looked taller and thinner than I expected. His hair was cropped almost to nothing and he had obvious implants in both temples – data-ports, maybe, or a socket for a brainweb. He didn't look like he'd taken transgravity treatments or spent much time on the surface. If anything he looked frail and fragile, even for an Earther. Which was odd because I knew he'd spent a lot of time on the surface six years ago: he was the man from Alysha's recordings, no doubt about it, the man I'd seen with Koller under the Monument.

His Servant identified him as Darius Vishakh. So why had Jacksmith said that that wasn't him when I'd shown her his picture? And why had Koller recognised his face this morning, but not as Vishakh?

His eyes got me. They had the wide staring madness of a true believer. A true believer in what, though?

'Agent Rause.' He didn't even look at Bix. 'I was expecting you days ago.'

'I'm only here to observe,' I said.

The marines led our tac-team on their pointless search. Vishakh launched himself along one of the corridors into a zero gravity conference room. We followed him inside and drifted in mid-air with two Fleet lawyers, all of us trying not to accidentally collide while Bix went through the questions Laura had prepared. We showed him Koller and Vishakh claimed not to have the first idea who he was. Same with the shells of Shiva, with Zinadine Kagame and Jared Black. He knew the three Fleet men who'd died in Mercy, he said, and then asked what progress we were making towards catching their killer.

I wanted to punch him. He didn't even try not to sound smug.

Bix asked if he'd sanctioned the executions of Jared Black, Zinadine Kagame and Agent Esharaq Zohreya. He asked in the flat monotone of someone who knew he was wasting his time. Vishakh's words were practised denials, terse but polite. Ten minutes after we started he'd failed to answer a single question with anything other than bland ignorance. Bix thanked him and headed out. The lawyers followed. Vishakh didn't move and nor did I.

I watched him manoeuvre in the zero gravity with practised ease. His body wore the atrophy of someone who'd spent years in orbit, but I knew that wasn't true.

It hit me then. This Vishakh was another shell. Superbly built and good enough to fool even me. The real Vishakh might be riding it or he might not. I figured he probably was because why not? But I couldn't be sure. I realised then that the real Darius Vishakh could be anywhere. He could be anyone. He might not even exist.

'Well, Agent Rause?' he said. 'Is there something I can do for you?'

'You can shut the door.'

The door closed. Good enough. I drew my Reeper and let him see it and then set it to safe and put it away. He didn't flinch.

'Really?' he said.

'I know this is a shell. And I know that's not your real face.' The shell shrugged.

'How do I even know you're who your Servant says you are?' Another shrug. 'You don't.'

For all I knew, the real Darius Vishakh had died years ago. For all I knew, he was several people at once all hiding under the same name.

'I want you to tell me about how my wife died,' I said.

Half a smile drifted across Vishakh's face. He didn't seem surprised.

'In a bomb attack, wasn't it?'

'She was playing you.'

'I don't know what you think I can tell you. The man who killed her was tried, found guilty, sentenced, and now he's dead. You know all that. You know what she did and you know why she ran.'

'Loki was the gun. I want to know who pointed him at Alysha and pulled his trigger.'

'What, exactly, do you think I can tell you?'

'You can tell me why you killed him.'

From the way Vishakh took that, I reckoned I was on the mark.

'Yeah. You were on Colony 478 when Loki died.'

'I have no idea what you're talking about.' The shell stifled a yawn. 'What are you trying to prove by coming up here? You know you're not getting off this station unless I let you.'

'I'm not trying to prove anything.'

I drifted around behind Vishakh to face the door and un-holstered my Reeper.

'If that door opens, I shoot whoever comes in.'

'Really?' He laughed at me and shook his head. 'Fine. So let's cut to it, shall we? Well played this morning. Clap clap.

Fleet have quite some explaining to do. But you've got nothing you can make stick and we both know it. We'll send our condolences for the agents you lost and remind you that we lost some too. We'll co-operate with your investigation while we both know it's going to get nowhere. Believe what you like about the baseless accusations of a dead spy or the murder of a convicted terrorist, but even if anyone here *did* have something to do with Alysha Rause's death, you're never going to prove it. You know that. So go home. Move on. We're done.'

I didn't move.

Vishakh kept his hands carefully where I could see them and drifted away across the room.

'You're still here.'

'I want the key to the data crypt Zinadine Kagame brought to Magenta.'

'I have no idea what you're talking about.'

'You want it opened as much as I do.'

'I doubt that.'

'If all you wanted was to shut Kagame up and wipe his list then why the charade at Mercy? You want to know what he knew.'

It was a good shell, well linked to the real Darius Vishakh – wherever he was – *if* it was Vishakh riding it all. Good enough to mimic the flicker in his expression that betrayed him. I took the data-safe out of my pocket and let it float between us.

'You know what I want more than anything?' I said. 'I want to prove that my wife wasn't a traitor. So how about you open that safe and we look at what's inside and find out. You and me together.'

Vishakh laughed. He didn't stop looking at the safe, though.

'How about I just take that off your hands? And maybe let you go?'

'What were you and Alysha doing with Rachael Cho six years ago?'

337

That made him frown. 'I don't—'

'Event Horizon.' Time to take a chance. 'Scratch that. I already know the answers. I know about you, Steadman, Nohr and Kettler. I know about Iosefa. I know about Steadman's pulsar data and what he was looking for.'

A flicker at the corner of his eye. Somewhere I'd scored a hit.

'Again, I have no idea what you're talking about.'

Liar. Alysha had been with Vishakh, trying to help him remember something. Something, if I'd put the pieces together right, that had eventually told him where to find the wreck that was about to be excavated from the Magentan Antarctic ice.

'What were you trying to remember, Darius? Why did you need Alysha's help?'

'Look me in the eye, Rause, and tell me that's Kagame's data.'

I looked him in the eye. The master of puppets behind Esh's killer. Maybe Alysha's too. 'It's Kagame's list. I stole it.'

He looked at me long and hard and then shrugged. 'OK, then. Let's see, shall we?'

A warning flashed in my Servant as Vishakh activated the data-safe and triggered the Tesseract intrusionware that Laura had piggybacked inside. Q-code cascaded into his shell and the Servant running it. The shell jerked. It flinched towards a desk console and then stopped. There wasn't much either of us could do except wait for the q-code battle to play out. Data streamed to my Servant and I streamed it to Bix. I had no idea what it was.

It lasted a few seconds before the Tesseract code died. Vishakh cocked his head.

'Is that the best you can do?' he asked.

I looked at what I'd got. The Tesseract's q-code had beelined straight into the heart of Vishakh's encrypted defences, looking for Kagame's key. It had retrieved something, but I had no idea whether any of it was what I was looking for.

'You tried your best, Agent Rause. There's no shame in that. I look forward to your co-operation in the hunt for whoever killed my men in Mercy.' He drifted a little closer.

Bix?

Dude! We just lost all our links off this station!

Execute the arrest.

Yeah, OK, but—

Execute the arrest! Abort the search, find a link, get that key to Laura and let's get out of here.

I looked at Vishakh again, sizing him up, trying to work out what game he was playing. Laura's attackware had actually worked? We'd taken the key off him? Just like that? But he was too calm. Or was that the point? Was that why he was talking through a shell?

'I'm done,' I said, 'And so are you.'

He smiled, and this time it was all teeth and venom.

'You're right about Loki. Tell you what – I'll do you a trade. I'll show you mine if you show me yours.'

I couldn't let myself believe that. 'What do you want?' Couldn't trust anything about him.

'Iosefa.'

Shit. All I knew was the name.

'What do I get?'

'Loki's accomplice.'

I took another punt. 'I know all about Iosefa,' I said. 'I know you're going after him.' Whoever the fuck he was.

Vishakh didn't say anything.

'Your shell's micro-expressions are very good,' I told him. 'They keep giving you away.'

A siren sounded. I saw his face change. I had no way to know what was coming through his Servant, but I figured the siren meant Bix and his tac-teams had taken matters into their own hands and issued the order for his arrest.

'Your turn.'

Vishakh broke into a smile. He shook his head.

'I don't think so, Rause. I don't think you have the first idea what Iosefa is. You don't get to play me twice. You don't get to even try.'

'I'm taking you back,' I told him. 'I've got one of your agents in custody. He named you. Darius Vishakh, I'm arresting you as an accessory to the murders of Jared Black, Zinadine Kagame, Tomasz Shenski and Esharaq Zohreya. You have the right to—'

He tried to laugh that off but his shell couldn't hide the tension of the man behind it. 'You have no jurisdiction here.'

'The Magentan government begs to disagree,' I said.

He went for something in the pocket of his jumpsuit and so I shot him in the chest. He was only a shell, but it felt good.

'How did you know where to look for the wreck?' I asked. 'Is it really the way Cho says? Did the Masters tell you?'

The shell looked at me then with weird wild eyes.

'Yes,' he said. 'They did.'

He went for the gun in his pocket. I fired three shots into his throat and watched as the shell collapsed.

22

FEEL THE BURN

The real Vishakh could have been anywhere. For all I knew, he was on the surface of Magenta already, laughing at us.

The door opened. Another Shiva Lee stared at me, floating weightless, and then went for the needler on her belt. Half of me stared back in disbelief at a face I'd seen disintegrate less than twelve hours ago on Magenta. The other half kicked hard, springing to the ceiling. I brought my Reeper to bear and triggered the code for the shuttle's electromagnetic pulse. The shell spasmed and fired an erratic burst at the floor. I put six rounds into her throat, face and chest. The recoil sent me spinning and crashing into a wall. The shell jerked and twisted. A spray of needles narrowly missed sawing me in half. I fumbled a thermal smoke grenade and launched myself out of the room. A thick grey cloud billowed behind me.

Rangesh?

The lights went out. A dull red glow sprang from the floor and ceiling in a sequence of bright arrows. Sirens sounded and the doors along the passage all opened at once. A message seared across my lenses, hammered through my Servant by the station: Decompression alert! Proceed to the nearest emergency evacuation point. The arrows were trying to guide me away.

My Servant pinged as its links recovered from the pulse and flashed back into life:

Dude! What the fuck?

Rangesh! Where are you?

Docking cluster. There's, like, another ship out here. It's totally big and it's sending a shuttle.

I bounced and kicked along the corridor, following the arrows, skimming the ceiling, tossing thermal smoke grenades ahead and behind me. A spray of needles fizzed from the smoke, peppering the walls at chest height. Shiva was coming and I couldn't see a damned thing.

Rangesh! Shut that jammer down and stop that shuttle!

On it.

The arrows led me to a corridor lined with emergency evacuation suits. I saw stars through the window of an emergency airlock. I snatched a suit and pushed myself along as fast as I could. I pulled at more as I passed, leaving them to float in my wake.

Got it! Key's gone, man! You did it!

The Shiva shell flew out of the smoke behind me, needler firing and tearing shreds out of the suits I'd scattered to drift behind me.

Underneath the adrenaline, something about this felt wrong.

My Servant accessed the airlock and opened the inner door. I launched myself into a spiral. Something sharp and vicious tore my leg. A line of white heat scored my back. I reached the airlock and dived inside and pulled the cycle lever. The door slammed shut. A spray of needles clicked off the armoured glass. My evacuation suit sprang to life, wrapping itself around me. My ears popped as the pressure dropped. The suit constricted, binding against my skin. My eyes burned. I couldn't breathe ...

The helmet locked over my head and sealed to the suit. My ears popped back. I felt a shifting against my skin, a pressure between my toes, my fingers. A hardening pressing against the backs of my elbows and knees, forcing them straighter as the suit compensated for the dropping pressure outside. I felt an uncomfortable squeeze between my legs as self-regulating microfoam crushed against me, moulding tight. Men had it worse, Esh once said. Now I knew what she meant.

The last air drained away. The outer door slid open. A pile of warnings lit up in my Servant. Droplets of blood floated around me. My back felt as though someone had set fire to it and my leg throbbed. I could see at least one neat needle-puncture in my suit. There were probably more.

The Shiva shell stared through the armoured glass of the inner door. I shot out the airlock controls. If I hadn't fancied my chances against a shell on the inside of the station, I certainly didn't fancy them in open space.

A pair of backpacks hung against one side of the airlock, each with a cluster of semi-rigid thruster hoses and a six-hour supply of oxygen. I ignored my Servant alarms and backed into one. The suit and the pack found each other, mated and locked together. The hoses snaked down my arms and legs, settling into position against my gloves and boots.

The shell slapped a breaching charge against the airlock door.

I muttered a silent apology to Rangesh and fired the shuttle's electromagnetic pulse again.

Nothing.

Shit.

The shell stepped back. I wrenched the second thruster pack free and kicked myself into space, caught the lip of the airlock door and swung myself out of the way as the charge detonated. A storm of fragments flew through the airlock in a white

343

wind of crystallised ice and gas. The Shiva shell tumbled out as the station vented to space, head over heels, trying to bring its needler to bear. I jetted into it, shoved the second thruster pack against it and then pushed away as the pack came to life and tried to attach itself. Before it had time to finish I fired into it. The thruster cylinders ruptured. Gas sprayed everywhere, throwing us apart, kicking us both into empty space in wild spinning arcs. My Servant wrestled with the interface to my own backpack, venting short bursts until I stopped spinning.

The Shiva shell froze. I watched it go, tumbling away into emptiness.

I was drifting a hundred miles up in an airless, weightless void. The wheel of the Fleet station looked small and far away. A colossal silence filled me. I was breathing too quickly, using up air at twice the rate of a practised spaceman. I'd been in zero gravity dozens of times in trips to orbit and back – but this ...

I was going to fall. For ever.

'Boss dude?'

Bix's voice in my ear was like nectar. The comfort of something I knew.

'Rangesh?'

'OK, man. It's like ... The incoming shuttle just mated to the docking cluster. I don't know who's on it, man, but I'll—'

'Rangesh!'

A dozen warnings were flashing in my Servant. I was leaking air. I was adrift in space. My suit had half a dozen punctures. Inside it I was bleeding.

'Dude?'

Deep breaths. One thing at a time. The emergency suit was tight to my skin. I wasn't leaking air from inside, only from the pack. My Servant was talking to the thrusters. I could move if I wanted to. I could get back to the station. There were a dozen sticky repair patches bonded to the chest and thighs of the suit. The punctures weren't so bad …

I started to laugh. Maybe that was the only way not to scream.

'Uh … Dude? What are you doing?'

I tore off a repair patch and sealed the first puncture. Then the next, and then the next. Slow and careful without thinking about anything else. Without looking at where I was or where I was going or how far it seemed to anywhere safe. Without listening to the pounding of my heartbeat or the churning in my stomach.

'Wishing Esh was here,' I said. 'Because she'd have aced this.'

The Shiva shell was a flickering speck growing slowly dimmer in the distance. One star among a million. Behind me the Fleet station turned, round and round. Below was Magenta, a colossal purple-tinged white.

Above, only a few hundred yards away, was another ship. It passed overhead, pulling away in a higher orbit. Painted on its belly was a symbol like an infinity sign enclosed by a star. If Esh had seen it, she might have reckoned it was a Fleet corvette.

The ship Chantale Pré had seen docked to the *Fearless*.

A heartbeat of silence, then: 'Yeah,' said Bix. 'She would.'

'The shuttle came from that?'

'Yeah. I think Vishakh's aboard. They're already prepping to leave again. It's locked down and refusing hails.'

'Stop him!'

'Out of my hands, man. You got to talk to Himaru. Fleet are yelling murder. You know, with the station half venting into space and stuff.'

'Can we catch him if he goes?'

A pause. 'No.'

'The data I sent—'

'Went planetside before the comms went down, man. Good work, dude.'

'Tell them—'

I could tell them myself. I pinged Laura and messaged the two Kutosov interceptors that Himaru had set to lurk in a higher orbit. I told them to move in.

Keon? Laura. What the fuck have you done? The Tesseract just went mental. Again.

I'm in orbit. I … I patched a link so she could see through my eyes. One of those times a picture was worth a thousand words. There's a shuttle about to—

The Tesseract issued an order for your arrest. You and Rangesh. There's a—

The decryption key in the data you sent—

Another ship up here—

It's wrapped in some sort of launcher, but—

The key was wrapped in something?

Then don't launch it! Laura, I think he played me.

Who played you?

Vishakh.

The Tesseract says—

I don't care what the damned AI says! Just wait until—

It's out of my fucking hands, Keon! Rangesh sent it everywhere!

It had been too easy. Vishakh had known I was coming hours before we'd arrived. He'd given me exactly what I wanted.

Tell Morgan to wait!

Fuck, Keon. Fine, I'll try, but fuck this and fuck you.

Laura cut the link. I pulled orbital schematics and an outline of the Fleet station. None of it made much sense, but that was what Servants were for. I could see the docking cluster and our shuttle. There were other shuttles too. Most were dark, but cabin lights flickered on in the nearest, visible through the cockpit windows.

The shuttle wasn't Fleet. It had the same symbol painted on its side as the corvette.

I pinged Himaru: I need you to stop that shuttle. Vishakh is on it.

Deep breaths. Slow and steady. So many stars. So much size. Magenta, white and purple and vast, spiralling around me as I tumbled ...

Two bright dots passed by. The Kutosov interceptors. They were so old that Vishakh's shuttle could probably outrun them. But they had missiles. Vishakh was a sitting duck.

They flew past.

I'm not authorising lethal force, Rause. The reply from Himaru flashed across my eyes.

Then track him! Don't let him get away!

I accessed the thruster pack and had my Servant target Vishakh's shuttle. It lit up in my lenses as I locked to its transponder. I told the pack to get me there as fast as it could. The suit responded with a firm gentle pressure, guiding my limbs, bending my knees and elbows, pointing the thruster nozzles to stop my spinning and take me back.

'Boss dude?'

The thrusters fired, gently at first, easing tiny corrections from my wrists and ankles. Magenta stabilised beneath me. I turned slowly until the wheel of the Fleet station was dead ahead.

'What?'

'You OK?'

I let my arms and legs almost fall straight.

'Why?'

'I got you on screen. Is that, like, spaceman yoga or something?'

My jets kicked hard as the refuelling arm disengaged from Vishakh's shuttle, each with a brief puff of white. Hydrogen crystals. The shuttle thrusters flared. The docking umbilicals disengaged. The shuttle started to move, inching out of its cradle. I wondered if they'd seen me, or if the shuttle Servant had noticed me pinging its transponder. I muted my own, too late.

'Is that shuttle armed?' I couldn't see anything obvious.

'Internal missile bay, dude. Not that they can use that on you. But, uh, you don't want to be in the way when he fires his rockets, dude.'

Rause? What are you doing? Himaru.

'The shuttle we came in. What about that?'

What needs to be done.

'Sure. Couple of Gatling guns and six long-range missiles.'

MagentaNet can track Vishakh in orbit or if he goes for the surface. The Kutosovs can follow if he breaks for deep space. He's not going to get away.

'So we could shoot him?' What's MagentaNet's polar coverage?

'We totally could, but we're not going to.'

Patchy. But there's nowhere there for him to go.

I was closing on the shuttle. It was clear of its cradle and starting to turn as it drifted back and away from the station.

Yes there is.

'Dude!' Bix sounded urgent. 'They're, like, lining up for a hard burn, you know? Get out of the way, man! Let it go!'

The shuttle was turning the open empty holes of its engine exhausts towards me. Vishakh knew I was coming. I could see other figures around it, spacemen in emergency suits evacuating from the station. But Vishakh didn't care. He was going to incinerate me.

Morgan just authorised Flemich to open Kagame's safe. Laura.

No!

Too late, Keon.

Shit. So we were going to find out the hard way if Vishakh had played me.

'Dude!'

'Can you cripple them or something?'

'No, man!'

Rause! Back off!

My Servant pinged an alert. It had scanned the unencrypted data I'd stolen from Vishakh's shell along with the key to the data-safe. Files on the trans-polar expedition. All of it. Dossiers on expedition members. Satellite footage of the site, updated daily. Every report the Institute had made public. All open source, but the satellite maps had notes highlighting the prefab huts around the site, all the machinery, the air vents, every way in and out.

No surprise. I'd been hoping for more.

'Dude! You're going to die!'

Rause! Back. Off!

I pushed my arms ahead of me, overrode the backpack's Servant and fired both hand thrusters as hard as they would go. The kick shot through me. I started to spin. I fired again, trying to angle myself into a trajectory away from Vishakh's engines. Maybe I did, but now I was spinning in fast circles, too disorientated to see where I was heading. Never override the thruster controls. Lesson number two, right after never override the safety protocols.

Shit.

'Boss dude!'

'Stop him!'

'Get out of the way, man!'

Rause! My men are NOT authorised to fire! Let him go!

My Servant took over. I felt a pressure on my arm and then a jerk. I stopped spinning almost at once. I told it to vector away from the trajectory of the shuttle engine burn. Himaru was right. I wasn't going to catch him. I had to let it go.

Flemich opened Kagame's safe. Laura again. The key worked! We've got names!

Vishakh's shuttle thrusters flared again. Stopping its slow spin. He was about ten seconds from a main engine burn. He was going to get away.

Jacksmith. Is Jacksmith on it?

If she wasn't then that was the proof that Vishakh had spoofed us. Because I got it now. They were both after the same thing. Something inside that wreck that no one else knew was there. Something they'd discovered twenty-six years ago in some dark corner of the *Fearless*.

I still had my Reeper. A Reeper worked just fine in a vacuum.

I aimed at Vishakh's shuttle and ...

Empty. I'd used everything I had on the Shiva shell.

I switched to the two sticky rocket-propelled tracker darts under the barrel, the sort we fired into pods to follow them. I lined up and shot them both. The shuttle was out of range but they were all I had. We were in space. Maybe they'd get there, maybe not. If they did, they only had a range of a few miles.

Yes. She is.

The trackers didn't matter. I knew exactly where Vishakh was heading.

I watched, floating away into the nothing, as the shuttle's main engines lit up and everything dissolved into brilliance.

IOSEFA

The Cheetah streaks through the Magentan stratosphere, cross-ing half a world in a quarter of a day, from New Hope on the edge of Firstfall to the deep frigid cold of the southern pole. Its rotors tilt and it eases with tentative care into a pit of snow pounded flat and cut deep into the ice. The polar storms, when they come, are viciously destructive. Winds of more than two hundred miles an hour drive chunks and daggers of ice the size of golf balls and knives. The lightly armoured Cheetahs cannot survive – hence the pit and an inflatable synthetic cover and the warren of tunnels carved around it. If a storm comes then the Cheetah will be buried but it will still fly. The tunnels shelter the drones and technicians who will dig it free. They are the only shelter in a world where the very air can freeze at night.

For now, though, the weather is bright. Magenta's blue-tinged sun glares in a vivid bright sky. Even so, the temperature is low enough to freeze the carbon dioxide in Kamaljit Kaur's breath.

The Cheetah settles. Its doors open. A small posse of scientists and technicians already waits to receive them. The air in the pit is kept warm by solar heaters and the waste heat of the tunnels, meticulously monitored to stay below the freezing point of the ice. No one pays attention to Kaur, the young meteorologist whose experiments and recording stations have nothing to do with the grand excavation of whatever lies under the ice. She catches a few phrases as she lingers, pretending attention to the unloaded cargo crates.

'... broken through ...'

'... possibility of working devices!'

'... evidence of Masters' technology ...'

'... media blackout ...'

The last catches Kaur's attention. Her Servant checks the local bulletin board. The news is mostly inane, devoid of detail as to the progress of the excavation and its discoveries. Routine security checks have been introduced after rumours that a journalist has reached the site. The rumours are not true, Kaur is sure of this, but the checks are real.

She walks into the tunnels with a drone wheeling her crate. A room has been set aside for her, little more than a nook carved into the ice tunnels and lined with insulation foam. She busies herself by becoming familiar with her new home. Memorising its layout as far as the security shells will permit. There are places a meteorologist cannot go.

The real Kamaljit Kaur woke hours ago in a locked abandoned hole deep in the warrens of Firstfall. She has no Servant. She has food and water for ten days and then she will slowly starve, but the door will unlock before then. She has a note with her, handwritten, telling her these things. Unpleasant and terrifying, but she will live. A necessary evil. The best that can be done. Better than murder. So she tells herself.

Inside the crate containing Kaur's experiments is an environment suit. She is permitted outside to set her recording devices and so she asks for clearance to reconnoitre the surface and look for suitable sites. Permission granted, she seals her suit. She makes her way to the nearest exit and climbs into the crunch of wind-carved snow. The ice is as hard as stone. Its jagged ridges are merciless.

She walks to the place where the first trans-polar expedition made its discovery: the shape under the ice. It's true that you can see it, a darkness under the translucent surface. At one end is a pit, heat-lanced out of the snow to expose the surface of whatever lies beneath – black and smooth. Kaur already knows that the Magentan scientists have used every tool at their disposal to try and cut through and have failed. Whatever material this is, it was not fashioned on any human world. This ship is a Masters' ship. It is *their* technology.

What matters is not the ship itself. What matters is what is inside.

'Hello, Iosefa,' she says.

EIGHT

ALYSHA

23

THE WAVEDOME

My Servant limped me back to the chaos around the Fleet station. Dozens of Fleet staff floated outside the hub in emergency suits. The Shiva shell blowing out an airlock had changed what had been a false alarm to cover Vishakh's escape into a real evacuation and our shuttle had become an impromptu lifeboat. We could have chased Vishakh, but this was where Colonel Himaru drew the line. I watched Vishakh's shuttle flare away and the two pinpricks of light that were the Kutosov interceptors burn after it. That was how the code of space worked. Sides didn't matter when it came to people adrift in a vacuum.

Esh's killer, taking the last of Alysha's secrets. I told myself it didn't matter, but it did. For a moment I'd almost had him.

The tac-team medic patched me up. I was going to have a nice scar across my back and one of Shiva's needles had punched through my calf; but they were flesh wounds that would heal easily enough. Bix fussed, trying to speed things along, until I sat him down and told him what we were going to do. After that it was just waiting. I sat strapped to a couch and looked at the data Laura had sent up. The sliver Kagame had brought from Earth to Magenta. The reason Jared Black, Vic Friedrich, Kagame, Shenski and Esh had all died.

Fleet Intelligence: Assets on Magenta.

Seventeen names looked back. Jacksmith topped the list. Nohr, Kettler, Becker and Steadman were next, and all dead. So were two former government staff. That left ten. Three were government staffers, mid-level civil service bureaucrats. Three were in the media: one channel manager and two news editors, all at the peak of their careers. Then came Selected Representative Siamake Alash, who'd come close to being the most powerful man on Magenta while I'd been away on Earth and who had a history of dubious relations with Fleet. There was Eddie Thiekis, the man who ran MagentaNet, who all but owned the entire Magentan satellite broadcast system and had already proved once that he could shut it down. That one hurt. Eddie had seemed decent. Now? I didn't know. I wasn't sure that I knew anything any more.

Alysha Rause.

I knew she'd be there. She had to be. I still didn't believe it.

The last name stared back at me hardest of all.

Tesseract One.

Vishakh's mole inside the bureau. Turned out Kagame hadn't known who it was.

I watched the feed from the interceptors as they followed Vishakh's shuttle. They were losing him. It was an attrition game that would take hours to play out, but it ended with Vishakh's shuttle in a polar orbit and the interceptors too low on fuel to keep up the pursuit. After that we'd rely on surface radar and imaging surveillance from high orbit. Vishakh would know exactly where to find the holes in both.

It still didn't matter. I still knew where he was going.

I pinged Laura and Bix: We need to talk. In private.

Then Himaru. For all I knew, the Tesseract had put him under arrest pending court martial by now, but I needed someone else I could trust. Someone who'd make sure Esh hadn't died for nothing. I needed him to do one more thing for me.

'He's going to get away,' Himaru said. It wasn't a question.

'Yes.'

I should have felt beaten but I didn't. Maybe it was the aftermath of simply surviving, but I felt almost ... free. Almost happy.

Almost. Something still felt off. Duping Vishakh had been too easy. Or was it simply that I wanted it to be that way because Alysha was on Kagame's list? Because I didn't want it to be true?

'I know where he's going,' I told him. 'I need a Cheetah fuelled and ready to go as soon as we get to New Hope.'

'I see.'

'And a tac-team.'

'Why not make it two?' Yeah. A slight sarcastic edge there.

'And I need you to keep the bureau away from me. I need you to shut them out.'

I didn't want anyone else knowing what I was doing. Kagame's list was, as Laura would probably put it, orbital shit-rain. Bottom line, none of us knew who we could trust any more.

'You don't ask for much.'

'You want a crack at Esh's killer? I can put him in your sights. On Magenta.'

A pause. Then: 'OK.'

'I owe you.'

'No you don't. But, Rause?'

'What?'

'Give me that fucker's corpse this time.'

'I'll do you one better,' I said. 'I'll get him in front of a Magentan court and bury him.'

Himaru grunted. 'I prefer my way. But OK.'

I left him to it and made a quiet pact with myself. If I managed to keep the promise I'd just made, I'd do whatever it took to see that Vishakh stayed on Magenta. Not Colony 478. Not where Fleet could spirit him away.

Then I fell asleep. It had been a long, long day.

Vishakh vanished somewhere over the south pole by the time Fleet gave us the all-clear to leave. The Kutosovs searching for him gave up before we landed at New Hope. I woke up and Himaru brought me up to speed on what little else there was to know. The burn from Vishakh's rockets had killed two evacuees. Fleet wanted him hanged, drawn and quartered; they also wanted me and Himaru extradited, probably so they could do much the same. At best the next few months were going to be made of paperwork, interviews, investigations and depositions.

'Tedious as shit.' Himaru laughed as he said it but he couldn't hide the bitterness underneath.

Vishakh had burned his bridges. We'd flushed him into the open. We'd cracked Kagame's list. We'd all but won, hadn't we? We weren't done, not yet, but what was left was mopping up the mess, right?

So what was the squirming in my gut?

I tried looking for the ship I'd seen passing over the Fleet station. The UNSS *Flying Daggers*. One of six ships built by Earth for long-term operations in space. Ambassador ships, the United Nations called them. What was a United Nations ship doing in Magenta? Why was it marked with the sign of a cabal of powerful Earthers obsessed with the return of the Masters? Why had they sent a shuttle to pull Vishakh out?

A message pinged into my Servant as we touched down in New Hope. Flemich ordering me and Bix to the Tesseract for a debriefing, and so he could arrest us for what we'd done in the morning and never mind cracking open a Fleet orbital. I ignored him, turned off my Servant and went with Bix and Himaru to the MSDF hangers where the tac-teams kept their Cheetahs. We were going to get Vishakh. We were going to make sure of it.

The Cheetahs were all gone. The last two had left while we were coming down from orbit, requisitioned by the Tesseract and packed with a dozen bureau agents. They were heading for Jacksmith's excavation. They'd figured, like I had, that that was where Vishakh would go. They'd gone to pick him up.

Himaru made a few calls looking for another. The nearest available was en route from Disappointment to make up the shortage but it was two hours' flight away.

Someone in the Tesseract had figured we weren't going to stop.

Someone had blocked me.

I pinged Laura: Who authorised the mission?

Morgan.

Why?

To stop Vishakh before he gets away, obviously! Keon, you can hardly blame the man for not waiting for you!

She had a point. And it didn't matter, right? Vishakh was on the surface where someone could arrest him. Didn't matter who, did it? Bix and Himaru wouldn't get to kick the shit out of him first, but so what? As long as he got what was coming to him, did it matter who got the glory? I didn't have to care about that, did I?

There was that squirm again.

Himaru clapped me on the shoulder. 'Two hours, Rause.' Short of hijacking an orbital shuttle there was nothing to do but wait. 'You could go home. Get some proper sleep. Figure out all the questions you want to ask when you have him manacled in an interview room ...'

'That what you're going to do?'

He snorted a laugh. 'No.'

'Didn't think so.'

'I want to see this ship.' He looked around the hanger. People were watching us. 'You and Rangesh should make yourselves scarce. If the Tesseract sends someone to bring you in, I don't really have a good reason to stop them.'

He didn't say it, but he had to be hanging by a thread himself after what had happened in orbit.

We left Himaru still looking for another Cheetah and took a pod from New Hope to the Wavedome. What else was I going to do? Go home and wait for someone to pick me up? Turn myself in like Flemich had said? Sit in an interrogation room for the next three days while the last act of the story played out without me? Because me sitting face to face with Vishakh, that sure as shit wasn't ever going to happen. Not after Koller.

'This sucks, dude.'

What would Alysha have done? Or Esh?

The Wavedome beach was quiet, the weather too violent to lure any but the most foolhardy onto the surface. I hired myself a wetsuit, crossed the sand and waded into the surf. Bix did the same, only he didn't bother with the suit. He picked his own spot a hundred yards further down the beach and waded out in his kaftan until the water was up to his thighs. He stood and stared out at the horizon. I knew what he was thinking. He was thinking of Esh. This had been her place.

The waves at the far edge of the dome were slabbing and breaking at almost thirty feet. I spotted six or seven surfers among them, the crazy ones. It wasn't so much the waves but that out there, beyond shelter, the wind was strong enough to pick a man off his board and hurl him into the water and the rain was a hail of knives. There were no drones today. Anything smaller than a Cheetah was helpless in all that wind. There was nothing to pull people out of the sea and rush them to Mercy, nothing to resuscitate them. The surfers were on their own. Just them against the elements.

Kind of how I felt.

The wind tore the breath from my mouth. The rain hammered the dome overhead. There were no drones with chameleon skins and particle beams today. No drones with microphones to eavesdrop. No drones or shells at all.

I walked into the water until it was up to my waist and then drifted, floating in the muted rage of the storm, sucked at and pushed by the ebb and flow of the sea. I thought of Esh bringing me to meet Himaru, the first time I'd come here since Alysha's death. And of Alysha, years before, a rare still afternoon, clear sky and bright sun and the black sand burning hot underfoot, meeting her for volleyball and ice cream and just to look at her.

People like us know when something isn't right, Alysha had once said. *That's what makes us good at what we do. Chasing that feeling until it goes away.*

I knew what she meant. I had that feeling now.

The grey churning sky fractured and swirled. Shreds of cloud ripped apart and crashed together. Beyond the cloud the horizon was a ruddy glow as the sun drooped towards the sea. The crash and roar of breaking waves filled the air and the water was laced thick with foam. Somewhere not far away another Magentan storm was coming.

Liss?

It took so long for her to reply that I almost thought she wouldn't.

Keys?

I told her, terse and quick as I could, what I thought I knew: that the prize at the heart of everything that had happened on Magenta these last few weeks had something to do with Jacksmith's excavation and something inside the wreck there. That Darius Vishakh had killed Jared Black, Vic Friedrich,

Kagame, Esh, Shenski and plenty more. That we'd flushed him out and tricked him into cracking Kagame's list, a list that proved that Jacksmith was a part of it. That Alysha had been on that list as well.

Something feels off, I said.

The Alysha I remember being wasn't a traitor.

No. She wasn't. Then help me.

How?

The Alysha I remember was the best detective in the bureau.

I'm not her.

You're close enough.

She didn't answer.

I'm almost sure it was Vishakh who guided Loki.

A pause. Where did it start, Keys?

Where did what start?

This. Vishakh.

With Kagame returning to Magenta.

What was the first thing he did?

Shenski had told me: the first thing Kagame had done was send him a message. *Darius had Rause killed* ...

So?

Walk it through.

I walked it through in my head. Kagame transmits to Shenski. Vishakh intercepts the message. Kagame's got something, but Vishakh doesn't know what.

So what? He makes a play to wait until Kagame starts talking and then takes them all out at once?

But he didn't wait, Keys. He killed them before Jared Black said a word.

He'd figured out by then that Jared Black wasn't Kagame?

No. Wrong. Vishakh was a lot of things but he wasn't stupid. If he'd known Black was Black and not Kagame, why do anything at all?

He'd disintegrated Black from the neck up, Servant and all. Which meant either he didn't care about what Kagame knew, or that he knew it already.

Why not just kill Black with the bomb?

What had he actually achieved doing it the way he had? He'd killed three Fleet men. Maybe one of them had known something Vishakh had wanted squashed?

If they had, I'd never know.

He'd certainly kicked over a nest of hornets inside the bureau. Couldn't have drawn more attention to the case if he'd ...

If he'd tried ...

A shiver ran down my spine.

Another ... What had Bix called it? A trompe l'oeil?

What didn't he want you to see?

He'd drawn in both Fleet and the Tesseract. So what else had happened while we weren't looking? Nohr, Steadman and Kettler, that's what. Three of the four people who knew what Jacksmith's expedition was really looking for. Three unexpected deaths all dressed up as accidents. None of them an obvious murder. Strange enough that an agent with time on their hands might have made the connection, but as it was ...

We'd opened a case on Steadman because of the bullet Chase Hunt had put in his head after he died. I'd seen the pattern because of Alysha's files ...

I hadn't been the only one to see them.

Chase Hunt. Liss.

Liss, what do you know?

Only what you've told me.

Chase Hunt has to be you, Liss. There's no one else.

But it isn't.

I don't believe you.

Then walk it through, Keys. What was the first thing she did?

Shot Steadman.

With what consequences?

We'd started an investigation into Steadman's death. Everything else had led from that. Jacksmith, the weather feeds, Kettler, the K-meth, Becker. Chase Hunt had stuck a murder-sized wrench into Vishakh's distraction. And who was that good for?

Someone else wants Vishakh stopped, I said.

Who?

You.

No.

Yes!

Why?

Revenge.

Keys! Stop it!

I tried to run it through again.

Vishakh wants Kagame and whatever information he's carrying dead. He wants Steadman's cabal dead, too. He's got Becker to do his dirty work but all three of them dropping at once is bound to raise an eyebrow. So he makes a real mess when he kills Kagame. Makes everyone look the other way.

OK.

But if they're working for Jacksmith and he and Jacksmith are in this together, why does he want them dead?

I couldn't get my head around how Jacksmith had turned on them either. The exchanges between her and Steadman didn't make them sound like enemies ...

Oh.

Shit.

What if I was wrong? What if Jacksmith *wasn't* up to her neck in it with Vishakh? But then why all the half-truths? What was she hiding?

Her name was on Kagame's list. Twenty-six years ago she and Vishakh had been in the same place at the same time for five months – on the *Fearless*. That was the first connection I'd found between them. The second was Alysha. Alysha had been watching Vishakh. She knew he was looking for something. She'd told Jacksmith. Jacksmith had warned her that Vishakh was a snake.

Kettler, Nohr and Steadman were on Kagame's list beside her. Traitors? I hadn't seen anything to say so.

Alysha was on that list, too.

I tried the alternative.

Jacksmith gets wind from Alysha that Vishakh's looking for the crashed ship. She starts looking as well. She brings Nohr, Kettler and Steadman in on it. Steadman because he can work out orbits and so might know where on Magenta to look. Nohr because ... because something to do with missing colonies? Kettler because ...?

Never mind. I was missing something, something that went back further. Save that for later ...

The first trans-polar expedition finds the wreck. Steadman goes digging and finds the fake weather reports. He blames Jacksmith. Jacksmith knows better but doesn't tell him about Vishakh?

But she *had* told him about Vishakh. It was in the recordings Bix had sent.

And then?

The excavation starts. Vishakh somehow gets wind of Jacksmith's cabal ...?

The first one to die. Even before Kagame. The first one was always the one to look at with the deepest care.

I pinged Laura: Jit Nohr. She was talking to someone in Fleet a few days before she died. About pulsars. Can you find out who it was?

Nohr was the first to go. Nohr was the weak link. Somehow Nohr had led Vishakh to Steadman and Kettler. Why not Jacksmith as well? Because by the time he'd made the connection, Laura had put her under protection?

Because she was careful, clever, warned and guarded. She knew who was coming for her and she knew why. He couldn't get rid of her quietly, not like the others ...

I closed my eyes.

So how did a man like Vishakh get rid of Jacksmith when he couldn't simply kill her?

With Kagame's list, that's how.

It *had* been too easy. He *had* played me. Maybe the rest of the list was real, maybe not, maybe Vishakh didn't give a shit, but he'd played me. He'd known I was on my way. He'd known the only play I had was Kagame's safe. So he'd quietly been ready to give me exactly what I wanted and tacked on a few names of his own. That was why the key had been wrapped in a launcher.

He'd never given a shit about Kagame's sliver. The evidence was right there in that room in Mercy where Jared Black's head used to be.

I pinged Laura again: I was right. Vishakh played us. Check the launcher code. Were *any* of those names real?

If they weren't, then Alysha being on Kagame's list meant nothing ...

I wasn't a traitor, said Liss softly.

But if Jacksmith and Vishakh weren't on the same side, then ...

Could Chase Hunt be a shell?

I'd seen the video from outside Mercy. The precision of Becker's execution ...

But if Chase Hunt was a shell then there had to be a pilot, and Jacksmith had a brainweb and had racked up hundreds of hours of practice and was probably the best shell pilot on Magenta. She could fight Vishakh at his own game ...

Shit. I'd got it all wrong.

There were still holes. Like how Jacksmith knew as much as

she did, and what Kettler had to do with anything, and who Iosefa was. But it felt better. The pieces fitted more smoothly than if I put Vishakh and Jacksmith on the same side.

You've done all you could, Liss said. It's out of your hands now. Go to the Tesseract and tell them what you know.

It wasn't that easy.

I told her about the moment I'd felt Esh's heart stop beating. I told her how Esh had figured the Wavedome was the perfect place to talk without being overheard. I told her Esh's secret that I'd promised to keep while she was alive. In death she deserved to be known.

It was still you, I said.

What was?

Maybe Jacksmith is Chase Hunt but it was still you under the Monument. You saved my life from those drones.

No, Keys. Steadman, Becker and the Monument. They were all the same gun.

But I'd *seen* her. I'd seen her face and I couldn't for the life of me understand why Elizabeth Jacksmith would disguise a shell as a long-dead friend.

Where are you? Laura.

Usual place.

Meet me outside. Now.

A part of me hoped it was true, that Chase Hunt and Jacksmith were the same. Laura could dig out the truth and everyone would be happy. Liss would stay free. My little secret.

I dragged myself out of the water and headed back up the beach. I saw Bix doing the same.

Who's leading Vishakh's arrest?

Flemich.

That was something. I'd known Flemich since before graduation. He'd been a mentor to Alysha. He'd come to her memorial. I'd spoken to him there. He'd been on the edge of tears.

369

I headed to get changed, but Laura was running through the Wavedome turnstiles, waving at me and at Bix.

'Get over here!'

We ran to her. She hurried us outside.

'I checked Nohr. Two calls on the night before she died. Both to orbit. Both to Darius Vishakh. Both very short. Then one coming back the other way, a lot longer.'

'Dude, what?' Bix almost tripped over his own feet in surprise.

'Fleet told you their end of the call routing?' That was probably more co-operation than we'd had from them in a decade.

'They really don't like Darius Vishakh up there right now.'

I faltered to a stop. Parked outside the Wavedome was a Cheetah, engines running. The back ramp was open and Himaru was waving at us to get in. Behind him I saw the rest of the team we'd taken into space. Two tac-teams armed and ready for bear, just as he'd said.

Laura turned grim. 'I told you Flemich's leading Vishakh's arrest? Guess who authorised Mercy to let Shenski's men in to see Jared Black.'

'Not Flemich?'

'Ninety per cent sure. And you know he authorised Walt Becker's transfer to data forensics? You know—'

'Three days before Alysha was sabotaged.'

'Yeah.'

'You think he's Tesseract One?' No. I couldn't take that. Not Flemich.

'I don't know what I think.' Laura shrugged as we ran into the belly of the Cheetah. 'Except that it's always the ones you least expect. Call this insurance in case, eh?'

The pitch of the engine whine rose. I squeezed onto a bench, still dripping in my wetsuit. The incoming storm was gathering strength, sweeping towards Firstfall to batter the city. I looked through the windows as we rose into the air, watching the first squall front come in. Himaru was watching it too.

'We're the storm,' he murmured.

I nodded. This time we were.

24

IOSEFA

The Cheetah ran ahead of the winds until we streaked into the stratosphere to arc over the bulk of the storm. Then we headed south. I was losing track of day or night and I needed to sleep. I settled to doze, hoping I'd wake to the flat eternal light of a polar summer where the sun never sets. But I didn't. Laura shook me when we were barely twenty minutes out of Firstfall.

'We need to talk.'

She pulled me into the cockpit, a big space with four seats: two pilots, a comms officer and a specialist for whatever payload the Cheetah was carrying. I wasn't surprised to see Himaru up there. I *was* surprised to see Jacksmith in the pilot's seat.

She threw me a glance. 'You'll forgive me if I don't get up.'

'What the hell is *she* doing here?' I looked to Laura, but it was Jacksmith who answered.

'This is my Cheetah, Rause.'

Himaru grunted something disagreeable. 'Strictly this Cheetah is on loan to the—'

'Mine.' Jacksmith was wired to it, I saw. Brainweb control. Flying by thought.

'OK,' I said. 'Let's start with this – did you shoot Steadman?'

'What? I was nowhere near—'

'Vishakh killed Esh and Kagame with a remotely piloted shell. You're an adept shell pilot—'

Laura rested a hand on my arm. 'Chase Hunt isn't a shell, Keon. I've got her DNA. I know exactly—'

She jerked in surprise as Himaru hammered a fist into the panel in front of him.

'Shit! We've been rumbled.'

A message pinged into my Servant. It came direct from the Tesseract AI: Agent Keon Rause. You are required to return to Firstfall immediately pending an inquiry into your actions over the last 24 hours. Failure to do so will constitute an offence under the Magentan Security and Integrity Act of 2162. The penalty for non-compliance is immediate discharge from service and a possible prison sentence.

'You get that too?' I asked.

Laura nodded. I didn't much care. I was already suspended with all privileges revoked.

'Tell them I'm kidnapping you,' said Jacksmith.

Himaru growled and swore. 'We've got two interceptors coming out of orbit at us.'

'What are they going to do? Shoot us down?'

'They just might.'

Through the window the sky was a deep midnight blue, almost black. I could see stars even though it was day. We were high. Twenty miles above the surface on the edge of space. High enough to see the curve of Magenta below.

'Can they reach us in time?'

'Yes.'

Flemich tried to call. I blocked him. He'd just say the same. He pinged me a minute later: Rause, you're being formally charged with dereliction of duty. That means criminal proceedings. Don't make this any worse than it already is. Patterson may have your arse covered, but if you want to keep your career then you want to be very compliant right now.

Yeah. I'd be quiet too. I'd be silent. 'How long have we got?'

'Right side of an hour.'

'Long enough for Doctor Jacksmith to tell us about Iosefa, then.'

Jacksmith didn't look up. 'I don't think so.'

I plugged my Servant into the Cheetah and pushed Alysha's video on to every screen. A grainy face popped up.

Me sorry, me friends, for what me do. Us know ...

That was as far as it got before Jacksmith killed it.

'Where the hell did you get that? Vishakh?'

I sent copies to Laura, Himaru and Bix and patched Bix into the feed from my Servant.

'Not Vishakh. Alysha. Steadman had a few seconds of it in his archives, too.'

'Nicholas?' Jacksmith almost exploded. 'The stupid shit!'

I set the video playing again. This time Jacksmith didn't stop it until almost the very end.

Me sorry me family. Me goes Magenta ...

'I was thirty-three when I met Darius Vishakh,' Jacksmith said. 'I'd just lost my partner and my mobility. The Institute offered me a brainweb. They said it would let me pilot shells. They didn't tell me about the six months of crippling pain. I tried to kill myself twice. Sanja-Mao was three years old. I barely knew her.'

She turned her chair to face us. 'When it was done they sent me to the *Fearless*. On paper I was researching the Masters, but the reality was a sabbatical. Several months away from everything. Fleet partnered me with a young officer whose experiences they

374

thought might mirror my own. I think they honestly meant well.' A wry smile. 'His name was Darius Vishakh.

'That video was in a dusty archive of trophies and relics from the first days after the Masters left.' She nodded to the screen, to the grainy face frozen there. 'Iosefa Lomu. Iosefa was one of the original settlers brought to Magenta. When the Masters left he joined the crew of the *Fearless*. A year later he stole one of the ships the Masters had used to travel to and from the surface. Not one of the ships they left for us, the ones built out of our technology of the time, but one of *theirs*. Story goes that the shuttles we knew how to fly were kept under tight security but no one bothered with this one because no one knew how it worked. So he just walked in and took it and was never seen again.' Another wry smile. 'The *Fearless* crew I met thought he was a myth but that video says otherwise. Do you understand what that means?'

I shook my head. Himaru shrugged. Even Laura looked blank.

Dude! That's ... Like ... No way! NO WAY!

'The Masters left behind exactly five ships like the one Iosefa Lomu supposedly stole. Believe all the stories and those ships can fly for ever, teleport, disappear and reappear at will, and disintegrate worlds. I'm not sure I *do* believe all those stories and nor should you. But this much is true – in the hundred and fifty years since the Masters left, Fleet haven't managed to get any of those ships to so much as turn on a light. It's almost certain that the wreck we're excavating is the ship Iosefa Lomu stole, but it's not the ship itself that matters, do you see? Even though it's priceless, we'll likely never get it lifted out of the ice. It's too big. What matters is Lomu. What matters is how he did it.'

It fell into place. Kettler's genealogy project.

'You had Kettler looking for his family!'

375

Jacksmith shot me a thin-edged smile. 'We were looking for his descendants. Anyone who might carry his DNA.' She sighed. 'Back on the *Fearless*, all I knew was that I'd found something special. I sat on it for a couple of days and then made the worst mistake of my life – I showed it to Darius. He understood at once that if the video was real then so was Iosefa. Which meant that a human had once interfaced to a piece of Masters' technology and made it work. And that, my friends, then and now, is the holy fucking grail.

'Vishakh confiscated the video on the spot. He told me it was meaningless, then that it was a prank, then that it was a fake. Next he threatened me with expulsion and arrest. When that still didn't work, he threatened Sanja. He didn't just say words when he did that, either. He rode a shell to the surface and showed me exactly how close he could get. I left the *Fearless* on the understanding that Iosefa's recording didn't exist, had never existed, and if I ever said otherwise then very bad things would happen to both me and Sanja.'

A message pinged into my Servant from the Tesseract: You are in violation of Executive Order 417. You are not authorised for Magentan airspace. Return to Firstfall or be fired on.

Jacksmith frowned fiercely. 'Are they serious?'

I checked. I'm sure Laura was doing the same. Executive Order 417 had been passed by an emergency vote of the Selected Assembly ten minutes ago at the request of Chief Director Morgan. All access to Magentan airspace was now restricted unless explicitly authorised.

Ten fucking minutes ago?

'What is this?' Himaru sounded like he didn't believe it.

'Because of us?'

Laura shook her head. 'Not *just* us.'

Tesseract One. Vishakh letting the cat into the pigeon-house. No one knew who to trust.

Rause! Flemich. We've got—

A pause. They were three hours ahead of us and two away from the excavation site …

'I've got a distress signal from—' Jacksmith.

'Holy crap!' Himaru sounded like his eyes were about to explode. 'That didn't just—'

The channel to Flemich was still open. I picked up, half expecting a trap, and found myself connected to the cockpit of Flemich's Cheetah, looking through his Servant and seeing the sky spin. There was a tactical overlay spread across it, projected into his lenses. Everything was a confusion of voices and messages all at once.

Break right! Break right!

'… under fire. Orbital source …'

Shieldwall one is hit!

The view lurched and shook as the Cheetah pitched sharply, nose-diving towards the clouds.

Mayday! Mayday!

'Multiple incoming. High veloci—'

Another violent shudder.

'One engine—'

Shieldwall one! Eject! Eject!

Flemich's head whipped to the side. I caught a glimpse of Agent Utubu in the pilot's seat, eyes wide. He looked paralysed.

All engines out. Shieldwall two going down. Grid reference Golf X-Ray one six by Tango Bravo two two.

'Get out! Get out!'

Repeat. Shieldwall two engines out. Ejecting at Golf X-Ray one six by Tango Bravo two two.

I looked out at our horizon. Up this high we could see for a thousand miles. Everything, everywhere, in every direction, was calm, still and serene. The clouds far below were so distant they seemed barely to move beneath us. The stars were fixed above.

If it wasn't for the vibration of the Cheetah's engines, I might have convinced myself we were motionless.

Somewhere over the horizon ahead Flemich scrambled out of his cockpit. Tried to. Their Cheetah was heading straight down, nose first. The air up here was so thin that they were almost in free fall. I wanted to turn it off. I didn't want to see this to its end.

'Anyone picking this up, it came from above. From above!'

He managed to haul himself out of the cockpit into the Cheetah's passenger module. Six other agents sat there, buckled into their seats. I knew them all. Every one of them.

Through his eyes I saw their terror. This wasn't what we did. We weren't trained for this.

Shieldwall two. Ejecting.

The Cheetah gave another violent shudder.

I lost the feed.

We all stared outside at the endless still horizon as if we might see them, somehow. The flash of some detonation.

'What the actual fuck …?'

'Feedback from one of the Kutosovs.' Himaru's voice was flat. 'The salvo came from the UNSS *Flying Daggers*. Both Cheetahs are losing altitude at a rate consistent with engine failure. All comms are silent.'

'Now what?' asked Jacksmith.

No one answered.

'They're going to shoot at us too, you know.'

Jacksmith started to turn the Cheetah. Laura snapped out a hand, steady on her shoulder.

'Fuck them.'

'Agent Patterson, I'm all for sticking two fingers up at Darius but I don't plan to die doing it.'

'The *Flying Daggers* is in a low orbit. She's over the horizon now. She won't have another window to fire for two hours. We're good until then.' She turned to look at Himaru. 'And you lot can shoot the fuck out of that Earth ship before they come back, right? Because what we just saw was an act of war.'

Himaru shook his head. 'Kutosovs are for chasing drug runners. Even if they can change orbits in time, something like that would shred them. If the *Flying Daggers* fires another salvo then our best chance is for the interceptors to engage the missiles themselves.'

Jacksmith took a deep breath and let it out, long and slow.

'Nicholas was the astrophysicist, but if their orbital period is only two hours, doesn't that mean they get two more firing windows before we reach the excavation?'

Himaru made a sour face. Yes.

'I was naive when I approached Darius that first time, but not stupid. I copied the video before I showed it to him. But it wasn't until Alysha told me what she'd walked into that I understood why Iosefa meant so much. Agent Rause, I wasn't entirely honest with you. She told me what was happening in Settlement 64. I showed her Iosefa's video. It was Alysha who worked out what it meant. She told me not to show it to anyone else, especially from the Tesseract. That was the last time I saw her alive. I'm sorry about what happened next. If I'm honest, I was scared. I thought maybe she'd died because of the video. So I lied to Agent Becker. I didn't tell him about it. I *did* tell Alysha that Darius was a snake, though. That bit was true. Can we turn back now, please?'

She was scared. I wanted to tell her we were all scared. We were just more used to it.

'Why didn't you tell me all this before?'

'I didn't know I could trust you.'

I growled. 'She was my wife!'

'I'm sorry.'

'Sure it wasn't because you wanted the glory? To be the one who—'

'Keon!' Laura grabbed my wrist. Tight. Hard. She was shaking. 'Not now. We need to—'

'I kept quiet because of Nicholas,' Jacksmith snapped. 'Sitting on that after Alysha died was like sitting on an anthill. Nicholas had been good to me when Sanja got into trouble so I showed it to him as well. He had the skills to work out the orbits and where Iosefa might have gone. He suggested we show it to Lars, too. They both understood straight away that it was Iosefa's DNA that mattered. Yes, it was our big secret, but it wasn't going to make just *us* great – Iosefa's too big for that. It would be the making of the Institute! Of Magenta! And it still could be, you know, if Vishakh doesn't get there first. And yes, we had our differences, and yes, we fell out, but I didn't want him dead, for fuck's sake! And then he was, and you were in my face asking questions like it was my fault. And it *was* my fault.'

'How did Becker know where to guide the first expedition?' I asked.

'It had to be Vishakh. I have no idea how he knew.'

Neither did I. The best I had was that he really had heard it from the voices of the Masters. That wasn't going to cut it. He could tell us later. After I finished hurting him.

Jacksmith finally unfroze Iosefa's recording. The only person not paying full attention was Himaru. He was looking outside, lenses full of sparks, mumbling under his breath to the Kutosovs that were coming to meet us.

Me goes Magenta home where all starts and ends. Me knows. Me hears them. Me knows when they go. Me stops them. Me keep safe me family.

'Me knows *when* they go,' said Jacksmith. 'We all assumed he meant *where*, not *when*. Then Jit and Nicholas started working together. Nothing to do with this, you understand. Jit wanted to fix *exactly* where Magenta was in space relative to Earth. Nicholas told her that looking at pulsars would be more accurate than looking at stars because the decay of their rotational periods would tell him *when* they were as well as where. But it didn't work until Nicholas twigged that the same question might apply to Magenta itself. Not just *where* we are relative to Earth but *when* as well. And then ...'

Laura screwed up her face. 'Are you serious?'

Jacksmith shrugged. 'Nicholas was. He and Jit used to meet up and get drunk now and then. He had a thing for her, which was why he was working on her pulsar theory – and Jit would have loved the idea that the Masters' ships are all time machines, too. If I'd known he had that clip ... I bet he wheeled it out and told her the whole story, right up to what Iosefa says at the end. Me knows *when* they go. And Jit could never have kept something like that to herself.' She shook her head.

Nohr had gone to Fleet for more data. She hadn't just gone to Fleet. She'd ended up talking to Vishakh.

'And?' asked Laura.

'And what?'

'Steadman's work. When are we?'

Jacksmith shook her head. 'It was just a theory. He never had the data to prove anything one way or another.'

'We have a decision to make.' Himaru got to his feet. 'Press on or turn back. We make it together. All of us. Each with one vote.'

Laura and Jacksmith immediately objected that all his men would presumably vote the same way he did and there were only four of the rest of us. We argued. Himaru got talking to the Kutosov pilots again about what they'd seen, where they were, how large the salvo had been from the *Flying Daggers*. We had Chief Morgan on the line telling us that we were free and clear to make whatever choice we wanted, suspensions revoked, arrest warrants recalled, clearances given, privileges restored, whatever it took if we could give him whoever was responsible for all this. By then we'd picked up the distress beacons from the two downed Cheetahs. The passenger modules had deployed chutes and landed intact. Whether they survived or not depended on what reached them first: a rescue team or the next storm.

Thirty minutes before the next firing window opened, Himaru outlined his plan and reckoned our chances of surviving a salvo were 'solid'. We voted nine to two to keep going. We made it anonymous but I was pretty sure the votes for going back came from Laura and Bix.

We started our descent ten minutes before the *Flying Daggers* came over the orbital horizon. We dropped below the clouds into howling wind and slanting hail, while high in the stratosphere the two Kutosovs sent to intercept us now flew side by side in our place, electronic emissions tweaked to look like a single Cheetah. We watched a hybrid display of radar and satellite as a new salvo of missiles streaked from orbit. I couldn't believe how long it took. For ten long minutes Jacksmith hovered over the Magentan ocean, angled into a wind that jerked us back and forth. The Kutosovs carried on straight and level twenty miles up. The missiles dropped through the exosphere, then the thermosphere, tracked on infrared by orbital satellite. The interceptors pretending to be our Cheetah held station until the last minute. Then they raced away. I watched the missiles track after them, but they didn't have the fuel to chase the interceptors back up out of the stratosphere. They fell and eventually disappeared into the cloud.

'Nice.' Himaru slapped Jacksmith on the shoulder.

'Expensive in fuel.'

Jacksmith waited for the *Flying Daggers* to vanish over the orbital horizon, then started the climb back above the cloud.

'Do we have enough to do it again on their next pass?' They were going to get at least one more.

'We'll be running on fumes by the time we get to the excavation site. But yes.'

No one argued. Laura muttered something about Vishakh getting away to orbit in his shuttle but that just got a flat shake of the head from Himaru.

'He's not getting away. What I want to know is what a UN ship from Earth has to do with any of this.'

Simple enough, wasn't it? Earth wanted Iosefa. They wanted him badly enough to start a war.

'Things on Earth aren't great at the moment,' said Laura.

Earth. Not Fleet. I didn't really see how that made sense, but politics never did. We were supposed to all be in it together since the Masters but it never felt that way. In the colonies we thought we were the victims, dragged across space by faceless aliens and dropped on hostile unfamiliar worlds. Five years on Earth had shown me the other side of that story. We were the lucky ones who'd escaped the famine years. We were parasites who'd sucked resources from Earth while its own children went naked and starving. And they hated Fleet so very much. Hated that it wasn't theirs.

I went into the passenger cabin to nap. Two hours wasn't much but anything was better then nothing. I woke again to the thump and shudder of the Cheetah dropping back down through the clouds.

'Hey, boss dude.' Bix saw me stir.

'How far out are we?'

'Ninety minutes.'

We were a couple of miles off the ground and diving. I pulled tactical displays to my lenses and patched into the feed between Himaru and Jacksmith and the interceptors. Our two decoys were in formation again, side by side twenty miles up, making themselves into a target. I made a mental note to find the pilots after all this was over and buy them a drink. I already knew what they'd say.

Happy to help. Esh was one of us.

The *Flying Daggers* crossed the orbital horizon. We were below the cloud now, flying over an icy plain. The track on the UN ship fragmented, exactly as it had done before. Another salvo of missiles. It took a few seconds for them to resolve into stable tracks. There weren't as many this time.

'Running out of ammunition?' Jacksmith.

'Unlikely.' Himaru.

We watched. Same as before. Tense and helpless. It either worked or it didn't.

Colonel, we're calculating a different set of trajectories this time.

I didn't know what what meant. Neither did Himaru, apparently.

Thirty seconds.

'Are they coming faster this time?'

Confirmed.

Sixty seconds. I could see how the missiles had separated into a wider spread this time.

Visual contact.

An orbiting interceptor passed thirty miles over one of the missiles heading towards us. It sent a brief sequence of video. Poor resolution, a camera zoomed in as far as it would go, at the limits of its stabilisation. A picture of a fat cigar with stubby wings behind the bright flare of a rocket.

Two minutes. The Cheetah's tactical computer was estimating another five before the missiles reached their targets. By then the *Flying Daggers* would be getting close to the orbital horizon. They wouldn't get another shot.

Colonel, that isn't anti-air. That's—

Sir! More launch flares from the *Flying Daggers*.

On the displays I watched the ship above fragment again, then resolve into another set of tracks. A second salvo.

Colonel, trajectory calculations indicate the first salvo is directed at surface targets. Repeat, first salvo is *not* heading for a high altitude intercept.

'Fuck!' Laura. 'They've seen us!'

'No.' Himaru. 'Not through all that cloud. It's a bluff. They're trying to flush us out.'

'Sure about that?' Jacksmith.

'Slow and steady, Doctor. Keep us low. They can't see us.'

We watched the missile tracks converge slowly on our position and on the interceptors above. They were all travelling at well over a mile a second, but on the displays they seemed to crawl like snails.

'Steady. Steady.'

The first salvo had resolved itself into a sort of pattern. A ring of six missiles with a seventh in the centre.

Two minutes to intercept.

I could feel them arrowing out of the sky towards us.

'Dudes? If they're blind, what are the chances of them actually hitting us?'

'Neglig— Shit!' Himaru. 'Down! Put us down!'

'What?'

'There! Put us down! Right now!'

The Cheetah lurched and dropped. High above us the interceptors split into two and bolted for orbit. The second salvo of missiles arced in pursuit.

'Down! No, not there, there!'

I had no idea what Himaru was pointing at up in the cockpit. Even when I pulled the Cheetah visuals all I saw was cloud and snow and a white field of ice ...

Was that a ridge ahead?

Sixty seconds to intercept.

The first salvo hit the clouds above us. Trajectory predictions showed the nearest surface impact would be more than a mile away. The Kutosovs in orbit lost their tracks. The Cheetah kept a running prediction of the missile trajectories. As far as I could tell we were good. None of the missiles were going to come within a—

Everything outside went white. The clouds above lit up with a dazzling inner light, brilliant bright as though the sun had gone nova overhead. The Cheetah's reactive canopy turned black.

'Oh, man!'

'Down! Now! *Now!*'

'What the *fuck* was that?'

An alarm in my Servant. A radiation spike. They must have figured we'd pull the same trick as we had on their first pass and they knew they couldn't do a thing about it. So they'd done the next best thing. They'd carpet-bombed us with antimatter warheads. Airburst detonations to set up a blast wave and swat us out of the sky.

I let that sink in. An Earth ship had fired antimatter missiles at the surface of Magenta.

'Brace brace brace!'

I curled up tight and waited for the shock wave to smash us into the ground.

25

ICE STATION FOXTROT UNIFORM

We hit the ground hard. The first shock wave slammed in half a second later, a thunderous impact and a roaring howling wind. The Cheetah shuddered and jolted. It trembled, the vibrations running into my bones as a wind howled and tore outside, singing through the Cheetah's wings and rattling its hull.

Slowly, the roar died away. We unpeeled ourselves from our seats and looked at each other, everyone silent. Then Bix started laughing. It was absurd, and I wanted to shout at him, but instead I started laughing too.

'Antimatter! Dude!' He was close to hysteria. 'They shot us with antimatter! And they missed! Like, they missed! With antimatter! How do you miss with ... like ... antimatter?'

I wiped the tears from my eyes and queried the Cheetah's Servant to see if everything still worked. Jacksmith was ahead of me.

'I need us dug out and the engines cleared of ice,' she said. 'But I think we can still fly.' There were holes in the cloud overhead now. Miles across. In the middle of each writhed a rising doughnut of white vapour. A freezing wind rushed towards them carrying a fine sleet of ice crystals. Ten minutes later they were ready to move. Himaru planted a distress beacon in the ice before we left. As far as the world knew, that was where we'd crashed and that was where we'd stayed. We sent one message to the Kutosovs to tell them we were alive. After that Himaru insisted on radio silence.

'I want us below the cloud again before they recross the orbital horizon,' he growled. 'No one gets to know we're still in play.'

Jacksmith took us back into the air. We flew on in silence, an hour of waiting to see what would happen next until Jacksmith started our last descent. We were back through the cloud when Bix picked out a signal that wasn't from the excavation site. Vishakh's shuttle. I thought for one wild moment it was one of the trackers I'd fired from my Reeper, but it wasn't.

'I guess I missed, then,' I said. I told him about firing my tracker darts at Vishakh's shuttle up in orbit. He laughed.

'I thought you were trying to, like, detonate his fuel tank or something!'

'I didn't have any real bullets left.' I tried to make it sound like a joke. It got a wry smile out of Himaru at least.

Laura raised an eyebrow. 'You thought he was trying to detonate a fuel tank right next to the Fleet station and you didn't try to stop him?'

Bix shrugged. 'Seemed, you know. Proportionate.'

Laura's eyebrow rose a notch higher.

Bix shrugged again. 'I really liked Esh a lot, you know?'

High from still being alive, all of us.

Jacksmith put us down half a mile from the excavation. The rest was going to be on foot through snow and ice. We kitted up in environment suits that were step-kin to the emergency suit I'd worn in orbit. We drew straws to see which one of us got to go after Vishakh's shuttle. I figured that was where he'd be, couched up in some rig, piloting an army of drones and shells to do his dirty work.

The short straw ended up with me. I gave it to Bix.

'For Esh,' I said.

'Thanks, boss dude.' He meant it.

Himaru sent one tac-team with Bix. Except for Jacksmith, the rest of us were going for the excavation. We were going to stop Vishakh's shells from taking Iosefa.

Sure you want to leave Jacksmith on her own?

I might have pretended I was asking so she'd have some protection, but mostly it was because I still didn't trust her. Himaru thought about that for a moment and then left one of his men to keep an eye on her and secure our Cheetah. It should have been Himaru himself and we all knew it, but no one said anything. Himaru had seen more friends die than anyone else. He was here for wetwork. If Vishakh ended up on the wrong end of Himaru with a gun, to tell him that Esh had once stood in his shoes and had had the courage not to pull the trigger. I'd tell him I'd promised I'd see Darius Vishakh stand trial in a public court so everyone would know what he'd done, because that was the way Esh would have wanted it to be.

If that wasn't enough, I didn't know if I'd try to stop him pulling the trigger.

We opened the Cheetah doors. The temperature dropped by about a hundred degrees. I stepped outside and didn't feel a thing.

'These suits are *good.*'

'We'll be fine as long as there isn't a storm.'

Himaru cracked the seals on the cargo hatch and hauled out two pallets. Each carried a tracked sled with a dozen kitbags. He shoved me and Laura at the first sled, Bix at the second, then unzipped one of the bags and handed out pairs of short skis to his team. A couple of minutes later we were moving, the sleds dragging themselves across the brittle snow with three bureau agents on their backs and Himaru and his men towed behind.

You have any idea how much resistance to expect, now would be a good time to share.

I didn't, not really.

Drones and shells. Hi-tech and fierce. It'll be like when we went after Kagame.

Worse, probably, but this time we were ready.

We stopped at a ridge before the crash site, a low rise of ice jutting from soft snow, harsh where the wind cut into it. Himaru ditched his skis and attached climbing claws to his hands and feet. He scaled the ice and set up a tiny camera. The feed flashed in my Servant. I cued it to my lenses. I could see the site's Cheetah pit a hundred yards past the ridge. To the left I saw a cluster of aerials and the guys that held them upright. From the satellite photos and the maps in Vishakh's files, the wreck was a little way past the antenna arrays.

Quiet, he pinged.

There was no movement on the surface, but why would there be? No one would come out into this cold unless they had to.

Going thermal.

The view changed. Everything became a near-uniform deep, deep blue except for a pale glow washing into the sky from the Cheetah pit. At first that was all I saw. Then I noticed other smaller wafts of what looked like smoke coming from the ground further away.

Ventilation ducts.

Himaru marked the three plumes past the Cheetah pit and laid them over our map of the site.

Mess. Kitchen. Dorms.

He shifted the view to the left, towards the aerials, zoomed in and picked out two more.

Equipment maintenance. Science. Don't know which is which.

I looked at the map. Vishakh hadn't known either.

Himaru switched back to the Cheetah pit and zoomed in close. Three bright rings flared around the pit. At the centre of each was a bright red speck.

Cameras. Lenses heated so they don't ice over. Probably not Vishakh. Not stealthy enough.

He scanned the ice again, a slow and careful panning from right to left, from the Cheetah pit to the antenna arrays. He found two patches of ice around the antennas that he didn't like. When he zoomed in I couldn't see anything except a slight change in the colour of the ice.

That's him. Tiny camera on a stalk, body buried in the ice, sinking heat there. So we assume Vishakh's still here, that he's been here for some time and that he knows what he's doing. He's set up a perimeter but he doesn't know we're here. With luck he doesn't know we survived. We keep it that way as long as we can.

Locate and secure our people, Laura said. First priority.

Then the items from the wreck, I added.

I noticed how everyone carefully didn't mention Vishakh.

Himaru tossed a handful of drones into the air, bugs no bigger than my thumb. They flew over the ridge. I tried to follow them through his camera but I couldn't.

OK. That's his surveillance taken care of. Deadly force is authorised to protect Magentan civilians or in self-defence. Do you agree, Tesseract?

Agreed. Laura didn't hesitate.

Verify targets before you shoot. Prep for shells and drones. The flesh and blood is going to be sitting cosy in their nice warm shuttle. For a bit.

Himaru flashed me a look. We both grinned. Vishakh might be expecting us at the crash site, but he had no way to know we'd spotted his shuttle as well.

Rangesh, locate your objective and hold position.

The ice wall was too steep and jagged for the sleds so we shouldered the kitbags and struggled up by hand. It was twenty feet high and the environment suits made hard work of it. On the other side was a drift of snow deep enough to bury a pod. Himaru flopped into it and sank almost out of sight. He wriggled a furrow on his belly towards the edge of the drift a few dozen yards from the Cheetah pit. One by one his tac-team followed. Laura and I went last. By now my Servant was picking up signals scattered nearby under the ice. As best I could tell they were from the living quarters close to the Cheetah pit: Servants transmitting emergency alerts. I didn't dare turn my own active to answer them. The moment any of us did that, Vishakh would know we were here. At least no one was howling for medical help.

Wait.

I checked the Servants against the site personnel roster. A few dozen scientists and technicians.

Doctor Jacksmith, can you verify names please? Laura.

Linking to the master Servant for the expedition was our best bet for finding where everyone was – but again, as soon as anyone did that, Vishakh would know we were here.

There are airlock seals between the Cheetah Pit and the living quarters and between the living quarters and the main excavation. Jacksmith pointed them out on Vishakh's map. That's where they're coming from.

Penned together. Makes sense. If it was me then I'd have an armed shell in there keeping watch and surveillance on both the exits. Any more airlocks?

One on the tunnels approaching the wreck and one controlling access to the science lab.

We crept low, hidden as best we could by the ridges of snow around the ventilation shafts. We split into pairs, two of us at each shaft, the last two keeping overwatch on the surface. I stayed with Himaru. He prised open the grille covering the shaft and then set up a line and tossed in a tiny surveillance drone, its vision linked to our lenses.

The shaft had a U-bend with a tank and a pump to collect any snow that fell through. Otherwise it was clear down to a second grille in the roof of the dormitory below. The mesh on the grille was coarse. The drone eased through the gaps. The dormitory beneath was empty apart from two technicians on the far side, grappling with a stack of crates on a cargo drone.

One of them? I asked. The plan was to make contact if we could.

We find the shells first.

Himaru steered the drone cautiously into the open and skittered it across the ceiling. The dormitories were split into two halves. Each had a shower block, toilets, a storeroom ...

Here.

Laura spat us the feed from a second drone. She'd found most of the station crew in the mess. They were sitting quietly doing nothing much. Two shells watched over them. I didn't recognise the shells, but that didn't mean anything. They were armed and obvious.

There are going to be drones too. Eye-spies. Any of them might be armed. Watch for civilians who aren't.

She was probably right. I guided Himaru's drone to one of the technicians moving the crates and landed it on the back of his hand. He looked down with startled interest and then my Servant crashed into his. I locked his communications down with my Tesseract codes and used his Servant to whisper in his ear.

'Agent Keon Rause, Magentan Investigation Bureau. Help is here.'

He froze. 'I—'

'Keep doing what you're doing. I need number and location of hostiles. I'm going to return control of your Servant. Show me where.'

I let him go and passed him the station map. He showed me where.

'They're *in* the wreck?'

'We broke through a few hours before they came.'

'Show me!'

He pinged a map of the wreck as far as they'd penetrated. I passed it on. It wasn't much.

Any of you know anything about these ships? Jacksmith?

Not this one, I'm afraid.

Yeah, actually. Dude, that totally looks like they went for the, you know, the bit with the hyperdrivey stuff. At least ... The bit people, like, think ... does ... You know?

Bix trailed off. A hundred and fifty years of access to their technology and not only couldn't we copy it, we didn't even know which bit did what.

No! I don't know!

'Hyperdrivey stuff?' Fuck's sake, Rangesh!

Wait! Navigation?

I guess.

'OK.' I turned my attention back to the technician. 'Act normal. Don't say anything. Don't try to spread the word. Leave that to us.'

How many of your squad do you need to take down those two shells?

Himaru didn't even stop to think. Three. One down each shaft. They'll hold until the rest of us find Vishakh. When we move in we hit them with a pulse. He patted one of the bags on our sled. That should disable them for long enough.

To Bix: You at the shuttle yet?

Close, dude. Few minutes.

We left three of Himaru's team lying in the snow by the ventilation shafts and crept towards the wreck. The expedition had used a heat lance when they first arrived, burning away the ice to expose the outer skin of the ship below. The shape they'd uncovered was utterly black and unblemished, blurring away under the ice at the crater edges. There clearly wasn't a way in.

I swapped a glance with Laura.

'You trust Jacksmith?' I asked.

'Right now, I don't even trust you,' she said.

We were close to the antennas and the two micro-surveillance stations Vishakh had set up. Both cameras now had domes over them, the result of Himaru's drones, the inside of each showing a fixed unchanging view of the ice. Short of treading on them, I figured Vishakh's cameras weren't a threat any more.

Himaru touched a hand to my shoulder. Careful. Vibration sensors.

We skirted the cameras, opened another ventilation shaft and rappelled into a cavern carved out of the ice. Vishakh's map marked it as maintenance and servicing for expedition equipment. It was empty. Quiet. Himaru sent a spy drone ahead. The maintenance cave led into a kitting room. Hazard suits lined the walls along with powerful battery packs, lamps and cutting tools. A passage led back into the bulk of the caves while an open airlock led into a second tunnel of raw ice, sloping down. Hard-set foam tiles had been bolted into the floor under a litter of power cables. A string of strip-lights hung from above, all haphazard makeshift work. A crude piece of graffiti pointed an arrow along the shaft proclaiming *This way to the aliens*. It was surrounded by signatures, most of the expedition team. I'd seen it before in some press release.

We held position in the kitting room. Himaru put up a second drone and sent it off down the passage to the living quarters. The first drone eased its way into the dark towards the wreck. It switched to thermals. I could see the hole where the expedition had finally found an entrance through the skin of the crashed ship. All the metal was an absolute black.

The feed died as soon as the drone crossed into the ship. Himaru grunted something rude.

Dude! Null-field!

Bix sent me a reference article. Something to do with the way Masters' ships worked. You wanted to talk from the inside of a Masters' ship to the outside world, you ran a superconducting cable through any convenient hole you could find in the hull, wrapped it in calcium-copper titanate and shouted loudly. There was a lot more, but the gist was that links didn't work. Something about the hull of the Masters' ships killed them dead.

How do you know all this shit?

Himaru was moving. 'What he's saying is that we have to go inside.'

'And that when we do we lose contact with everyone else.'

'One of us stays out,' said Laura. 'One of us goes in.'

'I'm going in.' I nudged Himaru. 'Take your men inside. You have to assume they're—'

The whump of a muffled explosion came over the link from Rangesh.

'Shit. Dudes!'

Go! Go! Everyone move! We're made.

Another muffled explosion came from Rangesh and the shuttle. I muted the link as Himaru and I ran with the last two men of his squad into the wreck. All our links died before we reached it as someone set off the electromagnetic pulse outside. That would shut down the shells and drones in the dormitories long enough for Himaru's men to take them out.

Wasn't going to help us inside the ship, though. Himaru flicked a grin back at me as though he was reading my mind.

'No links means no shells. Vishakh's not in the shuttle. He's here!'

He was right.

We ran through the hole in the hull. I picked up an expedition Servant at once on the other side. I threw my Tesseract codes and crashed into it, shutting it down, silencing it and stealing the video feeds from the linked cameras. Himaru flipped me a feed from another camera. Two figures stood in a room that was nothing but featureless curves of softly glowing white. I didn't see any controls and the only wires were a cabling conduit strewn along the floor. A man was stooped, pulling at something. Vishakh – or at least, the man I'd thought was Darius Vishakh from Alysha's recordings – sitting next to Tomasz Shenski.

A crowbar lay nearby. A woman stood watch beside him. Behind them both was a gurney with a corpse laid out on it, and then someone else slumped in an electric chair like the one Jacksmith used ...

The woman turned. I got a good look at her. Lieutenant Shiva Lee.

If these couldn't be shells then I was seeing the real Lee.

Esh's killer?

It hit me: was *she* Darius Vishakh? But no. She was too young. The real Vishakh had to be pushing fifty at least. Which made the man in there too young, too. So what? Surgery? He'd changed his face? That was why Jacksmith didn't recognise his picture?

The link died abruptly. The whine of a charging particle beam hummed out of the darkness ahead. A drone flew out of the shadows. Himaru's men opened fire. The sound was deafening. The drone exploded and Himaru tossed another half a dozen drones of his own into the air. They flew ahead, building a map that fed back to our Servants. For a few long seconds everything was quiet. Then a voice called out from ahead.

397

'You picked the wrong side, Rause! Your wife was smarter.'

I chambered a round in my Reeper. It wasn't necessary but I liked the way the sound of it echoed through the darkness.

'Send Iosefa out first,' I shouted. 'Then the rest of you, one at a time.'

A light bloomed ahead of Himaru, bobbing back and forth. A torch, perhaps.

'Lower the light!' Don't trust him!

I won't.

The light dimmed to a slit pointed to the floor. A gurney inched out of the darkness. Lying on it was a frozen desiccated corpse twisted into awkward angles. The electric chair followed, carrying an old man huddled under a blanket. He looked ill and frail and he was close to unconscious. I checked the expedition roster for anyone else in a wheelchair and came up empty; but I remembered what Cho had told me.

'Who's your friend, Vishakh?'

'Be gentle, Rause. He's not well and he didn't ask to be here.'

I sent the chair up the tunnel towards Laura. Whoever this is, they came with Vishakh. Willing or not, I don't know. Find out. Check him for explosives.

'How do you want to do this, Rause?'

How I wanted to do it was to toss a grenade into the room with Lee and Vishakh and close the door. But I'd told Himaru I was going to put Vishakh in court to answer for what he'd done, and so that was how this would end.

'Kit off. Pockets empty. Hands where I can see you.' I turned to look back up the tunnel. 'Patterson! What's going on out there?'

Laura didn't take her eyes off Wheelchair Man.

'Shells and drones neutralised. We're accounting for the station staff. I've cleared the second team to use heavy weapons on the shuttle.'

I laughed. 'Rangesh with a rocket launcher?'

Laura laughed too. 'Fuck yeah.'

Vishakh came out of the gloom, hands held high. I kept my Reeper on him and walked him out of the wreck. Once we were back in the ice tunnel I set a spider drone on him, wrapping him up good and tight.

I called to Himaru. 'You can bring out the last one.'

I left him to it. I didn't care how many pieces Shiva Lee was in when she came out. My promise only covered Vishakh.

We walked up the tunnel. I jabbed my Reeper into Vishakh's back.

'I know you played me on the station,' I said, 'I know that list of names is a crock of shit.'

He laughed. 'I have no idea what you're talking about.'

'Want to try again?'

'I slipped a sliver of steel into Loki's heart,' Vishakh said. 'I took a slice and ate it and then I burned the rest. He didn't have any last words but still I know who pulled his trigger.'

'Who?'

'Darius Vishakh, you jackass.'

The ground trembled and staggered us both, and then something came flying out of the wreck and flattened us both.

26

JAMIE

The blast came from inside the wreck, powerful enough that 'Vishakh' and I both went flying. I lay too dazed to move, thoughts scrambled. My skin tingled. I tried to work out whether anything actually hurt, whether I was injured. My Servant flashed warnings: elevated heart rate and adrenaline. Nothing serious. 'Vishakh' was trying to get to his feet. The spider ties were making it difficult. He couldn't use his hands.

'Laura?'

I heard her groan. Vishakh finally got up. He didn't make any attempt to run.

Himaru?

No answer. He was still inside the wreck. I picked myself up, fist clenched around my Reeper. I pointed it at the man I'd supposed was Darius Vishakh.

'Who are you?'

He laughed at me. 'Me? I'm Darius Vishakh.'

'You listen—'

Shiva Lee walked into the end of the tunnel from the kit room.

She was fifty feet away from me with a particle rifle levelled at us. I heard the whine of it. Vishakh – or whoever he really was – was blocking her shot, but if she had the rifle charged high enough then it would burn right through both of us.

Laura hauled herself upright to lean on the tunnel wall. 'Fuck!'

'Put your weapon down, Rause,' hissed Shiva.

'You killed Esh,' I said.

My hand was shaking from the shock of the explosion. Even from this range I might miss if I tried to shoot Vishakh, never mind shoot Shiva as well. But I badly wanted to try it.

'Put it down!'

'You're done. Don't you see that? There's no way out. The moment you came to the surface ...'

Everything I was seeing, Bix and Jacksmith were seeing too. By now Vishakh surely knew we'd found his shuttle.

'I ought to just shoot you,' I said. 'Both of you.'

Vishakh turned on me, still wrapped in spider ties. 'Maybe.' He shrugged. 'But what Agent Patterson ought to do is take a look at *this*.'

A video link popped into my Servant. I set a wall around it, ready to kill it if it turned out to be attackware like I'd used on him in the orbital. But it wasn't. I let it play, contrast and volume turned down in case my Servant had it wrong ...

A young boy was tied to a chair in a dark room. He was blindfolded and gagged but his head twitched from side to side to show that he was awake. I didn't recognise him at first. Then a blank-faced shell entered the picture and tore off the blindfold.

Jamie. His eyes were wide and terrified.

They were inside Laura's apartment. The shell took Jamie's head and forced him to turn and face the camera. I knew how strong those mechanical arms could be. Strong enough to snap a neck in an instant. I heard a strangled cry from Laura and knew she was watching too.

'Say the words,' said the shell. Its voice was soft, lilting.

'Mama? Help me? Please?' He started to cry. The video stopped.

Vishakh and I stared at each other. Laura sank to her haunches against the wall, moaning softly, head in her hands.

'No, no. Not Jamie.'

'Gun down, Rause,' Vishakh said. 'Do as the nice lady says and the boy lives.'

Bix! You need to get into that shuttle and shut them down! I nodded towards Shiva. 'Another shell? Or are you real this time?'

The pilot had to be on the surface somewhere. On the shuttle? Had to be – there hadn't been any time for them to stop anywhere else.

You killed Esh. The thought filled my head. And around it echoed another: *You killed Alysha.* Thoughts like those didn't care about anything except the pistol in my hand. Not about Shiva Lee's rifle or about Laura or Jamie. Not even about myself. I could shoot Vishakh here and now. The shell couldn't stop me. She'd kill me with her rifle and then Laura would have a few seconds as it recharged. Time enough to empty the clip of her Reeper.

Except she wouldn't. Not after what we'd just seen.

'You're going to take us out of here,' said Vishakh calmly. 'You're going to take us back to your Cheetah and fly us to my shuttle. Then we're going to leave Magenta. If you don't, that shell will snap the boy's neck. If anyone tries to interfere, if you try to sever the shell's command link, if the link fails for any reason at all even for a moment, the shell will snap the boy's neck. Do you understand?'

I nodded. I understood perfectly. I lowered my Reeper and put it carefully on the floor.

Rangesh! Back off from Vishakh's shuttle. Laura.

No! Jacksmith.

Ignore her.

You can't let them take Iosefa!

'Kagame was a bureau mole,' I said. 'He got right inside you, didn't he?'

So what's the call, boss dude?

Another shake of the head. 'Let me loose or the boy dies.'

I pinged the three men Himaru had left to secure the station crew. They were currently trapped behind the airlocks that sealed the living quarters from the science section and the Cheetah pit. They were getting ready to blow them open.

Dude? I'm at the shuttle. Do we go in or not?

'Keon ...'

Laura's voice was husky, but when I turned to look she was back on her feet. She had her Reeper trained on Vishakh. She walked towards him with slow deliberate purpose.

'Patterson!'

I didn't know what she was going to do. I knew what *I'd* do, and I knew what I'd do if Jamie was mine and if anything happened to him. But Laura ...

You can't let him win! Jacksmith again. Not after all this! I wondered whether Laura was getting that message too. Or whether she simply knew what was coming. Not after Nicholas and Lars. And twenty-six fucking years of being afraid.

Laura stood in front of Vishakh. 'Keon. Let him go, please.'

I flicked a command to the spider ties. Vishakh shook himself free and then slowly raised his hands.

'How do I know Jamie's not already dead?' Laura asked.

'You don't.'

Boss dude?

Don't do it! Jacksmith again.

I didn't put it past Rangesh to disobey a direct order. He

had a soft spot for Jamie. But he also had a tac-team with him. They didn't know Jamie, but they'd known Esh and they knew about orders. They'd be right there with Jacksmith. Don't let that motherfucker get away …

Laura fired her Reeper. The shock of the noise snapped me back. Vishakh screamed and clutched himself. She'd shot him through the palm of his raised hand. At the end of the tunnel Shiva sighted the rifle on them both. Laura held up her hands although she didn't put the Reeper down – not yet.

'So you're not a shell,' she said. 'Now show me he's still alive or that's just the beginning. I will murder you so slowly you'll think it will never end. Or your shell will kill us both and even if Rause here doesn't shut her down, how are you going to get away? We have your shuttle. You need a Cheetah. You need one of us to fly for you or you're fucked.'

Rause, what's the call?

Vishakh clutched his hand. 'Fucking bitch! I only need one of you!'

I walked past the two of them towards Shiva and the barrel of her gun, blocking her line to Vishakh and Laura. She had an easy shot on me now. As clean as you like.

'Go on, then. Vaporise me. Then Agent Patterson can shoot your partner in the head and you can go back to your stand-off.'

'Keon!' Laura again.

'Was it you who killed Alysha?' I asked. 'Or was it him?'

In my head I'd said Esh. I was close enough now to look her in the eyes. They were perfect. There was a fine long-healed scar that creased her temple. I could see the very slight twitch of her aim that came with every heartbeat. She looked so incredibly real. But she was a shell.

Boss dude? What's the call?

Take out the shuttle.

I didn't see what happened behind me. I didn't need to. I

heard the smack as Laura smashed the butt of her Reeper into Vishakh's face. In front of me Shiva twitched but she didn't fire. I was waiting for the moment when the rifle suddenly shifted aim, when she tried to shoot past me. If she moved then so would I, and then we'd see who was faster. She knew it would be her.

Vishakh howled in pain. 'It was the fucking Tesseract that killed your fucking wife! That's where it came from! Fuck!'

Shit, man. Sorry, Laws.

'I think Jamie's already dead,' said Laura. 'I don't think I have anything to lose. So I'm going to hit you again and again and again until your shell shoots us both.'

'Fucking psycho bitch! You know she really played you, Rause. She's known about half this shit right from the start, you dumb fuck!'

A new video link flickered into life in my Servant. The same scene as before. Jamie, tied and gagged in Laura's apartment. The shell was standing right behind him.

'Jamie?' Laura's voice sounded tiny.

Jamie's head twitched wildly, looking for the source of the sound.

'It's OK, little mouse. It's going to be—'

The link cut.

'It's not fucking going to be OK,' snarled Vishakh. 'Not unless you—' He stopped.

Shuttle secure.

I watched the shell. She didn't flinch. She didn't turn off. Her artificial eyes stayed locked to mine. I didn't know whether that meant she was running her own autonomous q-code now, or whether it meant ...

Vishakh. Vishakh was controlling her. The Shiva Lee inside the wreck had been yet another shell. And he'd been the one running her. The null-field meant it *had* to be him. *That* was the trap Himaru had walked into. And now here was another one.

I should just shoot him …

But I'd watched the shell as Laura shot Vishakh in the hand. It hadn't flinched. Whoever that man was, he wasn't Darius Vishakh. The real Darius Vishakh was someone else.

'Show me Jamie again.' Laura's voice had changed. There was a hollowness there now.

'Last time, bitch,' not-Vishakh growled.

The video link opened again. Jamie was still there.

'Fuck.' I heard the defeat in her. 'Give him what he wants, Keon. Please?'

I knew the look I'd see in her face if I turned. It would be a look that didn't waver, didn't blink, the same look I had right now staring at Shiva down the barrel of her gun. It was the look of someone who'd thrown away everything they believed in except one last thing. It was the look of love. She'd shoot me to save Jamie. She really would.

Had she known about Vishakh all along?

'OK.'

I backed towards not-Vishakh and pinged Bix: The shells are still up.

She'd told me about Vishakh and Loki. Right before she'd told me to back the fuck off.

On my way, boss dude.

How long?

Ten minutes. Maybe fifteen.

Too long.

Laura didn't take her eyes off me. The ice shook as another series of explosions rumbled through the station. I stopped, waiting to see what that meant. I didn't have to wait long. A frantic flurry of messages flooded my Servant. Himaru's men had set off their charges. Vishakh had booby-trapped the airlocks and collapsed the ice tunnels. The station crew and the last of Himaru's men were now trapped.

'Let's go,' said Shiva.

I stooped to pick up my Reeper. Laura shook her head.

'I think ...' She almost faltered. Almost. 'I think, Keon, I need you to leave that be.'

Vishakh turned and started up the tunnel. 'You—'

Laura shot him in the foot. He dropped, screaming. I stared at her blankly.

'Fuckface here isn't in charge.' She nodded to the Shiva shell. 'She is. Isn't that obvious?'

I looked at Vishakh writhing on the floor, howling, clutching his smashed foot with his one good hand. I wondered how much more he could take. Laura was right, though. Whoever was piloting the Shiva shell was calling the shots. The fact that Laura had shot Vishakh twice now and was still alive seemed proof enough.

I looked Laura in the eye. 'The shell's right,' I said. 'You pointed me straight at Vishakh.'

'Keon, I ... I don't think I can trust you.' You're closer. Is that woman a shell?

'I—' Yes.

'Alysha's dead. So's Esh. Jamie isn't.' Fuck.

'You set me up.' Now what?

I left my Reeper on the tunnel floor. I never took my eyes off Laura. She bowed her head and gave me the very slightest nod and then looked at Shiva.

'There's a Cheetah in the landing pit. You can reach it before the rest of our team gets here. Now that fuckface can't walk you're going to need Keon to carry him. That's my guarantee you don't kill him. Once we get to the Cheetah, Keon walks away. I'll fly you wherever you want. The Cheetah we came in hasn't got the fuel to follow you. The rest is up to you.' If it's a shell then where's the pilot?

I understood the blankness in her eyes. The shell with Jamie was expendable. There was a chance, if we did what they wanted, that Jamie might live. But whoever went as their Cheetah pilot was going to die. Laura knew it. She was making sure it was her. *That man isn't Darius Vishakh.*

Not-Vishakh snarled at me through gritted teeth. 'I think Rause should come too. He can hear some more about his wife.' *Are you sure?*

'Agent Rause will kill you if you're not very careful.'

Laura was watching me. I tried to read her face, looking for any hint as to what she was thinking, whether there was a method to what she was doing, some secret, some magic trick she was was planning that would save her and Jamie both.

Not after what you've done to him.

'That'll do,' said Shiva. 'Let's go. Rause, pick him up. Patterson, drop the Reeper.'

It's not someone on the shuttle.

Not-Vishakh somehow pulled himself up. There was blood all over the front of his environment suit, but he was full of coagulants and painkillers from his Servant now.

Then who? Jacksmith?

No.

Not-Vishakh cradled his hand, hopping on his good leg, spattering blood all over the floor. I didn't want to help him. I wanted to leave him to die, but for a moment now I had a doubt.

Someone who was already here?

'You're one cold fucking bastard.'

I blinked. Not-Vishakh hadn't been looking at Laura or at me. He'd been looking at Shiva.

On the expedition team?

The shell dropped a hand to her hip while she held the rifle on us rock steady with the other. She drew a pistol and shot not-Vishakh in the head. She lowered the barrel of her rifle a fraction and nodded towards the airlock into the kit room.

I stared in disbelief.

'Now you don't need to carry him. One of you misbehaves, I shoot the other. Move!'

She has Jamie, Keon. What am I supposed to do?

Laura started up the tunnel. I followed behind, dragging my heels, struggling to take my eyes off the corpse. Shiva with the rifle came next. The chair and the gurney tagged along at the back on simple follow-me algorithms. The man in the chair still looked unconscious.

Liss?

A long pause before she answered. Keys?

I need your help.

I hesitated as we reached the kit room. Shiva kept a careful distance, covering us with the rifle. She nodded to a storage cave melted out of the ice. Vishakh's map showed a tunnel through to the Cheetah pit.

'Through there. Patterson in front. You behind.' So that Laura blocked the way if I decided to run.

The woman who killed Esh is riding a shell in Laura's apartment. She has Jamie.

I'm not the police, Keys.

Liss! I'm ten thousand miles away and—

So?

This is Jamie and the Tesseract is compromised. I need you to be Alysha.

But I'm not.

I don't know who else I can trust.

I'm just a simulation.

I paused again, shivering at a spike of guilt. I think I just saw the man who killed you die.

Loki killed me.

I loved her.

I know.

I made you from that part of her.

I know that too.

Do you wish I hadn't?

We reached another airlock. Shiva ordered us to stop. She kept the rifle on us but there was a slackness to her face. Her head was somewhere else. She was inside her Servant. Distracted.

'Don't.'

Laura must have seen me twitch, seen the thought that two of us together could rush her here and now. Maybe one of us would die, maybe not, but the other one would have her cold.

I didn't move. The airlock door opened.

You're better than her, I said.

I'm less than her.

You're the best of her.

I'm the parts of her that you liked. The parts of her that she let you see. I'm not *her*.

We moved into the airlock. Shiva covered us as we donned hoods and masks ready to go outside.

Do you love me?

I thought she wasn't going to answer, but eventually it came.

Yes. It's the way you made me to be.

Shiva waved the rifle at Laura and then at Wheelchair Man. 'See to this one.'

Do this and I'll let you go.

Laura put a helmet on Wheelchair Man and secured the seals. Shiva watched closely.

I wish you were here to see me, Keys. To see this shell laugh and cry. Although it can't cry. But I wish you were here to see.

'Check it,' Shiva said. 'Get this wrong and your boy dies.'

I'm sorry.

You're sorry because you want something. You're sorry that this is what it takes to get it.

My turn to be silent. She was right, but I had nothing else left.

Laura looked over the seals and nodded.

They killed Esh, I said.

I know. I was there.

Shiva opened the airlock. Bitter cold flooded in from an ice-cavern filled with Cheetah parts. Spares and repairs.

Liss, I need you to hack a shell. I need you to save Jamie's life. Please.

We crossed to where the cave opened into the Cheetah pit. I shambled behind Laura, staring at all the things I'd done – felt forced to do – by my love for a woman who was dead. For my wife, whom everyone thought was a traitor. Someone it turned out I'd barely known.

The Vishakh from Alysha's files was dead. I'd seen him shot, right in front of me. It hadn't sunk in.

OK, Keys.

'You know we're on the same side when it comes down to it,' Shiva said.

I couldn't help a bark of laughter.

'I mean it. Alysha saw it. Maybe you're just too dumb. We're all just trying to protect humanity.'

'From what?' I spat.

'From the day the Masters come back.'

'You killed her,' I said flatly, then stopped so abruptly that the shell almost walked into the back of me. 'I know what Iosefa means. How are you protecting humanity right now? From what?'

'Right now from itself,' snapped Shiva. 'Move!'

I started to walk again. We were close to the Cheetah. Once we reached it, Laura was going to expect me to walk away and leave her to die, and then the shell was going to kill me.

'What did Alysha find that meant she had to die?'

411

'Don't be a dick, Rause. You answered that six months ago.'

'If you don't—'

A ping from Liss: I've found her. Can you cut the link to the pilot?

No.

Then there's nothing I can do.

Unless I kill the pilot?

That works.

And Jamie?

Alive.

I'll tell you when.

We reached the doors to the Cheetah pit. Shiva pointed her rifle. Laura punched the panel to open them.

Rangesh? How long?

Seven or eight minutes, dude.

Too long.

Laura. Do you trust me?

I saw her face. The dread and the anguish. The pleading in her eyes.

'Don't. Please …'

I scooped a pile of snow off the floor of the pit and lunged for Laura. I grabbed her wrist and pulled, dragging her out of the way and using her weight to throw myself at Wheelchair Man.

Shiva talked too much like Vishakh. I'd shown Jacksmith the picture of the Darius Vishakh from Alysha's recordings. She'd said she hadn't known him. I'd thought for a while she'd been lying. But she hadn't. And by now I'd figured out what she'd meant by a young officer whose experiences 'mirrored her own …'

Wheelchair Man. The real Vishakh was crippled, just like she was.

Shiva's particle beam came up. I threw the snow at her face, ducked and dived sideways. I heard the pop as she fired. Heat seared the side of my face. I didn't see what the beam hit, but it wasn't me, and that gave me a couple of seconds before it could fire again. I snarled and lunged for Wheelchair Man, tearing at the seals on his helmet. The real Darius Vishakh. I was going to kill him. I was going to rip off his head if I had to ...

'Keon!' Laura's cry was an anguished warning.

Liss! Now!

I tore the helmet from Vishakh's face. Shiva flew at me and drove a knife into my back. A sliver of ice stabbed through me, the blade already frozen to minus a hundred degrees, a cold deep enough to freeze the pain of the wound. But I wasn't the only one who felt that cold. Shiva threw me off as Vishakh snapped awake and gulped for air and choked on it, vapour freezing in his lungs. He coughed and gagged and tried to breathe.

The Shiva shell froze. Vishakh wasn't unconscious. He never had been. He'd been piloting the Shivas all along – the one inside the wreck and now this one. And I had him. I had my hands at his throat. The man who killed Esh. The man who'd told Loki how and where and when to plant his idiot bomb.

There was blood in my mouth. I shook myself and I staggered up.

'Keon!'

Vishakh had a pistol hidden in his lap. I heard something loud and then a hammer hit me in the guts. The strength went from me at once. I pitched back. When I tried to move, I couldn't.

The Shiva shell stuttered back to life. It lurched as through drunk, picked up Vishakh's helmet and fitted it back over his head. My Servant screamed a medical emergency. I didn't know how bad it was, but bad. Bad enough that I wasn't going to live for much longer without a lot of help.

You could have helped me there, Laura. You could have done something ...

She'd frozen. Caught between me and Jamie.

I tried to open my mouth and tell her that it was OK. That Jamie was safe.

I couldn't speak.

Vishakh wheezed inside his suit. Shiva lowered the ramp into the Cheetah. She grabbed Laura and dragged her to stand over me, a pistol in her side.

'I don't know why Alysha had to die, Agent Rause. All I know is that someone in the Tesseract wanted her gone. They paid me well to pull Loki's trigger.'

'Lauughn …'

I had to tell her about Jamie. I pinged her: Jamie. Alive. Safe.

Vishakh's chair hummed into the Cheetah.

Liss?

'Alysha crossed the wrong people, Rause. Just like you.'

The shell turned away and hauled Laura up the ramp.

Keys?

I forced myself to my hands and knees.

The ramp began to close. The shell turned back to me.

'At least she died quickly, eh?' She went inside.

Liss? I had to go after them.

I didn't have the strength.

You need help.

I know.

The ramp was almost shut. I managed to get to my feet. I was bleeding badly. Best I could tell I had one lung partially collapsed from Shiva's knife and getting worse. I didn't know exactly what the bullet in my gut had done but it was killing me. My Servant was working overtime with the environment suit's drug dispenser, but there was only so much it could do.

Jamie? He's really safe?

Yes.

You need to tell her. Tell Laura. Show her.

I tried to ping Laura again but her Servant wasn't answering.

The ramp sealed shut. The Cheetah's engines began to whine as they powered up.

You said you'd let me go, but you can't.

The Cheetah's cargo door was still open. My legs still worked. I forced myself towards it. Every step was the teetering walk of someone on the brink of falling. But I didn't fall.

You can't release someone from love. You don't have that power.

I could bleed out and die. That would do the trick, wouldn't it?

Goodbye, Liss.

No. Of course it wouldn't. I knew that better than anyone.

Please, Keys. Please don't. Please don't die.

I ignored her. What was there to say?

Keon? Keon! You need to live! I need to tell you. You need to listen. I know who Chase—

I cut the link.

I reached the door.

I dragged myself inside.

27

METEOROLOGY

The roar of noise and the swirl of air kept me going somehow. I needed that. I didn't want to know how much blood I'd lost or how much I was still losing or how long before it was *too* much. I shut my Servant down to shut it up. We were past that now. I'd saved Jamie, and Jamie needed his mum, and so I was going to save Laura too, but that wasn't where I found the will to haul myself into the Cheetah's hold. I found it because Vishakh had killed my wife.

A heaviness sank into me. I paused to catch my breath. I wanted to sit down and close my eyes. I knew that if I did, I'd never get up.

The Cheetah left the pit. It tilted, nose down, flying on its rotors like a helicopter.

At the front of the cargo hold was an array of monitors, the legacy of a seventy-year-old design and a philosophy of engineering that pre-dated the Masters. The display showed me everything I needed to know: the ice ahead and below; the excavation pit receding behind us; the cockpit, with Shiva's fingers wrapped lightly around Laura's neck as she flew; Vishakh in the passenger cabin, rummaging like a drunkard through the Cheetah's medical kits, breathing fast and shallow in his chair. Vishakh was fumbling as though he couldn't quite see. I hoped the cold had burned his corneas when it had burned his lungs, but more likely he looked out of it because he literally was – because most of him was riding the shell beside Laura.

Seeing the two of them, I figured how this was going to work.

I muted everything in my Servant that was going to scream for medical help the moment it had a voice and turned it on. I pinged Laura through the Cheetah's Servant to make sure she knew I was on board.

Laura?

I saw her start.

I need Vishakh away from the cockpit.

I couldn't see her face but I could see her hands on the Cheetah's yoke, knuckles clenched hard white. She pulled the Cheetah into a sudden hard climb. The engines screamed. The shell tightened its grip around Laura's neck. Vishakh tipped out of his chair. He crashed into the bench seats and flailed, tumbling to the back of the cabin.

I slid back through the hold and grabbed the ladder into the passenger module. I pulled myself up and threw open the hatch. The Cheetah was nose up almost thirty degrees, engines howling at their limits. Vishakh was on his hands and knees, trying drunkenly to claw his way back to his chair. I didn't know which one of us was in the worse state.

The Shiva shell had a gun to Laura's head. I grabbed Vishakh's ankle and pulled him towards me, letting the incline of the floor do the work. Shiva whipped round and levelled her pistol as we collapsed into a tangled heap. I slipped the survival knife off Vishakh's belt and held it to his throat. Maybe whatever q-ware he was running in that shell was good enough to shoot me again

417

while I used his own flesh and blood as a shield. Maybe, maybe not.

I need you to live.

Liss. They were just words written across my lenses. No sound, no tone, no emotion. But I felt the anguish. I knew it. It was already in my bones.

'Laura!'

I had to shout over the noise. Every breath I forced out felt like it might be my last. I had the knife at Vishakh's throat. The Shiva shell grabbed Laura by the hair and then pointed the gun at her head.

'Let me go, Rause, or I shoot her in the head.'

I growled in his ear. 'Let *her* go or I cut your throat.'

Keon! You need to live!

Laura didn't move. But I heard her. She spoke slowly and clearly.

'I've locked the controls to my Servant. So shoot me and enjoy your last few seconds.'

My vision was tunnelling. I was shutting down. Losing consciousness. Vishakh's feeble struggles were too much for me to hold any more. I saw Laura turn. She looked back at me, dull and blank until she finally saw me. Really, truly, *saw* me.

'Thank you,' she mouthed.

The Shiva shell turned her pistol back at me and Vishakh's body. Laura moved at once. She twisted out of the pilot's seat and jumped onto the shell's back, clinging to it and grappling the arm that held the gun. Vishakh started to struggle. My arm squeezed tighter around his neck. Shiva slammed Laura into a wall but Laura didn't let go.

'You killed Alysha.' Vishakh's fingers were locked around my wrist, trying to pull the knife away. 'You showed Loki how to build his bomb.' I squeezed harder. A last dying gasp perhaps but I was damned if Vishakh wasn't going to go first. 'You showed him when and where to set it!'

She was never on that train!

I got the edge of the knife to his skin. In the cockpit the shell twisted and jerked and lurched, trying to shake Laura off its back.

'She turned on us!' Vishakh snarled.

'She never was one of you! Never!' I felt the edge start to bite.

She sent a shell! It was a shell! Keon!

'Not Fleet, you fucking idiot!'

I pushed the edge into Vishakh's skin. He fought me all the way but he didn't have the strength. He wasn't born and raised in 1.4 gravities.

'Something bigger—'

I felt his blood running across my hands. It was warm.

Keon!

The Shiva shell finally broke free. It flailed an arm and smashed Laura around the head hard enough to knock her across the cabin. The pistol whipped towards me. A boom and a flash as the Shiva shell fired . . .

I felt the impact as the bullet hit Vishakh, caught between us. His targeting q-ware turned out not to be as good as he'd hoped.

More words from Liss flashed onto my lenses. I couldn't read them. My eyes were starting to blur. I clamped my arm tighter around Vishakh's neck. No need for the knife any more. I had him in a choke now.

'October.' All Vishakh's strength had gone.

The Shiva shell punched both fists straight into the Cheetah controls, dragging out a fistful of cables and connectors.

'Then . . . we all . . . go . . . together . . .'

The shell staggered and collapsed. Vishakh fell limp in my arms. And then we were floating and I felt a lightness inside me which I thought was death, but was actually the Cheetah as all its engines cut out at once, as it stalled and toppled sideways in the air. Laura must have disabled the safety protocols when she'd slammed us into that climb.

Made sense.

Pity, that.

She was moving. I watched her, paralysed. She hauled herself back into the pilot's chair.

The world turned slowly grey. There were still words written across my lenses. I forced myself to see them.

She isn't dead. Alysha isn't dead.

I frowned inside. That didn't make sense.

'I'm sorry, Keon! I'm really sorry.' I think Laura was crying.

Show her Jamie, Liss. Tell her who you are. Let her have that before we go.

'Why the fuck did you have to follow me?' She hauled desperately on the yoke.

'Engines, Laws. No … engines …'

You need to live!

I was fading. The roaring in my head was getting louder.

'Why didn't you just stay on the fucking ground?'

I love you.

There were more words. I couldn't make them out.

'Why didn't you just stay behind!' She was sobbing. 'You stupid … fucking …'

It started to sink in – what Liss was saying, what she was trying to tell me. I understood. Liss. Alysha. Even Laura. All the people we love, none of them are ever quite who we think. But love doesn't give a shit. Love is a terrorist and we're all just hostages.

The darkness filled everything.

ALYSHA

Kamaljit Kaur sits in the cockpit of a Cheetah flying a few hundred feet above the Magenta polar ice. A very angry man is shouting at her over the radio to bring the Cheetah back. He says his name is Colonel Jonas Himaru. He sounds in a lot of pain. In another life Kaur thinks she might have liked him. Now she ignores him.

Beside her Doctor Jacksmith lolls strapped into the co-pilot's seat. The moment just before Kaur stunned her lingers. Elizabeth Jacksmith was friend and mentor to Alysha Rause for almost a decade. The values that bring Kaur to where she finds herself – some of them were hers. The doctor is, Kaur thinks, a good woman.

Elizabeth had known her, despite the face she wears. She'd known as Kaur pulled the trigger.

The other Cheetah is a mile ahead and falling. The other pilot has worked hard to make her craft crash. Now she seems to have changed her mind. Self-preservation, Kaur supposes. Self-preservation can be the most powerful motivation of all. Self-preservation can make a person give up everything, even the people she loves.

The Cheetah ahead almost recovers from its death dive. The pilot levels the wings in time to bellyflop an emergency landing.

The Cheetah slides and slithers. Pieces fly off, snapped free by the impact, but the body survives. Snow and ice is little more forgiving than stone but the Cheetah was designed to be close to indestructible.

Kaur follows. The stricken Cheetah sings, wailing into the ether for help. Kaur listens, but no one transmits from inside.

She brings her Cheetah close and lands beside it, soft and gentle. She unbuckles and opens the door and steps into the bitter cold.

The rotors of the crashed Cheetah are mangled. One wing is cracked and has started to tear. Kaur climbs onto the roof and opens the emergency hatch. She jumps inside, the cold flowing in with her.

Laura lies slumped in her pilot's chair, wrapped in deflating airbags. She moans softly now and then. Kaur squats beside her. The Cheetah has protected her well. A little concussion, no more. She will live.

A shell lies at Laura's feet, wrapped around her chair. Hard to say how damaged it is, but it doesn't move. Kaur ignores it. She opens the hatch to the cargo bay. Down there is what she came for – the corpse of Iosefa Lomu strapped to a gurney, freeze-dried for a century and a half under the Magentan ice.

Iosefa Lomu. A human who once flew a Masters' ship. The only human who ever managed it. A Xen addict. A Magentan. She wonders, as she's wondered often over the last five years, whether the Masters made a mistake. The xenoflora of Magenta is compatible with human neurochemistry, something every-body knows, but what far fewer people know is that *compatible* is only the start of it. Now and then it does something vastly more. It wakes something up. Something latent, dormant, she doesn't know which. But something.

She's seen it.

And Keon knows, and Laura, and the Tesseract, and anyone who ever had anything to do with Alysha Rause's last case.

Alysha knew. This is why she never told anyone, not a soul, what she was doing. This is why she sent six soldiers on a secret mission two weeks before she died.

The xenoflora woke something in Iosefa Lomu when he arrived on Magenta more than a century and a half ago. A year later Iosefa Lomu climbed into an abandoned Masters' ship and spoke to it. And it spoke back.

A random accident? The right genes in the right place at the right time? It doesn't matter. Somewhere in the mix of Xen and Iosefa Lomu's genetic code is the key to the Masters. It is perhaps the key to humanity's salvation. That men will kill one another to possess that key is only the start of what it means.

Time presses. She needs to go.

She hears a moan from the passenger cabin. Darius Vishakh lies sprawled in a corner, smashed up and wrapped in a tangle of half-deflated crash-bags. He wears an environment suit covered in blood. Somehow he is still alive.

Darius Vishakh, the man who promised to smuggle her off Magenta when something far too powerful to fight became her sudden enemy.

She draws her pistol.

Darius Vishakh, who sold her out and set her up to die. Darius, who all but put her on that train while his puppet Loki quietly prepared to blow it up.

She aims a bullet at his face.

She thinks of Elizabeth Jacksmith, the friend who warned her that Vishakh was a snake. The friend who was an expert in shells. The friend who gave her the idea to maybe *not* get on that train after all. To send a shell carrying her Servant and dog tags instead and see what happened next.

And she did. And saw.

423

She feels the urge to pull Kamaljit Kaur's face to pieces and let the real Darius Vishakh see the truth beneath. But then she'd have to shoot him. It's not what Keon would have wanted.

She takes a moment to remember this. The look of him, broken and beaten and close to death.

'You deserve what's coming,' she whispers. 'Every piece.' For as long as he lives, she can watch him suffer.

Another man is wrapped under Vishakh, half crushed beneath him. Kaur drags him free, expecting another Fleet spy. Perhaps someone she met once, back when she pretended they were on the same side, if sides mean anything where the Masters are concerned.

She lifts his head.

And stares.

'Keon?'

The shock of seeing him numbs her more than Magenta's Antarctic cold ever could.

She needs to leave. She needs to take Iosefa and Jacksmith. She needs to get away while she still has the chance.

Keon's eyes open a fraction. He looks at her but doesn't see. He's dying.

'Laura?' he asks.

It cuts her that he says another woman's name. It shouldn't. It has no right to. But it does.

She finds the remains of a medical kit but Keon needs more than first aid. She can't save him, not here. He needs blood and a trauma unit. He needs it soon. She wonders for a short foolish instant whether she can take him with her. But anywhere she might hide is hours away and he doesn't have that long. Not even close.

She could take him back to angry Colonel Himaru. They have a trauma unit there. Enough to stabilise him. It's not far. He has that long left in him. It would save him.

Of course, she'd never get away again.

Keon or Iosefa.

'I'm sorry,' she whispers.

NINE

MERCY

28

EPILOGUE

I didn't remember much after Vishakh shot himself with his own shell, but I remembered a face looking down on me. It was masked in an environment suit. The memory was a fleeting flash snatched as I hung over the edge of the abyss. There was something about it, though. Something about the cock of the head. Something …

Comforting.

I was in a Mercy hospital room. Again. Doctor Roge was looking back at me.

'Rause?'

I made a noise that was an all-purpose question. I tried to look around but my head was full of clouds. When I moved my eyes the whole room started to swim.

'Blink if you can hear me. That should be enough to show your cognitive functions are back to normal.'

I blinked.

'OK. Now blink twice if you can actually understand me.'

I blinked twice.

'Excellent. I think that shows everything working up there as well as it ever did.'

He smiled. It was a good smile. I saw his eyes flicker, little sparks of light in his pupils as something flashed across his lenses. That faraway look of being somewhere else.

'Agent Patterson wants to know when you wake up. You OK with that?'

I grunted and nodded.

'Mercy's had you under for eleven days. That's why you're so groggy.'

I made another noise.

'Managed to save your lung but not your kidney. You've got an artificial one now. Well, I say artificial … Grown inside a pig. You know what I mean.' He laughed. 'You're missing a few other bits and pieces and about ten feet of miscellaneous intestine but Mercy seems to think you don't much need them. I don't know what happened to you, Rause. I don't suppose I ever will, but the trans-polar expedition is all over the news. A Masters' ship from just after the liberation, they're saying. Human bodies still inside. Lots of speculation about how it went down. That sort of thing. How it even got there. Not as much as there is about what else was inside. Speculation of some fracas in orbit, too.'

I shook my head. 'I didn't …'

'Been quite a couple of weeks. A lot of bad stories about what's happening on Earth coming in on the *Fearless*. Quite a thaw in relations between Magenta and Fleet. Us ignorant types are all guessing it's something to do with the expedition given that Doctor Jacksmith has been in the Tesseract ever since you came back. She's not the only one. Half a dozen scientists and technicians. Quite the discovery, eh?'

'What about Earth?'

A United Nations ship had fired antimatter warheads at the surface of Magenta.

He shrugged. 'Nothing new.'

I closed my eyes. I was too tired for this.

Roge backed away. 'You want me to put Patterson off when she gets here?'

I shook my head. 'No.'

I drifted away.

When I drifted back, Roge was gone and Laura was looking down at me. I didn't know what to expect after everything we'd been through, but there were tears in her eyes. She tried to blink them away but they grew bigger, spilling down her cheeks. She bent over me and kissed me on the forehead and then sat beside me and held me tight. I felt her shudder.

'Thank you,' she said.

'For what?'

'For Jamie.' She let go and sat straight and wiped the tears away.

'You look terrible,' I said.

'Oh, fuck off and get a mirror.' We both laughed. Or tried to.

'You OK?'

She shook her head. 'Not really.'

'Jamie?'

She looked away. 'We're all suspended. Best you know that. You, me, Rangesh, Flemich. There's still a warrant out for you. I'd take you in but, hey. Suspended ...' She looked at me, suddenly fierce and intense. 'How did you do it? How did you keep going on after Alysha ... After she ... After you thought ... You know. The bomb.'

'I didn't. I ran away, remember?'

She pulled herself together and told me in short flat strokes the rest of what had happened. Vishakh was locked in a secret cell somewhere in Firstfall. Koller had made a deal and started talking. Vishakh was the head of the serpent. The third of Vishakh's Dattatreya was dead – the man she'd shot through the hand. The man Vishakh had executed. So far we didn't know his name.

It was done. We'd won.

I thought she'd ask all the questions then about Jamie and how I'd saved him, the questions that would lead inexorably to Liss, but she didn't. She looked away and wouldn't meet my eye. They'd come soon enough, though. I knew that.

'You were going to crash that Cheetah,' I said. 'Even after Jamie was safe.'

She didn't answer. She still wouldn't look at me. I wasn't going to push.

'You were in bad shape,' she said after a bit. 'They had a mobile trauma unit at the base. I wasn't sure ...' She squeezed my hand.

Someone had carried me from our crashed Cheetah to another and then flown me back. Someone had saved my life. Himaru? Or had it been Laura herself ...?

'Vishakh was right. You played me to go after him.'

Laura shrugged and looked away. 'Someone had to.'

'You set me up.'

'I'm sorry it had to be you.'

'It's OK.' It wasn't, not really.

'It wasn't just you. Himaru and Rangesh, too. You can tell them, if it helps. Never hurts to have a few more people who hate me.'

'When did you know? About Vishakh, I mean.'

'Just before you clusterfucked everything by spooking Shenski.' She laughed bitterly. 'You were right about the names, by the way. Kagame's list. Vishakh really did give us the key but the launcher wrapped around it added a few names of its own.'

'Who?'

'Doctor Jacksmith. Nohr. Kettler ...' She paused.

'Not Steadman.'

'Yes and no.' She made a face like she couldn't puzzle it out. 'Vishakh added him but he was on the original list as well.' She took a deep breath and then let it out, long and slow. 'He added Alysha too.'

I let that sink in. 'She wasn't on the list?'

'No.'

I sighed. And smiled.

'We've been pulling them in. The people on Kagame's list aren't connected to Fleet. They're connected to Earth. To an organisation called *October*.' She shrugged. 'Don't get too excited. Kagame still tried to shoot you when he heard her name. That list doesn't really prove anything.'

It did to me. And that was enough.

'I saw you,' I said. 'After the crash. Standing over me. You carried me out. You saved my life.'

She shook her head. She was staring at the wall, so far away inside herself that I couldn't begin to imagine what she was thinking.

'Not me,' she said hoarsely.

'Then who ...?'

Nothing.

'Himaru?'

She bit hard on a knuckle.

'Laura, what?'

'You were going to die to save Jamie,' she said, without turning her head. 'I'm glad you didn't. Really, really glad. I don't think I could have taken that.'

'Do you think ... You know ...? When Mercy lets me out? Are we—'

'No.'

We sat in silence for maybe half a minute and then she left without another word.

I had a few more visitors over the days before Mercy let me go. Bix, pleased as punch to see me alive, gleefully ignorant of almost everything that had happened at the trans-polar camp until he and the other tac-team returned from seizing Vishakh's shuttle. There was some 'totally cloak-and-dagger shit' going down, apparently, about which he cheerfully knew nothing. Kagame's list was raising merry hell throughout the bureau. Was it real or wasn't it? Even if it was, the one name on it that mattered most of all was a cipher. Tesseract One.

We still didn't know for sure who'd let the Fleet men into Jared Black's room in Mercy. We still didn't know who'd given Becker his orders. Or Vishakh, come to that. Flemich had been in the frame for the first two, but he'd led the charge to stop Vishakh and almost died for his trouble, and now no one knew anything any more. Everyone would be looking over their shoulders until we knew the answers. I wasn't sure we ever would but Bix didn't seem to care.

'Not my world, boss dude,' he said.

Flemich came, poker-faced as ever. He was still suspended, like I was, but reckoned we'd all be cleared to work again soon enough. He told me he was looking forward to having me back. His smile as he said it didn't reach his eyes. Then he told me not to say anything about the *Flying Daggers*. The press hadn't got wind of it and it was to stay that way until someone with a clue worked out exactly what the hell we were supposed to do. Until we understood what Earth wanted, although I reckon we both knew the answer: they wanted what was in that wreck.

He didn't say much else.

Two weeks later I walked out of Mercy, the last of us to leave. I had a few more days before I was due to be discharged but apparently I had special dispensation or something to spend an afternoon outside. Bix picked me up and took me to the Wavedome. The weather was harsh but even so I was surprised to find the beach deserted except for a cluster of bureau faces. Flemich. Laura, a dozen others. Himaru with a limp, still recovering from the explosion in the wreck. I knew most of their faces. As we joined them, a procession of MSDF soldiers started out from the Blue Scallop. They were in full dress uniform and came at a slow, stilted march. At the head of the procession, mounted on a surfboard, was a coffin.

'Esh,' I said. It wasn't a question.

Bix nodded. 'Thought you'd want to be here.'

His hand was clenched around something. He pointed down to the far end of the beach where the waves come in hard and high.

'There's a wave there sometimes,' he said. 'When the winds are just right, when there's been a storm out over the ocean, the Meatgrinder turns on. Hits the reef out there and rears up like a monster, forty feet and slabby like you wouldn't believe. You take on the Grinder, man, you go in with everything. No fear, no doubt, nothing held back or it'll kill you. Earthers come to Magenta because there's no other wave like it. They cross the stars with their boards and take one look and go back home, but Esh would ride that wave like she was having breakfast. That's what she was, man. No fear. Always all-in. Man, I saw Esh do things on that wave like she could defy gravity. Crazy air.'

When he opened his fingers I saw he was holding a sliver.

'Esh,' he said quietly. 'Esh's memories.'

I didn't ask what he was doing with them. I didn't ask how he'd spirited them away from Mercy. Just watched as he slotted the sliver into a device the size of a knuckle pulled from the pocket of his kaftan. I knew what it was. An emergency secure eraser. I watched his finger hover over its little red button. I watched how his hand shook as he pressed it. I don't know how he could do it. I don't know how that didn't feel like he was killing her, right there on the beach.

Esh's memories. The digital remains a cracksman might have used to seed an AI core and plant in a shell. We could have brought her back the way I'd brought back Liss. We could have put her into a shell like Vishakh's Shiva, so nearly perfect I could hardly tell it wasn't human.

I don't know how he could do it but I was glad he had.

'I never quite figured out,' he said, a wobble in his voice, 'whether she was somehow still alive in there in some weird sort of way. But Esh would have said that only Allah can raise the dead.' His voice cracked as he said it.

I put a hand on Bix's shoulder as the procession marched in slow motion out into the surf. When the water was waist deep the coffin-bearers lowered the board into the waves. It moved steadily out to sea, driven by some unseen motor. A trio of Cheetahs flew over the dome and hovered out to sea, facing the shore. A hundred soldiers lined up and saluted as one. The Cheetahs dipped their noses. The coffin burst into flames, fierce and bright, and then slowly died away. The Cheetahs wheeled and left. The soldiers in the surf broke ranks and turned away.

Bix had tears in his eyes.

'This is what she wanted, man,' he said. 'She told me once. To totally go out in a blaze of glory.'

'She did that all right.'

He threw the dead sliver into the sea.

I offered Rangesh my hand. He shook it without hesitation.

'Care, dude.'

I left him there to grieve alone.

A pod waited to take me back to my room in Mercy. It was about to set off when Laura slipped in beside me. We sat beside each other in silence. She kept sneaking glances at me as though she couldn't find the right words. We drove from the Wavedome together, listening to the hammering of the rain on the roof, feeling the pod lurch as it was caught in sudden gusts of wind.

'Must be pushing a hundred miles an hour out there,' I said.

She nodded. She didn't look at me.

'You asked who pulled you out,' she said.

I'd written that off. One of Himaru's team? Bix, maybe? Did it matter? She'd almost lost Jamie and I'd almost died to save him. It terrified her. Last time we spoke she hadn't wanted to talk about it. Now she did? So be it.

The pod drove on. Laura didn't say anything but she took over the pod and set it on an aimless wander. We passed through the Squats and kept going down.

She was restless. She seemed almost ...

Uncertain.

'Where are we going?' I asked.

'Nowhere,' she said.

We passed the mag-lev station. The last place anyone had seen Alysha alive. I thought about Vishakh and his Shiva. I'd wanted him dead but at the same time I was glad he was alive. I wanted to talk to him now. I wanted to hammer the truth out of him. I wanted to do what I'd done to Koller, only a hundred times worse. I wanted to make good the promise I'd made Himaru. I wanted to see him stand trial and admit in front of everyone that he'd set Loki on his path. I wanted him to tell the world that he'd sabotaged Alysha's last operation. I wanted him to tell the world that he'd killed her, that she wasn't a traitor. I could have that now. I could actually have that. I could finally put her to rest.

'Does the stuff inside the wreck really tell us where the Masters went?'

She didn't answer.

I wanted to talk to Jacksmith. I wanted to ask her about Iosefa. There was probably quite a queue.

'Fuck!' Laura slumped, head in her hands. 'I don't know how to do this.'

'Do what?'

The pod was taking us back up now. Back to Mercy.

'This.'

She pinged me a handful of files. The first were a couple of video clips I'd already seen. The one from the ice rink when we'd been looking for Statton on the *Fearless*, of the woman in the background who'd moved in an oddly familiar way. Then the footage from under the Monument. The blurred snip of the woman who'd saved me there. The woman who looked like Alysha.

'It wasn't any of us who pulled you out of that Cheetah,' Laura said.

The last file was a DNA analysis from a hair recovered from a cheap hotel in the Squats. The place where Stephanie Wright was born.

Match probability 99.89%: Alysha Rause.

I shook my head.

Six years. She'd been dead for six years.

'I don't get it,' I said. 'Is it a hoax?' I didn't know how else to explain it.

'I don't think so.'

Six years …

'It's not real,' I said again. 'She's gone.'

And I didn't know why someone would do something like this or why, except that it had to be Vishakh, somehow, and we had him, and one way or the other I'd get to the truth.

The pod reached Mercy. We didn't say anything else. We didn't say goodbye.

I went back to my room.

I lay there, awake, thinking of Esh. Of Alysha. Of Laura. Of Liss. Eventually I told Mercy I was in pain. I coaxed it into

438

slipping me a sedative to help me sleep. I closed my eyes.

When I opened them again there was a woman by the door, half turned away, barely visible in the dark. Her hair was in a style I didn't recognise. But I knew her. I'd have known her anywhere.

'Liss?' I was dreaming. I had to be.

She froze.

'Keon?'

I knew that voice.

It hit me then: If it was true, then Laura had known days ago. Weeks. She'd been about to tell me when we were on the way to the excavation. And then she'd changed her mind.

I was dreaming. I had to be.

But then there was Liss. The things she'd told me right at the end, on the Cheetah as Vishakh and I killed each other. Things that made no sense then. But now they did.

Alysha turned to face me. Blood roared in my head. And I saw on her face a look of grief and joy and shame and hope and love and despair and a determined tragedy that no shell could ever feign.

Alysha. Flesh and blood. Back from the dead.

'Hey, Keys,' she said.

ACKNOWLEDGEMENTS

Thanks to my editor Marcus Gipps and the rest of the editorial team at Gollancz. Special thanks to my agent Robert Dinsdale who had to put up with the some substantial changes between drafts before it went any further. Thanks to Craig and Steve and Sophie and Stevie and all the other people whose names I don't yet know as I write this but without whom this wouldn't exist. Thank you to all the people who read and reviewed and said nice things or otherwise about *From Darkest Skies*.